RAGNARÖK

ARI BACH

Harmony Ink

Published by
HARMONY INK PRESS

5032 Capital Circle SW, Suite 2, PMB# 279, Tallahassee, FL 32305-7886 USA
publisher@harmonyinkpress.com • http://harmonyinkpress.com

Ragnarök
© 2014 Ari Bach.

Cover Art
© 2014 Ari Bach.
Cover Design
© 2014 Paul Richmond
www.paulrichmondstudio.com
Cover content is for illustrative purposes only and any person depicted on the cover is a model.

ISBN: 978-1-63216-622-7
Library Edition ISBN: 978-1-63216-623-4
Digital ISBN: 978-1-63216-624-1
Library of Congress Control Number: 2014949326
First Edition December 2014
Library Edition March 2015

Lyric excerpts from "The Minstrel Boy" (Traditional) by Thomas Moore (1779-1852).

Printed in the United States of America

This paper meets the requirements of
ANSI/NISO Z39.48-1992 (Permanence of Paper).

Chapter I: Utah

VIOLET JUMPED and hurtled toward the troposphere. As she fell deeper and deeper into the thickening air, the wind began to punch, then stab. She fell with no parachute, no personal descent thrusters, and no crash armor. All she had was a sticky suit, and all that could do was stick to things. Her only hope was her target. If she failed to connect with that target, the result could be bad, worse, or catastrophic: She could miss the target and fall to her death, splattered on the rock-hard salt flats below. She could slip into the target's jets and be incinerated utterly. If she were truly unlucky, Vibeke could pilot the shuttle fast and accurately enough to catch her, and she would never hear the end of it.

V team had spent the last week preparing for the jump. Veikko had infiltrated Skunkworks, no small task, and snuck a peek at the upcoming test schedule and flight paths. Varg and Vibeke ran simulation after simulation of physics and contingencies. Violet practiced the jump online and in the air over the Arctic Sea. They all surveyed the jump location and calculated the altitudes and atmospheric pressure. Vibeke studied the air of the Bonneville wasteland, the toxic air of old industries and old wars, obsolete poisons that lingered on like noxious vapors over a tomb. Varg showed her which abandoned skyscrapers she was most likely to get impaled on if the target dropped her over the ruins of Provo or the last surviving megaliths of Salt Lake City. Veikko programmed up a pretty simulation of what would happen to Violet's body should she fall all the way to the salt flats, complete with comically inappropriate sound effects. Absolutely none of that made her feel any safer as she fell at terminal velocity toward the white land below.

After falling just long enough to question if she missed the target, she saw it beneath her. A tiny black speck against the white earth, moving at exceptional speed. It looked fast enough to meet her right where it should. It was traveling at just over twice the speed of sound.

The shuttle Violet jumped from was moving at subsonic speed, so the acceleration when she hit the target would be fatal without an inertial negation field. The craft would at least be slowing down. It was on its way home after a test of its thermobaric thruster, the speed limit of which was unknown even to those who built it. From earlier tests monitored closely by H team, they knew it could pass Mach 40 with ease in the atmosphere and maintain 350 g's of acceleration for at least half an hour in space. That was only one of the reasons Valhalla wanted it.

The critical feature of the X-292 Blackwing Impact Resistant Plane was its flex-diamond armor. It made the craft so tough it could fly through solid rock. As Valhalla's last line of defense was solid rock, Alf thought it best that the craft not belong to anyone but them. Given Skunkworks's terribly overbudget development of the prototype, there would not be any more if this one disappeared in testing. As GAUNE had stolen the designs from an UNEGA company, which they later sent Skunkforce to massacre, Valhalla had no ethical problems stealing it.

Also appealing to much of the ravine was the idea of a new space-capable vessel. V had flown to Bonneville in Valhalla's only space shuttle, and it wasn't one of the finer models. It was a twenty-seven-year-old P-Zero that the ravine stole from the Crystal Methuselah drug gang. When the shuttle was stolen, the gang made no effort to recover it. Once plated in special thermophobic gold to prevent rust, the decrepit P-Zero shuttle developed "Purple Plague" and lost its shimmer within only two reentries. Thus it had to get TK chromed and appeared as the only silver vehicle in the ravine. The interior was as cramped as a boiler room and twice as hot. It was made for two people, and the retrofitting for four was known throughout the ravine as H team's worst job ever. Any team that used the P-Zero shuttle would relentlessly mock H over the two "jump seats," which were not so much seats as scraps of jagged metal with bumps in just the right places to irritate the rumps of their unfortunate passengers. Varg especially had height problems and had to man the weapons array by lying flat on his stomach under the front seat. Violet had donned her sticky suit en route in the cargo hold where the smell of old smart-foam made her eager to jump out.

She jumped with her inertial negation field off and set it only to turn on a fraction of a second before hitting the wing. The field would show up on the target's sensors, but without it she'd be turned into putty as soon as she touched the Blackwing. The field would also render the oncoming air stagnant within so it wouldn't tear her to shreds. It would even lessen the impact if she were to miss and hit the ground, but only enough to see that her innards exploded from her mouth instead of her back. Veikko had done a great job with simulations of both, utterly realistic except for the sound effect, a file he had labeled as Splort.

Recollections of the simulation ended when the field turned on too soon. She was right over the target when a jagged blue mist appeared under her, halting the airflow. Her inner ears told her she was no longer falling, the ground was moving up toward her. She was in pleasant, calm free fall. She was also visible to every sensor the target had. Nothing to be done for it. They knew she was coming, but it wasn't like she could turn around. Her perception aside, the field actually turned on only a quarter second too soon. Not a fatal mission error. In that quarter second, the target turned from a distant speck to a wall of black diamond wing right before her. Calculations had gone as well as could be expected, she would hit near the back. Advantage: It would give her plenty of objects to grab. Disadvantage: The time to climb forward. More time for the pilot to prepare. She elected to go for one of the tail fins and reached out.

Her hand stuck to the dark fin like a gecko to glass. The texture of the suit elongated, dozens of small sticky points held onto the craft and distributed her weight among themselves. A solid catch. No time to waste. Hand over hand she pulled herself down to the fuselage and began to scale forward. The inertia field prickled madly, deflecting and stopping tons of oncoming air. The still atmosphere would then fall back and pick up its original speed, leaving Violet in a near-vacuum pocket. She took a deep breath from her Thaco armor holds, but the sticky suit left no room for the exhalation system, the air sucked out from her lungs painfully with each breath. She got just enough to stay functional. The sooner she got to the cockpit the better.

She kept climbing, her suit like a shadow moving over the black fuselage. Her link told her one of the markings on the craft was text. No time to have it read the tag for her. She kept moving, stepping right on it. Apparently it said No Step. Her foot pushed it open, a minor vent cap that dislodged some ice. It was startling, but it didn't slow her down. She approached the ramjet intakes behind the cockpit. Severe air distortions confused her inertia field and weakened it. The air was hitting again. She ignored it. She was at the cockpit.

She took a thin, flat thermite charge from her back and slipped it into the miniscule seam between the unbreakable canopy shield and the unbreakable fuselage shield and detonated it. H had predicted that although the shielding was indestructible by conventional means, the bolts holding the cockpit door in place would not be, for rescue purposes. She detonated the charge and found that H was right. The cockpit shield flew back so fast it almost disappeared, leaving only an unsurprised and very angry pilot. Another inertia field turned on to cover the cockpit, a heavy-duty aircraft field.

When Skunkworks built the Blackwing, they devoted a special team to finding the right test pilot. Firstly, they had to find someone capable of using the direct brain interface. Not everyone's brain can interface with raw bolts of electricity from an array around their heads, but it was the only way to link a pilot to a craft with absolute unbreakable security. Valhalla never recruited anyone in the first place who wasn't compatible with a DBI. Secondly, Skunkworks needed someone who, in the event of a hijacker breaking into the cockpit, could fight them off in hand-to-hand combat. Keith Kalessin was chosen in part because he was champion of personal combat at his academy.

The instant Violet's inertial negation field had activated, the Blackwing's alarms sounded. Keith watched her connect, climb toward his cockpit and step clumsily on a vent cap. He smelled the thermite burning through his oxygen mask. When the canopy disappeared and he saw the figure outside, he already had his sidearm ready.

Violet wouldn't have lasted long if she weren't expecting exactly that. She watched him level his microwave at her, looking down her leg like the sight on a rifle, poised to kick. She let loose, and her boot knocked the microwave from his hand. The sticky suit held onto it, and she grabbed the weapon from her heel. The bolts of electricity around Keith's head doubled in quantity as he began to send alerts and warnings to Skunkworks. Violet couldn't allow that, so she used his microwave to fire a dull magnetic beam into the brain interface, dulling and warping the signals. He lost control of the craft, and it began to spiral and fall out of control. The magnetic wave also interfered again with Violet's inertia field. A jolt of motion seeped in like a hard slap on the back.

She let the force push her into the cockpit. Keith punched her in the face so hard that the field spasm felt like nothing. The microwave fell to the earth. She punched him right back, but he blocked. Violet wasn't easy to block. She realized she was up against one tough pilot. Her surprise lasted only an instant, replaced quickly by the worse surprise of getting slugged so hard in the ribs that she fell out of the cockpit and into the ramjet intake.

Her fingers barely snagged the intake vents and saved her from vaporization. Violet's annoyance was burning hotter than the fuel behind her. Her fingers stuck to panel after diamond panel, and she crawled forward to face the skilled, dangerous man who had just bested her. A man who now knew how she fought and knew she was coming. It was time for extreme measures.

Keith could see her escape the intake, but she disappeared as she crawled up the Blackwing's diamond skin toward him. He awaited the sticky devil, calculating her most likely attack. She could come from behind and drop in above him. As she would expect another punch, he would deny her that. Then, as she struck, he'd pull her in to break her in half. If she came from either side, she would be at the same angle he saw before. He could see the field generator on the back of her neck, so if he could hit it squarely, he could turn inertia against her, and she'd splatter like flies around him. Keith didn't expect her to appear in front of him, jumping from the nose of his jet.

Having climbed under the craft all the way to its exceptionally sharp front edge, Violet dimmed her field by 5 percent and leaped toward her enemy with the force of the jet's motion behind her. The Blackwing's inertia field was hit with an inverse Boolean effect and dropped to match. Violet was forced in at more than 100 kph. She aimed her foot at Keith's face with horrific force. His reflexes were superhuman, thanks to the superhuman reflexology project he completed in the academy. He managed to move his head and replace it with his survival knife just as her foot connected.

First Violet felt the pain of her leg breaking against the headrest, then the pain of a twelve-centimeter blade sticking through her foot.

She didn't grow any angrier at the pain because, though he had performed an impressive move, it had left Keith bent over to his side and without the benefit of his seat's protection. She unsheathed the blade from her foot and cut his belts in a split second. Keith managed two good punches in that half second, but they weren't enough to push her off him, not with acceleration affecting her at 5 percent—she weighed 250 kilograms.

And it was acceleration, not wind that she was feeling now. The craft was still out of control and speeding up in awkward bursts. They were going into a barrel roll and losing altitude rapidly. Whoever won would have a dangerous few seconds to right the craft and stop it from crashing.

Violet had to act fast. She linked her field back on full and grabbed his oxygen mask, tightly strapped to his head. She yanked the apparatus hard enough that it would snap his neck, or if he was smart, checkmate him and force him to follow the direction. He was smart, but he had lost. The move gave Violet enough leverage to shove him out of the Blackwing's field and he flew from the cockpit, hit by the air and speed.

As he fell to the ground with his personal inertia fields up and his parachute field ready to deploy, he was filled with admiration for the hijacker who evicted him despite a dagger in her foot. Then came the lamentation that if he ever got out of the desert alive, his salary would be docked until he could pay off the craft he had lost: 220,000,000,000 euros on pilot's wages.

Violet had worse problems. The Blackwing was in an uncontrolled barrel roll and losing altitude faster and faster. So fast, she calculated, that if she kept calculating, it would hit the ground before she finished. She sat back in the seat and let the electric bolts feel out her head. The interface loaded at once to inform her that she was not its pilot and that the ship would self-destruct in five seconds. She began the system hack, which back in Valhalla she had proven capable of performing in only seven seconds.

Skunkworks had included self-destruct mechanisms in all its craft for ages in case of theft. V team's research prior to the mission showed they had never sold a single craft without it since 2104. They had, however, lost the prototype for a boat back in 2193 that showed up for sale in 2194. Though the thieves in that case were all killed by

Skunkforce, it did strongly suggest that prototypes intended solely for testing were not granted their suicidal charges. Certainly one so expensive as the Blackwing wouldn't be an exception.

Seven seconds later, Violet had control of the Blackwing, despite the craft's solemn belief that it had blown itself to smithereens two seconds prior. In ten seconds she had restarted the computers and piloted the Blackwing out of its barrel roll. In twenty seconds she had taken the emergency auto-lattice polymer can and sprayed out a new canopy. In twenty-one seconds the Blackwing crashed full-force into the solid salty ground.

Despite every measure onboard, she felt it. From Mach 6 to 700 kph in an instant. As the concrete-solid salt split around the unbreakable diamond shields, she was pitched forward in a sickening explosive jolt. The thin new canopy cracked to the point that she couldn't see through it, but the craft's design did its job and directed the force away from the broken cockpit. The Blackwing held, and Violet managed to pull up out of the salt and back into fresh toxic air. She took inventory of the events and state of things. All were as favorable as could be expected. She welcomed a complex bolt of lightning into her head and told the vessel to set course eastward. North would have to wait until its tracking systems were disabled.

"Sloppy, Vi," chimed a voice in her head. She pulled off the sticky suit's face mask, leaving only her Thaco oxygen prongs.

"Vibs is right, that was a 'rocky' start," said Veikko.

Varg linked last. "I can't think of any salt jokes. But hey, knock knock."

"Who's there?"

"Skunkforce! Five wave hoppers on your *Arsch*, laser armament, unmanned. I'm shooting at the six that aren't there yet."

Microwave drones could be a real problem on most missions. They'd managed to spoil one of O team's attacks on an organ smuggling ring, they'd successfully assassinated Luka Carcass before R could reach him, and only a week prior, they'd shot down Luzie's experimental reconnaissance saucer. On the theft of any common aircraft, they could foil V team in a dozen ways, from recording telemetry all the way back to the North or simply cutting the wings off with their damn vibrating lasers.

Violet saw the red dots all over the Blackwing. Useless, thankfully, against its armor, they couldn't even make the slightest scratch in the black diamond. They could tear open the makeshift canopy and cut her to ribbons, but short of fifty more of the things appearing right in front of her, she could keep the canopy aimed away from them.

Eighty-nine more wave hoppers erupted from the ground immediately before Violet's position. Skunkworks wasn't going to let the master work go, and they'd committed their entire drone fleet to stopping it. The hoppers burst upward from their salt hangars and flew ahead of the Blackwing, accelerating toward its future position. They were far enough ahead that they could cut her off and cut her up. A turn away from them would only reduce her speed on the bank and let them catch up elsewhere. There was no way around it; she was about to be covered in them.

She had only one chance. Hoppers were piloted by programs. Good programs, programs that know how humans fly. All Violet would have to do was fly in so inhuman a fashion that the drones would lose her or crash. Crash appealed to her more than loss. The first drones were about to land on the canopy. She had only seconds.

Empty skyscrapers began to flash by her sides just as the last drones came into view. They followed her motion for motion as she dodged the towers and decayed factories. She wasted no time and made several hectic course changes that defied the laws of structural integrity and common sense. They continued to follow the craft as closely as possible without crashing, making meticulous course adjustments based not only on speed and direction, but on the programmed assumptions that the craft they followed would try to escape them while also trying not to crash. The latter assumption was incorrect and would prove their undoing as Violet flew directly through the side of an old office building, ripping it from its foundations and spinning it in the air 140 degrees. Most of the hoppers crashed right behind her, and the few that had made it to the Blackwing were sheared off as it passed through concrete.

The force cracked the makeshift canopy further and chips fell away. Chunks of wave hopper and office building poured in through the inertia field and cluttered the cockpit. The Blackwing wouldn't be able to take another hit until they found its proper canopy, but the mission seemed over for the time being.

With Skunkworks' external tracking gone, she quickly hacked into the Blackwing's tracking nodes and silenced them, then finally headed north.

As soon as Veikko linked in from the shuttle to tell her she was in the clear, the adrenaline died and she felt a stabbing pain in her foot. That reminded her she had been stabbed in the foot. The broken leg began to complain right after. She took some platelet packs and a quicksplint from the back of her suit and applied them to her foot and leg. She shot an analgesic syrette into her thigh, and it cleared the pain but not the uncomfortable position she had to sit in with her leg splinted.

Violet looked around at the debris collected from the hoppers and office building, all that fell into the cockpit gently after being struck at Mach whatever. Robotic parts, bricks, dust, two pencils from the office building, and half a wall poster of a cat hanging from a tree. She shoveled out the bits and pieces that shook most noisily in the insistent breeze. The half canopy took whatever air passed the triple field and focused it right on Violet's cheek. The little nuisances always seemed amplified after the bulk of a mission was over. She couldn't hit the fastest thrusters and be home in seconds, or she'd be spotted again. She had to wait for the slug-slow Mach 20 ramjets to get her up north.

It took half an hour to arrive in the seas north of Kalaallit Nunaat, where she splashed down and roughly slammed the Blackwing into some underwater rock. That concealed half of it and shattered the last of the makeshift canopy. She left the cockpit outside of the rock face so that she could make her exit. Water was pouring in through the fields and making them crackle badly. She hacked into the shutdown procedures and checked for any coded traps, all the typical thievery, before turning the primary power source off. That cut off the fields and the water flooded in instantly. Damn cold water.

She surfaced to see the old P-Zero shuttle hovering over her. It set down ungently on the water, and she climbed onto its flat chrome wing. A door opened on the slanted side and let her into the same smelly cargo hold she had leaped from hours before. Veikko rolled a scan jamming cylinder down the wing and into the water, then stepped out to toss several Ice-10 crystals in after. They quickly froze a few meters of the sea into a hangar around the exposed parts of the Blackwing.

So ended Project Bentley at 1640 hours on January 3, 2232. Calling it "Bentley" still felt strange. Even after Project Abruptum, Violet couldn't get used to having made a full spin around the alphabet. She might have been more sensitive to meaningless sentimentality on that day at that time because her parents had died exactly two years prior. She took no notice of the goings-on in her subconscious. She buckled into the cargo hold walls with Veikko for the ride north.

Varg chimed in via link, "Highly recommend we abort lift off, ditch this old junker and fly the Burp back home instead."

"Blackwing, Varg. Please don't call it the Burp," rang Vibs.

"Our shuttle is obsolete. We have a new space-worthy craft."

"One we can't show off. Not yet."

Veikko interjected, "Practically speaking, the Bur—the Blackwing has only one seat and no cargo."

"Okay," reasoned Varg, "you three take the P-Zero shuttle, and I'll take the Belch."

"Gaseous regurgitation," laughed Veikko. "Technically it may be a flatu—"

The sound of a light backhand resounded from the hold.

"Thanks, Vi," linked Vibeke.

Silence prevailed for twenty seconds before Varg spoke up. "If they didn't want us to call it a Burp, they shouldn't have named it B-I-R-P. Besides, it won't be a 'black' wing once we gilt it up."

"We won't," answered Vibs. "The flex-diamond hull is better than gold, TK chrome, even natural diamond. It will stay a Blackwing."

Veikko strained a full five seconds before trying to get on Violet's good side. "I vote for purple. The Purple Burple. There's some technical name for a burp, but I can't think of it...."

Violet was about to threaten a second backhand when she looked down to the white smart-foam and found it covered in blood. Her wound was leaking again.

"I have several fractures in my leg and an impalement through my foot," she declared flatly. Veikko looked down at her foot. Varg and Vibeke peered in from the flight deck.

Veikko replied, "Yes, yes you do."

All knew the shuttle was completely lacking in any first aid equipment, and Violet had already applied the best any of their armor had to offer. There was little to be done for the battered appendage. Violet stared at her foot uselessly and exhaled. Soon they would arrive at the ravine, and Dr. Niide would fix the wound. Vibs sent a quiet link back home so he could ready his surgical robots.

The knowledge that she would soon be perfectly repaired struck Violet the opposite way it should have. She felt a subtle wave of apathy. It was an odd thing to feel at the end of a successful mission, and Valkyries were taught to mention any psychological oddities they might experience. So Violet might have told her team that she felt like shit had Veikko not interrupted with a far more dire revelation.

"Eructation! A 'Ructus.' That's the term," he said, looking proudly toward Violet, "for a burp. Cetaceans call it *röyhtäily*." Veikko nodded. Pain seeped into Violet's foot, and the slow flight home in the P0S felt all the slower.

SIRAJ/ŢEPEŞ S.C.S. owned fourteen prisons, jails, and detention centers in Bharat. The Hugli River Detention Center was by far the most infamous of them. Built to house 6,000 inmates, it actually housed well over 25,000 the last time anyone counted, which was over ten years before Mishka was imprisoned there. The "Ergosphere of Kolkata" gave up on prisoner census after 2219 because none of the guards could accurately estimate how many prisoners thick were the piles on which the visible prisoners stood. Since then, matters had only grown worse as every disease from the bubonic plague to swine flu to the hemorrhagic strain of emu fever invaded and mutated amid the human petri dish into unnamable flesh eating pestilences. The culture that grew with equal virulence among the inmates was one of murder, cannibalism, and torture, so Mishka fit right in.

In fact, it was exactly where she wanted to be. Not that she wanted to be in prison, but she didn't have much of a choice. As long as she lived, Vibeke was going to chase her. From the events in Bangla, that much was clear. After a year on the run, Vibs had come within seconds of dragging her back to Valhalla in chains, and if capture by the Bharatiya Sthalsena was the only way out, it would have to do. She knew she'd be able to escape, so the only real loss was her new eye.

They confiscated it as soon as she was processed. She'd grown very attached to her eye in the last year. She wasn't happy about needing a new eye in the first place, but once implanted it grew on her. The poor thing transmitted from the possessions office until a cauliflower-eared guard smashed it under foot.

That was the least of her immediate problems. She was thrown into a holding room that rivaled the worst days of the old På-Täppan pile. She managed to stay atop the heap of people, which was so thick and unstable that she couldn't stand upright. All she could do was crawl cautiously over the mess of sweaty limbs, bleeding sticky prisoners, and shreds of prison clothing. Her own was in tatters within seconds; both sleeves and a pant leg were torn off by hands reaching for anything they could grip to pull themselves out of the mess. When they caught her flesh she twisted them off or bit them off. She had to lessen the number of oncoming attacks. One corner of the room had people piled so high they nearly reached the ceiling. She headed for it.

The instant she secured her penthouse, she began to plot escape. The ventilation shafts were unsuitable, as there were none. The heat was so intense and the air was so foul that she estimated less than an hour before she would succumb to the conditions and would be rendered unconscious or insane, as seemed the symptoms. Her first priority was defense. She elected to make a shiv. After fending off several attacks from her inmates, she took the time to break one of their legs more thoroughly than usual. She snapped his femur with force in the right direction to leave a sharp, jagged edge. The terrible sound kept attackers at bay for a time. She estimated the direction of the internal blade and sawed it free to create an opening, then reached into the wound and began cutting through the connective tissue of the hip with her fingernails.

No sooner did she have the bone knife in her hand and ready to go than the crowd crouched still, staring at just about the most disturbing thing most of the pickpockets and petty thieves had ever seen. Mishka had to smile with the knowledge that the creation of her weapon was a deterrent so strong she might never need to use it. Now her mind was free to contemplate an exit. The only one she could see was the way she came in. She worked her way across the man-pile to the trap door through which prisoners were dropped. It was within reach but flush sealed to the ceiling. So she waited. In only seven minutes, it opened to expel a bruised, beaten mess of a woman. Mishka used her as a step to the door, leaving her to presumably worse uses by others.

Microwave fire began the instant Mishka caught hold of the floor above. She took two stun rays to the wrist, losing her femur shiv as the door closed. She expected the crowd to attack her as she fell, but found them all keeping their distance, well aware that she might want to make another blade. Just then a valve on the south wall opened and a heap of humanity poured out into the adjacent ventricle. Mishka leaped and made sure that she was among them. The new room was bigger and smellier, though it had a floor instead of a pile. A sorting area where newcomers were forced by guards into whatever ring of hell came next. It contained men who hadn't seen her weapon-forging techniques, so as soon as she spotted a guard, she ran for him. In seconds she had cracked his armor like a crab shell. In seconds more she had his doleo and used it to send waves of pain through the other inmates who grabbed for it.

Having quickly mastered the new room, she hunted for an exit. This room had the same rotten walls as the last but no people-heap. The bases of some walls had serious decay. She was looking for something to widen the cracks when a three-meter-tall humanoid stomped up to her. She had fought enlarged gang members back with Valhalla, men who had every bone lengthened and every muscle bloated to provide a fearful visage to their enemies. It had worked so far for this man; he was still alive. But Mishka had seen the schematics. A solid surgery could strengthen a person if it added a decimeter to his height, but this oncoming thing must have added a meter and change. His bones were longer, but they were weaker. He bared his sharp black teeth as he prepared to grab her with a hand that could fit fully around her waist. She didn't even think of using the doleo as a simple baton to cause pain. She had to get to the wall over lines of cowering prisoners and oncoming guards. She extended the doleo to its full length and ran for Gargantua, forcing the doleo into his mouth to the back of his throat, putting him down to serve as her pole vault box. She flew over him into the wall with enough force to put a deep dent between two of the worst rotting breaches.

She felt cool air from the outdoors. So did others. Mishka elected to stand back as they started beating down the wall, savagely attacking their only hope of escape. Every guard left in the room was on her, and in numbers their armor would be harder to crack. She broke the doleo in half, knowing the inside of a doleo contains a powerful burst-discharge battery. Keeping the other guards at bay with a barrage of strikes, she tore the coating off the battery and threw it to the floor, then flipped one of the guards down and crushed the battery. The discharge nearly vaporized him within his metal armor. Bolts struck the other guards and knocked them unconscious.

Prisoners had since worked the wall loose and began to pour out. The first twenty men had been microwaved by outdoor guards. Another twenty still fled the heat and decay of the indoors before the crowd began to understand that death waited outside. Once they were finished dying, Mishka made her move. Shaking the powdered guard from his armor, she donned the hot metal and ran for freedom. It began to grow hotter as soon as she was outside, hit by microwave beams. She'd hoped to pass for a guard, but they either didn't buy it or didn't care. They were roasting anything that emerged.

The situation was difficult. Ten guards running at her on the ground. Ten more firing at her from walls and towers. Thirty corpses around her. Armor keeping the beams off but heating up badly. It would knock her out in under a minute. She burrowed quickly under the thickest concentration of bodies and forced the armor off herself. Microwaves were still hitting the body pile above her. Some were starting to burn. Luckily the ground guards were almost there. She heard shouting, and the microwaves ceased. Soon after, the corpse atop Mishka began to move. They were pulling it away.

Mishka rolled limply to get a view of the guard that was prodding the bodies. He was careless. She sprang and seized his microwave, then used its stock to knock off his helmet. He turned away but exposed his familiarly deformed, bloated ear. She shot through the front of his temple to blind him, and he dropped. Others were coming. She took cover within the bodies as guards opened fire again. She surveyed the weapon; it only had stun, burn, and dig functions. Dig would have to do. She fired at the fattest corpse in the pile and waited for fire to cease again. It ceased after only thirty seconds. Then she felt the guards prying again. They'd be more cautious this time. Using the guards' motions as cover, she worked her way into the hollow man. If he stayed facedown she could stay hidden. He stayed facedown.

Minutes later the guards had the situation under control. Mishka prayed they would skimp on proper investigation and cleanup. She waited almost twenty minutes, but nobody touched her makeshift tauntaun. She could just make out a hand grab the microwave she discarded. Her prayers were answered when she heard the bulldozer. She wasn't able to hold on to her cover for long as the bodies rolled, but she didn't need to; nobody was watching anymore. They pushed the pile straight into the Hugli River.

Once underwater, more accurately under sewage, she swam fast for the opposite bank, where only a razor-wire fence blocked the bank. Halfway across she emerged from the prison's link jam and ads flooded in. Behind the fence was a market. She cautiously surfaced and scanned for guards. None on this side, none watching from the other. All busy sealing the hole or dumping another dozer-load of bodies. She emerged from the river and spat out the foul slime that had seeped into her mouth, then climbed the razor wire. Climbing the stuff was never her forte in training, and her palms paid the price, but injury training was one of her best subjects. She topped the fence and dropped into the market.

She had three priorities: number three, find a new eye; number two, find her tank; but number one was something she could do immediately. She had to. With great urgency she scanned the signs and link labels of the market and found her destination. After her stay in the prison and swim through the sewage, she had little time. She ran, pushing aside anyone in her way, throwing the door open so hard it snapped a hinge. She jumped over the counter and grabbed a clerk by his collar. Customers ran, the clerk cowered in fear. He could see Mishka was desperate, ravenous, and homicidal.

"Please," he begged. "Anything you want! I'll give you anything!"

"Hand sanitizer!" she demanded. "Alcohol gel, antiseptic alcohol gel! Now!"

With her wounds clean and stinging, she broke open the store's first aid kit and regrew all but one cut in her skin. She stuffed the dermal regenerator in the elastic of her waistband. She ran back outside and quickly hid in an alley—the market was swarming with Bharatiya Sthalsena. She ducked into a weak crate and killed the man sleeping inside, then headed online.

She hacked the Bharatiya Sthalsena net in seconds. It showed every soldier on the streets. None were coming for her. Only a few were following search protocols. To the side of the operations files, she found records. Impounds. Impound lots. HRDC lots, HRDC unconventional vehicles. One listing for a four-legged tank. HRDC lot address—only three kilometers away. Back to the street ops pages. Personnel on duty. Bharatiya Sthalsena soldiers by height. Female. 1.87 meters. Hugli River Marketplace. One: Sanchita Patel. Highlighted, two blocks north, one block east.

Mishka sprang from her box and found her quarry. With the element of surprise, it was an easy takedown. Her uniform was a perfect fit, and her army ID chip was poorly implanted, easy to cut out of her palm. It didn't even have a removal detector. Mishka walked toward the impound lot and hacked back onto the authority net. The HRDC lot site had the easiest security yet. She created a new log: Sanchita Patel authorized to pick up white quadrupedal tank impounded four days prior. All too easy. As she approached the lot, she stuffed Sanchita's chip into her palm and hastily healed the last bit of skin. One handshake and her tank was hers.

Such as it was. Her quadrupedal tank now had three legs. She demanded an explanation. The HDRC guard shrugged. Who the hell would take one leg off a tank? She stormed across the lot looking for the missing limb. Nothing. When she came back to the guard, she seized him by the throat.

"That tank had four legs!" She checked the net logs. "It had four when it got here! You're responsible for this lot?"

He nodded, afraid. She caught a link going out. He was calling in more guards to ask about the missing parts. Guards that might not think she looked like Sanchita once they arrived. She couldn't waste any more time there. She jumped into the crippled tank and powered up its systems. Tripedal mode was about half as fast as normal. Still over 300 kph. It would do. She locked it in. The tank gave a jolt as it rotated two legs forward and one aft. She left as the new guards entered the complex, never learning that the arrivals wouldn't have known she was an impostor. Never learning that one of them, Ravi Vasquez, had removed the leg for use as a rocking chair. He would have been happy to resettle his grandmother back home and return it.

Mishka was already hunting the nets again for an eye and a leg as she galloped north. The leg was priority four, and Mishka knew the few places she'd have to break into to find a replacement. All high security. It might not even be worth the effort. An eye was priority three. Bharat was full of cheap eyes. In that same market was an AWB eye, which would, in theory, give her back her depth perception. But it could be hacked far too easily. A few kilometers south was a proper eye doctor, but his stock was limited to low-res wasteware. She kept searching for something useful. In Valhalla, Alf taught her never to fully eradicate the advertising that came with searches, but rather to filter it and skim it for potential results. Often someone was selling what they were looking for when all else might fail. As she drove right past the Vasquez residence, such an ad appeared to her.

"*Eye-Spy Yaugiku 1.2.1 by Krillco with 318 lenses. Capable of shrinking to one centimeter or expanding to three centimeters to fit any orbit and come out easy. Why take it out? Because this eye can fly. Link guidance can send your new eye half a kilometer in any direction with .25 kN of force. Great fun for the casual voyeur or a selling point for the professional private eye! Comes in white, black, blue, or made to match your natural appearance. 75,250 euros. See licenses required?*"

The loss of her old implant didn't seem so bitter anymore. If she hadn't lost it, she might never have met her new Tikari. And there was one on display at a convention at the Darjeeling Dome, right there in Poshchim Bangla. She lacked the funds and licenses, and the convention was closed for the night, but the latter problem solved the former two just fine. The white tank galloped north.

ALOPEX WAS running 477 distinct routines. About half of them were common ongoing processes to maintain the ravine, track teams, monitor security risks, and so on. Of the rest, there were a multitude of team projects that required special partitions, a few teams doing online work that required surveillance and security, and then some simple entertainment and dream link programs. There was only one medical program in progress. Medical almost always had priority over other systems. Of course, Alopex had never run over 70 percent capacity, so no programs had ever been overridden. There were only a select few programs that could override medical, such as the rampart system, HMDLR defenses, and some emergency shutoffs. There used to be one ultrahigh priority shutoff for an Ares Corporation hydromacrosis test, which could use 100 percent of Aloe's system and drop every defense Valhalla had. As Valhalla wasn't in the terraforming business, that program was not only obsolete but dangerous, so it was erased. In any case, the top priority running was a fairly routine program to fix a broken leg and stab wound in Violet's foot.

The second program was Alf's, monitoring GAUNE communications for the words "Wave," "Zombie," and "Mutagenic." All words commonly associated with wave bombs, "zombie bombs" to the vulgar public, "mutagenic weaponry" being the most proper term. High-level GAUNE chatter was filled with speculation about UNEGA illegally stockpiling wave bombs, but it was all mere speculation. There was no sign that UNEGA would build or deploy new weapons or try to fool the GAUNE weapons inspectors they allowed to supervise mutagenic wave studies. Alf was certain the threats were null but always kept an ear on the rumors. Given the severity of the issue and its potential to trigger global thermonuclear war and worse, he always had Alopex watching so that Valhalla might prevent any escalation before it grew unmanageable.

The third priority routine was unusual. It was normally a tenth-tier police monitoring program, but Vibeke had programmed it to go ultrahigh priority if it found a hit. In the year since she'd written it, the thing had never activated. For at least that one year, not a single cybernetic eyeball had been stolen. Mishka had bought her first replacement eye legally after some hard work in Africa. But the theft of a Krillco Eye-Spy Yaugika 1.2.1 from its showcase in Bharat was not to be missed. Alopex allowed a full three-picosecond delay in lower priority programs to deliver the news.

"Vibeke," called the fox. Vibs turned away from the clear med bay wall and brightened her link to see it clearly.

"Yes?"

"Cybernetic eye theft reported."

Vibeke barely registered it at first. It took her a moment to remember why Alopex would jump in at top priority to tell her. After that she realized it was obsolete, an old program now useless given that Mishka, last she saw her, had a perfectly good pair of eyes in her head. After the last chase through Bangla, Vibeke was sure of that. She didn't even want to think about it. They had Mishka trapped, and somehow the entire Bharatiya Sthalsena got in the way. It was the last insult in a frustrating year of near misses and hits that hit back. But in any case, Mishka was gone. Vibeke felt bad for making Aloe treat it as high priority. She would just ask one question to be sure it was a null report, and then she'd delete the routine.

"Don't suppose it was in Bangla?"

"Confirmed, northern Poshchim Bangla, Darjeeling."

Suddenly Alopex had her complete attention. Mishka was back on the map. Vibs immersed herself online where she stood and began reading every report and every detail of the theft, then of related local reports. She found the prison break, and it all came together—Mishka had avoided their capture by turning herself in to the Bharatiya Sthalsena. Their mass presence was to catch her, and she let herself be caught by an enemy she could escape rather than be caught by Valhalla. Cunning bitch.

VIOLET WIGGLED her big toe. Then each other toe. Her foot was back, but there was still some pain in her ankle. Dr. Niide looked over the foot and spotted a microscopic air pocket stimulating the nerves. He gave her a quick stab with a hypodermic needle and let it out. She walked around for a moment and nodded. Dr. Niide then simply wandered away.

After leaving the med bay, she found Vibs staring at the rocks. She poked her arm gently with no result. She must have been immersed deeply. And urgently given that she'd gone all the way in while standing. Violet linked in without knocking. Vibeke didn't notice her, but Violet could hear the reports. Eyeball. Bharat. She was looking for Mishka again. Violet logged out and pushed Vibeke over. She caught her oblivious teammate and carried her toward the barracks.

Vibeke had taken the results of Project Abruptum badly. Worse than Project Omfavnet, their previous run in with Mishka, which was in turn worse than Project Creative: the hunt for Mishka and Wulfgar that began nearly a year ago. But Abruptum was by far the most taxing because it was the closest they'd been. Before a *diabolus ex machina* that ruined everything, Vibeke had gone to frightening depths of obsession on that mission. Violet was still concerned deeply about the civilians Vibeke was willing to sacrifice, the risks she was willing to take, the irrational raw hatred that consumed her as they drew closer to Bangla. And it wasn't over.

Violet set Vibs down on her bunk and then sat down on her own. She stared at her. Peaceful on the outside, vacant. She might have been daydreaming. Whatever storm was pounding away in her brain, her body was perfectly serene. Skin pale and smooth, hair getting longer. She sometimes let the stuff grow and cut it instead of freezing it like Violet and the rest of the world. She kept turning it black as well. A strange habit that seemed to give Vibeke some sort of amusement or peace. Soon she'd have to cut it again or start welding it down for missions, which would be a good look. It was already down to the collar of her armor in back.

Cool blue and green armor. Violet's favorite in the ravine. Not least because of the body in it. Her eyes went straight for Vibeke's chest. Just plump enough to shift to the sides when she lay down. When she caught herself staring at Vibeke's breasts, she usually stopped, erased the thoughts as best she could, and focused on whatever mission or project they might have. They didn't have one just then, and her eyes were on Vibeke's hands before she noticed they weren't alone. Veikko's head slowly dipped in from the bunk above Violet's.

"Watcha dooin'?"

"Begging for trouble," she mumbled and lay back on her pillow. Veikko craned around upside down to look at Vibs.

"What's she doing?"

"I only peeked. The files said Bangla and eyeball theft."

"You worried?"

"No," she lied. "At least she has leads."

Violet did envy her that. The chase for Mishka was frustrating, but it was still a chase. Violet couldn't muster the obsessive hatred of Wulfgar that Vibs had for her nemesis, only an active vicious hatred that for the last year, had been dwindling from starvation. He was out there somewhere, but what of it? There was no trace of him. There was no murmur of activity, no hint of a gang reforming, not a single whisper on Earth that he was still alive. It was possible that he wasn't. Dr. Niide couldn't guess the damage done to his brain from the glimpse they caught of his head. It was entirely possible and, given the lack of developments, more and more likely that whoever stole his corpse couldn't repair it.

Violet had watched for medical logs, newly grown jaws, crushed corpses, and the like without leads. Unless he had elected to stay broken and faceless, he wasn't awake.

Vibeke snapped out of the net and sat up, reorienting herself to being in bed. Violet nodded to let her know how she got there, and Vibs nodded back. Violet was trying to come up with a subtle way to ask what Vibeke had found, but Veikko beat her to it.

"What news of the one-eyed monster?"

Vibeke link dumped the answer to her team. Her escape via capture, the stolen eye, all the peripheral notes. Violet took some time to look over it, all solid notes but nothing useful for finding her again. Violet was half-relieved at that. She wanted Mishka caught or dead but hated Vibeke's distance and cold bitter demeanor when they were on her trail. It was like all sense of fun got sucked out of her. Project Omfavnet was in Varg's opinion one of the most enjoyable cat and mouse games the Valkyries ever played, but for Vibeke and, by proxy, Violet, it was something like the road rash segment of injury training. It just grated and grated away. And it was coming again.

The door opened. Varg entered and jumped over Vibeke onto his bunk.

"That link dump came a second before I did, ruined everything."

"Sorry, Varg."

"My heart will go on…. So what's the point, though?" he ruminated. "We knew where she was, and she's not going to stick around Darjeeling."

"Didn't you see the link encryptions?"

Violet hadn't. Varg shook his head as well. All four dove back into the net and reviewed the logs. Vibeke scooped up a folder.

"See this? She hacked into the Dome's cameras when she went after the eye. Darjeeling's nets are so old that she could cream the security systems, but the security systems had no self-repair contingencies. They're still broken right now. They'll have to be reinstalled."

Violet didn't see the significance, but Varg caught it. "Her footprints are still there?"

Vibeke replied quickly, "She covered her tracks and deleted the providers, but you can see the routing they came from."

"The routing?" asked Veikko. "She was there in person. What's the point?"

Vibeke enlarged the coding prints for them to see. "Mishka was in prison. Her link was jammed. When she got out, it didn't hook into the Bharat nets. It went back to the last place she was logged into before she was caught."

Violet was amazed by the leaps and bounds of logic Vibs took for granted. She was only just grasping the train of thought when Varg derailed it to another track. He took the files and enlarged them further, looking over lines of code and text that she couldn't make out.

"And it's all black, Vibs. There's no code at all. It even lacked—" Varg's eyes lit up. "It had no contact barriers!"

Veikko seemed to understand it. All three were in on something, but Violet had no clue. She'd suffer the indignity of having to ask. Nothing new.

"What does that mean?"

"There's only one place that has no barriers."

And then Violet understood. In their hunt, V team had probed every job offer, every mercenary listing, every possible rumor of Mishka's specialties on every board and page she might have advertised on. They spent weeks browsing the Underground Nikkei and Dead List. They had a Chanscan reading the busiest, sleaziest imageboards and criminal channels for any sign of her. They even set an unnecessarily large partition of Alopex to look for codes and hidden messages in all of the above. But that would have defeated the purpose. Mishka wasn't talking in code to anyone. She was most certainly on her own. If she was online, she'd be offering her craft publicly. They knew she had work because they'd gotten in her way. Omfavnet cost her a pretty penny when an employer saw her clash with Valhalla and decided she was damaged goods. Project Abruptum began with a routine investigation. They had no clue at first it was Mishka working for Birlacorp in a black flag operation against themselves. But Birlacorp and Omfavnet Selskap had no listings anywhere V team could probe. C team insisted that there were none. That she must have handled it all in the real world.

C team was insistent about it because they didn't want anyone searching the one dirty corner of the nets that V hadn't searched. The only place online that Valhalla wouldn't risk sending Alopex or any but a senior team because the danger was too great. The only place so reckless it lacked contact barriers and risked all the demented minds who dared to venture there. The place they now knew for certain, despite the checks and assurances of C team, that Mishka had indeed been hiding.

"She's on the Black Crag!" exclaimed Violet. Her team stared at her, shocked. All four were suddenly back in the barracks.

Varg cringed. "Did you just say that out loud?"

"Oh shit," said Veikko.

Vibeke closed her eyes. Someone had said "Black Crag." It was only a matter of time.

"Maybe nobody heard," suggested Violet. "Maybe the—"

All four heard the link alarm. Then came an Australian voice. The most damnable voice in Valhalla.

"V team to C team office, please. Again," added Cato.

They skulked offline, and Violet's face burned red. They had made this walk four times before. Since they first asked for clearance, C had put a monitor on them. Every time they so much as mentioned its name, they got called into C's office for another little chat. The worst had been in September, and then they had only said the name because two and a quarter teams had just been slaughtered on it. It was the darkest day in Valkyrie history, and C team used it to teach them a damn lesson. And here they were again. Cato let them in with an expression that Violet wanted to rip off its underlying muscles.

Churro sat behind his desk looking like a disappointed father. Cato stood beside him, and Violet tried to amuse herself thinking of the man as a mother. She couldn't for long. The term "Thought Police" applied more accurately.

"Tell me, how many teams are there in Valhalla?"

Churro wasn't pulling any punches. He was in full cruelty mode from the start. Vibeke wasn't going to have it.

"We have proof Mishka was—"

"Tell me, Vibeke. How many teams?"

Vibeke stewed. "Twenty."

"And how many did we have in August?"

"Twenty-two. But—"

"Twenty-three. We had the beginnings of a Z team. We had," he said, smiling sardonically, "a whole alphabet."

Veikko chided, "The runic alphabet actually has—"

"We had, V team, nine junior Valkyries! Nine lives we do not have now! Why, V Team, do we not have them?"

Because of a race war. Because of a fight Valhalla shouldn't have been involved in. Because C team didn't do their job and watch over the junior teams. Because the junior teams got in over their heads. Because C team decided to kill nine hacked Valkyries rather than try to get their brains back. Not because V team said a damn name. Violet thought it all but didn't shout it. Vibeke shouted instead.

"You told us you searched it! You told us Mishka wasn't on the Black Crag. You missed the bitch, and you fucked up! We have proof that—"

"We didn't miss her," Cato spoke softly. "We lied to you."

They fell silent. Churro looked at Cato, then spoke again, calmly.

"We never bothered to check for her. We don't go there unless we have to. If a job can be done in five minutes on the Crag or five years in reality, we take the long road. Mishka isn't going to take down Valhalla. I doubt she wants to. She wants to be left alone. I won't tell you to leave her alone, but you need to think about your priorities. One is defense. The Black Crag *can* take down Valhalla. It damn nearly did, and you already seem to have forgotten it. You're still talking about that damn Crag. Why?"

Vibeke didn't lose a second. "Mishka's log from Poshchim Bangla shows—"

"Yes, Mishka is there," mocked Cato. "You did a great job. You're doing a great job and chasing a great chase. But it just ended."

"The hell it did," Vibs barked.

"The hell?" Claire chimed in. "Let's say there is a hell. Mishka's dead, and she's in hell. Do you follow? Do you drag Valhalla to hell with you?"

Vibs had the good taste not to answer the way she wanted to. Claire went on.

"It's not your choice if you would. If you set foot there, you put us all in danger. We told you we checked because we need it out of your mind. We still need it out of your mind even if you know for a fact she's there. We saw Mishka's missing barriers too. But did you consider what that little bit of clever tracking means? Without contact barriers, anyone there gives up all their security, all their protocol. There's no such thing as hack armor there, they don't have to wait for you to touch them to read your mind, they can grab you and kill you or reprogram you without any warning. Valhalla does not go there."

"We go there every day!" Vibs scowled. "It's called the real world. You can get shot, and you can get followed and get hacked. And it's not like we'd go in unarmed, all the shit they can do, we can do better. And we have Aloe to watch out for us."

"You're missing the big picture, Vibeke." Cato kept his voice soft and demeaning. "If you have our computer with you, they can take her over. Sure you know your net combat, and Aloe has the best tricks in the biz up her sleeve, but imagine what would become of Valhalla if she were taken over by a pirate? Or rogue company? There are things in this ravine even you don't know the danger of."

Bullshit. Violet knew. They showed her everything. There were no secrets, and she hated Cato enough to speak up. "Like what?"

"Like me," he replied in all seriousness. Pathetic. He leaned in toward Violet. He nodded severely, tried to be intimidating. Violet hated it when he tried to be intimidating. Violet's foot hated when he tried to be intimidating. Her foot decided to launch toward his throat. Cato would hardly be a senior team Valkyrie if he couldn't block a kick. In fact he might be called merciful for not breaking her leg again in the process. He didn't even flinch. He just blocked, stood, and spoke. "We're watching you like a Geki. You can't go, so try elsewhere. Or better yet, lay off the Russian sheila for a while and take a job from the crank file. Maybe nuke Tunisia. Meeting over."

Chapter II: Nikkei

THE FLIGHT to Venus wasn't scary. Dr. Mowat had been to Luna, Mars, and Station 9. Space flight was 90 percent dull and 10 percent beautiful. The accommodations on Venus weren't scary either. She'd have her own room. On Station 9 it was six people to a sleeping pod. Iwo Donatsu was said to have private tents for every individual. The colossal balloon that held the mine afloat was filled with breathable air. Earth air on Venus was like helium on Earth. So she'd be living and working within the balloon, the first time in space she'd have some space. Not the least bit scary.

The scary part was the airlock. It would contain a trace of Venusian weather. It would be purged of air, washed out with a blast of cleaning solution, and it would have a fast cycle of devoted oxygen to lessen the impact of the inevitable. But no matter what they installed, there would be a trace of Venus inside. A drop of rain always stuck to a panel or behind a screw somewhere, and rain on Venus is 700 Kelvin sulfuric acid. They wouldn't send people through if it still posed any risk. Legally they had to reduce it to a healthy ppm, but those last millionths were said to be damn potent and prohibitively expensive to reduce any further. Orientation said it was like inhaling a bit of Tom Yum soup.

She ran through the airlock and vowed never to try Tom Yum soup as long as she lived. The Iwo Donatsu lock closed and acquainted her with the balloon's atmosphere. It smelled fresh and alive, and somewhat artificially minty. The walls were all deep blue or green, the light cool and soft. Nothing like Station 9's nonstop brightness. Once inside, there was nothing to remind her she was on a hot orange planet, nothing to remind her she was in a mining complex. It was more like an undersea hotel, no doubt the merciful architect's way of letting the workers forget that they were, in fact, on planet hell.

There was one man in the lobby, dressed in shiny black rubber. He carried a microwave rifle on his back. He had no hair and no antenna, nor any discernible emotion. His voice was dead cold too.

"Dr. Mowat, you will follow me to your tent. I will carry your luggage."

"Whatever you say, boss," she sighed. He picked up her bags, heavy bags, like they were nothing. The gravity wasn't that different from Earth. She had just hauled the things in. She noticed the bumps around his sides. Powered armor or powered implants. His rubber garb was covered in too many pockets to tell which. She had to wonder if his extra punch was because he worked in the mine or something else. The man she was working for wasn't affiliated with the mines. None of his crew were supposed to be either. When she asked what they were doing on Venus if not mining sulfur, they almost terminated her contract on the spot. So she wouldn't ask here, and she wouldn't ask the man what his powered arms were for. He led her to a tram, and they sat down. As soon as the tram started, she could see the open balloon.

It looked bigger inside than out. A cavernous, foggy tunnel, half a kilometer high. The tram plodded along the very bottom, a long curved valley from which she could see the atmospheric refineries and storage bays. The refineries weren't as large as the complex of ducts emerging from them. Every meter of the walls had some sort of duct on it. Even over the hum of the tram, she could hear the throbbing drone of the air systems keeping them afloat and alive. Past the refineries she could see the city. There were tents right off of the track and tents all the way up the walls, accessible by ladder and positioned to offer a flat floor on what lower tents called their sides. There were no people to be seen. Everyone was either at work or asleep. The tram stopped at the far end of the city.

"You will stay in tent 390. You will be the only resident of this tent. Other medical staff live in tents 384–389. The hospital tent is straight ahead."

A giant tent, but still a tent. Two floors of light green canvas unmoving in the well-controlled air. She walked toward the tent, but the man motioned for her to stick to her own dwelling.

"You will not see the patient until tomorrow. You will be summoned."

He set her luggage down at her tent door and handed her a key card. Then without another word, sat on the tram and headed back to the lobby. A very cold reception. She found the tent to be as spartan as the rest of space, just a cot and a bathroom. She lay down and immersed herself in a memory partition. The net didn't reach to Venus, so she blocked out the world and slept in the files for the job to be done.

Dr. Mowat knew nothing about the client. She knew his injuries, his physiological scans, blood typology, immune system, and obviously she had seen images of his face—or at least what his face looked like before. But there was no name, no history beyond medical allergies (Novusazidocillin and Carbamazepine) and the injuries she was there to fix.

The patient was in a miserable state. Mutilated and murdered a year prior and whisked away without treatment. She had seen worse lapses in treatment and time. Many a businessman had been forced to wait in stasis for several years while his company or family saved up to hire her. Her last client back on Earth had slept for three years, unlinked and unconscious, while his spine was built, then scrapped for nonpayment, then rebuilt, then misplaced, then built again. So one year wasn't bad. What was bad was that he wasn't in stasis. He was awake and aware the whole time.

The patient refused to be knocked out. They resurrected him minutes after the murder without fixing a single thing and plugged his wounds for the trip to Venus. But he wouldn't go back under for anything more than a night's natural sleep. He had been living for a year with a smashed skeleton, no jaw, no legs, and no link. Dr. Mowat couldn't think of a worse kind of hell. Or one more easily avoided—if he could afford a flight to Venus he could have stayed on Earth and been fixed in a day. If for some reason he absolutely had to be in a Venusian sulfur mine, he still could have flown in a doctor like her within the month. And with a year to wait, he could have slept. But she was paid not to ask. And not to ask about the new jaw.

The nerve damage was minimal, and scans showed the loss of his jaw was physical trauma, no microwaves or burns or irradiation. He could have had a new normal jaw grown and attached without a problem. Same with his feet. But he had ordered some of the strangest modifications Dr. Mowat had ever seen. Mostly in that they didn't fit.

The jaw, when implanted, would be about two centimeters larger than his old one. Two centimeters isn't much in some engineering, but on a face, it's night and day. And this jaw wouldn't have skin over it. It was essentially a chain saw made to fit where a mandible used to. The inner teeth and soft tissue would let him eat and talk normally, but the outer teeth, jagged blades on a fast rotary track, were something not even the Cetaceans would ask for. Rumors of modifications for the Unspeakable Darkness contained massive fangs or horns and the like, but she'd never seen someone rich enough to get a jaw like this ever get anything so bizarre. Rotary teeth, structure extendable to half a meter, chrome plating instead of skin.

It was less rare for a man with a crushed skeleton to ask for a larger build and, given the funds, for some new intracranial armor and the latest designer marrow by Ossium. Almost half of her male clients ordered larger genitals. No reason for this one to be different. Link repair was common as cockroaches. A hidden link in the neck was not uncommon either. His hands would be bigger and stronger by far, and his feet—would also be hands. She had done palmed feet with opposable thumbs for Spetsnaz a few years back, the biggest paycheck she'd ever had until the Venusian client. She had no occasion to follow the soldiers' progress with the feet, all top secret, but she'd get to see it through this time. Two more months on Venus after the surgery. She knew nothing of the man so far but would be getting to know him very well.

She looked forward to it. He must have been a powerful man to afford what he was getting, to afford her and her trip to Venus. To be there at all. And to have earned the injuries she was treating—he was not mugged on the street. Someone had torn his jaw off, crushed him, torn his limbs apart. Someone hated this man. She looked over his external scans from before the incident. His face was not one to be hated easily. He was only just showing signs of his age, more signs of experience than midlife decay. His eyes especially, piercing eyes. There was a strong mind behind them, one strong enough to wake up day after day with an unset skeleton, with no mouth, with only something to do so urgent and so far away....

She had been staring at his insides and outsides all night. She was jarred awake by a page from the cold henchman summoning her to the hospital tent. The Donatsu medical facility was impressive, state of the art from Nippon, so they wouldn't have to send expensive doctors like her out too often. The programming went quickly. All his scans matched observations of his body. She had to correct for some necrosis that the calculations didn't expect, but those were calculations by programs made to predict a body's change over hours, not a year. Some of the skeletal damage was more severe than predicted. The mass of what crushed him must have been tremendous. There was also one more skewed prediction—his body was devoid of painkillers and showed no signs of sustained analgia field exposure. Over the last year his entire skeleton had been growing back wrong, and the tears in his flesh had been *cauterized* of all things. And he had not been living in an analgia field nor drugging himself into a daze. Who was this man?

Once programmed, the robotic arms took almost an hour to complete their jobs. The longest operation she'd ever designed. She watched the mechanical arms dig in to break all the misfit bones, inject new marrow, repair and plate the tissue in its new position. She saw the hands and handlike feet she'd grown on Earth attached and tested for reflex. And the jaw, that strange apparatus built by Fuji Automatic. They'd consulted with her over the last few months about nerve endings and skull sutures, so she knew what to expect, but to see the thing on his face, held on by bolts instead of muscle, teeth of glistening metal at the angle she devised carefully to not rip off his upper lip. A brutal mechanism. Yet it didn't ruin his face. He looked strong, unnatural to be sure, but not bad or unattractive. He looked bold.

The robotics and tools receded into their holds. The surplus tissue, 20 percent of his former body, took a last pathological scan and then incinerated, its ashes dumped into the boiling sulfur air, scattered to the terrible winds and burning rock below.

The patient awoke five minutes later. He was eager to stand, as all patients were. But unlike every patient before him, he was able. Dr. Mowat gently helped him up to his alien feet, and he stood on them, flexing his new muscles, popping his new joints. It was a reward in every patient to see the parts she constructed come alive. But never had she seen a man who lived a year waiting for them. It was a look of ecstasy on his face, a smile like no other that formed on his silver lower lip. He spoke, and his voice was deep, tremendously deep and half metallic. His voice from before must have been penetrating. His voice now certainly was.

"Dr. Mowat, thank you! I feel like a new man."

He put his new hand on her left shoulder. She couldn't even muster the will to say "You're welcome." His presence when awake was intimidating. His pleasure, being free of pain for the first time in so long, standing for the first time in so long, was radiating from him like steam. She stood and smiled, and regretted deeply how obviously she must have blushed.

The rest of that day passed quickly. It was all tests, which he performed perfectly, and scans, which showed a surgery gone well, flawlessly. She didn't dare to ask any questions. She was scared enough when he laughed or spoke a stray word. Every miniscule fiber of information she could glean from him was a treasure. He had been crushed by an animal. He had been awake because he lost his business empire and busily ordered his men in black to reassemble what they could from his meager Venusian holdings into something worth investing in.

As days went on, she heard more and more snips and bits about his enterprises. She wasn't a businesswoman by nature or education, but she could grasp his skills. Back on Earth he had a great company, and for every euro of it he kept one cent on Venus. Though he had no interest in sulfur mining, he gradually paid for repair and improvement work on Iwo Donatsu. Over the years he replaced so much of it that he owned it. He never told a single Earthside employee about the venture. He never even made a profit on it. In fact, once he owned the mine, he made certain its output never improved.

So in time he had an off-planet resort, staffed by 200 or so men loyal to him and nobody else. Filled with supplies to start anew should the need arise, not only lawyers on the strangest retainers in history or investment bankers ready to activate other hidden accounts but more. She asked what the "more" was once, and he almost told her before one of the black rubber men interrupted to dissuade him from answering, and raised a stranger question—he called the man "Little Boots." And the patient did indeed wear shorter boots than usual to fit his Spetsnaz feet. But lacking his real name, the nickname struck her as oddly childish.

As much as she listened to him, he seemed interested in her. What can a common programming physician say to compare with stories about conquering another planet? Every day she felt more and more inadequate, socially. Like she had nothing to offer. His recovery was so flawless she had no need to be there, so she thought. She was there as company and began to wonder why. She couldn't be so lucky as to have caught his eye. Not like that. He didn't give any hint of interest either and finally in passing mentioned that there was someone back on Earth. Though she wasn't sure it was his wife. She pushed for a little more about her, called the lady back home a lucky woman, but he shook his head.

"No," he told her, "I wouldn't say that at all."

After a month he asked her to take a walk with him to a disused part of the balloon. They passed some things she didn't expect to see. One was a giant mining drill. But this was a floating mine that collected rare, short-lived sulfur isotopes in the rain. She knew a little about Venus, but she had never heard of any purpose or even capability to mine the surface. Nobody had ever even stepped out onto the surface, she read in school, leading to a broken line of memorable first statements. "That's one small step for a man; one giant leap for mankind," on Luna, "I wish that the peace I see here could bless the Earth again," from Mars, "This one's for you, Mark Twain," on Halley's Comet. And from the only manned landing on Venus, "Oh my holy fucking shit I think we're on the fucking ground! Get us up we're gonna fucking die!"

She was surprised, almost disappointed that he let her in on so much. Even worried that he might not let her leave knowing what she knew. But she wouldn't tell him to stop. She wanted anything she could get of this man. No matter the cost.

They came to a storage bay set aside from all the others. It was white and subtly decorated. It looked almost like an Elline temple with the pillars. He opened the door and let her inside. The room was flooded with orange light, she realized, because it had a window in the floor. They were looking down onto the clouds and raw orange air. The rain dripping from the bottom of the balloon cast a rippling light on them both. In the room were two crates. Coffins, she realized. He put his hand on one gently.

"This was my brother. My twin. He met with the same executioner that cut me apart."

She couldn't think of a condolence to offer. She looked at the coffin and imagined a man like her patient within. She felt a stab of anger toward whoever did all this. He was the strongest, most noble, most passionately alluring man she had ever met. And the most cursed. Who would kill his family? Cut him apart and crush him? It was unthinkable. It was sickening. And to her, it was personal. Doctors take no oaths to bar them from feeling the pain of their patients, or the vengeance of them.

"Who? Who did all this?" she implored.

He took his hand from his brother's coffin and set it on the other. He looked at it gravely.

"In this coffin is something that she—that the girl who did this doesn't know I have. Something of hers. Something it would hurt her to know I have. At least that's what I hope. Tell me, my doctor"—those words, "*my* doctor," filled her with light against the dark facts she was learning—"if you could fix me after a year, what could you do with some body that's been rotting for two?"

The job he had in mind was perverse. She was sickened by it at first. But she had come to understand him in that month. What he wanted was possible. It wasn't even half as hard as his own surgery. The body wasn't rotting at all. It had been in stasis. A computerized brain, not a person but a simple A.I. with two settings, had already been programmed and set for the corpse. She wished that he could have reanimated his brother instead, to have given him back what he lost, for in that loss she now knew he had lost too much of himself. He had lost the pin in the grenade, the tourniquet that kept the madness in him from bleeding out.

If he had his brother again, he might have gone on just restarting his business. In that coffin on the right was a lost chance. A future that couldn't have been because some monster had burned away his brain. A future Dr. Mowat would have given anything to rebuild for her patient. In the coffin on the left was revenge, cruel and twisted, a future of pain, hatred, and blood. And that was the future she had awakened. The only future he had left.

So she gave him what he wanted. And she didn't hold it against him. She loved the man. She knew it in those last days. She could have told him. He might have even let her stay. But he was busy playing with his new toy. The doctor was, like so many with the privilege of knowing great men, only a pawn. A cameo compared to the star. She knew that what he was doing, what she had helped him to do, was wrong, terribly wrong. But he was an eccentric, all great men were. And he needed it more than he needed her.

She darted through the airlock and into the shuttle. Her eyes protected from the sting of sulfur by the sting of tears. She dared not look out the portal to see Venus fall away, and for the rest of her days on Earth, retired on the sum she'd been paid for that job, she never looked at the morning star again. She ignored the whole night sky and tried not to think about the man she met there, the man who she loved, or the unspeakable task she completed for him.

THE BLACKWING'S canopy was heavier than Tahir expected. He linked on highest crypto to Tasha and Toshiro.

"I've got it. Where's Trygve?"

"Monitoring the northern Skunkforce squad, too far to link to you safely."

"Relay to him, I've got the canopy. It's intact, but I'll need help. Tasha, bring the pogo. Toshiro, you—Ah shit, they're here."

The white landscape in moonlight was ten times brighter than the Skunkforce camouflage, nothing like the Thaco that could glow to match perfectly. The enemy was combing the place like ants, and they'd see the pogo as soon as it arrived. If T team wanted the rest of the Blackwing, they'd be fighting for it, and Skunkforce was no petty gang. Like Valhalla, they had a knack for trying out their research team's latest inventions in the field. Tahir had read Veikko's report from within Skunkworks: 70 percent humor, 25 percent information relevant to stealing the BIRP, 5 percent other. Other included the latest projects they were handing over to Skunkforce for aggressive testing. There were Gat-Zooks, Gatling bazookas. Tahir had to wonder why everything in recent years seemed all about antiquated spinning barrels, Gatling this, Gatling that. Easy enough to see these squads didn't carry them, much too big. But they would surely have the other prototype Veikko logged.

Flight capable spaz-razors. Tahir hated sharp objects. Microwaves burned and projectiles ripped holes, explosions were all kinds of terrible, but even in a blast it was the shrapnel he loathed. And Skunkforce would be eager to try the flying blades. He stood by the canopy and looked around for the pogo. He knew how Tasha flew. She'd have sent the pogo straight up from where they landed, and it would be coming straight down on the canopy. On him. He could sense Trygve enter his safe link range. Toshiro arrived at the canopy.

"What? You can't lift that yourself?" he whispered.

"You lift it."

Toshiro gave it a kick, it didn't move. He grunted, "I don't think they know we're here. Their search patterns aren't tactical. They're still just looking for their lost parts."

They felt a tingle on their shoulders, then the wind of a pogo overhead. They both stuck close to the canopy so Tasha would have only one target to avoid. Trygve linked in.

"Three minutes! Don't wait for me, tractor me up later!"

"Why? Did they see you?"

"No, dammit, they see you, or the black canopy! On the plateau to your north!"

They looked up at the plateau. There was nothing there. They kept their eyes on it. Then Tasha landed and the ridge sprang to life. Incoming fire, microwaves. Tahir saw something wrong instantly. The beams were hitting the pogo's dispersion field with red sparks. UNEGA signature microwaves. This wasn't Skunkforce. It was someone from across the pond. Skunkforce saw them and opened fire immediately. With the damn razors. Thankfully they were visible to the naked eye. Even in the dark, he could see the spinning blades. He dodged two. Toshiro ducked behind the canopy, and the razor bounced off. Tasha finally opened the pogo door.

All three began moving the canopy. Toshiro and Tasha used tractoring waves from inside the pogo hold. Tahir stayed outside to push it off any rocks or salt snags. They only had to move it a meter into the hold, but the damn thing was heavy as rock. Trygve was almost there. He'd make it on site before they lifted off. He might even get to help push the damn heavy fraggin' canopy before Tahir got hit by a—

The razor severed his head jaggedly from his neck. Half of Valhalla watched the signal as his vision rolled across the salt and went black.

"Inform Dr. Niide," stated Hellhammer. Most watching switched to Trygve's vision. He came to the pogo and kicked Tahir's head into the hold, then got to work on the canopy. Violet dimmed the live feed as Hellhammer spoke again. "That's the second time this month Tahir has been beheaded. I'd avoid him if I were you."

"I don't see why you sent them at all," argued Veikko. "If we're just gonna let the Burp gather silt, we don't need the thing."

"And it flew fine with the spray-on," added Violet.

"It made it through salt," said Heckmallet, "barely, but it won't do much more without the proper canopy, and we can't make a new one. We can't simulate the armor on that thing. We don't even have the exact specs for its old windscreen."

"I'm sure you could whip something up," said Varg.

"Of course we can, we are H team!" Hellhammer was in quite a mood. "But T has succeeded where you failed. We will have the canopy."

"Failed?" demanded Violet. "We stole the bloody thing! Did you want us to land and hunt for the bloody chunks of it while the hoppers were still on us?"

Veikko joined in. "Maybe we could have if we were in a better shuttle. The POS—"

"The P-Zero has a name," whispered Heckmallet. "It's called the Rubicon, and it's a fine shuttle."

All gathered spoke up. "No, it's not."

"Sucks."

"Terrible old heap."

"Wouldn't fly it to a landfill."

"Wouldn't last to the landfill."

"The trash would be insulted, worst shuttle ever."

"Smells like urine."

"Urine and poverty."

"The seats hurt my balls."

Hellhammer's avatar burned hotter. "Then have Niide remove them when he's done with Tahir's head. Get used to the P0—The Rubicon, because the Blackwing has no cargo capacity. It only seats one, and it's going to stay buried until H team's say-so."

He logged out in a puff of smoke. The flock of avatars hovered in silence around the T team feed. Tahir's remains and the canopy were safely in the pogo and headed home. Skunkworks and whatever UNEGA belligerents T had spotted were busy fighting each other far below. UNEGA, on American soil. Violet spotted a tarantula in the crowd and linked to him directly.

"You're more worried about that than the Blackwing, aren't you?"

"It is cause for concern," Alf replied. "But keep perspective. It doesn't affect us directly. I am far more concerned for a craft that can fly through our rampart than the petty squabbles of a cold war."

"But still, couldn't this heat it up?"

"Oh my yes, it certainly will, regardless of the motives behind it. We'll see the GAUNE diplomat banging his shoe on the table and UNEGA's feeble denials. If it happens again fortifications on every coast. New proxy wars. But both sides believe the other is stockpiling mutagenics. They don't want to fight, they fear it. And this may be selfish of me, but Valhalla does best when the giants are arguing among themselves. We can get away with more."

We can get away with more. Violet wondered how much V team could get away with.

"Damn right we can," added Veikko. "We should let 'em go to war. War is good for business, if you're in our business. And we are. Cuz it's our business."

Alf's avatar just stared at him.

Veikko shifted uncomfortably in reality. "How's the tank?"

"Ornery," laughed Alf. "She hesitates to let anyone else ride her. She has your personality, I think. Just a week ago she loaded her cannons as Cato walked by. But the other tanks like her and don't envy her limb count. A fine steed."

Veikko and Alf talked until morning, when the sun was almost close enough to rising to give the horizons some dim blue haze. Veikko maintained that as the most elite fighting force in the world, war would make them the most elite body on Earth. Balder maintained that he was happy for them not to be, given the price. Violet listened but didn't concern herself with the *Håvamål*-style discussion.

By the time Valkyries were leaving dreamspace for the cafeteria, H team was already en route to install the canopy and dry out the cockpit. T team had returned in the night and rushed Tahir's head and corpse from the pogo's stasis alcove to Dr. Niide. Tahir was in good spirits when V encountered him at the buffet line.

"It's mostly the cutting feeling, that itchy slice in your skin. Even the spaz-razors, even at two hundred kph you can still feel it. I just hate getting cut."

"Nothing to lose your head about," said Veikko.

"You know, you made that exact joke last time he got beheaded," linked Vibs.

"The razors are just nasty," said Tahir. "I'm ashamed we have the things. At least ours don't fly. Maybe we should rig them that way. Just keep them linear so the Tiks don't get jealous."

"No," Veikko explained. "They can turn in midflight too. Skunkworks' can be link controlled, very simple, not a tenth of a Tikari, but they're a little better than spear laun—Oh my goodness, is that spaghetti?"

Between the gray cubes and yellow hemispheres was a new bin of what appeared to be seasoned spaghetti. Quite a rarity so everyone in T and V took a generous helping. The two teams sat together by the fire, which was extra pleasant in the middle of winter. Being open to the sky, Valhalla still sucked down the frigid air from the surface and their suits had all stayed furry as they entered the building. Only now were they beginning to pull in their fiber.

"So anyways. We're in," said Tahir. He seemed to be speaking to the V team half of the table.

"In what?" asked Violet.

"For the Bla—for the.... The Cracked Blag. We're in."

"We're not going," grumbled Vibeke.

"Yes, you are," protested Toshiro. "C team forbade it!"

Violet dug into the noodles, which tasted nothing like spaghetti. Almost how she remembered fish tasting, a meaty flavor, vaguely acrid. But not bad, she had more.

"What's the point?" Vibs mocked. "We'd get our brains hacked, then C would kill us."

"Daaark, Vibs," said Toshiro. "My God, this stuff is good."

"What is?"

"Spaghetti à la Kjetil," he replied. "Really good stuff, suspiciously good."

"Suspicious?" laughed Veikko. "Like what, African conflict spaghetti?" He shoveled some off of Violet's plate despite having his own and slurped up a few strands. "Wow, that is good."

"You can't go yourself, Vibs," Tasha said, "but there's no reason you can't hire some goon to do it for you."

"Why didn't I think of that?" asked Varg.

Veikko choked down his food to blurt back, "Because you're a—" He stopped speaking as Kjetil emerged from the kitchen to refill the buffet. Veikko shouted out, "Kjetil! How'd you make this spaghetti? It's awesome!"

"No spaghetti!" he explained. "Centauri chitlins. Little gremlins have such long intestines!"

Toshiro pushed his main course aside in favor of some delicious green putty. Varg dug into the chitlins along with Veikko, who stated calmly, "You can really taste the chyme."

Violet didn't write off the substance but switched to brown cylinders for a bit. There was a novelty in eating something from another star system. In the common world, gremlins cost several thousand euros a plate owing to the difficulty of cloning and raising them on Earth. It was only by chance that F team raided an illegal cloning plant that specialized in them. They managed to send the living specimens to the proper authority but arrived back in the ravine with several hundred kilos of processed meat and offal. Both at the request of Kjetil, who had been sneaking the critters into various soups, flambés, casseroles, and other dishes.

"So you hire someone to scour the place for Mishka," linked Toshiro on high crypto. "They don't have to go through Aloe. You probably shouldn't use Aloe to contact them either."

"Classic spy handling," mused Vibeke. "We just need to find Fred Leiser."

"Who's he?" asked Violet.

"An unlucky fellow from an old book," answered Vibs. "Someone we can train to do our jobs and send us the results. Valhalla hasn't been big on agents like this, but it solves everything."

"Why haven't we been big on agents?"

"They always betray you or sell you out, and they always ask for things we can't give them."

"Ah!" said Veikko. "Mutual respect and benefit."

"We do hire out specialists, especially online," linked Tasha. "Nothing like the Blag, though. Actually I don't know of anyone who ever went there. Without dying, I mean."

"I do," Varg said. "A guy named Yoshi from the Nikkei Underground. Traffics information. My boss at the tofu warehouse hired him to scout all his illegal bets."

"Can he be trusted?" asked Veikko.

"No, not at all."

"Sounds good. What did he do on the Blag?"

"He bragged about it once when I passed him his share of Heinrich's winnings on a pickled pint game. Didn't get into specifics, but it involved mutant organ trading."

"That's odd. They do that on the Nikkei Underground. The Nikkei Underground's already one of the most dangerous, nasty sites around. Why would they go to the Blag?" asked Vibeke.

"Because the organs were intentionally mutated. They say Høtherus was one of the first people on the Cr—Blag. Though... wait, when did he disappear?" Varg scratched his chin.

"What will Yoshi want in return?"

"My boss, Heinrich, always paid him a percent. But he's into info rackets. Has a line of people asking him about anything they can't say on the wikis. Like my boss, he always sent me to get the insider rumors on contestants. Not who won before or who could swallow the most vinegar, but who was playing dirty, who was going to sabotage who. He always knew, Heinrich never lost a bet."

Veikko pointed out, "We do have tons of information."

"I don't think C would like us trading with it," Violet reminded him.

"C wouldn't like the icing on their own birthday cakes," said Veikko, "Fuck 'em. They had their chance to search the 'location' for her and lied. We won't sell him anything on Valhalla, no mention of Hall of the Slain. But we know loads on loads about the gangs, the companies. I can't believe we wouldn't have anything he needs. This is perfect."

"What about Aloe?"

"Log out," suggested Trygve. "Log in from somewhere else. You can still call her in an emergency, but that would alert C. You just need a mission cover for… what letter are you on?"

"C, actually. No name yet," admitted Vibeke.

"Obvious, Cra—Oh, never mind." Tasha looked down.

"Call it project Cato," said Toshiro.

"Might alert him," said Tahir. "What's a term for Cato that begins with a C?"

Tasha spoke fast before Veikko could answer. "What was your last C mission called?"

"After Alpha and Beta, we had to be more creative," said Vibeke, looking to Varg.

"But we couldn't," said Varg, "so we called it 'Creative.'"

"It's an unofficial mission. We don't need a name," said Violet.

"Sure you do. They're going to know about it once you find Mishka, or once you get home and ask for a heavy brain scan for parasites that only grow on the Crack Blag." Trygve nodded. "The ravine will know. It's just better to ask forgiveness than permission."

"We asked for permission," said Veikko. "We didn't get it."

"Well, then it's good that forgiveness is so damn easy." Veikko stood up. "We'll think up a name later. Let's plan this thing."

JABIR AL-HIMYARI'S cranium, cleanly severed high up the neck, had come to rest at Pelamus Pluturus's left flipper. The blood drained from it to stain his boot. A happy stain for Pluturus and given Al-Himyari's notorious chemical dumps into the Mesogeios, a relieving one. Though his acts as CEO of the YUP were infamous to Cetaceans, he was all but unknown topside. Landlopers had little care for what fell into the water where Cetaceans would breathe it, ingest it in the flesh of their prey, and die from its cancers or go insane from its diseases. Al-Himyari's head would soon rot and dissolve before the gates of the Ionian Colony, where Pelamus's father, a brilliant genetic engineer, had died from the pollution.

Two meters away, under his own desk, was the head of Harun bin Nusair. Nusair was the commanding officer of the Yuppies, a light name for a dark army. Almost two years ago, his attack on the Pluturus fleet killed Pelamus's sister. Pelamus's reign of terror against the Yuppie navy came to an end with the severing of Nusair's spinal column. At long last Nuala was avenged, and for that Pelamus was suddenly, unexpectedly overcome with a feeling of sorrow. Not for his victory, but the somber afterthoughts of a long hard path left behind. The Fish had killed the last fisherman in the pond. Certainly there were others across the seas—his brothers south of Suomi; sisters in California; the simplistic clan of Mariana; and the benthic farmers of the Atlantic. But none concerned him just then. Pelamus walked over to the financial mainframe.

A large obelisk in the room, black and glowing green at its seams, held the wealth of the YUP. From the obelisk alone, their funds were monitored, sold, bought, and held. Standard topside company business. No link could penetrate the obelisk, nor could any bank or police force freeze their holdings. Only three men in the world had access to the wealth within. Jabir Al-Himyari, Harun bin Nusair, and Steve Al-Sulayhi, Chief of Finances. Steve's head was in the hands of Captain Crockeri. Crockeri had proven herself in every single battle she fought against the Yuppie navy, and her place beside Pelamus was more than well earned. So she had the honor of hardwiring Al-Sulayhi's head into the obelisk, unlocking it, and then letting the head die while in its mechanical embrace.

As it registered his death, the obelisk began hunting for the CEO to input the new financial officer. As he was dead as well, it kept looking. Pelamus was careful to slaughter every employee in line, all the way down to Ellessey MacReedy, the spy who had informed Pelamus of the financial mainframe's order of succession. The human, traitor to his species, would be well rewarded by theirs. Having betrayed the YUP out of love for a Cetacean woman, he would soon be granted gills and fins and brand new eyes, the great vibrant eyes of a sea-dweller to replace the beady little lifeless orbs from which humans saw the world. And he would happily lose his link as well. Cetaceans in general had little need of the computer world. It was vulgar, ugly, and constant. Ellessey wouldn't miss it. He only needed it for a few more minutes.

Unaffected by the heads at his feet, he logged in and accepted leadership of the YUP, such as it was. Pelamus had truly wrecked the company, stealing their fleets, their resources, and killing a tenth of their worldwide employees. Before the end they were begging for bailouts. In Cetacean terms they were scaled, gutted, and undercooked. So thoroughly had the piratical rampage destroyed the company that what Ellessey would transfer to Pluturus from the obelisk was less than a third of what he had taken already. But it completed the hostile takeover, and when it was done, Pelamus was the richest Cetacean on Earth. His fleet was still the second strongest Cetacean navy. The Valkohai were technically stronger, but a military ruled by pacifists, never to see a fight, could hardly be considered a fighting force. Even among Cetaceans there were doubts that the fleet existed at all. In any case they would never fight with Pelamus. They were a defensive body. Cetaceans, until Pelamus, had no true offensive force.

And what to do with it now that he had one? Pelamus and his crew walked quietly from the blood soaked office. He walked with confidence that nobody would pester him, no employee alive would dare, no land cops would know of the massacre for quite some time, and even if they did, it would be a local police department against the joined militaries of the former YUP and of the greatest pirate ever to live. Pelamus was confident, and for his confidence, all the more barren of aspirations. The lack of an immediate need was haunting. Sickening. By the time Pelamus reached the hatch to his flagship, he was deep in thought, trying to recall his youthful dreams.

First as a guppy, he wanted to visit Atlantis. Then, as he grew older, he wanted to meet Poseidon and Neptune. Eventually his father took him on a package trip to Atlantis and let him shake the fins of furry costumed actors playing each god. Now he mused, he had such plunder that he could retire into a trough of his own, buy most of the Pacific, buy Atlantis, and hire Neptune as his personal fry cook. He laughed. His more serious dreams, he recalled, were those inspired by the books he read after school. Those in his grandfather's mildewed library. When he set out under Jolly Roger, he donated them all to the library in the bay by Alexandria, and it was there he set his course.

The great fleet headed northwest toward the Kemet Nile. Pelamus headed to the berth deck for a walk. On the bulkheads were more reminders of his youth. Wood carvings along every surface and stanchion depicting his grandfather's exploits. The founding of the

Ionian Colony, carved by Breluga the Elder in 2191. The defense of Patmos, 2192 by Vermircelus. It was Pelamus's favorite as a tadpole because of the guts on top of the pile of gold. The first gill implantation unassisted by land robotics, carved by Breluga in 2197, his last work before he died. Shot to death while visiting a land museum displaying his works, shot eight times, then stabbed in the chest with one knife and beheaded by another. By humans. The damned filth, the apes from which Pelamus was ashamed to have evolved.

He stewed and mused about the state of land races as they passed the Suez gates, which Pelamus was amused to know he now owned. His mind passed from fantasies of revenge to fantasies of superiority, and even, for a moment, of equality. His father once said that peace was no fantasy. That Cetacea could live in harmony, even in trade with the land. Unlikely, Pelamus snorted. But then he came to the very last carving. Untitled, carved by a convert from the far north in 2204. Pelamus had seen the man. He was still mostly man when he made the thing. He died a Cetacean a few years later. Nuala had been at his funeral where he was sent into the darkest deep. But his carving depicted what he claimed to be "An accident waiting to happen." A disaster for men but, the artist bragged, a Cetacean dream come true.

His father didn't want him to hear just what, and the artist never explained. Pelamus had to guess. He stared at the carving for hours, as he had done when he was young. The curves and pits warmed his fingers, and he ran them over the smooth dark wood. As a child he was fascinated by the strange land formations. Jagged rocks around a deep ravine. The ravine was filled with buildings, land buildings. Ugly boxes like they loved to build. And in the center was a giant tree. Too big to be real, reaching up all the way to the sky, which held two moons and no sun. Every carving in the boat had a sun and a moon, save for this. Two moons. And the narrative pieces: Water flooding in from the ravine's edge. Fire leaping up from the boxy structures. And one Cetacean man, one who looked remarkably as Pelamus would come to look, holding a trident up with one hand, catching a drop of water in the other. A mystery.

After docking at the library, Pelamus went straight for the art section. He studied the symbolism of every carving done undersea. Within an hour he understood the two moons—night without day. That meant the location was either far north or far south. In two hours he was buried in a pile of literature on the history of the arctic circles. By nightfall he was studying geographic records of pits and canyons. A week passed before he discovered a science journal that shattered the mystery. In reading a one-page update on an obscure experiment that failed miserably, Pelamus became a believer in his father's peace. And he had a purpose in life greater than any pirate had before him. He was to be the messiah of the seas, or the harbinger of the next deluge.

The road ahead, he knew, would be difficult. He broke down his mission into outlines within outlines, goals to reach goals to reach goals. He consulted his captains and some scholars of the library. He sent for humans to scour the nets. He would need humans. Cetaceans, for all their enhancements, were only at their best in water. And half the key to peace was very far from the sea. Half of the key was in a place lacking not only water but proper air. A place so far away it cost a life's fortune for every kilogram sent, and the key hidden there was listed as weighing 250,000 kilograms.

But that meant money and work, and nothing else. Pelamus had more than enough in the bank. The other half of the key was that ravine. No science journal even hinted at where it was. It had been top secret when it began and was a closer kept secret now. There was only one lead in fact, one left by the absolute destruction of every other. Though the science journals offered no clues, a paper record in the pits of the library held accounts of financial transactions for the Ares Company, mentioned only once in the journal as the company responsible for the ravine. On page 1902, a mildewed and decrepit page, was the listing for payments on the delivery of several million euros of parts to…. Redacted.

Of all his time in the library, Pelamus had never seen a censored word. Censored in bonding grease marker, and that meant it was censored while at the library, or at least after the volume headed underside. He marched to the eldest librarian present in the hopes he might remember something, anything about the desecration which could cost Cetacea everything. Pelamus and the seas were in luck.

"They gave no names. Just four humans who wanted to look through our collection," said Dewey Otlet Putnam LaFontaine the

Fourth. Not only the eldest librarian but the eldest Fish in Abu Qir colony.

"Anything you remember will help, no matter how—"

"Little? Child, I'm senile as silt. I remember their shiny suits, I remember the books they wanted, I remember why they wanted them, and I remember what I bought with the gold they handed me."

"Gold?"

"They paid me off, son. There was something dangerous in our books, something that could get them all killed. Now I was appalled at the thought of censorship. If they asked to take a line from Twain or a word from Shakespeare, I'd have kicked them out then and there. But they found their books and gave me a corvette's worth of solid gold to take out a few spots in a tax log, a company financial serial from the last century, and a science magazine we threw out a decade ago. Hell yes, I took the money."

"Do you remember what they crossed out?"

"Son, they paid me another corvette not to ask."

"What do you remember about them? Do you know where they were from?"

"The two that spoke most had Norsky accents. Maybe Sversky. 'Nother said a little, Elline. They didn't let on much, but you know who did? The fella looking for 'em. Unspeakable Darkness fella, you know them?"

Pelamus nodded.

"Well, they wanted to know the same damn thing, and they didn't have a lick of gold, so they left empty. But they did know *who* they were looking for, just not where."

"Who were they?"

"Hall o' the Slain. And boy, there's two times you hear that name down here. Kids who want a horror story and scarred old pirates like you. Pirates who know that the name means Davy Jones. Pirates who know not to chase whales and pirates who know when to leave well enough alone." He leaned toward Pelamus. "And I know you ain't not none of them."

Pelamus headed back to his ship with his mind racing. He had heard the name before on two occasions. A survivor privateer whose ship was blown out of the water and a survivor privateer who died with the name on his lips. Neither reliable. As the name was all but a myth, they likely attributed it out of fear for whatever really attacked them. But he was in a library and he had a name to look up. So there he stayed for another month as his crew sought out to hire humans to do the parts they needed humans to do. And Pelamus studied. He studied on and on, day after day and found only enticing snips and quips about the most severe of rumored bodies. In all the time he studied, he became certain of only two things.

First, that whatever else was false, the Hall of the Slain was real, and it owned that ravine. Second, that the Hall of the Slain was full of humans. Humans make mistakes, so the great fearsome Hall of the Slain would too. And if it took a hundred years, he would catch them when they did. The instant they set foot on dangerous ground, he would be there to take them.

V TEAM set foot on the Nikkei without Alopex's protection. All they had of Alopex were a few security programs, which they stuffed into the net partitions of their brains before heading south. A Valkyrie's net partition is already an arsenal of fatal coding attacks, immune software, spyware, ad blocking protocols, hacking systems, and defensive mechanisms ranging from common virus scanners to a last case amputation battery, which could cut off the part of the brain interfacing with one's antenna. Such a battery would render the user unable to link to the net or Tikari forever. They would lose that sacred insect, that body part that made them a Valkyrie, but it might save their life. If all else failed, they could always call for Alopex, but that would alert C team, who they'd taken great care not to alert.

That was why they waited nearly a month after their last run-in with C, running plain dull missions to save plain dull lives and plain dull companies until Churro's eyes found other problems to spy and the stink of Cato's breath was a distant memory. Despite worrying about C team for an entire month, they still lacked a C name for the project. Violet had no ideas. Vibeke's were all deemed by Veikko to be too dull, whose own were deemed by all to be too obscene. Varg's was the front-runner for a time until the others looked up what it meant. Its cancellation was a sad loss as the word really rolled off the tongue.

When the time finally came, they logged in from AleGel. Valhalla had "aggressively disassembled" the company several years prior to V team's beginnings and kept its contents on hand for various mission purposes. Their old office buildings in Norge and Empresargentina often came in handy for luring targets into false organizations; their fleet of limopogos was frequently called in for travel requiring some degree of class (and as often for Valkyrie nights out); and their website proved an invaluable asset for excursions into the net that were expected or required to be traced. V's first step was to hardwire in to the Tromsø office netscape and repeat the words "Black Crag" over and over until they were certain that C team didn't monitor the AleGel server.

Tiwaz team was more than happy to watch C from back in the ravine, one Tikari per member. V's own Tikaris were all safely chested with their AIs online, so the team appeared to be eight rather than four. As Valknut wired in to the AleGel net, T reported that Cato was busily hacking a Zolfo isotope shipping satellite, Churro and Claire were asleep offline, and Cassandra was a potential threat as she was looking over V team's psychological data. According to Toshiro, she had linked to her team some time earlier to explain that she expected V to do exactly what they were doing. Churro had fortunately believed V team's assertion that they were linking out of Alopex and heading south to look into illegal port mods in Ersfjordbotn. Cato backed him up over Cassandra, certain that his fearsome display would deter the team and set them straight.

As Cato had failed in every relevant way, V team found themselves untraced atop the second most dangerous site on the nets. The surface of the Nikkei was notorious on its own for sleazy companies, illegitimate hiring practices, and the production of about 70 percent of the world's spam. V team's anti-advert brainware was already on overdrive to block the common Nikkei commercials. Once they hit the Undernet, it would likely not be enough to deafen them to their surroundings. They could already feel scans pushing at their temples. Invasive probes that hit their links hard enough to warrant forced deletion from their defenses. A random seller would only be declined; to get itself deleted, something would have to have tried to hack them, to reprogram them to buy Skuzz or scamware. Varg took a peek at some of the programming caught in his filters.

"I just caught a strange one," he reported, "It looks like a typical pirate store, but if you enter the site, it implants nerve impulses. Makes you feel your skin is burning away. No sales in it, no purpose."

"Must be from the RIAA," explained Vibs. "They released a bunch of those in the 2100s. Ancient programs, easy to catch, but some are still circulating."

"Nasty. Oh wow, just blocked this one—an inception that you need more penises. 'Medical-West Consortium can give you more! Limit 4 in Kentucky and Saudi Kemet.'"

Veikko laughed, "I just got one for Kruschev's Funerary Services. 'We will bury you. Offer not valid at Disneyland, postmortem burials may cost extra.' Sounds legit to me."

"Let me know if one starts with a C. We still have no name."

"You think too much, Vibs. Crisco! I got one for Crisco. Weird, that's hardly Nikkei materi—Aha. It's really swill oil sold under the real deal's label. They skim it out of raw sewage."

"I like Crisco," added Varg, "the name, I mean. And also the shortening."

"Well, pick fast." Violet had spotted the black and yellow mark. "Here's the Undernet access."

The Undernet trapdoor was no more than a warning label on the Nikkei planetoid's lowest layer floor—"Warning: This site will destroy your brain." A spamwriter looked at them with disdain, shaking his head in disappointment, knowing the sickening goings on beneath that label. Veikko saw him and caught his attention.

"Hey, spamboy, is 'Crisco' a good name for a mission?"

"You'll die down there, slick. Crooks in those parts 'il eat you and your pals alive," he muttered as he floated away.

Veikko laughed, "That was a yes. Let's do it! Crooks who know pick Crisco."

He leaped onto the trapdoor and fell out of sight. His Tikari's avatar followed immediately. Violet noticed on the spamwriter's words, "Slick," that they all had a shiny black appearance. Though they had signed in through AleGel, they still had their obsidian avatars from Valhalla, avatars being a brain setting rather than a net selection. It wasn't a flaw, necessarily. Some parts of the net recognized them as the Obsidian Order. Balder once explained that a couple of lurkers even knew they were the netside visage of the Hall of the Slain. A good thing for the most part. People who recognized them as such knew they weren't to be messed with. Violet hoped it would work to their advantage. She hated the feel of an overlooked mission element no matter how positive its effect. She had to wonder just what else they'd overlooked on their first rogue project.

Vibeke followed after, her Tikari disappearing with her into the warning. Varg and Violet jumped last, Tikaris silently following them into the pit. And it was a pit. The Undernet looked little like the warm colorful planetoids of the common web. Where most sites loaded as globes to be wandered, the Undernet was a vast funnel with nine distinct levels. The top level was called the shooting gallery and had become a sort of proving ground for the virulent ads of the region. When they'd logged in before via Alopex, they could bypass the common entry and land anywhere they pleased on the Undernet, all without a single advert passing Aloe's natural security. Without Aloe they came in like the rest.

The shooting gallery didn't look all that bad. It manifested as a long circular garden with plush grass floors. Most of the avatars seemed benign, just common topside users who weren't there for any specific criminal activity but wanted to see the forbidden zone. Taking up a third of the circle was the Lower Mantle Bulwark Orientation (LMBO), a castle forged from stolen code and illegal barrier coding. There one could find the legends of the illegal net. Omar, The Octopus, The Hypocrites, and the infamous Caesar all worked from the LMBO, wreaking havoc upon the topside nets with hacks the common net user couldn't fathom. Hacks that even Alopex couldn't implement. Valhalla had once tried to engage Caesar to break into the Gallia Database, but he declined, having broken in some years prior and not wanting to repeat himself.

Valknut suffered the indignity of having to walk through the landscape, unable to simply appear where they wished. They'd have to make their way down each ring from portal to location specific portal, treating the vast rings like a combination lock to find their man. And like the rest of the net, they'd have to deal with the same dangers.

Violet spotted the first threat coming from far away: a Skuzzbot. It had no avatar, but against the limp code of the walls, it stood out as a blister in the VR. Contact barriers were still in play so it couldn't hack her and make her buy the deadly Skuzz, but the bot would monitor her and learn what she was after, then disguise itself and wait to be touched. Veikko had spotted it first and hit it with a delay code.

There were several others incoming: Silkbots, zombieware, zombified users sent recruiting, fractal theft algorithms. Violet even spotted a transcription bubble floating ominously around the ring. Alopex could have burst it in an instant if she were there. But rogue as they were, V team couldn't do a thing but avoid it. It would eventually find a user and take over their monetary implant back on Earth, alter their RNA transcription to produce physical worms, and then release the parasites to infect the innocent in reality, where contact barriers sadly didn't exist.

"Yoshi is in the Deutsch section of the gambling sack," said Varg, "We have a long way to go."

The avatars followed Varg as they descended from level to level, trying to stick near to the German routes and portals. Level Two sold pornography. Pornography even Varg was loath to witness. Most was thankfully nothing particularly worse than what appeared topside, merely made more scandalous by merit of its location. The appeal of the forbidden. But some corners of the ring didn't display what they sold. That was their advertisement, that they wouldn't even show their stock on the illegal Undernet. The team moved quickly, not wanting to even consider what might lurk inside those rooms.

Having lost their appetites completely, they arrived in the third circle, where the illegal foods trade thrived. Where illegal high concentration livestock farmers hocked their abused goods. Where foie gras was advertised openly, where endangered species were sold by the premium cut. But the crowds on the third circle didn't flock to eat beef. A crowd on that ring meant someone was online offering the real forbidden fruit—Soylent goods. Human blood was common enough, but all hell broke loose when an avatar appeared offering genuine human meat. It was often a lab growing the stuff illegally, but if ever a live farm went online, it was in the third circle.

They dropped quickly to the fourth, the Black Nikkei itself. Arms dealers, illegal medical stores. It was estimated once by Forbes that the amount of cash flowing through the fourth level of the Undernet was ten times what passed through the top five subconglomerate companies topside. There were so many avatars Violet could believe it.

V team had browsed the ring a hundred times for Mishka. But that was under Alopex. It looked completely different as a common user. They couldn't instantly see the true identities of the anonymous around them anymore. Violet was surprised to find a few were black solid blanks like their own. She wondered if any might be from Valhalla, seeing right through their own from Aloe's eyes. Common detective work could resolve her curiosity about some of the crowd.

The biggest transaction in the ring was coming to an end. Violet used a plain Bryce hack to listen in. It was a matter of shipping rights. Heavy load transportation from Mars to Earth, massive payment, massive security. She didn't try to trace any of the avatars, but some were obvious. WYCo wasn't even disguised. Xorats was there, evidenced by a poorly hidden provider log. Zaibatsu had two avatars present. She'd have to trace to learn which, but if they were on the Undernet, one was likely Yakuza. The avatar she guessed was the Yak won the contract as V team left the area. Violet followed her team down to darker circles.

The fifth circle was a thick swamp of anonymous hate. Primarily a ranting zone, the arena was also rife with duels. Where offended parties from above came to settle their disagreements without contact barriers. Here they would take each other's hands and fight to the death with their cruelest hacks. Many of the avatars were frozen as statues, duels in which both had become caught in infinite loops, their bodies dying off in the real world, and their brains stuck forever in their final feuds.

Ring six was a smattering of political dissident sites and underground religious groups. One log bore an icon of a crescent moon and star—Muslims, according to an old briefing. The label had a musical code under it, and Violet glanced at it to listen. It was a chant of sorts. It seemed fairly innocuous, unlike the formidable police tracking codes that stuck to any user walking in or out of the place. Other religious symbols appeared, but Violet wasted little on them. She only glared angrily at one Russian Cross, and then they moved on.

Ring seven was dominated by gang disputes. It was there that Bruise and Kigali En Ligne fought the war that lead to the Black Crag itself, that killed the most junior teams. Violet had been there not too long ago to clean up the aftermath. It was a sad place, made all the uglier by its garish militaristic designs. Thankfully ads and malware were now all but absent. The people deeper down the cruel vortex meant business and would happily spend their time tracking down an author or programmer if they were attacked.

The eighth level was the most massive. Divided into ten sacks, it housed the most colossal fraud ring in existence. Each sack held an organized crime syndicate or illegal action zone. The mafia owned the first. The next was empty, having housed the Orange Gang a year prior. It hadn't filled in, to Violet's surprise. It was seen as cursed. She grinned at that back in the real world. The level was so massive the team clung to their Tikaris and activated Geryon systems to bypass most of the netspace, a process taking longer than walking but avoiding confrontation with the illegitimate businesses that might have disputes with the black avatars that once foiled their projects.

They skipped the Unspeakable Darkness's sack where body modifications were bought and sold. Many of the mods were illegal and dangerous, but those there to buy were in no fighting mood. They just wanted their teeth implanted with venom glands, and that was fine by Violet. They skipped the Yakuza sack, which seemed to be celebrating the deal made a few circles up. And finally they came to Bulge Five, the gambling sack.

It was a rowdy place full of pitfalls of damaged coding. Everyone was shouting. All the link labels were in different, larger lettering. When Violet looked at one to have it sounded out, the thing screamed at her. It was nothing like gambling sites on the common net. Those sites ran in euros and legally checked and monitored every bid. Nor was it like the Nikkei nets, which ran in untraceable Yen instead of tracked euros. It was more like a den of rabid animals, or what Veikko explained as a "Mosh Pit," a long banned musical ritual where people danced by running into each other as hard as they could. The metaphor was apt. People everywhere were trying to grab each other without permission. The contact barriers kept bumping the avatars back at odd angles.

What Violet could make out amid the shouting was confusing to say the least. A large pit bull avatar was calling out stakes for some sort of match. Violet looked directly at the board icon, but it wouldn't say what sport, only the names of the contestants, which sounded like pet names instead of human. Beside that kiosk was a political betting stand. The bet was on a senate vote to censure a group of GAUNE subsidiaries. It had few takers, but the ones there were double blanked. It would take Alopex to trace them completely. On her own Violet couldn't find the avatar's name but a quick penetrative scan revealed them to be logged in from a GAUNE senate chamber link.

Varg and his Tikari were making a thorough search of the region. The sack churned slowly under their feet, showing them every dirty game from Interzone Inc. to the remains of the Purple Gang's betting businesses. Violet was tempted to ask how their old boss Hrothgar was holding up when Varg found his man. The team headed for a small kiosk leaning against the debugging gutter of a Russian Roulette casino. It was programmed in rotting wood textures with a text sign that bore no link label. Violet couldn't make it out at all. Her text software called the left letter a backward E, and the other two just looked like smiley faces. Whatever it said, Varg recognized the old man inside.

And he was an *old* man, a wrinkly, liver-spotted mess of an avatar with brilliant white hair, about ten strands of it on his entire head. He was speaking in a low curdled rasp to an ASD avatar. Valhalla had considered using ASD avatars in the beginning, the constantly shifting face and scrambling voice provided extreme anonymity and left other users guessing as to what was behind the mask, but obsidian black offered the same without the confusion or implications—ASD avatars were generally used by drug enforcement, and given the nature of some of Valhalla's contacts, they didn't want to be suspected as such. The old man handed his customer a folder, and the strange thing logged out. He looked at the faceless obsidian crowd.

"I don't serve blacks," he grumbled and closed his kiosk window.

V team looked to one another briefly, then all to Varg. Varg shrugged, even online with one palm up and the other down. He walked up to the closed front and used one of his borrowed Alopex routines to force-start the portal. The old man was startled but more angry than afraid.

"Obsidian goddamn Order. I know about you! White knights in black armor. You *schwarzes Glas* always trot around the place and never buy."

Varg replied quickly, "Today we're buying, Yoshi."

He was surprised. "Who says my name is Yoshi?"

"Your sign and our pals in Deutschland GmbH."

"I know a lot of Germans. Not many of 'em are my friends. Who sent you?"

"Think pickles."

The old man lit up. "The game boys! Pickled Pints and Hungry Hungry Hobos! Always sent that same kid, KolossalKnockwurst69. How's he holding up? Didn't seem like the type to hang out with your order."

"He died, I'm afraid. Skied off a cliff."

Violet was growing concerned again. Varg had to get into the man's good graces, but they were on territory that could reveal an identity if they weren't careful. But then, Varg had to give him something. All he would buy was information. If Yoshi could be bought for outdated tales, it would be well worth the risk. She trusted Varg and said nothing. The old man was suspicious again.

"You kill him?"

"No. He was a good man. A strong man, and the world will miss his good looks, his singular wit, and his robust—"

"We need information," interrupted Vibeke. "We need someone who can search the Black Crag for us."

Yoshi considered the gravity of their request. He nodded solemnly. "I can climb the Crag. But for that kind of work and that kind of risk, you'd have to give me the kind of tips I can retire on."

"What do the rich people need to know?"

"Three big questions people want to pay for today. Answer a couple, and I'll do your dirty work."

"You got it."

"Alright, first, whose probe's gonna get to Barnard's Star first?"

"UNEGA," Vibeke stated without skipping a beat. "The propulsion system on GAUNE's probe had superior acceleration at first, but it's reached its top speed. UNEGA never gave a press release, but Pan Fleet intercepted a telemetry link that shows their probe is still accelerating, which is why they're neck and neck right now. UNEGA's will enter orbit in four years, six months ahead of GAUNE's. GAUNE knows it and can't do a thing. None of that should be public for another couple weeks, but if you're selling the information, you better be sure Pan Fleet isn't the one buying. They've killed two vendors already."

Yoshi was very impressed. "Do you have a copy of the telemetry link?"

Vibeke held out her hand. Yoshi considered it for only an instant before accepting. Vibs transferred an ancient site map to him, one from the AleGel accounts where she had stored the telemetry before heading out. She had expected it would be the second top seller for information before they left, and the top seller they had access to. The top seller was something they didn't know, and it was to be Yoshi's second question.

"Where is Ellessey MacReedy?"

"We don't know," she answered honestly. News of the YUP traitor was the highest commodity on that side of the globe. Valhalla analysis was almost certain that the pirate they'd once encountered was behind his defection. Most of the planet thought a Cetacean had something to do with the company's downfall, but nobody had any clue where they hid MacReedy. Valhalla had no reason to look into the matter, so the former human, now partway through underwater modification surgery, was going to stay on the loose.

"Alright. Third question," Yoshi began. None of V team was sure which bit of intel he'd put third. Vibeke was banking on the identity of the Carson Robber. That was intel she'd be happy to deal out, having discovered the missing Carson Bank detector logs by accident while looking for Mishka. Varg and Veikko were both convinced he'd want to know whether Zaibatsu was going to purchase Nabisco from GAUNE. Months earlier Nabisco had unveiled Calabi-Yau Breakfast Cereal, the world's most technologically advanced cereal, which offered six dimensions of flavor, but they discovered too late it did so at the cost of quantum diarrhea. GAUNE made money in the end off the drugs to alleviate the problem, but with its stock lower than ever, many expected UNEGA to buy Nabisco at a low point and thus control a major part of GAUNE's food supply. Violet alone guessed what Yoshi would ask next. "Who stole the Skunkworks prototype?"

All four cringed to hear it. The question they knew the answer to but couldn't answer. Violet spoke quickly, she thought, because she wanted to offer something else. She couldn't admit to herself that she wanted to move on out of fear Vibeke would answer him.

"Can't say. But you can keep the software you use on the Crag. It's a Gullinkambi system that'll let you look through the entire Crag site code in seconds. It works on any website. You could strip bare this entire ring of the Undernet with it." She produced the program in her hand to let him see. She had forgotten that Veikko designed their copy's icon: A blue rooster with a gold comb. Thankfully her avatar had no face to keep straight.

Yoshi looked at the blue rooster, one of Alopex's finest routines. H team had developed it a few years back to speed up searches in high risk areas. C team claimed to have used it on the Crag a year before. It would, to Yoshi, be one of the most valuable tools imaginable.

"Tempting…. But why can't you say who stole the prototype? You know who, don't you?"

"We can't say."

"I'll tell you fine folks what I'll do. I'll take your blue bird and that juicy bit about Barnard and scale the Crag for you if you'll answer one more question. Just yes or no."

"Deal," stated Vibeke.

Yoshi looked directly at Violet's avatar. He might have looked because she was offering the Gullinkambi program. He might have looked at her randomly of the eight avatars present. But to Violet it felt like he knew exactly who she was and knew exactly what she'd done. His eyes narrowed, his wrinkles grew deeper, and he put the fate of the mission right into her hands.

"Was it you?"

Violet tried to think. She could say yes, and he'd find Mishka. She could say no, and he'd simply believe her and leave it at that, and do as they asked. But the way he looked at her, directly at her, the thief herself: he might have known already. It might be a mere test to see if she'd offer the truth or deceive him. She didn't have Alopex hiding her face, only an avatar this time, and who knew what programs Yoshi had to detect lies. She should lie to him either way and let the project fail if it must. But then Vibeke would never forgive her. Not for losing the last hope they had of finding Mishka. And what exactly would be lost if she told the truth? One man who sold—*sold* not gave away, not acted upon information—would know that the black avatars stole the thing. He'd sell it to Skunkworks of course, but what could they do about it?

They'd already seen T team, and everyone knew the Obsidian Order online were a dangerous gang. But then again—

"Yes," said Varg. And it was done. Yoshi smiled and laughed. He linked something to a faraway user, then closed his notation window.

"Don't worry, I won't tell the skunks. They don't pay well enough!" He turned to Violet. "Hand me your cock. I'll scour the mountain for your friend Mishka." V team was stunned. Through their avatars he must have sensed it. He went on, "I deal in information, kids! Mishka told me who the Obsidian Order were in exchange for a tip on Birlacorp."

He jumped out of his kiosk with a dexterity that mismatched his avatar. He took the blue rooster icon from Violet and integrated it into his net partitions. Then the back of his head popped open to reveal ocular hookup protocols. He let them see what he saw as he jumped down toward the next ring. The project was on course.

Looking through Yoshi's eyes, they could get a hint of the programs he was using. Beside the new blue Gullinkambi program, there were about fifty icons for net security. Some they recognized, others they didn't. It was rude to look around at the man's brain, but Violet couldn't resist peeking at some of the program specs he had running. One was an illegal log deletion protocol, another was an avatar speed alteration buffer so he could trick sites into letting him move at illegal paces to surprise or escape an enemy. One was a false contact barrier so he could pretend to let people in without doing so. He sensed her looking at it.

"That one doesn't work on the Crag, dearie. Nothing works on the Crag."

Yoshi left the sack and hopped down to the airspace of ring nine, the lowest of the low, the anus of the entire net. Violet had never seen the place before from the common net. It was, in theory, a visual micro-weblog conglomeration. But she could make out no images. The ring cycled so fast she couldn't focus on any single thing. It was like a whirlpool over which Yoshi floated calmly toward the center. She could see how the board acted like a meat grinder, some of the avatars had programming to view the board, but at the cost of their sanity. It would have their brains functioning at impossible speed, doing severe nerve damage. It was a sort of drug for net users who had exhausted the rest of infinity and now needed the most extreme just to feel anything at all. The ring, it was rumored, contained as much information as the rest of the net combined, but it was all a waste. Whoever looked into the abyss would be devoured by it—the promise of all the knowledge in the world at the cost of the inability to use it. An eternity of heightened awareness as your body rotted away in a comatorium or died at home. A living death.

Yoshi came to the void, surest access point to the Black Crag. One could log on to the Crag itself, though they'd be killed instantly by whatever might be waiting for them. One could enter the void of the net from any access point and try to find the Crag, but the Nikkei Undernet point was situated directly over it. The Crag didn't respond to calls like common planetoid sites above, where one could simply state the address and the place would appear. It was a site that worked on its own terms, ones not understood by its own users. Nobody understood how it let people bypass contact barriers. In theory, no part of the net should have allowed it. The one inviolable rule of electronic communication was that nothing could be forced on you. Even in the void between sites, that rule was in force. But once a person set foot on the Crag, everything changed.

Yoshi set down, and they could see the netscape from his eyes. There were only a couple hundred users, visible ones at least. He put out a heavy array of feelers and detection routines so that if anyone approached, he'd know. The appearance was indeed that of a black rocky mountain, riddled with grottos and cells along a single spiral road climbing up the steep cliffs. The few avatars were like a line of parasites roaming across it. Yoshi was about to start up the Gullinkambi program when a large gargoyle avatar approached him. He kept his distance, as did the gargoyle. A standard assurance on the Crag. The gargoyle spoke in a high, weak voice.

"Would you like to buy some fresh baked cookies?"

"No, thank you, I'm just heading to the financial sector," he replied. The gargoyle moved on, and Yoshi thought back to his watchers, "I assume you didn't want any local value pairs? They make fine souvenirs, but who knows what else he baked into them?"

V team didn't respond. Yoshi headed as promised to the financial sector, a short ways up the Crag. He glanced down at the rock, nothing like the colorful plastic and glowing cartoon labels of the rest of the net. It was meaty, flaking like dead skin. Its resolution was grainy but not low. The place wasn't cheap, cheap as in the Undernet just looked like a lack of textures and poorly assembled polygons. The Crag looked like it had been meticulously designed to feel gritty. More than that, it felt not so much like a mountain as a giant animal horn, owing to the swaying deformation of the road and the sinewy layout between the ingrown caves.

All the avatars kept their distance. Everyone on the Crag was cautious in the extreme to let others know they would do no harm, and wanted no harm done to them. Some were blanks, others were beasts. One avatar was a perfect likeness of Abraham Lincoln, another was just a mess of legs and eyes. But all were whisper quiet. It was oddly like the atmosphere of a library site. Though library sites lacked the glimpses Violet could see as Yoshi passed various grottos. One held a pharmaceutical meeting, clearly labeled as the KVH drug company meeting with members of the Janjuweed. Another held what looked like a classroom. All the student avatars were joining hands with a tentacled being, repeating a mantra, preparing for some unspeakable ineffable something.

The financial sector made more sense. There were mercenary ads. Any of them could be Mishka. They were as simple as "Have microwave, will travel" and complex as a total readout of available militaries and off-planet resources. Conventionally, one would have to reply to each ad to learn the identity of the poster. There appeared to be under fifty mercs so it was a possibility, but one to be avoided if they could find Mishka's ad, buy her services, and lure her into a trap. Or better yet, simply trace the origin and find her unannounced.

Yoshi produced the Gullinkambi and set it on the pathway so it would recognize the site to be hacked. Once activated he would be able to see names and providers behind each page. Yoshi would only need to log the results, return to safety, and V could handle the rest. He prepared to activate the little blue rooster.

Suddenly a bright flash illuminated the Crag. There was a disturbance on the road nearby. A small avatar of a little green man with a giant wrinkly brain was destroying a larger troll avatar with something that manifested as lightning. Dozens of avatars looked on as the very lifecode of the troll was spewed onto the Crag for all to see. It wasn't like the scattered programming in a disarming protocol—it was brain code getting deleted. Incomprehensible strands of information that made up the user's consciousness and thoughts getting ripped to shreds. The troll avatar remained on the cliffs like a corpse, hollow now and transparent but lingering, sickly. Violet could almost smell it. The little green man wandered away, and the denizens of the Crag returned silently to their business. Yoshi activated the Gullinkambi.

It didn't work. The Crag stayed opaque and black. The ads were all highlighted, but whatever part of them was inside the site coding wasn't revealed. Yoshi tried again with the same results. Avatars around him could see what he was doing. One laughed. He linked back to V team.

"I saw the code for the ads. It's not a problem with your rooster. It's the Crag. It's invulnerable."

Vibeke replied, "Go ahead and start clicking the ad links. Just log their contacts one by one and come back. We can handle it from there."

"No, let me try one more thing first. Your rooster is only set for noninvasive penetration of the site's code. I have an intramarkup hack. If I apply it to the Gullinkambi, it should be able to see through the Crag. It'll damage the permissions a little, but it's a website. It won't feel anything."

Violet watched as he applied the new coding, a rather brilliant modification. She felt some trepidation at his last words. If any site could feel, it would be this abomination. She reminded herself the rock walls were just site code. He activated the modified Gullinkambi, and they could see inside the Crag.

They saw eyes. There was a grotesque crablike face inside the rock. Yoshi staggered back. They could see more. Inside the spiral rock crag was a gigantic face with several mandibles, feelers, and eye stalks—and it was looking at them. Not only at Yoshi but right through his visual link to V team. The Gullinkambi cut out. The stone went black again.

"Okay, guys," Yoshi stuttered, panicked, "I'm coming up topside. You can keep your program."

Yoshi began to skip across the cliff toward the portal to the common net. As he did the Crag began to shake. It was the first time

Violet had seen an earthquake online. Avatars began to tumble down the sides.

"What the hell is happening?" asked Veikko.

"The Crag is moving," said Vibeke plainly. She spoke as normal, but Violet could hear something in her voice. She had never seen anything like it either. The Crag continued to shift. As Yoshi fought the local gravity settings and ran for the portal the mountain began to turn onto its side. That helped Yoshi for a moment, with the Crag turning he was almost to the edge, almost to the portal. He leaped for the junction and looked in the clear when a gigantic black claw appeared from under the mountain's edge and grabbed him. Its chelae squeezed down on the old man, and he vanished in a gruesome puff of pixelation. The visual link cut out with a sickening yank, as if their eyes had been pulled out with it.

V team stood on the eighth ring staring at the hole. Violet tried to understand what they'd just seen, some sort of advanced site AI or a defensive mechanism? No other sites had anything like it. She had never imagined anything like the face she'd spotted within the Crag— the Crab. A crab's face within a mountain-sized shell, a face that would be haunting her dreams. Its eyes were....

Still looking at her from the pit. The crab's face had emerged from its mountain shell. It saw them from the void, even after Yoshi's link went dead, the Crag was watching them from below. Four of its eyes breached the portal on their long stalks and stared. As they stared, the black avatars began to crumble. Violet couldn't tell what it was at first. It was a hack completely unlike Alopex's but every bit as powerful. Their avatars fell away and revealed their residual self-images. At horrible resolution, with no added trackability, they suddenly looked a lot like themselves. It could see their faces. And they couldn't stop looking at its grotesque visage. Angry at being hacked. Anger radiating impossibly, tangibly from those hot flat eyes. Violet's only consolation was that it was a site looking up from the void; they were safe. She hoped.

An instant later, the deadly claw reached out from the pit and landed on the spinning vortex of the bottom ring. The entire Undernet shook. The spinning ring shattered with sickening lag. Textures across the Undernet began to lose resolution. Motion became jerky as it hit, freezing up and making sound chirp painfully as its stream broke up. Violet couldn't grasp what was happening. The Crag was not only moving but disrupting the Undernet. It shouldn't have been able to touch the damn thing at all, only users could step onto a new site, not another—

"It's not a site!" shouted Vibs. "The Crag's not a site! It's a user!" And what they were seeing made sense. The contact barriers didn't exist because the people there were walking on a person. They accepted it in as soon as they touched it. And their hack, the Gullinkambi, it could see through page code but not a living avatar. Yoshi's modification could. He had just tried to peel the skin off of a person, and now the person was very pissed off.

V team began to run for the higher rings, toward the logout protocol. It was difficult amid the lag. Time kept freezing, and by the time it caught up, there was more and more damage. The rings shook and jammed. Their visual output lost resolution or flashed out entirely for several seconds. Avatars tumbled down the walls as the Crag's gravity coding took them over. The Undernet was getting deleted by its claws as they climbed.

They jumped off of the unspeakable pornography ring just as a claw hit behind them. Obscenity spilled from the stores into the void by the terabyte. Violet saw Varg recall his Tikari, still a separate avatar but one revealed as a mechanical caterpillar. It coiled around him as in the real world. She did the same with Nelson and hid him in her chest. What avatars the Crag didn't crush and destroy outright were landing on its massive shell, the mountain where its native avatars, like lice, would begin to devour them, or beat them away toward the void in fear. V team climbed as fast as the new gravity would allow. The Crag followed, slowly clawing its way up the rings, smashing them along with any users who hadn't yet logged out in the panic. The log-outs jammed the top door to the Nikkei. A crowd of frightened criminals, mutants, and perverts formed to block the way. The top rings had escaped. The middle rings were blocking the door. Those from the lowest rings were doomed.

"We need Alopex!" Violet shouted.

"C will know!" Vibs replied.

"Fuck C team! It won't matter if we're dead."

"This will make every news log on the planet anyway, trust me. Call Aloe!"

All four activated their emergency calls. The information tore through the Undernet ceiling and into the Nikkei, and from there back home. It hit every link in Valhalla. C team saw V's signature, and Cato cursed loudly before running to a pogo to find their real world bodies. Alf and Balder halted their chess game to monitor. T team recalled their mosquitoes and headed for a pogo. R team rushed onto the Nikkei to begin rescue procedures. Half the other teams in Valhalla began monitoring. Alopex's priorities also shifted like an avalanche. The fox manifested at the Undernet portal.

Violet began to feel nauseated from the jerking lag and fits of deafness. The Undernet was breaking up around them. The crowd of remaining avatars was blinking and shifting rapidly from their own contact barriers mashed against each other. Suddenly Alopex broke through. Seeing the crowd, she first tore a new portal into the underground, programming a fifteen thousand channel log-out complex to get rid of the crowd. Trolls and Skuzzbots began to pour out onto the Nikkei floor before the eyes of startled stockbrokers and business avatars.

The Crag's legs were almost upon the top ring. Some of the spambots tried to attack it to no avail. They burst into code as they hit its thick armor. A kind of hack armor they'd never seen before. What kind of mind was inside that thing? It had clearly grown beyond all common capabilities for avatar scaling allowed online. Its destructive power was beyond comprehension, as if a thousand denial attacks emanated from its every limb. It forced physics onto every site it touched, like its presence made the net vulnerable to earthly peril. And it came so close now Violet could see its eyes again, glowing yellow within red from behind the crustaceous spiky mandibles and claws.

Another leg emerged from the mountain shell and reached straight for V team. Alopex emerged through the emptying portal and assessed the threat. Within a thousandth of a second, she ran every denuding program she had on the beast. Her trace program hit it first with no results. Her invasive trace couldn't penetrate it either. Half a dozen more programs failed before a scanning cloud routine running off the surrounding netscape contact points made it through: The user was Bill Ulster from Amarillo Texas, 176 kg, fifty-four years old, multiple arrests for net crimes, disappeared twenty-one years earlier, the same day the Black Crag went online. Alopex attempted to disrupt his link to no avail. It was a tunnel-penetrative tomography link. His higher brain functions were taking place completely online.

V team climbed topside into the Nikkei. The market was mayhem, in chaos from the influx of spambots and fleeing porn connoisseurs. The logs and news volumes were getting flooded by users and programs alike. Violet saw an economic log toppled and smothered by a crowd of gamblers. Debuggers were at the rim of the portal trying to keep the code-rot at bay. A monetary planetoid above was falling into the Crag gravity and several dead avatars lay scattered, either crippled users or improper log outs, some disfigured by the Undernet collapse missing texture maps, others mutilated with their nurbs ripped off. The Alopex system felt out for V team and ingested them, resorting their link from AleGel into herself. New safety protocols loaded instantly.

The rest of Alopex jumped out from the pit. Violet was about to ask if she'd neutralized the Crag when a claw erupted from the ground. The thing had torn all the way through, up to the proper Nikkei. It began to prop itself up as the Nikkei began to fall into the void left by the Undernet's destruction. Orbiting logs and company sites disappeared, going offline to escape. One hit an immersion log-out error and got impaled on the top of the Crag's rising spire. Its segfault lines cracked open, and the lice swarm crawled inside. The whole planetoid, once labeled as XeServ, went dead black and crumbled to binary.

Alopex was busily scanning for any weakness. It took several seconds, an eternity for Alopex, to find one. And only one. In order to maintain a site-like gravity and enormous size, the user had put a great deal of dependence on physical simulators. He was so invested in the sims that the Crag very nearly functioned in netspace like an animal in the real world. Alopex could work with that.

The little white fox representing Valhalla's mainframe grew to several hundred times her usual size. She adjusted her physical simulators to match those of the Crag. Because Bill Ulster's brain was totally immersed in the net and fully dependent on the simulation, his avatar's destruction would render him brain-dead. Alopex was vulnerable as well. The Crag was a powerful being, the most powerful user her logs had ever recorded. All things being equal, they'd have a fair fight. But a fox is more agile than a crab. The fox attacked.

What denizens hadn't logged out of the Nikkei stood still. Across the offices and markets of the Nikkei, what appeared to be a 300-meter tall fox was wrestling with a 300-meter long black hermit crab with a mountain for a shell. The Crag hit Alopex with its limbs, shaking the Nikkei and causing a painful lag across half the local nets. Back in Valhalla, lights flickered. The ground code broke further under their feet. Large chunks of the planetoid were now falling into the void. Veikko fortified their island with new locking protocols as the access tower beside them fell into the great 404.

Alopex bit into the limb and tore it from the Crag, throwing it into a log silo, which broke apart beneath it, leaking news tickers everywhere. The Crag was unstable. Aloe stayed on top of it from there. She didn't let it get another foothold. She bit and tore into every appendage it thrust toward her until it was crippled and fell onto its side. Then she went for its eye stalks, scratching monitoring programs out of the thing's face. The mandibles fell and rendered its action protocols null. Deeper still she dug into the shell, ripping out meaty chunks of net code, then avatar code, and finally brain code. It was a grisly victory. What was left of the Nikkei was covered in crab guts and crag rocks. A puff of Aloe's super-realistically simulated hair was clogging the mass debugging gutter, which was already on overload trying to deal with the destruction of the Undernet and several trillion terabytes of Nikkei programming.

From the dead Crag's shell, its native avatars were wandering away. Some looked at V team, but none tried to attack. Their days of contact barrier violation were over. A familiar brainy green avatar spotted them, bowed to them, and logged away. Alopex took a last glance at them, scanned for their safety, and blinked out. Violet and team just stood, awkwardly, on their island of green plastic netscape, surveying the chaos around them. Ragnar and Ruger hopped down from a floating chunk of stock market without a word. The rest of R team waited above.

A familiar blue rooster floated down from the sky, losing feathers as it flapped its wings. The Gullinkambi landed at Veikko's feet and crowed. He scooped it up and nodded to Ragnar, who activated his regional log-out and swept the teams offline. Violet awoke in the cold empty office from which they'd logged into AleGel. R team was absent; they'd logged in from Valhalla. T and C teams were standing over them. Tahir and Tasha looked like kids caught stealing candy. Most of C team looked stern but stood silent.

Cato stood alone before them all. Violet thought she heard more audio lag. She touched her link instinctively, that horrible squeaking of broken sound stream was back. It took her a moment to realize it was the grinding of Cato's teeth.

Chapter III: Ukiyo

YAMASA-KAIUN WAS making too much money. It was making too much money and not giving half enough of it to Zaibatsu, so Zaibatsu offered an ultimatum: forfeit its earnings for the last three years or be dissolved into another more sycophantic Zaibatsu subsidiary, the YUP. Neither was an option. Their earnings had all been responsibly invested in more ships, better safety features around its islands, and advertising for maritime transportation. To give up and be assimilated into the YUP was just as impossible, because a few days before the deadline, the YUP personnel arranging the takeover ceased to exist. So when Yamasa was set to go rogue and die fighting the Yuppies, the Yuppies never came. The entire navy seemed to drop off the face of the Earth, or at least into storage under its oceans.

The board was uncertain how to proceed. It could be a ruse by the YUP to lure them into lowering their defenses, though in truth they had none. It could be a mislaid file in Zaibatsu HQ that let the situation dissolve. It could be any number of things, and all that the owners of Yamasa could agree on was that they wanted no part of what was to come. They had to sell it all while they still had it to sell.

The Ukiyo ferry service went first and for the most—sixteen ships and the rights to every port and route to the biggest floating city in the Nihonkai. Various other assets sold over the course of the week. Some sold to Zaibatsu, though peacefully and with no sign of the Yuppie's infamous armed hostile takeover tactics. Others sold to companies in GAUNE, some of the ships to private citizens from all over the globe. Everything found its place in the great material continuum. Except for Hashima. Nobody on Earth wanted Hashima.

It was a ruin that over the last couple hundred years had attracted a few photographers, documentarians, and larpers. It was a solid source of revenue for Yamasa until the mid-2100s, when enough of the world had modern ruins to make travel to the obscure island not cost-effective. With no buyers on the respectable markets, it went for sale on the Nikkei. No offers. Even then, weeks before the Nikkei crashed, it looked like Hashima would stay the only holding of Yamasa-Kaiun, as the executives fled for private islands and the employees followed the ships or hunted for new work.

And then it got an offer. Indeed nobody on Earth wanted the place, but someone on Venus did. An anonymous bidder. His bid wasn't much, but it was the only bid. So passed Hashima into the hands of Wulfgar Kray. As it happened he was already on his way to Earth. Wulfgar's shuttle set down on a broken concrete plain. Its thrusters blew debris in all directions, off the seawall into the ocean. The landing skids cracked the ancient concrete further. The airlock opened, and a pair of handlike feet walked on the Earth for the first time.

Crews from other shuttles ran from their transportation to search the island for unwelcome guests. They found it calm and abandoned. They headed into the dead buildings, sifting through splinters and rocks, and over the seawall to scan the water. As they secured his new abode, Wulfgar activated his new link and looked around. The net was not as he'd left it. It changed every hour, and after a year it was a whole new species of net. He ran a quick search for the Orange Gang. It turned up in historical cyclopedias and little else. He ran his own name, even less.

He had something of a blank slate. He had some resources, funds, manpower. He had a new toy that kept him very happy. And he had plans. Two distinct plans. First, revenge on Violet MacRae and her family of Valkyries. He knew where they lived and had some firsthand, though severely outdated, intel on the place. Second, he wanted to rule the world. Or at least most of it. Violet and her team had disassembled his gang in weeks because, despite its influence, it was fairly small. The greatest gang in history was, in the end, small potatoes compared to any average conglomerate. So the first step was to take over any average conglomerate. The first move to the first step was a company.

He'd arrived too late to buy up most of Yamasa. He could have made something out of the Ukiyo ferry services. With a monopoly on a commercial sector's traffic, he could own the commercial sector. With a commercial sector, he'd have access to every company and prospect within. But KeiJu had beaten him to it. Even if they hadn't, the price for the Ukiyo lanes was beyond his capabilities. He'd exhausted every cent from the sale of Iwo Donatsu in buying, then moving, home. He brushed off his feet and pulled his short boots on. Men were already unloading his desk and boxes.

"All the way down," he reminded them. "The very bottom." He had moved from one mine to another. One floated high over the acid land of Venus, and one was carved deep into the earth beneath the Higashi Shina Kai. Mines had advantages in every field but good looks. Security was one of his favorites. The office from which he ran the Orange Gang was in a common København skyscraper. If the police had ever found it, they might have leveled the building. If someone wanted him out of Hashima, they'd have to dig for years. With all the fortifications he planned, it would be an impenetrable underground lair.

But to afford it all, he needed the Ukiyo lanes. To any legitimate businessman, the fact someone else owned them would have been a problem. To Wulfgar, the legality was only a short barrier to be leaped past. After he woke from his first night asleep under the earth, he ordered his men onto the boats. There were two boats left on Hashima, included in the deal. All it usually took to bring tourists to and fro. On them his men mounted guns. One microwave battery each, the only two they had. If Wulfgar lost his first skirmish, it would be weeks before he could find new tools and men to try again. The ships headed for Ukiyo's port in Tottori. Ukiyo had already left for the year, but there would still be a string of cargo vessels bringing the floating city any new food and supplies it needed. A thin string. A weak string.

In one day, Wulfgar had seized five of its ships. Their crews were bribed or executed and replaced with his own. There was no break at all in the cargo, nor anything unusual in the reports and logs. Wulfgar's hackers deleted any hint left online that the monetary implants signing for each package weren't correct. In two days they had all sixteen ships of the Tottori Ukiyo port and the port and the receiving personnel of Ukiyo. They were mostly the same people, just paid a bit more.

Despite their new pay, they complained bitterly to the shipping company about not having enough. Since they had bought Yamasa's shipping rights, KeiJu found the whole thing nothing but trouble. The ships cost too much to maintain, the port cost too much to handle, and the crews were demanding more money. They began looking for a buyer. Wulfgar was spending what little fluid value he had on bribes and Hashima, so he couldn't buy yet. All he could do was see that nobody else did.

His hackers wrecked KeiJu's credit with every net attack they could. They made certain the news heard of the impossibility of making a profit off Ukiyo shipping, stories which greatly amused the Yamasa executives as they reclined on the sunny beaches of Novo Yugoslavia. One day KeiJu's sole owner, Hideo Duplantier, was visited by his banker. He didn't know his real banker had been murdered. He had never met the man in person. The new banker gave him some documents to sign, ones he said would relieve the stress of the Ukiyo lanes by diversifying this and amalgamating that. He didn't care just what. He was at his wit's end. He didn't notice that one of the documents was a will or that another effectively declared bankruptcy. He was quite surprised the next day when WGUSMW, a medical company, came to repossess his lungs. He explained to them that he'd never bought lungs from them. He begged them to let him keep the lungs for one more day as he sorted out the problem. But in the end he simply gave up, his life was in ruins and his business defunct. He went under the knife and died hoping someone else might breathe easier with them.

Wulfgar suddenly found himself inheriting all of Ukiyo's shipping contracts and equipment. It all transferred as per the will to a net avatar known only as "Little Boots at Hashima," real identity unknown. He was able to make the systems run far better than his predecessor, mostly because he didn't have himself sabotaging the whole scheme. With Ukiyo's shipping in his arsenal, Ukiyo itself began to fall. The mayor of the city began to sense things were amiss one day when the ships began delivering recording devices and cameras he hadn't approved. The captain explained brusquely that they came free with the food, and that if one stopped coming the other would follow. It took a few meetings of that sort before the mayor was completely in Wulfgar's pocket, but with the threat of blockade from their own lifelines, he and his crews began installing the spycams themselves. From then on, Ukiyo and its shipping worked flawlessly. Solid businesses under the leadership of one of the finest leaders of his time. Though nobody knew who that was.

Wulfgar sat back as his feeds and money flowed in. He spent his time online watching the Ukiyo markets. The crimes were petty, the businesses mostly legitimate. There was nothing to hold on to, no real prospects. As his grasp on Ukiyo became hard as iron, he began to realize that he had caught little more than air. And then, one day, he found he'd struck gold. Quite unexpectedly, the Nikkei collapsed. Literally, under the weight of a giant crab. The loss of the semi-legitimate Nikkei, its illegitimate Undernet, and the ultimate in depravity—the Black Crag—hit the underworld hard. Tens of thousands of criminals needed new places to deal, and many were distrustful of the nets.

More and more of them began to meet in the real world. Still in yen zones, still in secluded rings, but now in the void of the ocean instead of the net. That arrangement was especially happy for Pelamus Pluturus. He kept an entire fleet in the Nihonkai to ensure his meetings with the Yakuza went well. They'd won the contract for Mars, but he didn't trust them. He was about to spend most of his YUP plunder on them. Meetings at Ukiyo went on and on as the Yakuza and Pelamus representatives argued over budgeting. They argued with raised voices. Raised voices shouting extremely high prices.

Wulfgar knew he had found his next mark but couldn't quite figure out what the mark was. He knew it was on Mars, so he started spending his Ukiyo earnings on a return to space. He knew something heavy was coming back to Earth, so he looked into stealing the Solar Division of FedEx or PortuCorreio. And he knew the Yakuza already had the contract, so he began assembling an army.

"YOU CRASHED the entire Asian stock market!" Cato shouted. "Into a mountain!"

"It was actually a—"

"Silence, Veikko! You have lost the right to talk in this ravine! If your memories had shown one second of contact with that, that *thing*, you'd have lost the right to *breathe*!"

C team had utterly devoured their memories. Cato took Violet's and picked them apart violently, quickly he said to be certain they hadn't brought back any cragware. But she knew he delighted in the pain caused by an in-brain memory sweep of that depth.

"Do you have any idea the gravity of what you've done?" he continued to rant. "How deeply you've violated the treaty? And don't tell me it was only a black market. You know damn well the black markets hold more sway than the proper. I've seen some fucked-up shit in my time here, Valknut, but this is by far the most fucked-up shit that Valkyries have ever fucked!"

"Then where are the Geki?" whispered Vibeke.

"Do! Not! Speak!" he raged. "If the Geki came into my office and burnt you all to cinders, I would thank them and light a cigar on your flaming corpses! I would take up smoking to *want* a cigar to buy to light on your smoldering flesh! You want to know where the Geki are? I don't know where they are. They never came here because they have nothing to ask, and if they have nothing to ask, it's because they know who hired Yoshi already. They know all about you lot. You want to know what they're up to? Look at this mess!"

He forced a graphic into their visual cortices. Burn victim remains. Badly burned, utterly destroyed. Chunks of fat still boiling.

"Look and don't damn forget! Amarillo, Texas. Bill Ulster. The Geki seem to blame the Crag more than its inciting idiots. But Alopex already killed the man's brain. The Geki burnt his body as a message. A message to you, V team. To you and Greta Klein."

He dredged up a picture of a frightened sixteen-year-old girl. Red hair and freckles, a skinny kid with round cheeks.

"She's alive, don't ask me how, but she—"

"Sorry," interrupted Varg, "who is Greta Kline?"

"Yoshi. Your damn friend Yoshi. Her link won't work again, and the kid's scared shitless, but the Crag didn't kill her. But she has been warned. As have you! And if I so much as guess that your team is doing anything that could endanger Valhalla again, I will summon the Geki myself and have them burn the eyes from your damn miserable fucking skulls! Am I understood?"

"No," stated Veikko. "Your accent's just atrocious. It's 'understood,' not 'ahnda stewed.'"

Cato froze. He stared at Veikko for an instant, then spoke again calmly.

"You will not search for Mishka again. If we get intel on her, W will scout it out." He leaned toward Vibeke. "You will never, not ever, set your eyes on her. And from this day on, your team won't run a mission, won't leave the ravine, won't make your bladder gladder without running every drop by us."

Veikko giggled.

"If you laugh again, boy, Dr. Niide will spend the night making you new teeth. Now get the bloody hell out of my office."

Violet stood up to leave with the rest when Cato put his hand on her shoulder.

"You stay here, sheila. We've something to discuss."

Violet stopped. She was suddenly overcome with happiness. She was happy because she knew, not hoped, but knew without a doubt that once the others had left, she was going to reach into Cato's ugly olive drab armor and rip his balls off. She'd savor his screams and howls as she twisted them away, breaking the cremaster muscles and skin, then hold the orbs before his eyes, kick him to the floor, and stuff them down his throat. She was considering how best to finally spit on his face when he spoke again.

"Sorry about all that, all for show, you know? You did a damn fine job down there."

She hated him all the more. She had no clue what shit he was pulling, but he only had a second left of it before she implemented plan T.

"I want to talk to you about something you saw on the Undernet. A meeting you peeked in on. I'm not your enemy on this one. If you listen to what I have to say…. I know you loathe me, but listen for just one minute. I'm gonna make you lot the heroes of the ravine again. Tell me, Violet, how would you like to save all humankind?"

Violet's team stood on the rocky floor outside of C team's office. Veikko broke the silence. "I think she's gonna rip his balls off."

Violet had been in there for several minutes, and no nurses were on their way. Vibeke was afraid for her. She couldn't fathom why Violet and not herself would be held back. She felt sick from the fiasco. The net had seen worse; this wasn't even the worst net disaster of the year. Months earlier the entire Kelpo net fell apart, killing hundreds of users. Before that the British Columbia link service went out and sent over 9000 businesses into bankruptcy. The Nikkei crash killed only a couple dozen when all was said and done, and those were all criminal slime anyway. And it wasn't Vibeke who did it. The Geki were right; it was the Crag. It was Bill Ulster. Their provocation meant little to nothing.

"And stuff them down his throat, just wait, the nurses will be here any minute," added Varg.

But they didn't find Mishka. All trace of her was gone now. With the Crag gone and the Undernet with it, Mishka might respawn her mercenary marketing on any of the lesser Undernets. Even if she did, Vibeke wouldn't be on the case. She'd watch Veikko's kids take the woman down. W team, babies. None of them had even died yet. Some in the ravine said the teams just kept getting better and better. Maybe it was true. Maybe Wart and his crew would never die. They'd just outshine V in every way, capture Mishka, save the planet, and leave Vibs with the damn coffin on her collar, the last time a junior team member got herself briefly killed.

Violet stepped out of the office. Her armor was sadly devoid of blood. Cato closed his door behind her. He looked happy enough. And Violet didn't look half-mad either.

"What did he say?" asked Varg.

Veikko hurried to ask, "Did you rip his balls off?"

"Did he give you more shit about the Nikkei?" questioned Vibeke.

"Where are his balls?"

"Are you okay, Violet?" Varg whispered.

"Did you stuff the balls down his throat?"

"Geez, Veikko, his balls are in his pants. Let the girl talk," Varg finished.

Violet considered how best to summarize. "When we were down there, I saw a meeting on the Undernet, something about a major shipment from Mars. Apparently C is always on the lookout for that one spec. There's something there that could.... Well, Cato wants us to talk to Alf. We need to run an investigation and.... He said if it is what he thinks it is, we have one hell of a mission to do."

"Great. New crap," muttered Vibeke.

"He did say we'd get to save the planet," Violet pushed.

"I'm all for that," added Veikko. Varg nodded as well.

Vibeke thought about the situation. V team hadn't had a global save yet, even T had topped out at half a continent. If she were ever going to give up on Mishka, the time was now. Or at least time to stop thinking about her and move on to bigger fish. Save the planet. Maybe see Mars. All the Valkyrie fun and games. She managed to spit up the words.

"Yeah, let's do it," she said. But felt deep down like it was just another insult, another reminder of failure after failure to destroy the bitch to end all bitches. Vibeke would give the new mission her all, but felt like, after the Nikkei and Cato, the day couldn't get any worse.

"Veikko, Vibeke, Violet, Varg," linked Alopex, "Hangar 18, Walrus Detail."

THE FOX shrieked and fell under the treads. Carrie hit the brakes, and the snowcat ground to a halt. Snorri hopped out into the snow to take a look.

"Is it okay?" Carrie shouted.

Snorri checked over the poor creature. It was dazed but still alive. He took off his right glove and stroked the animal, felt along its ribs and limbs.

"I think so!" he called back. "Just stunned."

He lurched back through the snow, cradling the fox in one arm and pulling himself up to the cab with his other.

"What are you doing?" asked Carrie.

Snorri looked at her, then the fox.

"Could still be seriously injured," he explained. "I'm not leaving it out there."

"We can't keep a fox where we're going."

"Why not? We had a parakeet on Luna. That's a bigger deal than this."

Carrie didn't reply, it was no use. If Snorri got his mind around something, there was no point in arguing. She'd just stay silent as the man tried to explain a damn fox to the project supervisor. The snowcat plodded east. They had one more day to get to Kvitøya before the melt got bad enough to break ice. *Funny*, Carrie thought, *we're trying to melt the ice on Mars, and we can't keep the ice frozen here on Earth.*

They arrived at the ravine. As it happened, the project supervisor thought the fox was adorable. That didn't stop her from sticking the couple in a corner barrack not a meter away from a dead rotting walrus.

They fell asleep despite the smell but woke up their first day to the blast and splatter of an inept technician trying to dispose of the walrus with mining explosives. She ordered them the next morning to help dispose of the walrus chunks and mop up the ravine floor. Two programmers mopping up guts. Carrie was about to quit right then and there, but Snorri reminded her of the contract. Two years on the Ares Project. Finish the contract, and they'd have 137,000 euros each and islands named for them on Mars. Bail, and they'd spend the time doing hard labor. They got on their knees and mopped up dead walrus.

No day was ever so bad as the first. Leo the fox recovered fast and grew popular among the scientists and construction personnel alike. As Snorri began programming the pattern extraction algorithms for the Ares computers, he put Leo's face on the hard drive icon. Soon after, Leo was the mascot of the whole project. And what a project it was. A year earlier one of the Ares whiz kids had invented "hydromacrosis." He had altered the Aufbau Lattice in hydrogen in such a way that it could, given the proper Zeeman kick, form the same lattice in any other hydrogen atom it touched. An infectiously obese Aufbau. He had quickly altered a liter of water and found that it suddenly took up three liters. It also lost the ability to freeze at anything but near absolute zero or boil at anything short of fissile temperatures.

As other scientists back down south applied the principle to make supercooled water systems, the fifteen-year-old genius Valfar Bakken sailed north to Kvitøya to work on the most profitable project his invention could accomplish. Mars had water but not nearly enough of it to terraform the planet, nor was the temperature of Mars high enough to keep the stuff liquid. And he had invented subfreezing water that took up three times the volume of the natural stuff. All he had to do was invent a way to force it to infect the Martian polar caps in their entirety.

He had demonstrated, in a most unscientific move of drinking his "fat water," that it was in fact drinkable and usable by the body. Later tests showed that fish could breathe it with no problem. It had exceptional heat insulation qualities, and it kept its original mass. Only the molecular density and gross volume changed. It was great stuff. If little Valfar had owned the patent instead of his native company, he might have been rich. But as it was, Jamaica owned all the inventions of its citizens, and the same company that owned Jamaica owned Ares.

So Valfar headed north, bundled in jackets and thermal underwear, to tell Snorri what he was doing wrong.

Snorri detested the upstart, but it was still good work. It would pay very well, and when he was offered a second contract, he took it, this time for four years. He forgot to ask Carrie. She headed home, two years older and two years richer, leaving Snorri and Leo to the cold north. That suited Snorri just fine. He met Veronika when she came in on the next boat. Within the month, they went to Maximilian Quorthon, director of human resources, to marry them. The project grew and grew. The ravine was carved deeper and deeper into the rock and in the center, Valfar's magnum opus began to sprout. The YGDR S/L system grew like a tree. The engineers and construction details kept armoring the sides, but the actual power source, the thing that could create the Zeeman kick, had to be grown from a chemical bath. Snorri couldn't fathom the thing. It was so new, and he felt so old in those days that he never tried.

His only concern was the overrides. He was there to program the computers, not to learn about the thing they controlled. By the time Snorri and Veronika were welcoming a new bride, Kristina, into their marriage, he had most of the system complete. Quorthon was governing an entire village of company men, women, and others and had Snorri program up a village counsel. And Valfar, the day after he finished the giant twisted tree of a power plant, began work on the fat water. He had calculated that in order to spread the Zeeman kick to an ice cap, he'd need just under 1,000 kilograms of fat water. A mass three times the size of 1,000 kilos of normal water to coat the big tree. Engineers built the distilleries deep in the ravine caves. They built three massive specialized tanks near the YGDR S/L to hold the stuff. They sent Ares the bill for fat water distillation, just over 75,000 euros per liter.

As the stuff came out drop by drop, Valfar began to pester Snorri more and more about the override programming—about backups for it, backups for the backups, a dozen layers of activation security, backups for the security—so much programming he had to give Leo an AI to handle it all. "Leo" referred only to a computer by then. The fox had died at a ripe old age in Snorri's lap. As the fat water was finished and Valfar began to stick it to the YGDR S/L, Snorri was working up the nerve to ask Quorthon's daughter on a four-way date and the Ares

Company was running out of funds. Mars was far away, and the executives were coming to realize that they might not be able to afford sending the thing there. The news sent Valfar into a panic. As soon as he heard about the possible shutdown, he ran to Snorri and began reviewing the overrides again.

"Damn it, kid," Snorri objected, "I've shown you this crap ten thousand times. It's as secure as it gets! This thing can't turn on unless you and fifty other men give it the go-ahead."

"The fat water's *on* the power system, Snorri. It's there and ready to go."

"And if it goes to Mars someday, it'll take them a year to activate it thanks to all this junk."

"Look, Snorri. You know how this thing works. We don't want it here a second longer than it has to be. I'm going to start taking the fat water off tonight if we don't hear word from central."

"Why? Why are you so damn uptight about it sitting there?"

"Because it reaches the top of the ravine!"

"And?"

"Think about it, Snorri. It triples the size of the water it touches. If it activates here and touches the ocean, Mt. Everest would go under."

That same night, the Ares executives in a rare moment of corporate concern and wisdom decided the thing was too dangerous to leave intact. Or even on Earth. They had funds to ship 10,000 kilograms to Mars. Not enough for the whole thing—the power plant weighed ten times that. But they could move the water supply and keep the Earth safe. Valfar supervised as they siphoned off the fat water and shipped it to Spitsbergen Spaceport in the massive safety tanks that took up the rest of the budget to move. As the rocket took off, Ares Corporation went out of business.

With no more company, the hundred and fifty residents of the pit lost their contracts and transport fees back down south. But not many really wanted to leave. They had a home in that ravine, a chance for life away from the company betrayals and fights and life they'd left behind. Almost everyone stayed. Valfar never got used to the cold, but he managed to keep busy. He focused on the trivialities of life in the pit. He built a movie projector from scratch and downloaded half the movies on the net to the thing. Quorthon brought in a few new cooks and kept the ravine alive and very peaceful.

Snorri finally asked Quorthon's daughter, Merrit, out on a date. She hit it off with his wives spectacularly and moved into their cabin not long after. Snorri had built the place out of brick, not too different, he said, from laying out binary. In his spare time, he'd work on his chronicles of the Ares Project and the ravine, or sleep with his gorgeous and plentiful wives, or retrofit the Leo program with new tricks and gizmos. As its AI developed, he decided to make a few changes to the original fox, which reminded him too much of Carrie. The last wife who got away. Not that he dwelt on her loss too often. He had Veronika, a master programmer. Kristina, a master climatologist. And Merrit. She had the most beautiful voice he'd ever heard.

"SO WE go to Mars and boil the fat water before they can bring it home?" asked Violet.

"Fat water doesn't boil," explained Vibeke, "not short of fission. We should let them take off, then send the transport into the sun."

"Exactly my thoughts, Vibeke," Alf said with admiration, "but not Valfar's."

Valfar began in his unintelligible accent, "The sun is a fusion engine. In the same way deuterium accelerates fusion, fat water is a 'quantum isotope' of sorts. Its infectious rate is amplified by the internuclear energy and the shattering electrostatic force is exponential due to my tinkering. If a single drop of heavy water entered a fusion reaction, the result would be extraordinary."

"So this stuff," asked Veikko, "can destroy the sun too?"

"Oh no! Not at all," explained Valfar happily. "The sun would do great. It would grow up to be larger than Woogie 64 and Canis. In fact Canis Majoris may well be a fat-water-based reaction. The sun would love fat water. It's only the planets that would be destroyed," he smiled proudly, then frowned.

Varg asked bluntly, "What about a fusion bomb on Earth? Standard Tsar Yield?"

"Nothing like the sun with all that fuel," Valfar stated confidently. "It would only annihilate the Earth, likely the moon but no more."

"Oh thank goodness," sighed Veikko. "So what can we do?"

"Fission will destroy the water. The orbits of each hydrogen atom are so distant that the electron is already past the Coulomb barrier. It makes for very weak fissile material. It just falls apart."

"So we need to get an A-Bomb to Mars?"

"That's the only thing that would do it."

"But this is all speculation. We don't know yet that the fat water is involved. All we know is that someone is bringing something heavy back from Mars. Your first task is to learn what. If our fears prove correct, your first priority is mere prevention of its return. There are still some hopes of using the device and making Mars another habitable planet. I'm sure you know how dismal attempts have been so far. The Qahira project is the most successful attempt to date, and it only managed to thicken the air with minimal oxygenation. If the Ares water leaves Mars, we'll consider the atomic solution, but bear in mind the state of earthly politics.

"Some in UNEGA blame GAUNE for the Nikkei collapse, given that a Texan destroyed it. GAUNE is still complaining about the Blackwing and rumors of wave bombs. Consider what a nuclear explosion on Mars might trigger. We must consider that a last resort. Or penultimate. Even if the fluid makes it to Earth, it's useless without our little ash tree. We need only stay where we are. If the Ares is completed and ready to do its worst, we have a rampart to seal it off and Alopex to keep it unplugged."

"And if all that fails," said Veikko, "the Earth gets flooded and the Fish take over."

"Destruction of the Ares fluid is still an option, Veikko. We already have a nuclear weapon on Mars, or at least the PRA does. But this is all conjecture. For now, your mission is to track down the Yakuza involved and learn why they're going to Mars. If they're going to excavate a Martian rock for display as a sculpture in some company office building, we can leave well enough alone."

"So we're Yak tracking today?"

"We are."

It was a clever but simple process to attract them, one Veikko had designed for Project Nepenthe in a stroke of subtle genius. Find someone to kill, make them step on Yakuza toes, follow whoever they send to execute the unfortunate.

"Is there anyone we want dead?"

"Only you, V team," linked Cassandra.

Kabar rang in next. "Arms dealer in Empresargentina. But it has to look like an accident."

"We need a bombing," sounded Necrosis. "I guess you could kill someone, but we can't let the Yaks take credit."

"We've got one," called Wart. "Yaks would be perfect. The Keres in Karpathos had us doing surveillance a week ago on Omar Sedaris, guy in Barcelona who was planning to bomb a Zaibatsu office. They took him down and moved on, was only a small part of their Barcelona clean out. But Zuhoor Sedaris is pissed as hell and she's gonna pull something, we think, on Tuesday. We were gonna hand her to the police, but she's a nasty, nasty critter."

"Zaibatsu would want her dead naturally. The Yaks would make perfect sense. We're certain they don't know about her, though. He never registered any of his kids."

"Does she have a link?"

"Yes, sending provider listings now." It appeared in V team's heads, "MÁSmóvil, easy hack. You want us on it?"

"If you want to stay."

"Fo sho," linked Veikko. "Go ahead and plant a claim on Zaibatsu's transportation grids, ultraheavy cargo from Mars. Let the Yaks see it and any replies but not Zuhoor. I don't want her receiving congratulatory e-mails and wondering why. We'll head out today. Just link us her—What does she live in?"

"Omar's mansion. Beautiful treehouse grown from a massive modified Eucalyptus. Address on its way."

"Nice," lauded Varg. "My parents almost moved into an Oak, but decided it was unnatural and got an apartment."

"Alright, we'll hang in the branches and—"

"They might see us."

"Figure of speech, we'll 'surveil the premises' and wait for the Yaks to come knocking. If the Yaks still work the same way, they'll be from a detachment of the Mars crew. We'll follow them. If they go to meet for Mars details, we follow. If they head for a Yak stronghold, we'll try brain hacks."

"And if they're unrelated? Not Mars personnel?"

"W, you go ahead and stay on their netside communications. Hack them in Espana and see who they inform of the completion. Put a burr on that, and we'll see which Yaks get it in their hair. But I think they'll head to the Mars crew directly. That's how they did it when we were on project Nepenthe."

"Alf, thoughts?" asked Vibs.

"Sounds sound. You may be heading off planet again, and in a hurry. See that Eric loads you up for space, and get backups made."

They nodded. Backups were always an ominous precaution. And not much of one, as if they died, the backups would be of little consolation to the deceased. V team headed to med bay. They'd done it before. Any time a team headed off planet on a mission, it was standard to have their memories backed up on the med bay computer. The lipid polarity drives could store several brains apiece, but it was only raw data, memories like so much video. If they were to die permanently on Earth, Valkyries would generally try to recover what they could of the brain and keep the memories on file. In space losses, bodies were rarely recoverable so they backed people up in advance.

Skadi ambushed them on the way to the med bay. She jumped out and hugged Veikko full force, and one of their usual matches ensued. Skadi always won. She was simply stronger, and Veikko would have to tap out before breaking a rib. She snuck in a kiss as he squirmed.

"Getting backed up?" she asked.

"Everything but you, I'd rather forget," he coughed.

Violet walked on, having heard their flirtations before. Skadi kissed him again.

"You can try," she said, squeezing him tighter. He couldn't speak. Finally a snap resounded through the air. Skadi let go.

"Damn it, Skadi," he wheezed.

She just laughed. "Well, you're going to med bay."

She sauntered off.

"God, I love that woman," he said genuinely, though clearly in pain.

Niide fixed his ribs—she'd broken three—with only a two-minute delay, having had his scans prepared from the last time she did the same. He quickly turned to the backups.

"Over to mmmm, Basher," mumbled Dr. Niide. Violet thought it was peculiar to name the medical backup drives Bonecrusher and Basher or why three drives had two names. Vibeke could read the text labels on the machines but didn't get the names Bones, Crusher, and Bashir either. In any case they hooked into the third drive and started uploading. It only took a few minutes but always carried an unpleasant flicker of the old images, more often than not ones that they didn't consciously remember seeing. A disorienting feeling.

Once finished they headed out to the pogo pads. Their uniforms turned black, standard for unknown territory. With their memories safely stored away behind them, they and their brains headed out to Espana, well aware at how much couldn't be transferred. A person's mind is a great deal more than the raw data that could be uploaded, more than memory alone. Their thoughts, feelings, consciousness, whatever made them who they were couldn't be logged on lipid chains. The transfer always reminded Violet of that, always made the mission to come feel like it would be the one on which she'd lose them.

SHIKA SAID nothing for the entire ride. She found small talk unbecoming of assassins. For the two years she'd worked for the Yakuza, she'd conducted herself with the utmost respect and professionalism. Usagi on the other hand was running out of fingers. There were soldiers, and there were fools. Shika was a soldier. Shika hated working with fools. She wouldn't give Usagi the chance to blow a mission. She made it clear; Usagi was the pilot and nothing else. Shika would do the job.

Shika did the job. Ten seconds landing. The target saw them but didn't flee. Shika played it calm. Scanned for detectors, none. Touched the door, let it go clear, introduced herself. Confirmed the target, are you Suhoor? Sorry, Zuhoor. No, I didn't know it meant rose, that's very sweet. What was that? I can't hear you with the door closed, ah, thanks! One shot to the link, one to the forehead, one to the heart. Quick local scan, no detectors, no police links. Departure, back to the pogo. Job complete, send confirmation. Code Seikou. Take us back. We don't want to miss the meeting.

Wunjo Team intercepted the confirmation link. Common Yakuza coding to the Zaibatsu hub. Yakuza cryptography was simple enough for Alopex and carried no internal detective algorithms. Nobody working for Zaibatsu ever paid for that extravagance. Widget stuck a burr onto the provider log and let it go to work. It passed five rerouters in the Zaibatsu mainframe, then passed on to their I/O port. The I/O port had caught one of their burrs a few months prior, so they had Alopex time some cloaking code to activate at just the right time. The burr deleted itself as it entered the port. The port sent it out. The burr recovered itself immediately and followed the last transit protocol: Ukiyo City delivery daemon.

V team tracked the Yakuza pogo without moving from their hiding place in the alley. Veikko had spent nearly an hour adorning their own pogo with garbage from the finest dumpsters in Barcelona. It took the Yakuza nearly a day to get off their butts and wipe out the competition, which concerned W team as Zuhoor's last bomb components would arrive later that day. Still, all worked out, and the pogo had some truly revolting trash to disguise it beyond the normal goldtop chromatophores. Like their uniforms the chromatophores could assume any color and even some patterns, but nothing beat the rotting banana peel and crumpled Rockdelux with which Veikko had lovingly endowed the windshield.

Sadly, all things come to an end, as when the Yakuza pogo neared the edge of tracking range. They had to lift off and let the garbage fall by the wayside. After a quick hack to silence the litter detectors, Varg hit the accelerator and followed the Yaks northwest. Walter saw their course and nudged Wart, who linked to Veikko.

"Do you want us to head to Ukiyo?" asked Wart. "Looks like your mark's going the wrong way."

"Affirmative, my fungal friend. Head on over and see if Ukiyo's having a Yak convention."

Walter and Widget linked simultaneously, "You got it, Veeks."

W headed for a pogo in Valhalla. V followed their mark toward the Golfo Vizcaya. They kept a wide twenty-kilometer distance from the Yaks, the maximum with which they could safely keep the thing in their sights. Yakuza were notoriously brutal to anyone they suspected of following them. Dr. Niide had, in total since beginning his work in the ravine, reattached twenty-nine Valkyrie heads due to Yakuza swordplay. They'd never lost a head from a Yak fight, but the second man named Borknagar, from one of Balder's early teams, was killed permanently by a slash high up on his neck that severed his brain stem in just the wrong place.

The Yak pogo made a sharp turn at the coast and headed due west toward GAUNE. Over land a twenty-kilometer distance is filled with other craft. It's nearly impossible to see someone tracking you. Over the ocean, twenty kilometers means nothing. If one pogo follows you and the rest follow shipping lanes, you've caught them Valhalla used the trick often. The Yakuza too valued the technique. But unlike the Yakuza's, Valkyrie pogos were fortified for extended undersea travel. They hit the water as soon as they reached it and continued to follow the Yaks.

As soon as they were deep enough to hide their wake, they could see the red lights of the Euskaldunak Cetacean colony below. At that depth, at dusk, they could only make out the shapeless glow, but Veikko explained, "It's shaped like two crosses, lauburu crosses. One of the better-armed colonies, they had a fight with the SI before it was banned. I got in trouble for laughing about it in school once. Honestly a bloody fight between Fish and Loyolists was all good news to me. Still had to come here on a field trip from Itämeri. You'd be amazed at the language barriers down there."

The Yaks made another course change, an about-face toward Asia. Vibeke calculated their course—Straight for Ukiyo. Varg brought the craft to a halt. Veikko linked back to W team.

"All roads lead to Rome. We'll stay here until they're well out of range, then head over. What's your ETA?"

"We should get there about nine hours before your Yaks," said Weather. "Directions?"

"Wait for us on the city. Don't spend all your money on porn."

"Confirmed, half on porn, half on drugs."

W linked out. The craft slowly sank toward the colony. Violet sat back and watched a fish swim by the side window. They'd only need fifteen minutes before the Yaks would be long gone, but those brief pauses always hit her the hardest. It was too short to do anything but too long to hold still. She'd mastered holding still while getting stung by flies at Achnacarry. She could lie motionless for more than a day if detectors were looking for her. But there, in a pogo with no threat at all, time acted strangely.

Violet was always aware of being useless to a mission. She wasn't often a fifth wheel, but in thinking back on the Nikkei disaster, she realized she hadn't actually done a single thing but run away. Not that any of them had done any good, but the Spanish mission hadn't even seen her outside of the pogo. She'd resigned herself long ago to an idea of the team with Vibeke as the brain, Varg as the muscle, and Veikko as the master of the craft. It left no question who would do what but seemed in recent projects to leave Violet as "that other girl." Why else had she been picked to steal the Blackwing herself. Everyone else had specific roles to play. Another abysmal line of thought she was getting herself into. She looked out the portal for a distraction and found an obvious one.

It looked rather like the fish that had just passed. A tall, thin, one-man craft. A one-man *Cetacean* craft. It made no contact, just looked them over. Veikko said nothing, so Violet wasn't concerned. He had a sixth sense for when the Fish posed a danger. This one, he just watched, so she followed suit. The craft luminesced once, red, and swam away.

"Just one blink. They know we're not broken down, probably want us to go."

Violet asked, "In a hurry?"

"No, we can stay the full fifteen. They're never in any hurry."

A short time later, they lifted from the sea and started toward Ukiyo. Ten thousand kilometers. With a long wait ahead, Violet leaped into the net. A clean, polished net with full Alopex protection. Three other black avatars popped in behind her. With only hours to Ukiyo and the fate of Earth in the balance, the team made the best of their net time by watching all the funny kitten videos they could find and forwarding the best of them back to Valhalla.

A few servers south and a transfer protocol away, Shika was reading up on more pressing matters. The first real world meeting with Pelamus had gone poorly. He was offering most of the former YUP holdings but not the navy. That made sense, he was Cetacean. But the whole reason Zaibatsu wanted them in on the deal was to seize a real navy. They had the weakest sea force of any major UNEGA outfit, and general assembly was powerless or unwilling to stop predation within its companies. Zaibatsu, as part of the charter, couldn't have any military of its own, so that fell to the less-than-legal divisions. The Yaks had beaten out the Unspeakable Darkness at the last net meeting. They had the contract, but if they didn't get a navy out of it, Zaibatsu would replace the Yakuza as its favored knuckle. That would mean an intraconglomerate war.

Both Shiro and Ota were going to be in Ukiyo to see that it didn't come to that. With two oyabun on the way, security was going to be as tight as possible. A new difficulty given the changes in Ukiyo. For the first time on the floating city, they had found detectors and monitoring bugs. All were cleaned out of course, but it meant someone new was onboard, someone disrespectful of Ukiyo's blindness policies. So after Shika dropped her useless companion and rendezvoused with other security, they'd be on the hunt. If someone was planting bugs in Ukiyo, they were desperate. If they were desperate, they wouldn't stop at the removal of their tricks. They would send agents. Spies into the next meeting. It was inevitable: before the week was through, Shika would be adding another new stripe to the dragon on her irezumi. It had thirty-five so far. A thirty-sixth for Zuhoor. If she could catch four more spies in the next day, she'd have a full dragon.

Wart linked to V, "Arrived at Ukiyo. Standing by."

Veikko paused the kitten playing in zero gravity and linked back, "Any sign of Yakuza activity?"

"Nothing yet. We've put our Tiks in the air sniffing for skin dyes. So far we've got some temporary motion tattoos on kids, holographic tattoos on adults, mod-ink on the modified, and various other colorful insignia but nothing big under fine suits. Nothing like the Yakuza. Your ETA?"

"Nine hours now, puts the Yaks at just over eight. Likely their next event is tomorrow. Intel on any good hotels?"

"All hourly, all full. Lots of good hides, though. We're keeping to the back of a lamp locker. Did you see the one with the guy brushing the Maine coon's teeth? It's all 'yowmrowmowow.'"

"Negative, we'll keep an eye out for it, top priority."

W linked out, and they flew on into the night. When dawn broke, V was at the edge of the Nihonkai. They couldn't see the sun or the sea, only a monsoon. Violet thought, growing up, that the tropical Scottish storms were as bad as skies could get, but Ukiyo was in the midst of the Arashinigatsu, a hot winter monsoon that began in the early 2100s, around the same time Kvitøya thawed out. None of the causes were of as much concern as the results—pogos try to stay a fixed height above the ground. On land, it meant they gently bounced along and absorbed most small shifts in height. Over water, they caused a light ripple beneath them. Over waves, they followed each and every wave up and down. The Nihonkai had three-meter waves, and Veikko was getting either airsick or seasick. He couldn't tell which because the air and sea had merged.

Rain wasn't falling in drops. It was just a solid wall of water flowing constantly downward. Varg flew with great care, letting the auto-navigation do its work but not the autopilot, which would likely have sent them into the sea bottom with the constant lightning skewing its sensor array. They'd decelerated to a snail's pace, and it was a relief when Varg finally spotted the Ukiyo link label.

"Three minutes and we'll hit the Ukiyo grid. Then it'll clear up."

Vibeke had been reading Ukiyo specs for the last hour. She quietly added, "Then parking's the problem…."

As promised in three minutes, they fell from the cloud bank into the crystal clarity of Ukiyo's fake weather, drizzling lightly below the torrential rain and black sky just atop the grid's edge. Ukiyo itself sat in the middle of the open airspace, a wooden city under a great tan canopy. At a distance it looked like a giant motionless buoy, a tall column in the center for the canopy and a stout squareish plain on which the city rested. Even from a kilometer away, they could make out the huge lanterns, banners, and mountains of apartments built atop stores atop walkways. The main street itself was completely hidden behind kiosks and side markets that hung off the sides like moss.

They unclingered their microwaves and handed them to their Tikaris. Veikko's carried his own and Varg's, Violet's and Vibeke's held their own. Sal, Bob, and Nelson flew toward the city where the weapons could be sneaked in covertly. Pokey stayed on Varg disguised as a bandolier.

"MORNING, FELLAS," linked Weather. A large mechanical grasshopper greeted them, floating in the air in front of the pogo briefly before flying back to the city. Weather continued. "We spotted our first Yak today. Couple of them arriving, and a few coming up from subsurface condos. Security's tight, personnel twitchy. Bugs everywhere, the Yaks have disabled a ton of devices and complain loudly to the locals every time they do. No concentrations forming yet, no Cetaceans. Looks like you didn't miss the big show. We're coming out of the lamp locker, gonna get some pierogi at Reštaurácia Radičová. High up the center column, good view."

"Stay high," replied Veikko. "We'll take the main street when we get there."

There were few other vessels in the air, but the ocean was full of docked boats, ships, pogos, copters, hovercraft, surface skims, blimps, and spinners. Luminescent algae patterns lit their way to the valet system. Varg let the pogo down to a meter over the still water. A small hoverbot came out to scan them.

"Four persons, one craft, 900 yen. Save 250 yen by parking underwater?"

"Yes, please," Vibs called out. An autoparker linked out to the pogo, and Varg handed over the controls. It took them to the Delta quadrant, row 5, space Q and set the pogo down on the water where a small punt was waiting. They hopped onto the rickety little boat and locked the pogo, then watched it sink down to the Strawberry level. The boat headed for the city. The thing was terribly slow and made several detours to pick up new customers.

Vibeke ventured a subtle hack on the parking system to look for the Yakuza pogo. It came into the weather grid seconds after she began. They'd passed it in the storm. Two persons, one craft, 700 yen. Cancel parking, drop off only. Only one to drop off, 150 yen. Four-minute wait for the boat. It would call their boat. Vibs had Alopex give her a programmer signature and altered the system so the Yak would take a different boat. Best not to be seen at all. Six-minute wait for boat. Shika cursed quietly, and Vibs logged out.

The punt finally came to its dock, a small portion of the larger dock used by the massive cargo ships. One was present, towering above them, its deck almost level with Ukiyo's. V team disembarked and began climbing the 224 steps up to Ukiyo's main level. Their suits turned gradually to match the brown wood tones. Other tourists didn't seem to care. Their outfits were blinking green to red and flashing skull cartoons and rainbows. The walls of Ukiyo didn't stay wood colored either. Link windows opened along the hull of the city and began to speak.

"*Irasshaimase!*"

"*Irasshaimase! Welcome to Ukiyo!*"

"*Irasshaimase! Only 200 steps to go! Do you not liking to climb so much? You can sail to Ukiyo too! Parking in Tottori is free, and we boat you! 4000 yen is you at the top!*"

"*Irasshaimase! You may not do drugs here!*"

"*Irasshaimase! The child is forbidden in forbidden child zones! You can place the child in our daycare place for 600 yen per child!*"

"*Irasshaimase! Only 100 steps to go! Do you not liking to climb so much?*" It went on, playing out in broken English designed to instill a deceptive feeling of superiority in tourists.

Every step creaked slightly, all cantilevered out from the main hull, a deep weathered wooden shell that held the lower innards of the city. Employee housing, storage, and the like. At 214 steps they came to the guardhouse and weapons check. A guard gave them all a quick scan, their armor hid everything they had kept, and he waved them on. A small traffic jam waited at the top few steps. In the confusion and crowding, they called in their Tikaris.

Nelson was on the spot. Swooping down to the level of the crowd's feet. He flew in and adeptly dodged all the moving legs on his way to Violet. He made it from the low air to her palm in seconds flat, where she holstered her microwave and allowed Nelson back into her chest. Vibeke's Tikari flew in next. As skilled as Nelson, it darted between oblivious bystanders and dropped her microwave directly into its holster before climbing into the vent on her armor.

Sal, Veikko's Tikari, was slightly weighed down from holding both boys' microwaves. He aimed straight for foot level but drooped and stuck his front right wing into the wooden step with a quiet thud. His legs were holding the microwaves, so he tried to swing them up onto the deck to free his limbs. It worked too well and threw Varg's microwave directly into the small of a guard's back. The guard turned and looked, but luckily saw nothing at eye level.

Sal pushed his way loose and went for the microwaves. Veikko's was easy to find, but Varg's had bounced off the guard and was lying in the busy walkway. Sal rushed toward it. He tried to grab it but accidentally grabbed the trigger and gave a tourist a hot foot. As the tourist shouted and ran, Sal picked up the second microwave and darted for Veikko.

He smacked into the side of Veikko's head and knocked him into Violet, then went for Veikko's chest before handing over the microwaves. Varg's fell and landed directly in his hand, while Veikko's was stuck awkwardly half out of his chest. He quickly removed and holstered it and checked around to make certain nobody had seen the fiasco. Aside from a shouting tourist and a confused guard, they were safe. They stepped up to the deck.

It was loud. Thousands of voices mashed into one chattering buzz. It was bright. Even after they dimmed the link labels, there were neon labels on half the buildings, talking moving posters on others, vibrant floating ad-bots, and shouting marketers on stilts between kiosks. The place didn't look all that different from the worst of the Nikkei—utterly stuffed with shops, stores, malls, swap meets, kiosks, bathhouses, miniplazas, sales centers, eateries, and the occasional wholesaler. Between these structures, where normally would have been streets or paths, were pedestrians crammed shoulder to shoulder, not so much like sardines as carbon atoms.

Up close the urban sprawl was even more impressive, built up to give the effect that they stood, as they approached the main road, in the middle of a valley. Especially in the center, wooden shops on stilts on other shops rose almost all the way to the canopy itself. Giant lamps of old Asian design lit the shadows and tinted the last neutral colors into more brown woodiness. They could smell the fishmonger forest, though the link said it was still far away. Flyers for wig shops and porn haunts stuck to their boots. Various food courts belched their odors onto the plaza, hoping to lure a hungry patron, odors that soaked into every last raw cherrywood wall.

Another grasshopper Tikari floated briefly before them, then flew up top to direct their eyes to the restaurant where W team waited. All

W team had their Tiks in orbit, blending in perfectly with the air traffic of ad-bots and security cameras. Vibeke's parking hack announced that the Yak had arrived at the dock clockwise from their own. Violet spotted a perfect place to see the incoming mobster, a flat-topped building high up the outer mountain range.

Not to risk anyone seeing their microwaves, they climbed a series of gutters, slant roofs, scaffolding, and open windows to make the spot. The crowd on every level of the hill was too distracted to notice their abridged ascent between walkways, and the target building was a bookstore so it had nobody outside to watch them arrive.

Looking down over the edge, they saw the guardhouse crowd. Violet sent her Tikari back out to survey it for Yakuza ink. Nelson spotted not only Shika but two other Yakuza. None of the three spoke to each other, but one raised an Alopex alert. He was already labeled from an old N team mission, Shiro, an oyabun. Leader of an entire family. Vibeke sent out her own Tikari to keep an eye on him. Veikko put his on the last. Widget linked in.

"We've got a guy named Ota, two Tiks on him and his guards. He's the head of Aizukotetsu-kai, master of all the Yaks in space. We've got a few more previously labeled members, mostly lieutenants."

"And, Veikko," added Wart, "guess who I spotted?"

"Who?"

"Hokkaido Joe!"

"Lovely," muttered Veikko. Project Nepenthe had introduced Veikko to the most annoying, irritating, despicable loudmouthed bastard in the history of the Yakuza. For hours of the mission, he'd kept the man's company, waiting for him to spill the beans on who manufactured the memory drug, and he gave up nothing. Not because he was being careful, not because he didn't know, but because the squeaky voiced idiot had to talk about every damn irrelevant subject in his tiny brain at every chance he got. He even bragged about losing a pinky for it. Veikko finally snapped and killed the bastard, dragged him back to the ravine, and hacked him posthumously to get the information. He was livid to discover Niide resurrected him, and Balder sent him back to Nippon before the Yakuza noticed he was missing. Mission appropriate, but Veikko really, really wanted Joe to stay dead.

Once on the main street, a pattern formed among the Yakuza. The first few met with another tattooed batch, and more and more, like drips on leaves falling into a common river of Yakuza, flowing straight for the meeting place. V team followed from the rooftops, working their way toward a degraded district of rotting wood and rotting moral fiber. Disney stores gave way to porn stores, porn stores gave way to dissident stores, and in the deepest reaches of the capitalist meadow, the herd of Yaks came to a stop in one unlabeled barn that the Ukiyo denizens seemed to avoid.

MOST OF the team kept their Tikaris back from the entrance. They were small but not invisible. Violet sent hers to the ceiling, where it deployed a tympanum to the surface and got echoey but discernible results, or at least it would when the crowd grew silent. Vibeke kept hers aloft to spot newcomers, and Vcikko's mantis took to the walls of the shed opposite the target. Varg's still remained stuck to his person.

The influx of Yakuza slowed, then stopped. There were some untattooed men but no Cetaceans. Silence descended over the table within. Violet linked audio to her team and W.

"*Ohayo gozaimasu*! Oshi will speak first, for Zaibatsu."

"Respected brothers and Cetacean representatives, we have the ultimatum from the executive board. We are willing to proceed without the naval concessions."

An uproar sounded in several languages. Violet couldn't make much out of the rabble, but she caught basic snips of "Bullshit," "Fucking Bullshit," and "Motherfucking Bullshit" from the loudest screamers. When the outrage calmed down, Oshi spoke again.

"It is Zaibatsu's intent to trade the—"

More shouts and jeers sounded. Zaibatsu was, in effect, selling the Yakuza out. They would still do all the work and take all the risk, but other Zaibatsu companies would reap the benefits. Oshi began again when the crowd ceased.

"The Yakuza *will* have a navy! We will, in time, control the seas—Sorry, the surface of the seas, for Zaibatsu, but we will do so with a fleet produced by Stechrochen GmbH. To *our* specifications, with the liquid funds acquired from the Cetacean deal."

Mumbles sounded from the crowd instead of angry cries.

"As this is an internal matter for Zaibatsu," continued Oshi, "I assume your friends underwater will not object?"

"Captain Pluturus will be advised," called one of the crowd. "But I expect he'll be pleased."

"Thank you, Kansha. Masamune will now address those present."

After a moment, Masamune began. "Ohayo Gozaimasu, to address Oyabun Ota and Oyabun Shiro: Randaquivila has loaded a blocked partition in my brain with the technical specifications for the transpor—"

He was interrupted. There was more mumbling, then shouting from elsewhere in the room.

"One representative!" Veikko recognized Hokkaido Joe's voice. "You said just one! Who's he?" Sounds of a fight broke out, more indistinct shouting. Then Joe screamed in his most aggravating voice, "He's not with the sashimi! He's a spy! He's a spy, spy boy spy! Break his link! He's a spy!"

V team prepared to move. Veikko linked to W team, "Expect break, you stay high, we stay low. Girls on spy, boys on Masamune."

A fight was breaking out below. Violet's Tikari picked up microwave fire, then extensive microwave fire. A man with a burned face bolted from the building, chased by several Yakuza. Violet quickly sorted out their priorities. Save the spy from the Yak stampede. Follow the spy. Determine loyalty, motive, threat, potential as ally or threat. Act accordingly.

Veikko and Varg would be capturing and hacking Masamune with Walter and Wart. New team: Violet and Vibeke on the ground, Widget and Weather in the sky. Vibeke linked out to all.

"I'll keep V's pogo. Boys take W's."

Wart sent out a link dump to Valhalla of the meeting and important points. Violet called her Tikari off the roof and told it to follow the burnt man. Vibeke sent hers straight down through the roof of the building on which they were perched. As Violet darted away to follow the spy from the rooftops, Vibs looked around the room. It was emptied of people. She scanned for combustibles; there were none. She had to work fast. She stood and leaped to the next building after Violet. The Tikari kept scanning. There was a boiler. It would have to do. Her

Tikari landed on it, and she told the wings to superheat as it crawled up toward the valves. It clamped the valves closed, and she put the wings on overload for a few seconds, then let it make an escape.

As Vibs hit the next building, the boiler exploded and sent the wall crashing down on several pursuing Yakuza, blocking the path for more. She figured five stopped, twenty slowed. A good start and an unseen cause. They'd assume the spy had grenades. Their resulting caution would slow them further. Violet could see the burnt man clearly from her Tikari if not the rooftops. She let it fly on its own. It was hard enough to look through the bug and run at the same time, let alone over slanted, patched, and duct-laden ceilings. She leaped to a third and knocked a panel loose. Her foot fell right into an attic and caught as she pulled it out. She didn't fall, but it was getting problematic.

Vibeke was close behind but moving slower, falling back briefly to tractor any debris she could into the way of the remaining Yaks. She caught a straggler on the head and tripped up two more, but there were still four hot on his tail. It would have to do. She couldn't risk hitting a front-runner and revealing herself to the Yakuza. Violet kept ahead, making good time on the rooftops and staying even with the target. Her Tikari stuck to him and two Tiks from above, W team's, stayed high to offer maps. Widget rang in.

"He's sticking left, likely heading to the center. Could have headed outwards by now."

Weather added, "Not hearing any links out of him, nothing incoming. If he has backup, they're keeping quiet."

VEIKKO AND Varg had stationed themselves on the roof of the original meeting. Audio yielded nothing about what was happening inside. They'd seen two major entourages escape, but both carried old link labels, all men protecting their family heads. None named Masamune. He was still inside with—Wart linked his estimate—twelve men.

Veikko linked to Varg for real-world cover and lay down on the roof. He went netside and felt around in the building. Four signatures he could tap, more he couldn't be sure of. These Yaks were highly secured. He couldn't get names on any of the few he could even be sure existed. He pushed Alopex's denuding routines in and could see a few more men, but it was clear a hack was hopeless. Even if he could find Masamune, his internal wetware would be even tougher. They weren't going to hack him without a cerebral bore on his head.

Veikko burst out of immersion, and Varg knew what that meant. He took a concussive charge from his back and set it on the roof, five seconds. They ran and leaped over to a scaffold on the adjacent building. Peering down, they saw the charge go off and collapse the roof. Two men left the building. Veikko put his Tikari on them for a moment before Walter's arrived to see them out. If one was Masamune, Walter would take him. But that was unlikely; he'd have more protection. Varg took the lead and jumped down into the hole.

He landed flat on one Yakuza, knocking him out. He could see eight. He couldn't see the ninth because the other eight were protecting him. Very likely that was their man. He linked out for backup. Wart's Tikari arrived first with Veikko's, which stabbed the first Yak to raise a sword. Varg in kind unfurled his Tikari and let it assemble into a long blade. Veikko landed. Four Tikari and two Valkyries against eight Yakuza and target. Easy day.

VIOLET SAW the spy run up a flight of rickety stairs and into an unlabeled building. It was hard to tell where one building ended and the next began. So cramped and complex were the walls, he could have just run into a single room or a massive complex. The bundle of shacks had too many exits to trust. She had to follow him in. She kept her Tikari low to the ground and sent it crawling in, then took a low stance herself outside the door.

The Tikari sent back scans and video: it was a bathhouse, foggy and hot. Numerous *baishunfu* and customers. Even more potential escape routes. Violet glanced from customer to customer. Most were looking bewildered toward the northern door. The Tik went north. Another room, four doors, one woman looking toward the western. She went for it. A long hallway, numerous doors, and no customers. One door was broken, however, the last one. He didn't know the layout. He was just trying to lose the tails.

Weather rang in by link, "End door leads outside, saw him dash through an alley into a kitchen. Heavies threw him out of the kitchen. Headed center again from the next road."

Violet sent her Tikari out the door and up to watch while she headed back into the fold. She jumped down from the bathhouse entrance and almost landed on Vibs. They were both headed to the alley corner. Violet's Tikari caught sight of the target again but had difficulty maintaining a lock on him—he was headed through a crowded and canopied section of food court. And they weren't the only ones who saw him. Few of the following Yaks were still following, but one woman was well ahead of the pack and listening out for links so broadly all the Valkyries heard her.

Shika heard the kitchen security linking out and knew it was her man. She knew the restaurant. It was near the core of the city. He was heading inward. Likely reason to head toward the core—to get to the canopy.

"Usagi," she linked, "bring the pogo over to the top. Let it rest on the canopy. If you see a burnt man emerge, tranq him and pick him up. I'll follow."

"Roger roger!" she linked back. She linked back unsecured.

Vibs heard it and linked to their own pogo. She didn't bring it out of the water yet but powered up the systems.

Shika cursed Usagi's name. The link had come back without a security signature. It was open. Best to leave the ditz out of it and take the man while he was still in the city. He was emerging from the crowd and running up stairs to a mezzanine. She knew the place. Long stairs, elevator closer to her position. She let the two other followers run past her to chase the man up the stairs and headed for the elevator. Slow elevator, but she wasn't going to call the thing. It was in the down position. She took a running leap and clawed up on top of it, then kicked her way up to the next level with enough force to break open the door. A few noncombatants ran. She headed for the stairs.

The two other remaining Yakuza chasers tried frantically to get through the crowd. Violet and Vibeke were right over them. They'd lost one, but the remaining man would be an easy takedown. Out of sight so intervention at that point was best. Widget confirmed their man was nearing the top of the stairs. They could catch up. Both jumped and took down their respective Yaks. They hit their heads hard on the floor as a few civilians looked on. Vibeke would deal with the bodies and give them some stun juice. Violet headed for the stairs.

Just as she reached the bottom of the case, she saw the burnt man running back toward her. He was coming down the stairs, and his good eye looked scared as hell. He paused and saw her. He must have recognized her as a threat because he halted. Glanced back up, then jumped down from the middle of the flight into a chicken coop. Vibs was closer now. She finished her stuns and followed him.

Violet suddenly saw why he had jumped. Why he was coming back her way. At the top of the steps was a very mean-looking Yakuza woman. Probably the last Yak on his tail. An angry, cold-looking woman whose glare struck Violet strangely for a common combatant. She knew this one would be trouble.

Exactly what Shika was thinking. The lady at the bottom of the stairs had armor on, camo armor. Must have been working with the spy. Good prospect for fucking up badly and torturing the answers out of. Shika knew other Yakuza would find the spy, but nobody else was looking for this girl. And Shika had the high ground. She drew her swords.

Violet recalled her Tikari. She could see a microwave on the Yakuza's hip and could have drawn her own, but the swords were a clear message—they could shoot various conflicting beams at each other for half an hour with no clear result, or they could settle it now and settle it fast. As Vibeke ran past a cloud of feathers to follow the spy, Violet grabbed her knife from the air and began walking up the wooden stairs. She knew how to use the low ground to her advantage, and she knew the appearance would make her opponent overconfident. Shika brandished her swords and headed slowly down. Numerous men from a nearby *kyabakura* stood on a porch to watch and make bets.

VEIKKO AND Varg had Tikaried three Yakuza and shot two before Masamune and his personal guards squirmed out through a back window. Veikko shot the wall with a heavy repulsion beam and knocked it over. Varg gave chase, and Veikko, having been knocked off his feet by the force, stood up to face the one Yakuza who had stayed behind. Two were on Varg's tail, but Wart and Walter had their Tiks ready to take them down. The man who stood before Veikko was short. Upon realizing how short, Veikko cringed. He'd seen the man before.

Hokkaido Joe shouted happily, "Raoul? Is that you?"

Veikko groaned and rubbed his eyes.

"Holy shit, it is you! How you been—Hey, you killed my man! You the enemy, Raoul! The enemy. En. Em. E. You goin' down, Raoul! You goin—"

Veikko hit him with a microwave in the chest. This time he took no chances. He stood over the body, set his microwave to deep fat fry, and let loose a scorching bolt of energy into Hokkaido Joe's head. The brain, such as it was, was melted in seconds. Vaporized in seconds more. Veikko kept the beam on until the very atoms of brain started to lose cohesion. Not even Niide could recover the damn bastard now. He gave the crispy head a solid kick, and it fell open with a burst of ash. His top mission priority complete, Veikko ran after Varg to save the planet.

SHIKA LEAPED from six stairs up and brought her right sword down on Violet's arm. It deflected off her armor, but Shika wasted no time in striking again, alternating swords and forcing Violet back down the stairs.

Violet was surprised by the ferocity of her attack. It was as fast and skillful as something she'd expect from an elder team member. It was all she could do to block the strikes, several every second all aimed for her head or unarmored portions of her suit.

Shika grew frustrated at Violet's blocks and pushed forward faster, trying to knock Violet off her feet. She made certain Violet had no chance to counterattack, kept her completely on the defensive. It was difficult, more than anyone Shika could remember fighting. The girl was skilled, but she had no idea what Shika had in store for her.

Violet finally caught a fraction of a second gap in Shika's attack as she adjusted her grip on her left sword. She knew it might be the only mistake her opponent would make, so she took it for all she could. She dragged her Tikari blade down the sword and twisted it at the hilt.

Shika was still adjusting her palm and the sword flew from her grip. Violet was about to press the advantage and strike her neck when she saw from the corner of her eye something that terrified her.

As the sword flew from Shika's hand, panels on its hilt were opening. She heard a click like the one her Tikari made when it engaged its launch systems. While blocking Shika's right sword, Violet glanced at her ear and saw a second link. She realized just in time to fall back instead of striking—Shika's sword was flight capable and link controlled.

The sword engaged its main thruster and darted for Violet's head. She fell out of the way just in time. Shika set the sword to orbit her and spin, creating a field of sharp metal through which Violet couldn't strike. Violet set her Tikari to defend, matching the orbit and keeping the spinning sword from shredding her. That left Shika with one sword free and Violet with nothing.

Shika was amused when she saw the girl's knife start defending. They were more evenly matched than she expected. But still not evenly. Shika pressed her advantage and made several strong thrusts with her right blade.

Violet flipped back farther, away from the stairs, but unable to stay beyond the sword's tip. It grated into her armor and slipped onto the soft zones, cutting her deeply. Shika kept moving closer. The cuts grew deeper and deeper. Violet tried to find any nuance in the terrain or her gear to take the advantage but found nothing. She was going to die.

And that, she remembered was her advantage. She could die, if she did it right. She crouched down, a fatal move. Shika used it as expected and stabbed down deep into Violet's shoulder. The blade entered her torso, down through her lung and diaphragm, into her intestines. Pain shot through her like electricity, but as she expected, the sword stuck. Violet jumped back with the sword inside her, disarming Shika.

Shika didn't stop. She recalled her other blade and moved in to behead her quarry. She wasn't surprised to see Violet try to pull the sword out of her body but was shocked at what came next. In her last seconds of life, Violet readied Shika's sword, recalled her Tikari, and leaped at her with two blades.

The advantage was finally Violet's. Injury training suggested she had about thirty seconds left before she passed out from blood loss. The wound in her shoulder and back sprayed blood like a pump, numerous major arteries were open. She had to work fast.

Shika defended every blow, still amazed at the girl's resilience. She couldn't allow her to control her sword, so she set it to fly. The flaps on its hilt opened, and the thrusters turned on maximum, burning into Violet's hand.

Violet gripped tighter, the flames cutting their way into her fingers. Injury training kept her on target—the muscles in her fingers had ten seconds left before they were cut. Enough time. She began to catch on fire across her arm and chest as she continued to swing the blade, which fought her with every last ounce of thrust. But she could handle it for just one more instant. Violet attacked Shika with all she had, pushing her into the stairs, stabbing and swinging for her neck, her head, and her heart.

Shika began to flee. She'd killed the girl. All she had to do was outlast her final sprint.

Violet wouldn't let her. She set her Tikari to fly from her hand and impale Shika in the stomach. She was using her sword to defend against the stolen sword in Violet's hand. The Tikari blasted in, and Shika recoiled, grabbed for her belly, and in that instant, lost. Violet took the moment for all she could and swung Shika's sword through her temple and into the wooden post behind her, severing the top half of her head.

Violet fell back to the ground and turned on her air field, creating a vacuum that stopped the fire that had completely consumed her. Shika's swords fell motionless. Violet's Tikari bolted from Shika's stomach and flew for Violet's chest, then hid safely inside. Blood continued to spurt from her wounds for a few more seconds, and then her heart gave out. Violet's brain squeezed out one last thought—*I should have just shot the bitch*—and then she fell dead on the wooden planks. Men at the kyabakura accepted their winnings and losses.

ALOPEX TOLD V team of her death over their links. Vibeke cursed and linked to the pogo. She'd have to get Violet into its stasis field fast.

After the chicken coop, the spy was nearing the center pillar. Vibs called her Tikari in close and fell back to the side alley. The Tik saw him reach the center pillar, nearly a flat wall up close, and begin cutting into it with a razor torch. She called up architectural plans. Hollow interior, bilge pumps, and rudder controls, open air above with a one-way field on top. He could get out that way but not back in. The portal of wood fell, and he climbed inside the pillar. She didn't send the Tik in, but it saw him climb straight up. Someone was going to meet him on the canopy, but a Yakuza pogo was inbound as well. Vibs linked her pogo to leave the water.

By the time Veikko caught up, Varg had just microwaved the last of Masamune's escorts. All lay atop a restaurant's roof, which was accessible by ladder but hard to see from the street. Veikko joined him just in time to see Masamune pull out a compressed pistol. The flat card popped out of his pocket and expanded like papercraft into his hand. He leveled it at Varg. Diving out of the way, he linked to Veikko.

"Kill?"

"Knock out," he replied. Veikko's Tikari jumped at the man, but Masamune was extremely fast and managed to shoot it out of the sky. The bladed projectile hit its right wing and bent it. The Tik quickly limped away from the fight in repair mode. Varg used the instant the gun was off him to draw his microwave and fire a stunning beam. It hit Masamune full on, and he fainted, but he must have had an emergency protocol—his link broadcast his location in twenty very specific directions along with an SOS. As Veikko tended to his Tik and Varg pulled a cerebral bore out of his pocket, Walter linked in.

"Twenty Yaks around the city just started running. Seven close to you. First arrives in forty seconds. Want our pogo?"

"Please."

There wasn't enough time for a full hack, so Varg stuffed the bore back into a chest pocket and grabbed the feet while Veikko grabbed the head. Wart called the second pogo out of the water. By this time three pogos were heading illegally from the parking zone toward the city. Automated police drones were already in the air, and one unconventional spybot was taking notice. It began sending a report to Hashima Island about the mess.

"Twenty seconds, two more in thirty, get out now!" linked Walter.

Veikko and Varg exchanged a glance, moving the body was too slow. They had to risk a race against time rather than a race against Yakuza encumbered by an unconscious man. Varg raised his sword high and cut off Masamune's head. They had a few minutes to get it to the pogo stasis field and a few hours to get it back to Valhalla for a proper hack. But by the time Varg had put the first aid plugs on, the first new Yakuza were on the scene.

Veikko microwaved the first to pop up over the rim, but the second scaled a gutter and popped up behind Varg. Varg dropped the head to stab him with his Tikari, and Masamune's head rolled down the slanted roof into the crowd below.

The crowd scattered fast at the sight of a severed head. Varg jumped down immediately to recover the cranium but found himself surrounded by six men. All with swords. He had his own drawn when he landed so he engaged the first. Veikko shot the second, but as he aimed for the third, a man tackled him from behind on the roof and a struggle ensued. That was no problem for Varg of course. He had his sword. But he didn't have many choices in how to use it. All six Yaks were skilled and left him precious few opportunities. He was constantly defending their jabs. Luckily they were close, and his armor was deflecting most of the hits they got in. Before long two of them stood in proximity, and he could strike at their necks. He hit both in one swing and sent their heads to the ground. Right next to Masamune's. One Yak slipped on one of the heads, and Varg swung down quickly—on his neck. Varg dealt with the problem of the oncoming Yakuza but quickly found himself trying to sort Masamune's head from the seven rolling down the street.

Veikko microwaved his first attacker, but a second Yak quickly distracted him. Then another. He had two men on his tail, and with his Tikari awaiting repairs, his only weapon, the microwave, was occupied deflecting their shots. If they reached him they could kill him by sword. Wart's and Walter's Tikaris were in the sky, but Veikko needed a fast escape. W team's pogo was heading for Varg to preserve Masamune. He could see V team's wet pogo, not flying for Violet but toward the canopy. He could only hope it flew past him before the Yaks caught up.

As he scaled a scaffold toward the balcony, he could see it wouldn't. He quickly reached into his back armor for an explosive. He pulled out a fluff bomb, not much, but it would work on wooden scaffolds. He stuck it to a stud and set it for five seconds. He made the balcony five seconds later with the realization that the balcony was supported, at that time, solely by the scaffold. The bomb went off. Both Yakuza fell to the ground, and the balcony shifted forward rapidly, about to plummet into the street. He knew he couldn't make the next building if he jumped. The balcony slipped from its last tethers and began to fall.

It fell right onto the side of the gold pogo. Wart had remote flown it in just in the nick of time, and Veikko rolled with a few scraps of wood into its back hold. Veikko took over the controls and headed to Varg, who was accidentally kicking the closest head as he tried to chase the rest.

VIBEKE AIMED her microwave for V's pogo and tractored herself up. Taking the controls, she sent out a wide low-level interference pulse. It knocked all the police and parking drones off her tail and left her one Yakuza pogo to fight. She lifted up to canopy level and saw the situation: the spy was running across the canopy, and the Yakuza pogo was firing at him. Projectiles, likely tranqs. Still she had little choice. She opened fire on the Yakuza pogo before it saw her. The microwave beam popped and crackled along its hull, and it went down.

Usagi jumped from the pogo seconds before it hit the canopy. She rolled down the fabric. The burning pogo tugged half the panel down as it hit, and the hull flames set the edges on fire. Usagi was surrounded by flames on all sides but down. *Nothing else to do*, she thought. She jumped and fell toward a marshmallow stand filled with soft white sugary goo. The soft mass roiled and rippled, the owner of the stand carving bits from the vat to sell to tourists. Usagi's neck hit the vat's hard metal corner and snapped instantly.

Vibs spent a tenth of a second wondering what substandard flammable material the canopy was made from and went into rescue mode. She dove for the spy and braked just ahead of where he ran, opening the side door. He ran in without question, and she took off, closing the doors behind them and leaving the rest of the Valkyries behind.

"You're a chick!" he coughed.

"Wow!" She couldn't miss a beat if she was to pass as his intended rescue. "You really are a great spy. No wonder he hired you to fuck up the Ukiyo job."

"Fuck you, broad, just take me to Türkiye."

"Türkiye? I'm from a different safe house. You got the coordinates?"

"Of course I have the coordinates, doll. Now move your ass."

Vibs would have to fly toward Türkiye immediately to conserve her deception. She linked on top security to Veikko to let him know she was on her way. Abandoning Violet dead on the street left a sick feeling in her stomach. But W and the boys from V were there. Violet would be fine, she told herself as she flew out of the calm air and into the storm.

VARG JUMPED into W's pogo and tractored the batch of heads in behind him. As the pogo took off to get Violet, he sorted through the heads, kicked the wrong ones out of the open door, and stuffed Masamune's into the stasis chamber. A second later he landed at the bottom of the stairs, crushing Shika's body into the wood. He jumped out and grabbed Violet's corpse. It was pretty bad, covered in cuts and burns and severely exsanguinated. Still salvageable, though, and her head was fine. He crammed her into the same stasis chamber and took off.

As he headed for W team, Wart linked in.

"Leave us and get to the pit. We'll find another way home."

Veikko didn't ask any questions, he set the pogo to land by the med bay and let it take over. As soon as he left Ukiyo's weather, the flight got rough, painful, and sickening, but they didn't turn on the manual controls to ease the flight. They just strapped in and set the autopilot for speed, no matter how nasty the trip.

Wunjo rendezvoused in a small Thai restaurant on the opposite side of Ukiyo from the action, where dozens of fire drones extinguished the canopy.

"Terrible business, that fire," said the waiter. "They say severed heads were rolling down the streets, dozens of Yakuza killed, buildings falling down."

W team averted their eyes. The waiter continued, "Almost the worst incident this week."

"I'M NOT angry," explained Wulfgar. "I'm disappointed."

Somehow Red thought that was worse. Red Boots, he reminded himself. And the man before him was Little Boots, not Wulfgar. He wasn't supposed to know that name. In fact he was certain that if W— Little Boots knew that he'd heard it, he'd be dead, and there would be a new Red Boots.

"So you really have no idea where Yellow Boots is?"

"N-no, sir."

"The reason that troubles me, Red Boots, is that he's exactly where he's supposed to be."

"Sir?"

"Yellow Boots checked into Rüveyde Hanım exactly as he was supposed to in case he was found out."

Red had nothing to say. That meant everything was okay. Somehow, Yellow had escaped the Yakuza and made it to his check-in point. Made it there fast. Maybe all wasn't lost?

"Do you know why that troubles me?"

Red was seconds from dying, he knew it. Little Boots could surely see him sweating. He must have known, but he wasn't letting on. He suspected Red of lying, or incompetence, and he couldn't prove a thing against either. He wasn't lying, but he had been terribly incompetent, unable to find Yellow Boots in the chaos at Ukiyo. Knocked out in the fight and awake only after the action stopped.

He had nothing to say to the man's piercing gaze. Little Boots stroked his fierce metal jaw and exhaled. Disappointed.

"It troubles me because you didn't fly him there. Which means someone did, and according to Yellow Boots, it was a woman."

Red stood motionless. There were no women, not a single one in the Wolf Gang. How could one even know—

"Are you afraid of something, Red?"

He was so afraid he couldn't speak. He froze up.

"Look, Red. Martin, your name is Martin, right? I'm not going to bite your head off. I'm not even going to fire you. I just need to find out how Yellow Boots got to the safe house without you. I need to find out who now knows the location of our safe house in Türkiye.

Chapter IV: Türkiye

VIOLET WOKE up feeling euphoric and tingly. She was lying on a table, above her the sickly green med bay lights. She ran through her last memories: fighting a Yakuza woman, dying at Ukiyo, mission inconclusive when she died.

She looked over her body. Dozens of healing cuts and two robotic arms digging into her belly to fix the organs. She couldn't feel anything in the area. She was under extreme analgia fields. For the better, she recognized. She had no desire to feel her duodenum getting sealed up.

"She's up," called Varg. "Hey, Vi. I hope you don't mind, we all watched your fight with the Yak while you were out, well done!"

She couldn't speak.

"Mission?" she linked.

"Got Masamune's head right here. H is hacking it now. Vibs dropped the spy off in Türkiye, and W headed over to watch him. Marks at 88 percent. You got a 99.8 percent for your sword fight."

"Nice," linked Violet as she let her head fall back and allowed sleep to carry her away.

The next day, Masamune's intel belonged to Valhalla, and V team was reassembled to read it.

"The Yakuza are planning to bring the liquid components of the Ares Project back to Earth. They're working for Pelamus Pluturus, a pirate responsible for the destruction of the YUP. Pluturus can have only one plan in mind—to take over Valhalla and reintegrate the Ares Project in order to flood the globe."

Alf stopped speaking and sighed.

"E Team will see that the Yakuza are not able to bring the Ares home. This is obviously our top priority for the time being. Valknut, we need you to follow the spy that Vibeke delivered to Türkiye. If forces are working in opposition to the Yakuza, we need to know who they are and what they plan to do."

W team linked in from Türkiye.

"The spy seems to be named Mehmet Aga, or at least that's what he told the medic. He used a public medic near the safe house for his microwave burns. We hacked the funds he spent, and they came from a small account opened from Hashima Island, an old mine and tourist trap."

"V," said Alf, "I want you to join W team in Türkiye and follow Aga wherever he goes. If Aga leaves the planet, V will follow. W will monitor the gang's earthly assets in Istanbul. L team will check out Hashima. Any other matters?"

Nobody spoke.

"Very well. Head to the pogos, and Don't Fuck Shit Up."

V TEAM arrived at W's roost across from Aga's safe house. Wart filled them in on recent events.

"He met with a man in a black rubber business suit. The man called him 'Yellow Boots.' The man in black called himself 'Red Boots.' He seems to have been Aga's actual escape from Ukiyo before Vibs picked him up. We hacked back to Ukiyo and found he was knocked out in the first volley during the meeting. He informed Aga that Vibs was not his intended flight to Türkiye, but neither seems to know what to make of it. Red Boots informed Aga that 'Little Boots' was very upset."

"Little Boots? What's with the boots?"

"Well, that seems to be the designator for a rank in the gang. The 'Wolf' Gang."

"Wolf?" asked Violet.

"The Wolf Gang. Caught it when Red told Yellow off about trusting a female pilot when there are no women in the gang."

"What else?" Violet pressed.

Weather explained, "Nothing else. Aga sticks to the safe house, no visitors except for a hooker and pizza delivery. I checked out the prostitute, looks genuine. Walter checked the pizza out for messages or contacts and came up dry."

"More greasy than dry."

"Where did Red go?"

"Headed to Ukiyo, Widget's on him there."

Widget linked in, "He eats, he sleeps, he wanders. Harassed a shop owner about fumbling a deal but hasn't given any info on the gang."

"So what's the call, V?"

Veikko thought for a moment. He looked to Violet. Violet was agitated. The mention of a Wolf Gang had her mind racing. Likelihoods and chances. She told herself there was no chance it was Wulfgar. He'd not name a new gang anything so obvious if he were alive. All signs pointed to dead. No, it was just a gang. She shook her head as if to say she didn't consider it a possibility. But her mind still raced.

"We infiltrate," decided Veikko. "I'll pose—"

"I wouldn't," said Wart. "He and Red exchanged some serious coding when they met. Nothing we can even guess at."

"Hmm. Well, I'd like to monitor a bit closer than this, maybe bore the guy. Any ideas?"

Varg asked, "How often with the prostitutes?"

"Just one so far," said Wart, "but he put the call out on the local Craig, unsecured."

"Let's meet him there," said Veikko.

It was only two hours before Aga sent out an unprotected link to the Craig. He headed straight for the escort section and started looking over the available women. Violet, Weather, and Widget all posted their likenesses, Vibeke being recognizable. Veikko operated a covert hack into the four other available avatars and exchanged their likenesses for Larry, Moe, Curly, and Shemp to ensure he selected a Valkyrie.

After a brief study, Aga selected Violet and Weather and gave them a bathhouse address along with 750 euros each. All signed off.

"Oh my goodness, I've got nothing to wear," Weather realized. They'd have to stop by a clothing store on the way. As they selected appropriately inappropriate robes, they tended to another matter.

"We need working girl names," said Violet. "The Craig numbers won't do in person."

"What kind of names do they have?"

"I don't know, sexy names, I suppose? Like Jasmine or Jade?"

"I don't feel like a Jasmine or Jade," said Weather. "How about Violet and Heather?"

"Sounds good, I'll be Heather."

They chose a matching pair of revealing robes and left their Thaco armor with the boys. Weather concealed a cerebral bore in her new handbag and both kept their Tikaris securely chested. Microwaves were deemed too bulky and left behind.

They went to the bathhouse and met the doorman.

"We're here for Mehmet," said Violet.

"Last door on the left," he replied and let them in.

It was hot and humid even in the small foyer. A hall stretched off to the left, and they followed it to the end. The heat was even worse, as though there were a fire behind the door. Weather knocked. No response. She tried the knob, and it opened, vomiting steam out into the hall. They removed their shoes and walked in.

"Welcome, welcome, ladies," said a figure shrouded in mist.

"Hello, Mehmet," Violet tried to say in a flirtatious voice. She in fact had no idea how to sound flirtatious and sounded drunk.

"Come closer, let me see what I bought!"

They walked up to him and saw him clearly. The big potbelly wasn't the problem. He was hairy. Absurdly hairy. Nearly everyone Violet had met until that moment had been depilated and given a haircut, then taken Alopigaid and grown no more. Even Vibeke used the stuff everywhere but her scalp. Mehmet appeared to have not only a thicket of curly black hair covering every part of his body but a tuft of the stuff on his upper lip. Violet had never been so revolted. It took all her training not to gag at the sight of his furry form.

Weather seemed to take the sight better and spoke first. "So what can we do for you tonight?"

"Hmmm," he purred, "come closer, you, the blonde one." He pointed to Violet.

Swallowing her disgust, she walked up to him and knelt down centimeters from his lap. She let her robe slip halfway off her right shoulder.

"You're very pretty girl. Very pretty. Do you like pretty things?"

What kind of idiot question was that, she wondered. Concealing her ongoing repulsion to the man, she nodded slowly.

"Would you like to see something pretty?"

Oh dear God, she thought. She knew what he was talking about and knew the things were the least pretty parts humans had. She turned her cringe into a smile and nodded. He began to loosen his towel and stand up.

He fell back down to the bench with the bore on his forehead.

"Thank fucking Odin," Violet shouted. "You couldn't have done that sooner?"

"I did it as soon as he wasn't looking at me!"

"I was down there for half an hour! I almost saw his... his... willy!"

"Well, you didn't, shall we get on with the hack?"

"It would've had hair, Weather. I'd be traumatized for bloody life."

"Shush, let's get on with it."

Weather stood guard as Violet immersed herself in the bore. The first thing she saw was heavy hack armor. She linked to Alopex to solve it and move in.

His brain was dimly lit and loosely partitioned. Once inside she only had to skip over the barriers from functions to memories to active thoughts. He didn't have much in the way of active thoughts, all were related to his grotesquely hairy member and Violet kneeling before him.

Preconscious zones had more to them. Violet deleted the sexual aspirations and sent the rest as a brain dump back to Valhalla for analysis, then started looking around herself, monitoring the info stream and origin pool. She saw the faces of the other Boots men, some absurdly buffed out henchmen in armor. Black armor, familiar black armor. She'd seen it before.

A second later she'd have recognized them from Wulfgar's rescue. The men with the high powered wraparound microwaves who took his body after it was crushed. But before that, she saw his face. Or at least half of it. Wulfgar Kray with a metal jaw. And a deranged look in his eyes.

Death had changed him. He was still composed, but the insanity that took over when he bit off her hand was closer to the surface. Present right behind his eyes, seeping out. She thought briefly that she'd killed the man and left the monster. It was frightening, genuinely scary in a way she had to actively think to control. She was face-to-face with Little Boots. His image flickered out of the origin pool and on to Valhalla.

They would know. She'd found Wulfgar again. She was suddenly delighted. She'd found him, and she was on the team actively working his new gang. She would get to take him down.

Violet heard a scream. She unlinked herself immediately and turned to see Weather clutching her face. She saw blood coming from under her hands.

Violet ejected her Tikari and told it to kill. She didn't know who was in the room yet, but she sensed their shadows in the mist. She trusted it to avoid Weather and herself and find whatever target had attacked. She grabbed Weather and pulled her down to the floor, then entered her Tikari.

She came to its eyes just as it sliced through a man's neck. It targeted the next man, and she saw his microwave pointing at her—at her Tikari. She flew down toward his stomach and ran him through.

Violet returned to her own eyes and scanned the room for more men. She saw none. She kept her Tikari alert and looked to Weather.

Her eyes were fried out. The door opened again. Violet readied her Tikari in the air. She elected not to kill the next man to enter. She'd fight him and learn who he was first. Her Tikari would kill anyone else coming in.

Violet leaped up and kicked toward the newcomer's head. The robe she was wearing caught her leg and wouldn't let it swing that high. She lost balance and fell back onto her left hip. Suddenly the man had a microwave on her. She called in her Tikari to cut off his hand. It did in an instant. She grabbed his hand off the floor and pried his microwave from it. He didn't make a sound.

Violet scrambled up as best she could in the absurd robe and leveled the microwave at the man's head.

He was dressed in black with a black hat. He stared at her with what looked almost like a grin.

"Who are you?" she demanded.

He smiled. "I've already linked out. They know you hacked Yellow Boots. They know you're here. They will kill you both."

Suddenly Violet heard a secure link from across the street to her and Weather. It was Veikko. "Jammed him, didn't get out."

"Who are you?" she asked again.

"Fahrenheit. You killed The Elbow and Jimmy Pig Lips."

Violet winced at the strange names.

"We'll bore him later, just kill the fucker!" shouted Weather.

Violet assessed their priorities and agreed. She shot him in the heart with a full beam, and he flopped over onto his side.

"We've gotta get you home," she told Weather.

"No, clean up first. We can't let them know we hacked him."

Weather ejected her Tikari and started to look through its eyes. She linked to Veikko, "We need Valkyrie microwaves in here now!"

Violet checked the bore on Mehmet's head. It was complete. She removed it and put it on Fahrenheit's head. Weather, adeptly using her Tikari's eyes, began moving the dead men into a pile in the corner. She nodded to Violet.

Violet recalled her Tikari to her hand and held it as a knife. She pulled up her robe and headed to the door. With no suit and no microwave, she went slow, scoping out the corners and clearing the hall methodically. No more hostiles were coming.

Varg arrived soon with their suits and microwaves. Violet changed fast as Varg used her microwave to disintegrate the first two bodies, then once the bore was complete, turned the last man to ash. The room was thick with the smell of fine cooking. He tractored the ashes into a small mass and dropped it into a dispersion toilet.

Violet set the bore back on Mehmet and linked in. She posted a simple hypnotic that he got laid and fell asleep. It wouldn't hold up to scrutiny, but unless he got hacked by Wulfgar, and he went straight for that memory—Wulfgar.

Violet couldn't believe it. As they ran from the building and returned to the pogo, she kept replaying his face, his mutilated metal face, in her mind. She'd found him: the man who hunted her, who had eaten the flesh from her wrist, whom she had killed. She said it over and over to herself. Her hunt was suddenly active. Weather took to the pogo, and it launched to take her to Dr. Niide at top speed. Varg and Violet returned to their room with the rest of W team.

HOURS LATER they had watched Aga return to his safe house and monitored him for any signs of awareness. He showed none concerning his hacking. They got a link from Valhalla as soon as Weather arrived.

"She has new cosmetic implants but seems to prefer looking through her Tikari. Eccentric, but that's nothing new here. If that's what Weather wants, that's how she'll see."

Weather would be fine. Violet asked Balder about something even more pressing. "And the intel?"

"Well, you found Wulfgar. Congratulations on that, Vi."

"Permission to take him down?"

"L team is on it, already at Hashima and ready to infiltrate. Aga has a ticket to Mars on the third—"

Violet considered L team, not without a bit of envy. Would she return from Mars to find that Wulfgar was dead? She calmed her mind, assuring herself it would be okay if he was. But she felt distant from it. She was at least present at his last death. This time she would be in a transfer orbit when they went in, out of range of Aloe or even the common Earth net.

But such was saving the world. She exhaled. Vibeke suddenly elbowed her in the side. She didn't know what to make of it. Then Varg spoke up.

"Request V team exchange with L."

"Request denied, you have experience with Aga, you should be on Mars."

"Respectfully," said Veikko for the first time in his life, "we have more experience with Wulfgar Kray than L team, and a senior team should head to Mars for the more important project."

Alf sounded amused. "You raise a good point, V, but—"

"Fuck buts," said Vibeke. "You're not sending Laguz to end our arch nemesis while we're in cryo."

Our arch nemesis, she said. Vibeke had never called Wulfgar her own. Violet felt a sudden throb of gratitude and camaraderie. When she had simply given up, her team fought for her, and Vibeke had taken her nemesis on as her own. Violet wanted to speak but found herself choked up.

"Have L monitor," said Veikko. "We'll kill Wulfgar when we get back."

"Inefficient, V," said Balder.

Varg retorted, "Aren't you the one who held up Ehwaz for a year and a half because of an incident involving your—"

"Okay, okay," interrupted Balder quickly. "Granted, but seeing his gang doesn't bring back the Ares is your top priority. I'll have L team monitor Hashima passively."

"Good," said Veikko.

"So how about Mars?" asked Vibeke.

"Well," explained Balder, "Yellow Boots is definitely part of a Wolf mission to Mars, but he seems to know nothing of its specifics. Not locked in a hidden partition, not disguised or camouflaged. Very strange. But the bore says he does have a ticket to Mars for the third."

"I suggest we take the flight on the first. W can monitor him here while we're gone. But we'll arrive before him, and he won't get the chance to recognize Violet or Vibs."

"Excellent. I'll speak to our allies there and inform them of your arrival. E team may join you soon. Their intel suggests a heavy Yakuza presence heading to Mars in two weeks. It looks like the Wolves are ahead of the Yaks in a competition to ship and sell the Ares water to the Fish. A lot of animals on this project. Speaking of which, have you named this one, for the records?"

"Daunting."

"Appropriate, V. All sounds good. Get your asses to Mars. Oh, and V team—"

Veikko replied, "Don't Fuck Shit Up?"

"It's under the redwood."

Balder closed the link. Nobody on V team knew what he meant. All looked to Varg, but he just shrugged. There was no time to delay; the flight to Mars left in two hours. Wart flew the pogo to take V to the spaceport. Veikko handled the ticket hacks as they flew. The Marsden family would find themselves rebooked for the next flight, and Valknut team would go in their place. Walter and Widget took off to monitor Aga and see that he made his own flight. If he changed his plans, V team would be headed for Mars with no hint of where to begin.

MOST OF the Nikkei Underground was back to its horrible normal state. Only the space where the Black Crag once stood was different—there were now 450 Black Crags. Once the secret of the original was out, imitators took over the space and offered an expansive variety of barrier-free sites.

Mishka chose the second tallest in the hopes it would lack the overgrown popularity of the tallest but still offer plenty of work. She was quite right. It held less than 15 percent of the avatars but almost as many job offers. Assassinations, illicit deals, information trafficking. She checked the local regions first, from UNEGA Bhaarat to Persia, but there was little paying well and not obviously a trap.

She stuck to the Crag and opened her own listing, the same as she had on the original Black Crag: Single Assassin, dual cutter rifles, one tank, top skills, and ready to prove them. She kept it open to anyone on the continent, off continent for a fee. And she waited.

She wandered the Crag with protective whiskers out, a popular measure now that people knew why the contact barriers were down. She recognized several alcoves from the original Crag, or at least new alcoves mimicking them. There was a Thuggee alcove, several Muslim alcoves free from the police that monitored them on the Nikkei underground, and one new alcove she'd never seen before but recognized instantly. It bore the same cross she'd once worn on her Tikari. A Russian cross.

She entered the alcove and saw the decor. Icons of ikons, saints. Copies of prayers long forgotten, written in Cyrillic. A blank avatar in priestly garb approached her. The whiskers highlighted him, and her defenses went active, ready to kill him.

"I mean no harm," he said.

"I know," she replied and lowered the defenses. "This place...."

"You're Mishka, aren't you?"

She was stunned.

"I'm Nikita, Sasha's boatswain mate, from Carrier Dva. I recognize your avatar."

"You survived!"

"Barely. My body is crushed and in stasis. So there's not much to lose. I thought I could continue Sasha's mission online, the only place I can still move. I tried on the Undernet, but it was too risky. But now that we have so many crags...."

Mishka used the lack of contact barriers to hug him and kiss his cheeks three times. It turned out he had a modest following already. He told her about the remains of Sasha's crew, how most had dispersed and taken work as it came. But he and a few other faithful held out hope of seeing her again and began their ministry partly in hopes of finding her.

They spoke for hours about matters of faith and felony. She promised to visit his body in Krym when she had the chance. He promised nothing less than the resurrection of Sasha's regime. Mishka was hesitant to accept it. Her belief was undiminished, but her enthusiasm was. She admitted she had little taste left for Africa.

"Nor do I," said Nikita. "But I've always liked the north. Much cooler."

"I liked the north too, once upon a time."

"Ah, there's more to the north than your old friends and nice weather. There are people with open minds. People who listen when you speak."

"You think there are converts?"

"Well, no. Not short of the seventh seal breaking open before their eyes. But we believe the seals will open, do we not? The Christos may return in our lifetime, or may not. But if he does, that's where I'll be. I have nothing to do now but wait, and welcome those who will wait with me. What of you?"

"I have a few things to do while I wait."

"People to kill?"

"Vibeke isn't a person."

"And revenge is hardly Christian."

"Iisus has to forgive me for something."

"Then I ask only one thing. Pray. Open your heart and ask for a sign, a real sign. If revenge is in God's will for you, he will deliver it. But if it is not, when you pray and you feel deep within that this is not God's plan, you must give her up. Abandon your plans for vengeance. Can you do this?"

"I think I have to, don't I?"

"Certainly not. We all have free will. The entire point of free will is that we can choose to follow God's path or choose to stray. Only with the freedom to sin, can we truly choose to be good."

"You have Sasha's way with words."

"And you have his blood. Don't spill it without reason."

They parted, and Mishka headed back to her advert. It had a single reply. She moved to touch it, but first she gave a moment to superstition and thought to herself. *Whatever this response tells me, this is the path I'll take. If it tells me to quit and be a nun, I'll walk back to Nikita's alcove and stay there forever. If it tells me to run from this assassin's life, I will. But please, God, please let your will give me the one thing I want most. Give me Vibeke.*

She touched the response, and it loaded Vibeke's face.

The job came from Türkiye. An assassination with a torture and fact-finding bonus. One female, about twenty, organization unknown. Vibeke. Posted by an agent named Red Boots linking out of Hashima Island. Mishka accepted the project before asking a single question. She was in shock. Never had any prayer been answered so resolutely or fortuitously. Never. She was face-to-face with proof of God. And God's will was her own.

Red Boots gave her all the info she needed, and more. Mishka knew where Vibeke was based better than Red, though she could hardly march into Valhalla to kill her. Of more interest was the Wolf Gang itself. Though Mishka couldn't surmise that the Ares Project was at stake, she assumed that V team was working on taking the gang down. A covert hack into her employer's visual cortex revealed their motive—Wulfgar Kray was behind them.

Vibeke would be on the hunt behind Violet as she tore into her nemesis's new gang, and Mishka could work with that. First she bought some pond surveillance drones and stationed them around Hashima, uploading her own mind's images of each V team member along with specs for Valhalla pogos, the P0S, and various covert vessels they might use.

Next she headed to Türkiye and monitored the safe house personally. She arrived the day after a fight in a nearby bathhouse. She interviewed Yellow Boots, Mehmet Aga. She recognized the tiny skin spots of a cerebral bore and the sound of a Valkyrie hypnotic suggestion. She asked to look into his brain, and after getting permission from Hashima, he let her proceed.

She unlocked the fight without a problem and saw Violet and Weather do their work. Vibeke wasn't among them, but she wouldn't be far away. She only had to find where V team was heading next. Nothing useful was said in Aga's memory, but it was clear they were on his trail. Odd that V team should be following him when they must have known the gang was in Hashima, knowing all Aga knew. What would send Violet after a lowling when Wulfgar was so close?

Aga explained he was heading to Mars. He didn't know why. He'd receive instructions there. V team had two courses: they'd head for Mars, likely before Aga left; or they'd head for Hashima, which quite impossibly, they hadn't already done. *There must be something damn important on Mars*, she thought. Mishka hacked into the local spaceports and looked for sudden changes in passenger lists. Two cancellations, one priority bump. She examined the bump. Four individuals bumped for four different individuals. The clear sign of a team. A sloppy team that should have bumped some random passengers as well.

Her course of action was clear. She knew where they were heading, but the security around the spaceport was prohibitive. Security on Mars, however, was nonexistent. It was a wild frontier. An ideal setting for an assassination or four. She hacked into UNEGA's security grid and gave Sanchita Patel a promotion in lieu of her "Missing" notice, then used Sanchita's new status to book herself an emergency ticket for the fifth, as the team would surely be monitoring Aga's flight on the third.

As she waited, Mishka visited the minicrag and shut down her advert. Then she headed for Nikita's.

"This is a gift," he said. "Seldom are God's plans so clearly revealed."

"And seldom are they so kind."

"If they're kind indeed. Surely God is leading you to Mars, but…. 'When God hath ordained a creature to die in a particular place, he causeth that creature's wants to direct him to that place.'"

"Ephesians?"

"Frank Herbert's *Dune*, actually. Let us pray."

VALKNUT LANDED safely in the white zone, and Wart dropped them off.

At security, they Tikaried their weapons and sent them to the hull of the next shuttle, where they welded themselves on. V team would have no weapons nor Tikari on the flight, but also no expectation of a need for them. A space flight was the most secure, safest way to travel in existence. Not a single incident of any kind had ever been reported on a public Mars flight, so they were content to keep their weaponry in the only place it could make the flight unseen—welded to the sub-aileron plating.

On their way in, they spotted a few of the other passengers. Three were dressed in black, the same black rubber business suits as the Wolf Gang. V team noted them and watched them carefully. They were easy to spot as all three had big potbellies, exactly like Aga's.

The shuttle taxied out and lifted off, taking them up to the Lasswitz, their transfer orbit liner. As the shuttle docked, the Tikaris broke off and affixed themselves to an inconspicuous beam behind the Lasswitz cockpit assembly. V team meanwhile followed the bulbous men to the cryo-bay, where they were uneventfully sealed in. The cryo-locks couldn't open before the Martian shuttle docked. They would pose no threat.

Varg also remained in the cryo-bay. He had no interest in spending an entire month on the cruiser awake. Veikko and the ladies elected to try it, get to know the people on board, play games, and see the stars. Varg snapped instantly into the cruiser dreamscape and headed for the orgiumorium.

The liner taxied into high Earth orbit and prepared for its primary burn. The Valkyries had all experienced the feel of 20 g's in pain training, so the 3-g acceleration of the burn was nothing to them. Others were less experienced and required nausea preventatives. Several begged to go into cryo but had to remain seated for the duration of the burn. As soon as the burn was finished and the Hohmann transfer had begun, fourteen more passengers headed for the tubes.

Violet and Vibeke undid their belts and floated free, their first time in null gravity since Project Monolith. Veikko remained seated. They looked to him to see why he remained.

"I'm gonna level with you two. I had a barf bag filled up with the perfect blend of ramen, cheese, and lemon juice to 'spill' on you, but I left it on the shuttle by mistake. That's really the only reason I stayed up, so I'm gonna tuck my tail and go to bed now."

He undid his belt and floated away. Violet was happy to see him go. It was nothing against him in the least, but suddenly she was alone for a month with Vibeke. She felt a flutter in her chest at the thought of it.

Of the other four who remained awake, two were a couple that stuck to their room, one was an old man who had brought physical books to read, and one was a social engineer who seemed eager to meet the girls but too timid to say hello.

Violet and Vibeke checked out their berth. The wall was drastically curved, the waking module being much smaller in diameter than the three cryo-modules. With 148 asleep and six awake, there were still quite a few empty berths. The room was small but not too much smaller than the one back home in the barracks. It also had four bunks like home, but here each was covered in a net. The bathroom on the side was also far more complex, coming with ten paragraphs of instructions for the zero-g toilet.

The link faded out as they left Earth's orbit. Those who stayed awake were still able to immerse themselves in the ship's dreamscape, but full immersion in Earth's net was impossible at the quickly growing range. Vibeke thought ahead and stuffed forty books into her memory partition, including Burton's complete *1001 Nights*, which would more than cover the month long trip. Violet had packed a few literature files as well but not nearly enough. She'd have to link into Vibeke to borrow a few more to pass the time, if reading were her chosen activity. But it was not, and nor was it for Vibs.

The two simply talked, for hours on end. About old missions and life before Valhalla, both were surprised at how much had been left blank over the last year, how much had gone unsaid. They talked until their voices went hoarse, and then they talked by link. Violet wasn't used to talking by link with someone right in front of her but got used to it fast, able to eat and talk at the same time. They could even chat while exercising, leaving their breath unaffected.

They spent a great deal of time exercising together in the gamesphere. Half arcade, half gymnasium. The gymnasium side was required. Cryo prevented atrophy but a month without gravity would wither the muscles of anyone left awake. The rules for waking travel required two hours per day, but even on the first twenty-four-hour stretch of dimming and brightening hall lights, the two logged ten hours each in the gym. Zero-g exercise was absurdly fun. The weight simulators took a dozen forms and allowed pinpointing of each muscle. The outlined routine was fairly dull, simply designed to work out each muscle group few by few, but freestyle workouts could fill ten hours easily without repeating an activity.

And they could fill that ten hours a day with more than idle chat. They linked back and forth without repeating a story. Violet was especially happy to hear Vibs talk without the net backing her up. She was less intimidating a wit. Still incredibly smart but when she heard Vibs admit she had no idea about the names of the first Mars colonies, Violet nearly spit out her freeze dried ice cream. She seemed all the more approachable, not that she hadn't been before, but without her cloak of knowledge, she was finally just human. *And all the more beautiful*, Violet thought. As they spoke, Violet often found herself transfixed on Vibeke's link, its end blinking as she thought to Violet. Violet had never considered how oddly intimate it was to have someone else think straight into your mind. It wasn't intimate, she reminded herself. Everyone spoke by link. But with Vibeke, having her thoughts flow in while she strained on the resistance bars or crunch pad.... Violet was in heaven.

As was Nate the social engineer. Watching the two work out in nothing but sports bras and shorts. Nate was very happy with his decision to stay awake. It was already well worth the nausea of launch and the gravity of the burn. Nate was now alone with two beautiful women, whom he had no idea were romantically incompatible. With him.

After a few days, he finally worked up the guts to approach them as they left the showers.

"So I hear Mars is incredibly vibrant!" he shouted. The two stopped and floated before him. "Red I mean, I hear the shade of red is like nothing on Earth. I mean—it's not on Earth but—I have to go."

It took him another day to try speaking to them again, though he still had little success on his own. Vibeke broke the ice out of pity.

"So what brings you to Mars?"

Violet was oddly offended to hear her talk to someone else. She told herself it couldn't be jealousy. Vibs could talk to anyone she pleased, but after days of nothing else, the new conversationalist was terribly unwelcome to Violet.

"I'm a peace envoy. For the PRA."

"I thought they were at peace," said Violet curtly.

"Well, they are now. It's my job, my duty to see it stays that way." Pride oozed from his pores. Violet nodded in repulsed amusement. He clearly took it to mean she was impressed. "I'm actually one of the most skilled negotiators around! Have you ever heard of the Evergreen Ecoterrorists?"

He knew he had them hooked. A threesome was all but inevitable once he told them how he had peacefully resolved the dispute between the E.E. and Asda. Nate had single-handedly ceased the bloodshed from corporate police, who slaughtered any E.E. members they could find. He had, without assistance, negotiated the truce between the furious E.E. and its arch nemesis, the number one polluter on the continent. Yes, that treaty was all Nate.

Violet and Vibeke by contrast had only met the E.E. once, a few months before Nate, having killed eighteen of them when they threatened to bomb a meat-growing lab.

"Oh, I must have shot like ten of the fuckers," bragged Violet.

"I got at least five," added Vibeke to the man's horror. Violet was thrilled that Vibs was still on her side.

She turned to Nate as if telling an anecdote about sports. "The trick to busting up an E.E. cell is to throw a match into their explosives and watch 'em flee one by one. They just keep coming out the door like bang bang bang." She mimicked shooting each one as they came out.

Vibeke was back in warrior mode. Violet was relieved to think they were the insiders and Nate was…. Just Nate.

"You should have seen her," she told the disgusted passenger. "Shredding 'em with a big fat JVX D1."

"No, a JVB. I don't like the D1."

She had Vibs talking guns. She'd never return to Nate's "peace" bullshit.

"You don't? What about the hair trigger? Just the slightest caress of your finger and bam."

"Exactly, the JVB doesn't just go off on the first tap, you need at least two fingers to make it blow."

Nate frowned as deeply as he could, but the ladies didn't even notice.

"It takes two fingers because it's a loose trigger," said Vibeke.

"It has generous allowances," defended Violet. "The D1 will go off before you can get your fingers in the trigger guard. It misfires if you pump a cartridge into it too rough."

"It can handle a hard pump if you keep it well lubricated."

"Well, I prefer the solid ka-junk of the JVB."

Nate pushed off and floated toward the kitchen. Violet looked perplexed.

"What was his problem?"

"Guess he didn't like guns," answered Vibeke.

"We were talking about guns?"

Vibeke kicked Violet's shin, sending them both into a gentle spin. Violet lightly slapped her, and the two enjoyed a lighthearted shoving match through the gangways back to their room. Violet loved any such moment of physical contact she could steal from Vibeke. For the last year, she'd satisfied herself with pokes and bumps and innuendo. But it seemed different in space, and not because of the gravity.

There was some hope that with one month awake and aware together that something more might happen. But it wasn't to happen that day. Vibeke asked if Violet would be bothered if she took some time to read.

"Not at all," said Violet. "I've got Cloutier's *Maze* series myself."

Vibeke was surprised that Violet had brought any partitioned books at all, but had to set her straight about the series. "No, don't start on those. You have to read *Antechamber* first."

"I read it."

"You read it?"

"Not on text obviously, but yeah, I finished it online."

"You read a Cloutier book? Doesn't seem your kind of thing."

"No, but you said you liked it, so I gave it a shot."

"A 780-page shot?"

"Well, it's mostly because of Mishka."

Vibeke almost jumped at the name. "What?"

"You said you couldn't stand to read it again because it was one of her favorite books, that you used to talk about it with her. So I figured I'd read it so you could talk about it with me and then Mishka wouldn't own a good book in your brain."

Vibeke paused. "That's actually really sweet, Vi."

Violet blushed. Vibeke's warm response was worth the 780 pages of pretentious nonsensical bullshit. So they read together when not asleep or in the gym. They didn't see Nate in the gym anymore, suspecting he actually monitored to make sure he only attended when they were out.

On day nine however, he approached them brazenly.

"Sorry about a couple days ago, ladies, I just… have some strong feelings about violence, as a social engineer and peacekeeper."

Violet was disgusted and said nothing. Vibeke was more kind and tried to put the man at ease. "We were just kidding, you know. We're not murderers!"

Nate breathed a quick sigh of relief. Violet rolled her eyes. This again.

"We're not even into guns really."

Violet didn't know why she was being so social.

"Oh that's great!" laughed Nate, his hopes regrowing. "So where were we before that?"

"The red planet, I think."

"Oh yeah! I hear it's bright candy apple red all over."

He was cutting into their time together again. Violet elected to end the conversation for good. "I've heard it's actually more of a pink color. Hey, Vibs, do you remember that hot pink Uzi that Katyusha had? With the modified clip?"

Vibeke didn't but wanted to see where Violet was going. "Yeah?"

Violet turned to Nate. "It was real easy to change ammo, see, the front lip on the ammo clip was bent inward so it fit real close, same with the back."

"Oh," said the oblivious peacekeeper, nodding.

"Yeah," Violet continued. "There's nothing like a tight pair of lips around a hot pink clip."

Nate turned bright pink himself. He departed, and they didn't see him again for the rest of the trip.

"That was in poor taste, Vi."

"Actually I hear they taste really—"

"Odin's balls, Violet! He's gone, you don't need to keep it up."

They floated toward one of the sun domes.

"Sorry," Violet said.

"You don't need to apologize for joking," Vibeke sighed.

"I mean for scaring off the third wheel. Just wanted you to myself."

"Aww."

Violet pushed against the window strut and turned herself toward Vibeke. She could have told her that she wanted her to herself again, with more meaning. Vibs would get it. If she didn't know already. Violet had hid her infatuation for a year, and she doubted she'd done it very well. Part of her said Vibeke knew everything. She was that smart. She couldn't possibly have missed it. But another part of her said Vibeke was just like her, socially inept when it came to such things. She might not. But if anything were to happen on the trip, it would need to be out in the open. Violet tried to approach the subject cautiously.

"You know in two years I never asked about your first time."

"First time in space?"

"Yeah, if 'Space' is a girl's name."

It was one subject they'd avoided in all their conversations. Vibeke knew exactly how many kilograms Violet could lift with a broken arm, and Violet knew exactly where on Vibeke's body she could safely fire a restrained microwave beam to kill someone standing behind her, but neither had ever asked about a past girlfriend, let alone each other's sexual histories. For a year they'd avoided it like stepping between snails.

Vibeke asked, "Counting Mishka?"

"Egads, no!"

"Then never. You?"

"Counting Gabrielle?"

"Hell no."

"Then me neither. We never actually did...."

They floated silently for a moment.

"Guess we're fighters, not lovers," said Violet.

"I don't think so. Veikko and Skadi seem happy enough. There's plenty going on in the ravine."

Violet was hopeful. "So you would, if you met someone?"

"Would have to be a hell of a girl."

"So nobody you know now?"

Vibeke knew how Violet felt and knew the question for what it was. She didn't know why she'd never told Violet she had moments when she felt the same way about her. Now was certainly the time, but nothing so clear traveled her nerves.

"There's one girl, but nothing could ever happen."

Violet simultaneously hoped it was her and hoped it wasn't.

"Why couldn't anything happen?"

Vibeke was tempted to lie and say it was "in-team romance" but that would reveal everything. She could more easily tell Violet the truth, if not the fact the truth was about her.

"She reminds me of Mishka."

Violet very much hoped it wasn't her.

Vibeke thought for a moment, then continued. "It doesn't leave this dome, but honestly, I think I'm broken. Useless for anything romantic now. Because the things I fall for are the things I fell for in her. So anyone I love, I'll be terrified of. Afraid they'll betray me. Afraid I'll have another girl to hate. And this girl, the one I like... I can't afford to lose her like that. I need her. Even if it's just as a friend."

Violet was deathly scared that she was talking about her. And even more afraid she was talking about someone else. She didn't want Vibeke to have a closer friend. But she didn't want Vibeke to fear her. She didn't want to remind her of Mishka, not in any way. There was no good solution. Not for Vibeke at least. For Violet things seemed simpler.

"It's obvious what you should do, then."

Vibeke was very surprised. "What's that?"

"Try her out, and if you lose her, you lose her as a friend. Won't matter. You'll still have me as a friend."

Vibeke didn't know if she said it because she knew or because she didn't. She tried to think of a response that wouldn't openly declare her love as if from a balcony.

"I really couldn't stand to lose her."

Violet needed to know, desperately. She stared at Vibs until she looked back.

"I can't speak for your crush, but for what it's worth, you'll never, ever lose me."

Vibeke might have shed a tear if gravity held its sway. "Thanks, Vi."

They floated and took in the sun, warm behind the protective layers and warm inside despite themselves. Violet wanted Vibeke more than ever.

Vibeke, however confused, knew she was in love, and for a moment, she forgot the implications and let a slow shiver fill her body, arms and legs and chest. She was so overcome that if Violet had reached over and touched her just then, they'd have tangled up and not let go until Mars.

But Violet was still uncertain. Hopeful but daunted by what Vibeke had said. More daunted than any mission had ever kept her. She had to know if it was her. She said it as clearly as she could stand.

"It's too bad we don't want each other like that," she ventured.

"Yeah," said Vibs. "We would've had another activity to pass the time."

Her words turned Violet on like she'd never felt before. It was no answer, but Vibeke saying it felt like an electrical shock and its tingling aftermath. She couldn't respond, not for real.

"You mean loading each other's Uzis?"

Vibeke laughed, "You're such a lech!"

"What? We're talking about guns."

BALDER UNLOADED another clip at the Martian terrorists. It didn't feel the same as firing on Earth. Not because of the weight or oxygen-deprived atmosphere. It felt different because he had too much sympathy for the terrorists. If they were terrorists at all. Their targets were always military or police. Their cause was just, in Balder's opinion.

The PRA demanded only one thing—that Phobos be allowed to govern itself free of direct company interests. They'd still pay taxes, and they'd still obey UNEGA directives, but they could do so in their own way without Zaibatsu enforcing it with decimation. One tenth of Phobos was sold into slavery on Mars. Who wouldn't have expected those slaves to rebel and start bombing their owners?

Balder had enough of it. He wasted the clip into the newly thickened sky. Once it was spent, he set down his rifle. And that night, he spoke to his team.

"We're fighting on the wrong side of this war. If anyone disagrees, they can leave." Nobody left. "Then we're all on the same page. You three will stay here and sabotage the Martian forces. I'll see if I can meet with the PRA. I'll head out on my skiff at the end of the extra forty. Any objections?" Silence.

Balder skiffed out at the start of the new day, after the forty-minute hour that constituted a Martian midnight. He headed for the Ocampo crater where the satellite tracked the last band. He was unarmed except for his Tikari, and when they came, they surrounded him with a force larger than anything intelligence suggested they had. If they tipped that bit of intel, it meant they didn't expect to let him leave. Or live.

He was sealed into a plastic pouch and thrown unceremoniously into an armored landskiff.

When he arrived at the tunnels, he was cuffed and dragged to their prison. It was empty. The PRA didn't generally take prisoners. But they knew he was from an independent body, not from UNEGA or GAUNE. And they knew he came unarmed to meet them. They had to find out why.

"Why?" asked the woman. She was a beast in stature, six foot six and muscular enough to match Balder. She had short black hair and a sleek face. She wore the torn remains of a Zaibatsu space suit around her actual suit.

"My team got involved on Zaibatsu's side because we had to protect our lone interest on Mars, a water tank near the North Pole. You were raiding silos in the region, and we couldn't have you raiding ours."

"What's in it?"

"Water. Fusion sensitive and infective of other water sources."

"How forthcoming. What's your name?"

"Balder."

"Niana. General."

"Pleased to meet you."

"What do you offer?"

"Leave our water tanks alone, and we'll leave."

"And if we prefer you fight for us? We've seen your organics. We could use those, I'm sure you guessed."

"We can't stay here forever. It's not our war. And we can't leave you our organics."

"Sure you can. I don't expect you to stay forever, of course. But you have no need for organics back on Earth, if that's where you hail from."

"It is, but my people don't just trade arms."

"You came here to trade. You didn't come here to sit in prison and chat."

"I offered to leave. You can't have our organics."

"What if I had something to offer you?"

"I'm listening."

"We know about the Ares Project, and we know what's in your water tanks and exactly where they are. We know that if you're the interested organization you must own the rest of the Ares. Am I right?"

"Yes."

"So the last thing you want is for those tanks to head home, yes?"

"Yes."

"We have a fission bomb."

"You? You have a fission bomb?"

"Mmhmm. We can annihilate the fat water for you. Of course we'd need your organics to do it."

"Ah. You want us to hand over our organics because you have an atom bomb, let me guess.... From the Høtherus incident. You have a nuclear weapon you can't use without its living components, and you want me to hand over that capability. Make you a nuclear force. Do you really think I'd agree to that?"

"You will."

"I most certainly will not. We're not in the habit of giving nuclear bombs to terrorists."

"One nuclear device, and we'll spend it on you. Here's the deal— you give us the organics to arm it, and we coil them around your water supply. We set it off, solving your problem and making ourselves known as a nuclear force. No one need know we have no more nukes. You are, essentially, disarming us."

"How can we trust you not to nuke one of your own targets?"

"Easy, we'll give you the trigger."

Negotiations continued. Balder and his team would spend another two months on Mars. They set one of their eggs to grow the arming device for the PRA's bomb and kept the wormy appendage that triggered it. Balder was expected to take it home, but in his time with the PRA, he came to understand exactly how they worked. They would never use the bomb on a civilian target. That much was certain.

He got to know Niana better than he knew the PRA division she commanded. He got to know her better than her first husband did before he was killed by Zaibatsu's assassins. Valhalla thus gained a link to the PRA something like a medieval wedding, a political wedding or its opposite, a romantic treaty.

In the end, Balder hid the trigger in one of the Barsoom colony's air gardens. There it would live as a giant earthworm among the other organics, unrecognized in plain sight. If the PRA should need their bomb, Balder would tell them where to find its trigger. And if Valhalla ever needed to destroy their unusual water supply, they'd need only find the trigger and use it, as the PRA left the bomb attached to the center tank, its organic components freezing in the Martian arctic until awakened.

Balder and Niana ended their affair as he left for Earth. He heard her speak when she came topside to list demands or announce new campaigns, and he sabotaged a few Zaibatsu shipments to Mars as a sign of affection. Within a year, Phobos was independent of Zaibatsu and the PRA went to sleep.

Then eight years later, Niana received a transmission from Balder. It said nothing of the bomb or the battles or their brief romance, it read only "Take care of my kids."

"I STILL have nightmares about that thing from Project Kolossus," admitted Vibeke.

"I never got nightmares, but I can imagine."

Two weeks of nothingness had passed. Violet and Vibeke hadn't read a word of their books. Violet hadn't steered the conversation back toward love or sex, nor had Vibeke.

They talked over their hours in the gym, and then in the showers, in the sunrooms and in their berth but never went back to that moment, though Violet thought of it constantly. She hunted for ways to return but what came was too obvious. There was no segue, no excuse. She'd have to say it outright, and that tempted her from time to time. But her friendship with Vibeke was so strong and so important to her that she didn't want to ruin it either.

The risk was too great, and the reward too unlikely. She couldn't just ask if Vibeke had been talking about her. Not even counting the risk she'd answer it was someone else.

"It's Tasha, you know," said Vibeke.

Violet's heart nearly stopped.

"Tasha?"

"That anonymous paragraph in *Hávamál* last month. It's Tasha. She gave it away when she referenced Las Vegas. T team had just been there the same day."

"Oh." Violet breathed again.

It was all small talk. The prolonged avoidance of the subject both wanted to settle.

"Mars is supposed to be really hot. Indoors, I mean. You see nothing but red out the window and you feel nothing but heating systems behind it. The surface temperature is freezing, but you feel hot all the time. Even out in excursion suits."

"I won't object to that," said Violet.

"They have a plug-in simulator in the arcade."

"Nah, feels too much like practicing for the mission. We'll be there soon enough."

"Two and a half more weeks. Our voices will run out again if we don't do something other than talk."

Violet was sick of small talk. "I'd like to do something other than talk...."

"I think the arcade has a movie database."

That wasn't what Violet meant. "Yeah, that sounds great!"

There were 9,656 movies on record, dating from 1927 to 2231. They began with *The Rock* and *Armageddon*. Violet found the older movies slow and only intermittently interesting, but Vibeke watched them the same way she read, and Violet could stand to sneak a peek at her as she drifted away into Alcatraz or the least realistic spaceflight ever pictured in the history of cinema.

The computer quickly learned their taste and gauged their personalities. It knew their interests better than they'd ever learned them, so for ten days the arcade kept them entertained. Violet noticed, and hoped Vibeke didn't notice, that the monitors watching her were leading to more and more amorous movies. They both enjoyed *The Matrix* so the computer showed them *Bound*, and once the monitors caught Violet's heart rate skyrocket during the sex scene the statistics condemned them to seeing hotter and hotter love stories, then sex stories, then by the time they were getting bored with the medium, it was running nothing but erotica, which was for the most part about as realistic as *Armageddon*'s space travel.

Still, watching women on the screen while sitting next to Vibeke was intoxicating. She couldn't move, though. They were reclined on a semigravitic bean blob, and both were afraid to make any sudden motions. The popcorn had remained untouched since *La Vie d'Adèle* for fear of reaching toward one another. They couldn't allow their hands to collide when the screen was displaying such things. But they couldn't turn it off for fear of appearing prudish or uncultured.

Violet's lips were chapped from resisting the need to lick them, a motion that could be misinterpreted by Vibeke in the worst possible way.

Vibeke ignored the discomfort in her legs rather than uncross them.

And both were afraid to talk. It simply wouldn't do.

"Oh is that the book guy?" said Violet, looking down toward the gym.

"We've been hogging the screen. We should go in case he wants it."

"Definitely."

Abandoning the arcade, they hit the gym oblivious to the kinky imagery still rattling around their subconsciousnesses. The workout felt different for both of them, though thinking themselves invulnerable to cinematic sex, neither had much of an idea why the burning of their muscles felt more tingly or the sweat smelled better in the air.

Violet kept her eyes on Vibeke through her workout. Watching her glisten and grunt. She wanted Vibeke desperately and cursed the last weeks of stagnation. She kicked the hell out of the tibialis resistor. She had to do something, anything. Not to solve the mystery of who Vibeke was talking about. It was her, or it wasn't, and she wanted Vibeke the same in either case. After her set she shut off the machine and floated over to Vibeke.

Vibs finished a set of pulls and looked to Violet, breathing heavily and sweating buckets. Without gravity to drip, she was coated with a thin layer of water, shimmering.

"Want to go sparring?" asked Violet.

They hadn't fought each other since the flight began. Vibs reiterated why.

"It's a bad idea, Vi. There's no doctor here, none like Niide, I mean."

"You're right. We never stop until we break a limb."

"And there's no real reason to, zero-g sparring isn't supposed to be very fun. All bouncing and spinning."

"No, you're right, it's a bad idea."

"Right. No good."

They took a few seconds to catch their breaths and nodded at each other in affirmation that it was a bad idea. Violet stared at Vibeke. Vibeke stared back.

"So you want to go sparring?"

"Yes."

They toweled off quickly and floated into the padded ring. They tried to bow but instead awkwardly folded in the middle. Violet let out a short snort of a laugh. Vibeke giggled. They pushed off.

Violet's first punch sent her spinning but didn't connect. Vibeke took advantage and kicked her in the back, sending Violet into the ceiling and herself into the ropes. Violet rebounded fast and darted into Vibeke, pinning her for an instant before they both bounced together toward the center.

They continued as trained. Calculating their moves for the likely motions to result. Moving to cause the most damage without losing control. Not all the damage they could. With Niide already thirty million kilometers away, they'd have to fix anything broken on their own so as not to alert the ship's doctor. But it was still a Valkyrie match and bruises began to emerge. Sweat began to form again and flick from their skin with every hit.

And then Violet grabbed Vibeke's arm. She grabbed Violet back and tried to put her in an armlock. Violet spun upside down and grabbed her again, then wrapped her legs around Vibeke's left thigh. Trapping her. Squeezing her. She was squished up against Violet, covered in sweat, breathing heavily, and close enough to look straight into her eyes. Violet was looking up to her, face only centimeters from her breast. Vibeke tapped out.

"Recover," she said nonchalantly.

The two pushed off to their corners. Vibeke found herself uncomfortable. She had some idea what they were getting into but didn't care to stop. After a moment they both launched into each other. This time they failed to spar; they only grappled. A tangle of limbs spinning in the middle of the ring. The noises they made sounded like the movie they left running in the arcade, grunts and gasps. By the time they twisted each other into a solid state, Vibeke had no illusions whatsoever about what was happening, and Violet had no inhibition against it.

"There's nobody here," said Violet. "It's a ghost ship."

"I know."

Violet let go and pushed off into the ropes. Vibeke floated slowly to her corner. They stared at each other. Violet undressing her with her eyes. She'd seen Vibeke naked a hundred times, but this was drastically different. Still clothed she was sexier than she'd ever appeared. Violet's mind raced, thinking of nothing but what she'd do to Vibs if she so much as made eye contact.

And Vibeke could feel it. She knew the stare she was getting from Violet, knew it all too well. It was the way Mishka looked at her. And in that moment, she thought of betrayal. Of the hunt.

Violet was oblivious, too in lust to think straight and too close to the object of her desire to imagine she was thinking anything else.

Vibeke felt ice cold. Sweat freezing on her skin. A chill in her spine. She couldn't be betrayed again, not by Violet of all people. She needed Violet. She loved Violet. And all she saw in that moment was Mishka's gaze. The look that disrobed her, the look that caught her escaping from the carrier with Balder. All betrayal, both of them hurting each other more deeply than Vibeke ever knew she could be hurt.

Vibeke bowed. Violet didn't understand at first. Slowly it dawned on her that it meant sparring was over. She bowed instinctively but remained lost. Breathing hard and confused as hell, she tried to reassemble the events to mean something more sensical. They had gone sparring. Nothing more. She didn't know why she said it was a ghost ship. She wasn't implying anything. It was just a random statement without meaning. Surely Vibeke knew that. She didn't need to say anything.

Vibeke's mind raced, her Tikari antenna snapping under Mishka's fist, killing Sasha, Mishka's escapes, the near misses, the hatred.

"Just one round, then?"

Violet couldn't keep sex out of her mind. She wanted Vibeke more desperately than she ever had before.

"Yeah, I'm not feeling it."

Vibs wanted to gut Mishka, to eviscerate her and watch her innards spill out onto the concrete.

"Me neither, let's shower off."

Showers, dear fucking hell, thought Violet.

"Yeah."

They floated to the showers and linked them on. Both their hearts racing for opposite reasons, they arrived at the sonic barrier. Vibeke began disrobing exactly as she always did. Violet did the same. Just like normal, because nothing abnormal had happened.

Vibs floated into the shower first, and its hum filtered her sweat from her skin. Violet floated in after and cursed the vibrations, the absolute last thing she needed to feel just then. They tried not to look at each other, though they'd seen each other in those very showers every day of the trip. Vibeke spoke, her voice distorting in the sound waves.

"Did you know this was the first transfer liner of its kind?"

It was more refreshing than the showers. Violet jumped in.

"No, no I didn't. What kind is it?"

"They call it Lasswitz class. It differs from the old Čapek class in that the thrusters are quark inversion like Valhalla instead of nuclear."

"That's so interesting!"

"Yeah, the Lasswitz liners are really amazing. They're expected to be in use until 2300 at least."

"Really built to last."

"Yeah."

The small talk continued until they made it back to the berth and strapped into their beds. By then it had transmogrified into something slightly deeper, the usual quality of the conversations that kept them awake until the next morning.

"My parents were in Inverness when they met," began Violet. "Apparently they got into this big fight the first time. They were at a murder mystery dinner, both dragged along by my grandparents. So they're at the front bar where you pick up your names, and both of them reach for Robin the Highlander. My dad is like, 'I get the Highlander, I'm from Inverness,' and my mom says 'The hell you do. I'm from Inverness too,' and my dad says 'I was born in Dornoch. Where were you born?' and she frowns and says, 'Glasgow.' He goes, 'well, that settles it, then. I'm the Highlander,' and she says maybe they can make a new tag and both be highlanders, and he says 'No, there can be only one! I'm the Highlander. You can be the wench from Glasgow, bloody keelie...,' so she took Jeanette from Hoorn, and she turned out to be the murderer, and she got to kill my dad. So every year for their anniversary, they'd go to some dinner and kill each other."

"Sounds almost Valkyrie."

"I can't even imagine what Valkyrie weddings would be like."

"Well, Viking weddings lasted at least three days, asked for blessings from the gods, and then everyone marched to the marital bed with torches and marked their first legal mating."

"How sweet."

"Do you ever want to get married?"

Violet thought about it briefly. "Sure, we can have the liner's captain perform the ceremony, and Nate can watch our first legal mating."

Vibeke laughed. "Me neither."

They paused, the long sort where neither knew if the other had gone to sleep. The kind that had become common after a month of staying up until morning just talking, ruining their sleep schedules. They could each duck into the dreamscape and see, but both were afraid to go and find themselves alone. Despite the tension and strange moment in the sparring ring, both found themselves happy to have so close a friend. For the first time in ages, Violet thought of Vibeke as her closest friend and not at all as something to be courted. It was a comfortable thought, a happy one that she wished would persist.

The next few days it lasted. But it faded. Every visit to the gym, every conversation, every covert stare wore Violet down as it did every time she tried to convince herself to think of Vibeke only as a friend.

On the penultimate day of the trip, she finally came to understand that no matter what she did, she'd not be able to eject Vibs from the core of her affections. However Vibeke felt about her, it was hopeless to convince herself that she had to be a friend or that she had any value so great she'd have as a lover. And Violet resolved that somehow, some day she'd possess her utterly, romantically, sexually, mind and body exactly as she wanted her, no matter what the cost. Because losing her teammate and losing her friend were not so terrible a fate as regretting that she'd left some stone unturned, some chance untaken.

The last night of the journey, she slept, determined to tell Vibeke everything, to demand she admit her own feelings and give in. The trip to Mars would be the last time they wasted such a chance. The trip home would be completely different. And the stay there would be different too, a burning hot stay on the bright red planet—Varg and Veikko be damned. To hell with the mission. This was the moment everything changed.

The Lasswitz turned and burned to slow down and slipped into Mars's orbit. The Martian shuttle docked, and the Tikaris broke away from the liner, heading for the shuttle's ailerons.

Violet slept through the braking process and awoke hours later, ready and resolved to speak to Vibs. She slowly opened her eyes to the bright berth. She saw Vibeke—floating right between Veikko and Varg, who were both strung out on adrenaline from their wake-up procedures.

"I fucked forty-seven women in the dreamscape!" shouted Varg.

"Twenty here, but I was—I won the Hold 'Em tournament three nights in a row, and—and I came in second twice. It was awesome! I made like 40,000 euros and then, then I gave it all to the Armor for Orphans fund!" Veikko's face went flat. "Why the hell did I do that?"

"What did you two do?" asked Varg cheerfully.

"Nothing."

"Nothing."

Varg and Veikko didn't know what to make of it. They did nothing, apparently. *Nothing to tell, then,* Veikko thought, and he went on to regale them with the specifics of his straight flush—clubs, nine to king.

The crowd slowly floated to the shuttle and took their seats. Violet never had her chance, but she didn't regret it all that much.

Nothing would have come of it anyway, she told herself. The landing was smooth under the thin Martian gravity, and the taxi to the spaceport took nearly an hour. They left it intentionally long to give the newcomers their safety lectures.

"Martian air is currently only 45 percent as thick as Earth's sea level and contains almost no oxygen. Never go outside without your oto-equalizers and a supply of oxygen appropriate for your activities. Never go outside without a warm jacket, even for a moment. Though the cold may not feel bad at first, you will get frostbite within ten minutes of exposure. Never forget that terraforming is only in its earliest stage. The effects don't change the fact that this is not a planet fit for life, and that life is now your own."

The sight out the windows was far less red than Violet had expected. They were in fact on a brown planet, not a red one. *Disappointing*, the word echoed through her mind for several reasons.

"We are now docked at the Valles Marineris Spaceport. The airlock will open in twenty seconds. Mars net will be available to your links in thirty seconds. Please follow all safety instructions at all times, and enjoy your stay on the red planet!"

It wasn't red. It just wasn't as red as she thought it would be.

Chapter V: Barsoom

THE TIKARIS began to unweld themselves from the shuttle's plating. Vibeke's broke free first and started to help Varg's, which had the most legs and would take the longest to break free. Violet's and Veikko's joined in as they escaped, and soon the group was fluttering across the tarmac, trying to hold up Pokey in the thin Martian air while also juggling four microwaves.

They weren't spotted on the tarmac, but as soon as they opened one of the luggage portals to the spaceport, two engineers took notice and ran for them. Nelson and Bob dropped their microwaves and sprang into action, flying for the engineers. Landing on their necks, both Tikaris tapped their quarry with the sedative needles on their front feet and flew back to close the airlock. Pokey was best suited for the tough inner door's crank so he started the instant the outer door was closed.

A small pop resounded in the luggage room, but nobody was there. Everyone was still unscrewing the cargo cylinder from the shuttle. The insectoids flew better in the indoor air and carried Pokey up to the ventilation system and, from there, to the intake to await their owners outside of the security zone.

V team was among the first off the flight. They quickly jogged to the terminal exit, then to the edge of the superstructure and awaited their Tiks. Sal spotted them under the vent and began unscrewing it, quickly magnetizing each bolt so as not to drop them. He was about to lift the grate upward into the vent when he realized it opened outward. The grate fell two meters onto Varg's head, knocking him over onto Vibeke.

Violet went into attack mode instantly, and Nelson felt her state, so he flew to her fast and landed in her hand as a knife, dropping her microwave on the floor at her feet. Bob seemed almost offended and flew to Vibeke for solace, and then Sal joined the rest as fast as he could, leaving three microwaves on the floor. That also left Pokey all alone in the vent system, unable to fly down. Varg recovered and looked up to see what dropped the grate just in time to see Pokey walk off the edge of the vent and fall right onto his shoulder, knocking him down again onto the floor.

Pokey immediately saw the microwave pile and realized he'd left Varg's sidearm up inside the vent shaft. He linked through Violet to ask Nelson to recover it, so the knife left Violet's hand and flew up to dislodge the weapon, which fell onto Varg's head just as he made it up for the third time.

By some miracle, nobody saw the Tikari fiasco happening in the corner. All four humans finally turned their Tikari back to control mode and chested them, Varg's around his torso. The team then holstered their microwaves, cursed their bumbling instruments, and headed for the conveyor.

There was no view in the underground conveyor train to the Barsoom Colony. Only four hours of darkness that somehow made the month-long space flight seem shorter.

The large-bellied men from the flight sat beside V team, so nobody from either group felt very vocal. Violet examined them, certain they were Wolves. They had the disgruntled pride she saw in so many Orange Gang members, that subsurface snarl that said they hated the world and loved hating it. If anything they were caricatures of the Orange Gang, more extreme versions. When the conveyor stopped at Barsoom, V team rose to depart, but the three men remained to head farther north.

Veikko linked, "We can't risk sending a Tikari to track them. Varg, throw one a node if you can."

Varg took three nodes from one of his Thaco pockets and linked out, "Distraction."

Violet immediately shoved Veikko into the railing.

"Don't you grope me, you bloody pervert! I oughta kill you! I *will* report you. You'll lose your job over this!"

She slapped him and continued. "I swear, I've never met such a pervert in my life. I should rip your bloody arms off and stuff them down your throat, I swear to God, you bastard!"

She gave him one more slap as the doors opened, then stormed out into the station. Varg and Vibeke caught up. Veikko exited the conveyor last, cradling his cheek.

He linked, "I missed you in cryo, Vi."

She linked back, "We missed you too, you gropey bastard. Varg, did you get a node on one?"

"All three, great show," he replied.

THE ARCHITECTURE of the Martian colony was nothing like that of Earth. Everything was redundant, inner and outer windows, inner and outer halls, inner and outer lobbies with inner and outer reception areas. Every wall was two walls, the bulky mass that protected from sandstorms and thin air, then the inner wall full of heating systems and soft paneling. Even the people dressed in layers: pressure suits opened to reveal jackets, jackets opened to reveal thermal suits, thermal suits covered underclothing. Valhalla's multipurpose garb would offer all those layers and even oxygen on the surface, but it stuck out on Mars as if they were wandering naked.

Thoris Hotel was something like an arcology in that it contained everything an entire city would need, as did all separate structures on the red planet. It made its own air, drilled and refined its own water, and was run by its own devoted company. The hotel's layout was completely unearthly. It took up far more horizontal space than any Earth contract would allow, spreading across three square kilometers of the brown sand, but standing only two stories tall. Nearly every wall was blue. Green moss-like fluff grew by every UV protected window, modified land algae with a high oxygen output.

Unlike the alien world they lived in, the people were utterly human. Few were modified, and some lacked links. They were quiet, as were the halls and even the humungous atrium. Veikko hacked into the hotel's system to program reservations for the team. The only four-person rooms available were the Marsden family's and one reserved for but canceled by the 19/50 Club. He looked up the club on the common Mars net and found they'd canceled their low gravity plans and were staying on Earth for the month. He linked out to the team and programmed their variable ID implants to show the names of the club members, luckily two male and two female.

The hotel check-in went smoothly, and they headed for their room. Veikko entered first and was the first to see the woman sitting on the first bed. She sat motionless as Veikko drew his microwave in surprise. The rest of V team flooded in and took up arms as well. The woman just smiled.

"What are you doing in our room?" asked Veikko.

"Ah, but it's not your room, is it? It's the 19/50 Club's."

"Who are you?"

"There is no 19/50 Club, you see. We forged it so you'd take this room so I could see you all for myself."

"You have ten seconds to say who you are, or we use a bore to find out."

"I'm Balder's wife. And he calls you his kids, so I guess I'm your momma."

The team considered it.

"Bullshit," Veikko replied.

She just laughed. "My name is Niana. Head of the Phobosian Republican Army. Ya heard of me?"

Violet hadn't. Varg lowered his weapon and spoke. "Yes, he's mentioned you."

"What does he have to say about me?"

"Nothing that needs to be repeated," he said aloud. Then he linked to the team, "We can trust her. There were only three people still alive who knew Balder got hitched: Balder, Niana, and me."

They lowered their weapons and took seats around the room.

"So I'm gonna brief you, and then you can brief me. Balder didn't tell me much as Mars comm is unsecured, but if he wanted me to meet you, it's likely about the Ares Project, am I right?"

Veikko nodded.

"Well, here's the situation. We have a fission bomb stuck to it with an organic detonator. We don't have the trigger, so I assume Balder sent it with you?"

"No, no, he didn't give us an organic trigger."

"Odd. Well, perhaps he doesn't want you to nuke the thing. Why don't you fill me in?"

Veikko started. "There are two companies trying to bring the Ares home. The Yakuza"—Niana cringed—"and a new gang calling themselves the Wolf Gang, run by the remains of the Orange Gang. We're here to stop the Wolf Gang, another team is coming to deal with the Yaks. But nuking the device is very much what we'd like to do. He didn't give us a trigger, though.... Is there any chance it's here?"

"Not likely, unless he told you otherwise."

Vibeke spoke. "It's under the redwood."

Violet remembered Balder's last words to them. "Is there a redwood tree on Mars?"

Niana grinned. "It's the tall one in the center of the atrium. The sneaky bastard. He left it here for us all along. Come with me."

She led them out of the room. They spoke by link.

"Easy day, we nuke it and head home to kill Wulfgar," said Veikko.

"I don't think so," said Varg. "I spoke to Balder about the situation here a few times before. He mentioned a nuke in the power of Valhalla's allies but said it was an absolute last resort for an apocalyptic scenario. He wouldn't use it unless it was absolutely necessary. He'll want us to foil the Wolves, not risk a nuclear blast."

Vibeke agreed. "Tensions are high on Earth. A nuclear blast here could start a war. Varg is right, we need to focus on the Wolves."

"But he gave us the location for the trigger," said Veikko. "Why would he do that unless he meant for us to use it?"

"Worst case scenario, we blow it in space if it lifts off." Violet considered. "It's an organic trigger, right? It'll work on extranervous link."

Vibeke was impressed. "That's right. We could hit the trigger here when it was in transfer orbit, and it would still go off."

"So we focus on the Wolves first," said Veikko, "and keep the trigger on us at all times."

They arrived at the atrium's garden. It only produced 12 percent of the building's oxygen but held most of its flowers and trees. A few lone wanderers were spread out around the plants. In the center was a giant tree, the biggest Violet had ever seen. She assumed it was due to the low Martian gravity. Niana lead them straight to it.

"The trigger is two meters, a chain-link worm. Standard organic trigger, it can smell your intent. You can squeeze its head, tell it to set off the fireworks, beat it to a pulp, but unless you actually mean to set it off, and you have to really mean it, it denies the signal. It'll recognize me and Balder. We'll see if he set it to recognize other Valkyries. If not, you may not be able to set it off."

They looked around the redwood for any sign of a worm. Other large organics roamed the garden: a tall red hairy blob with two feet and two eyes, spybirds like those on Earth, and Octosqueegees, cleaning the windows. Earth had banned most organics after Høtherus, but Mars needed them. Animaloids designed to survive outdoors, to serve any purpose from food to work horse.

Vibeke pulled out her microwave and aimed it for the ground. Before anyone could ask what she was doing, she sent a low audio pulse into the dirt. *A good idea*, thought Violet, it would force the worm out of the ground. And so it did. Niana spotted it only seconds later.

She pulled the long chain out of the dirt and handed it to Varg. It beeped twice.

"It likes you! He must have programmed it to recognize your sort. Pass it around!"

Varg handed it to Veikko, and it beeped twice again. To Vibeke and Violet with the same results. Violet examined it. It was very much like an earthworm, grayish pink with a thick band around its head. The body, though, was twisted into a five-centimeter-thick chain. *An impossible shape for anything alive*, she thought. But organics were a very strange technology. Varg took the worm and wore it like a scarf for safekeeping.

The five returned to V team's room and further discussed the situation, sharing all intel from each side. Niana told them that the remains of the PRA were at their disposal as long as they were on Mars before she headed out, back to their base. V team contemplated their next move. They would follow Yellow Boots once he arrived, of course, but none were completely content just to wait and see what he did.

YELLOW BOOTS arrived on the next shuttle. Two Tikaris were there to watch him. Hanging on the ceiling, Violet's observed him getting off the shuttle and walking into the baggage claim. But it saw something else, a man behind him. Also wearing a black rubber business suit.

Violet's Tikari stuck to Mehmet, while Veikko's stayed to monitor for more Wolves. It counted eight men in black, all with a similar build. They watched Mehmet and the chubby quorum check into their rooms without incident. For two days the men didn't move. They stuck to their rooms immersed on the Mars net, doing nothing notable, or wandered the hotel, still doing nothing notable.

When it came time for the next shuttle to arrive, Veikko sent his Tikari to count men of similar bellied build and garb. The team sat in Tarkas bar, snacking on spicy synth beef sticks while it worked. The Tikari had counted four new men when there was a commotion in the jetway.

Veikko turned up his tympanum to hear what people were shouting.

"I want every room searched.... They're here without question... I want them brought to me."

Veikko could tell it was a female voice.

"Kill the three if you can, but the girl lives. I need her alive."

It sounded bad.

"Vibeke Dyrsdatter, extremely dangerous."

"Uh, Vibs...?"

Vibeke looked into Veikko's Tikari feed just in time to see Mishka coming out of the jetway with four security guards.

She turned pale, livid. Before she could tell Veikko to send his Tikari into her heart, an alarm sounded. It was broadcast across the link and by sound in the halls. But the link also carried an image. Vibeke's picture, clear as Mishka remembered her. Consider extremely dangerous. Apprehend at all costs. Kill all accomplices.

"We've gotta move!" whispered Veikko.

Half the bar was now looking at them. At least two Barsoom cops among them, already reaching for sidearms. Varg tightened the trigger worm around his neck. Vibeke and Violet were ready to go.

"We're surrounded," said Violet.

"Almost," replied Veikko.

He leveled his microwave at the bar's window and fired. The team had their mask fields up within a fraction of a second, before their ears popped. The cold still hit them like Kvitøya ice. All four jumped one floor to the ground and headed for the nearest rocks. Microwave beams burned the rusty dirt around them as the police fired. Violet's suit absorbed a few hits, as did the others, but they made it to the rocks alive. Veikko's Tikari flew from the window into his chest.

Violet spoke first, "I'll leave my Tikari here to watch Aga, but we need to find somewhere safe."

"There's nowhere safe," said Vibeke. "She has the entire Martian police force after us!"

Varg linked to the three, "The PRA will house us!"

"They're in a crater across the planet from here!"

"Then we better get going," muttered Veikko out loud.

Inside, Mishka heard the alert come in from the police, all four spotted. They'd blown out a window and gone outside.

"Follow them!" she demanded.

"We can't, we can't go outside, it's—"

Mishka grabbed the officer by his collar. "I'm following them outside right now. I expect your men armed and armored behind me *immediately*, is that understood?"

"Yes, ma'am!"

The police scrambled to get into outdoor gear. Mishka didn't have any, but she had oxygen, and that would have to be enough. She linked into the local map and found the bar where they'd escaped. It was on the same side of Barsoom but almost a kilometer north. She calculated the distance given the cold and the air available in her jumpsuit. She could make it.

Mishka fired at a window, and it blew out onto the surface. Travelers ran for cover and oxygen masks fell from the ceiling across the terminal. Mishka jumped out the window as her escorts pulled masks on.

"Who the hell is this lady?" one asked.

"Manifest listed her as Sanchita Patel," said the commander, "a Red Beret Havildar."

"Damn, I can see why."

Mishka ran north. The cold cut into her painfully. She ignored it. She readied her microwave.

Veikko linked into the local police net and hacked the PRA files. He immediately found the most recent sight listings and checked the Barsoom file. Most recent contact with PRA: 3.5 years ago. Spotted in Aureum Chaos 14km east of Barsoom Colony.

"We head east," said Veikko authoritatively. The others had no reason to question it. They had to get moving, and that was as good a chance as any other.

As soon as they left the rock, Mishka spotted them. She couldn't outrun them, and if she reached them it would be four to one. Mishka linked to the police and demanded a rover sent to their position. Then she ejected her eye.

The eye shot for V team at top speed. Mishka aimed for Vibckc's head. At top speed, though, it couldn't correct its course fast enough, and it flew by her, missing her by centimeters.

Violet, running behind her, saw it. "Black dot!" she called out, not certain what she'd just seen.

But Vibeke knew the file by heart. It could only be Mishka's new eyeball. "Microwaves!"

Violet pulled hers out but couldn't see the dot. Mishka slowed it down and reversed its course. At half speed she shot for Vibeke's temple. This time it could correct course. Violet spotted it coming and fired a wide beam in its direction. The eye briefly shorted out and fell to the rusty surface.

Mishka cursed, her link to the eye was disrupted. It would come back, but that wouldn't be critical—her rover was on its way.

She linked to the rover and told them to run the four down, disable them at any cost even if it meant wrecking the rover. Its driver, Com Stockins, was more than happy to oblige. He floored the accelerator and careened toward the group.

V team was only a hundred meters from the first canyon when the rover caught up. Six gigantic wheels with a small cabin on top. Violet fired at the rover with no effect. It was mostly just rubber. Stockins laughed at the detector warning.

Mishka's eye came back online, the link restored. She sent it after the rover to see V team crushed. The rover made it to their position when they were thirty meters from the canyon. They split up, girls left, boys right. The rover followed the boys.

Varg was beginning to feel tired, and when Varg got tired, he got lazy. Not lazy meaning he slipped up, but he wanted to resolve the situation as easily and quickly as possible. Thinking fast, he took his microwave and fired at the ground with a strong repelling beam. Holding on tightly, the beam jumped him like a trick pool shot up over the rover's wheels and smack into its windscreen.

Com was surprised but unconcerned. He swerved to throw him off. Varg hung tight and turned, firing a lethal beam at the driver. The windscreen deflected most of it, and Com was only sunburned. He swerved again.

Varg used the motion to vault around the windscreen to its left and came in feetfirst, kicking Com out of the open cabin and into the wheels, and under the wheels.

Mishka cursed. She saw it happen and saw the rover slow. She sent the eye at top speed to hit Varg, but Veikko saw it coming and fired another wide beam to disrupt it.

Mishka screamed in frustration. They had a rover now. She'd not catch them anytime soon. She linked into the police and told them to monitor the rover's position, but she knew it was a lost cause. Given a perfect vehicle for Martian terrain, they were uncatchable. But Mishka reminded herself, the police were her first avenue of capture but not her best. She knew they were following Yellow Boots. All she had to do was the same.

Violet broke off the rover's tracking pip, and Varg drove the four down into the canyon and toward the last known location of the PRA. There they disembarked. The sun was going down, dim by day and growing darker as night approached. The air grew even colder, and their suits grew as much fur as they could.

They found no sign of manmade caves before it grew dark and didn't want to risk illuminating their suits. They gathered into a small nook in one of the cliffs and went to sleep for the night, huddled together for what little warmth they could keep.

VIOLET AWOKE to the sound of voices, carrying softly through the thin air.

"—happy to see you!"

"I thought ya might be. Looks like you have the entire force after you now. Now you know how we've lived for the last twenty years."

"I don't envy it," said Varg.

Niana continued. "So where are you headed next? Trade us this rover, and we'll take you anywhere you please."

"Violet?"

Violet snapped to attention.

"Where's Aga?"

She looked into her Tikari. She had no second link control of it that far away, but it could still send encrypted information and video over the common Mars net. It was adeptly following Aga under its own AI. She consulted its geolocator. He was north of Barsoom on the conveyor, headed farther north.

"Approaching Acidalia Planitia," Violet reported.

"Varg's tagged Wolves are there too. Nelson reads them on the same conveyor, two cars ahead."

"They're heading toward Vastitas Borealis. That's where the Ares water tanks are. I suppose you'll be wanting to catch up to him?"

"Yes," said Veikko, "but we can't risk the conveyors anymore, and this rover is short range. Do you have anything that can take us that far north?"

"Sure we do, but you're not going to like it...."

They boarded the rover, and Niana took them to a small tent fort hidden in the canyons. Several PRA men in stillsuits erected another tent across the rover. In the central sealed tent was an impressive heating system and a table covered in printed maps.

"You have nearly 3,000 kilometers to cover. It takes the conveyor two days. We can get you there in one week."

"Nothing faster?"

"The conveyor is the fastest thing on the planet. And you'll be traveling by organic runner."

Indeed they didn't like it.

"Are you kidding?" asked Veikko.

"Nope, organic runners are the second fastest thing on the planet. Faster than that rover, faster than any skiff that can go that far. But that's not the bad news. Bad news is that they live for five days. You'll be walking the last two."

Violet took a deep breath. They'd be heading north to the Martian lowlands, and they'd be walking for two days in the waste. It would be a superhuman feat just to survive. She spoke up. "I've got my Tikari on him. We've got the detonator here. A Tikari can sabotage a whole hell of a lot."

"But it's on its own," explained Veikko. "You won't be able to control it directly, only send it orders via common hackable net links. We need to be there, and just hope we can get there before they take off, before the Yakuza arrive."

"And before Mishka arrives," added Vibs. "She'll know what we're here for. She'll be on her way."

"Let's just get to it. The sooner we leave, the sooner it's over," Veikko added.

There was no more discussion. Niana took the team to the PRA zoologist. She then programmed six eggs as runners. Within an hour they were ready to hatch. Within five, the giant furry monsters were grown to adulthood.

It was frightening to see anything grow so strong so fast. The incubation system was massive and immobile, preventing them from simply taking eggs along to be grown after the death of the first batch. The runners themselves were mostly legs with only small bodies and no heads. They had eyes on the fronts of their torsos, four each, but no mouths or any other orifice. They wouldn't eat. They were born with all the energy they could consume in the form of Microstorage ATP. Only a kilogram of their body mass, but enough to keep them alive and running nonstop.

The zoologist explained that their DNA was based on snow leopards, but there was nothing of it visible in them, save for the fur. They were utterly alien, designed for the sole purpose of Martian travel. Violet would have preferred a pogo or even the POS, but the Martian atmosphere couldn't sustain an airfoil field and actual space-capable vehicles were as rare on Mars as astatine on Earth. She tried to think of any possible way out of the walk to come, but in every instance, it was the best shot they had to catch up to Yellow Boots.

And presumably Mishka. Nelson didn't show her with Aga, but there was no question she'd be on his tail. She was looking for them, for Vibeke specifically. Violet couldn't fathom why after a year of running, she was finally seeking them out. Perhaps it was because of that year of running. Or perhaps it was something more urgent.

There was no more time to think. They strapped onto the runners, Violet and Vibeke on the first, Veikko and Varg on the next. Two carried nothing but supplies, survival gear, and a few landskiffs to use once the beasts died. On the last pair, Niana sent the zoologist's apprentice and a PRA lieutenant to monitor the beasts and take care of the Valkyries' Martian survival. She knew they were tough, but they were from Earth. No matter how they trained for Mars, they'd not grown up in its wastelands. They each carried more supplies. The apprentice carried egg harvesting tools, and the lieutenant kept an assortment of conventional explosives. Varg retained the nuclear trigger around his neck. Aside from carrying the ultimate destructive power in the universe, it was pleasantly warm and stylish.

There was no discussion or training for the ride. Anything they had to know, they'd link once underway. The zoologist tapped into the animals' self-grown wetware and programmed them to go as close to the Ares as possible, and then Niana gave them a slap on the rump, and they were off.

THE FIRST two days were an uneventful misery. The lope of the runners was possible to sleep through, but only just. Most of the time, V immersed themselves in a local network with a Tikari flying overhead as lookout, Vibeke's small red Tikari by day and Veikko's larger Tik by night. Staying aware in their bodies was to be avoided at any costs. A standard chemical cocktail kept them from freezing to death. Even under their furry suits the temperatures were below freezing at night and little better by day. It was an enduring pain that didn't quite go away online.

Over the rumble of waking motion, V team got to know Weasel and Spit better. Weasel was born on Phobos. He lived there with his parents until age twelve, when they were evicted to make way for a Zaibatsu executive. They were shipped to Mars and placed in Ylla Colony in housing one-tenth the size of their Phobosian home. Weasel couldn't stand up in Martian gravity, Phobos being nearly weightless by comparison.

"If an Earther jumps on Phobos, they don't come back down. On Mars I was like putty, took me years to stand up. I was twenty before I was able to work. Wanted to be a fauna engineer, but the terraforming companies were already dying out, giving up. Nobody was hiring. Nobody was working, started to riot instead. First time out of our little house with my parents and I saw them killed by Zaibatsu cops. I got carried off by PRA members, they took care of me.

"They asked what I wanted to do, and I thought they meant for a career, so I told them I wanted to design animals. The PRA doesn't do that shite, but they were using what few organics they could steal. Already had a zoologist, but she took me as an apprentice. Genius woman, Karrine. Can stretch a scrounge beetle to clean up an entire tent, stretched these runners to live five days. Most live for two, there's only so much energy you can squeeze into 'em before they burst. But she found a way to, well, I won't bore you, but these beasts are the fastest runners ever to exist. Only downside is they can't stop. Their muscles would petrify with acid if they did, have to kill 'em to stop 'em."

It seemed cruel to Violet, but Weasel pointed out, "No brain, no pain." Organics weren't animals. They were biological machines. They had roughly the same intelligence as flies, a few hardwired behaviors and nothing more. Still, gripping onto the white fur with her own suit growing fur to match, she had to wonder if humans were much different. More nerves, but where there are nerves, there's consciousness, or so she had learned in school. It was amusing to think of plugging into school a few years back while tied to a strange furry mass of limbs cantering across brown Mars.

Before long they could see the second sign of the old terraforming attempts. After the thickened air, there was snow. Never falling snow, it had last snowed actively while the machines were still on in 2218, but dirty patches of the stuff littered the ground.

"The machines were monstrous," explained Spit as she retied her long hair. "They created humidity, but they put out ten times more smoke than water. They did more to wreck Mars than make it livable. I didn't care about Phobos when I joined. I just wanted to take down the machines. By any method. Basically I wanted to blow shit up, and they gave me the bombs.

"Of course, I got to care a great deal about Phobos after I joined. And Deimos, a lot of people don't realize the PRA is as much for Deimos as its original moon. UNEGA rapes the moons for the good of the planet and gives nothing back. They take the people, the resources, use them for docks or testing grounds. The last time a wave bomb was tested, it was on Deimos, and they have the mutants to prove it. The zombies, the diseases.

"We don't attack civilian targets, but I'd stick around if we did. Civilian is another word for company man. The processors, the pencil pushers, and penny pinchers, they do as much to torture the moons as any cop. Any army."

Violet realized as Spit said it that fighting the PRA on Earth might have been her job had she stayed at Achnacarry. She grew uneasy at the thought, or perhaps it was at the terrain.

The land grew more rocky and uneven. The runners could see and adjust for obstacles, but they didn't care about any nuance to the ground that wouldn't trip them up. They went top speed over any bump, and that could result in a massive lurch to anyone hanging on. Violet took another nausea tab from her Thaco pockets and checked in with Nelson.

Aga was about to reach Vastitas Borealis and disembark the conveyor. All four Valkyries entered full immersion into Violet's Tikari feed. Aga met with two men in black rubber suits. They took him to a sport utility skiff, and the skiff headed east.

The Tikari stayed glued to the underside of the vehicle and soon gave them their first look at the Ares tanks. They were identical to the three tanks near the YGDR S/L system in Valhalla. Tall, round silos reinforced by buttresses. Thinner on the top and bottom, intended for transportation. They were too far to tell if the nuke was intact. Next to the tanks was a large tent to which the skiff traveled.

The Tikari took to the sky and surveyed the area. There was no sign of Yakuza, nor of any organization but the Wolves. It snuck into the tent and revealed a small complex of buildings. It was able to identify some as barracks and one as a mess hall, with one small storage building. Nothing else. There was no ship under construction, no rocket pad, no visible means of transportation.

Nelson took to observing the behavior of the men. There were too many of them to count living at the facility, but none of them seemed to be doing anything. They talked, they wandered the thin Martian net, they ate and drank and slept, and they did no work whatsoever. V team couldn't put it together.

Spit called them out of immersion with an alarm link. As they came out, she shouted, "Avalanche!"

They had run into an area of mountainous high snowdrifts, one of which was falling down, disturbed by the runners' footfalls. Varg was the first to draw his microwave and fire. He fired a wide spread on the weapon's normal mode, turning some of the snow to steam. Violet and the others did the same, but as the runners neared the accumulation zone of the fall, the microwaves only turned the snow into scalding water, and they had to stop firing.

They had given Spit enough time to reach one of the gear runners and pull out their avalanche safeguards. A giant Mylar bubble inflated around the runners, who continued their canter as if inside a hamster ball. Immediately the ball ran over rocks that burst it, and it began to deflate.

"Don't worry," shouted Spit, "they're only meant to last a minute. It'll get us out of the avalanche. Cut it if you can when it falls on us."

Violet and the team did so, firing thin beams into the Mylar as it floated down onto them. The runners headed for the holes, and all six burst out into the bright, snowy landscape. Weasel gave his beast a pat on the back, and they ran on north.

As the snow pack let up, they began to see the next result of failed terraforming. One of the first attempts involved a plant that took in the carbon-dioxide-thickened air and output oxygen. Called the white weed, the stuff managed to take in plenty of carbon dioxide and grow over massive swatches of the planet, but it put out little oxygen, only a half of a percent of what was expected.

It was neither white nor a weed, Violet recalled from school, but a yellowish fungus that grew like a weed. Far worse, in fact. Its tendrils would take root in any living tissue that touched them. That included the runners.

"They'll go down in this! Get ready to bail," shouted Weasel.

The runners had taken them four of the five days possible, not bad in the long run, but a day for the runners meant five on foot. They'd arrive far later at the Ares, just in time to meet E team and fight the Yakuza. Not a problem as the Wolves didn't seem to be doing anything. Violet's Tikari had witnessed numerous Wolves come and go. None did anything to move the Ares.

Tendrils began to root into the runners feet as soon as they left the snow. Their feet were tough pads, and they lasted several kilometers into the thicket, but soon the tearing sound of broken fungus resounded from beneath them. They started to slow and then stick, and finally they fell to the ground where tendrils began to devour them.

Violet could feel the tendrils trying to reach into her boots, as if they sensed her inside. She was unnerved by how fast they tore into the beasts, which shook as their muscles seized up, going still after the long run. Weasel wasted no time with an emotional farewell. He went to each beast and cut them open with a laser tool. From each he took a few tiny eggs, the next generation of runners to incubate once he got back to the PRA.

They took the landskiffs from the packs and rode them across a few kilometers of the white weed, hoping they'd outlast it. But at the end of their range, the skiffs only took them an infinitesimal portion of their journey. The weed persisted.

Without a word they abandoned the skiffs and began to walk. The white weed grabbed at them with every step but broke off unable to penetrate their suits. The expanse of it went to every horizon. The six stuck to any snow patches they could find, but for the most part, they were stuck on the gripping plain. Walking felt good, though. After four days tied to the organics, Violet could finally stretch and pop the joints in her legs. But walking got old after a few hours, and as night fell, she realized they couldn't lie down to sleep on the white weeds, or they'd be consumed in minutes. They walked until dawn came, and the first patches of weedless land emerged. They slept in the first one that would fit them.

Finally in sleep, they monitored Violet's Tikari feed. Aga had left by skiff. Violet abandoned him at the conveyor and recalled her Tikari to keep watching the Wolf site in case anything happened. Without the Tikari present at the conveyor station, she missed watching Mishka arrive to collect her eyeball and lie in wait.

Fewer and fewer weeds appeared as they trudged farther north. There was little snow accumulated in the lowlands. Mars was back to brown rock. The team talked by link with Weasel and Spit, slept for three hours each day, and walked for twenty-one and a half. Violet found herself wishing there were a private link she could share with Vibs to recapture some of those funny first days on the shuttle, but the brown planet insisted on itself, the terrain just uneven enough to demand her attention. Until a simple encrypted link came from Earth.

"E grounded, Y shortly."

E grounded. Surely it meant E team wouldn't be following the Yakuza, who were soon to arrive. They didn't bother to link back to ask why. The Earth to Mars communication was as good as public, and they wouldn't be able to say. But it meant a drastic change in their mission. They were now in charge of seeing that the Yakuza didn't get the Ares back to Earth. They had expected the Wolves to try taking it first, but it was now becoming clearer it was all an act of misdirection. The Wolves only wanted to make the Yaks think they were after the thing.

That would explain E team's disappearance. A gang war between the Yaks and Wolves on Earth must have erupted. They were either preoccupied with it or prevented from flying by it. It all came together. Mishka was working for the Wolf Gang to see that they couldn't inform anyone of the fake operation, a random net meeting that gave Mishka the opportunity to kill her old pals. With the Yakuza in a space race, they'd have left their home turf unguarded. Wulfgar was going to seize Yakuza assets while they desperately clamored for something Wulfgar never wanted in the first place.

V team was 300 kilometers from the Ares when they began seeing shuttles in the sky. The Yaks meant business. They were likely using their regular fleet to build a rocket capable of taking the Ares home. A massive undertaking. There was hope in that, the bigger the operation, the easier it would be to foil. A couple malfunctioning thrusters would negate the need for the fission bomb, at least for a while.

But their arrival also meant security, more than the fake Wolf tent. At 200 kilometers they heard the first growl.

"Guardthings," said Weasel. "Security organics. We have a few outside the main crater. Extremely dangerous, resistant to microwaves. Those things in your chests are knives, right?"

"Right."

"I hope you keep 'em sharp."

Three of the monsters appeared on the horizon. They were kicking up dust, running toward them. Vibeke and Veikko ejected their Tikaris and prepared to fight.

The guardthings bore even less resemblance to any earthly animal blueprint than the runners and went for broke in the teeth department, having six legs ending in two ten-taloned feet each, uncountable eyes, ears, and nostrils, several tusks and like a starfish, a central stomach orifice surrounded by sharp fangs. Things as nightmarish as the Kolossus.

"Their weakness is the nerve cluster on the tops of their backs," explained Weasel. "Sever any part of it, and they'll go down. But it's surrounded by a carbon-fiber-grown spinal column. Look at the bumps along their spines and cut between them, try to get through the cartilage disks. It's the only way."

"Not the only way," shouted Spit as she took a box of explosives and wired it. She quickly arranged the contents and then gave the box a kick. In midair, the box began to burn like a roman candle, slashing through the air toward the first guardthing. When it hit, it exploded, sending chunks of the head guardthing across the rocky field, cracking the bulk of its torso in half. She began to wire a second crate, but the guardthings drew close enough to leap and pounced toward V team, one at Varg and one at Violet. Vibeke threw her Tikari to Violet, who held it firmly and ran under the monster to avoid its initial spring. Its underbelly teeth cut into her head, through her welded hair but no deeper than the skin. As soon as it was behind her, she leaped for its short tail. It wasn't enough to hang on to, so she leaped again and tried to get on its back.

It fought her viciously, but its limbs didn't reach behind it. It kicked back with its hind legs, and its talons scraped over Violet's armor. She severed the tendons on one, and it crouched briefly, just enough for her to climb up onto its back. She sunk the blade between its vertebrae, but it didn't die. It started bucking, clawing at her as best it could. She stabbed again. This time the knife went deeper and the beast went down.

Violet rolled off and looked to the other creature. Varg had cut it in half with a single swing.

THEY SLEPT that night in the warm guardthings' fat. They were fairly lean, but the three of them easily housed six sleepers. Veikko and Weasel slept in the exploded remains, Varg and Spit embraced under the halves of Varg's beast, while Violet and Vibeke shared the tight interior of Violet's animal.

The air was frozen as night took over. Painfully so, despite the suits and chemicals. Nelson was stowed away in a corner of the abandoned Wolf camp, hiding from potential witnesses. He had nothing to report. There was no distraction from the frozen air. Violet lay next to Vibeke, afraid to roll over toward her. But she could sense Vibeke was shivering too. She needed permission, so she suggested something she knew wouldn't work.

"We could put up vacuum defenses on our armor," suggested Violet.

"They use pressure for power, won't work in air, even this thin," Vibeke replied.

Just as planned. "What can we do?"

"Just spoon me."

Bingo. Violet did so, delighted to hear the words. She squeezed Vibeke hard enough that the shivering in her arms refocused into her grasp. It was the closest Violet could get to anything physical with Vibeke so suddenly she didn't mind the cold. She considered pressing against Vibeke's chest, but she'd no doubt know why and might make her stop, brush her off into the cold again. Violet wouldn't feel much under the Thaco fur anyway.

She focused on the gory surroundings to eradicate any desire. She listened to the drip of blood and fluids from the inside of the beast, felt how it matted down on her armor's fur. Despite using oxygen prongs, she could smell the guardthing's blood and fat, iron and a sickly sweet stink. She tried to smell Vibeke's neck to no avail.

"Do you...." Violet linked.

"Do I?"

"Do you have any regrets about the trip?"

"No, I thought it was lovely. Do you?"

"No, no, of course not."

Vibeke said nothing. She thought of the awkward moment in the sparring ring.

Violet thought of her resolution to tell Vibeke everything. Cut off only by Veikko and Varg. Not by anything else, she told herself. They were alone now. She had no excuse. She was courageous in the extreme, or she wouldn't be a Valkyrie. She had to tell herself that five times before she was able.

"It is me, isn't it? That you're afraid of?"

Vibeke said nothing.

"Then tell me it's not, because it would be a real load off. Tell me nothing could ever happen between us, that you don't want what I want. And you know what I want, you have to. Tell me you don't want it too, that you don't wish we'd locked ourselves in that berth and locked lips for thirty days."

Vibeke found herself angry at Violet's forwardness. "Which lips are you wishing we'd locked?"

"Wow, I meant kissing, but since you mention it—"

"Stop."

Violet cringed, letting guardthing blood into the corner of her mouth. She knew Vibeke was angry. Well, if she'd pissed her off anyway, there was no sense in stopping there.

"Look, I have something I have to get off my chest."

"Unless it's your Tikari, now's not the time."

"There will never be a good time."

"I'm tired, Violet."

"Me too, Vibs. I'm tired of the charade that we're not in love. And if it's because you're scared, then I'm tired of you, a Valkyrie, not conquering your fears. I'm tired of wasting time, because every second I'm not holding you is a waste. I'm tired of wanting you from afar. Staring at you, listening to you, getting myself off to you—"

"Stop, now."

"Stop what? It's a compliment."

"Right, that's all, a compliment."

"Exactly. Like your perfect arse and succulent tits."

"And your complete lack of decency."

"And the way you sleep sometimes with your hand on your—"

"And the way you're too fucking stupid to know when to stop."

"And the way you're too fucking smart to do what would make you happy."

"Well, thanks for the fucking compliments, Vi."

"You too, cunt."

Violet felt a prick of something that wasn't entirely negative, as she'd expected rejection to be. Something like sparring, it hurt to get hit, but it felt good to fight.

Vibeke felt only anger at Violet's tactlessness. She'd just said it, openly. She resented Violet above all because she hadn't had the guts to say it openly herself.

"You're a crude one," said Vibeke.

"I mean it complimentary like."

"I'm glad we're so complimentary." Not what Vibs wanted to admit. "I mean—"

"We are perfect for each other, you know."

Vibeke couldn't deny that. Lying about it would send her stomach through her throat, and Violet would know it. That would encourage her even more. But nothing could happen. They were on the same team. They had to put each other's lives in their hands daily. She was afraid of what might happen, of being betrayed again by the last person she could take it from. But that was a fear, and Violet was right about fear. She could admit the truth. She had to.

"…Yeah, I know." She said it so begrudgingly it was like Violet asked her to clean a plumbing fixture. She knew why, Vibeke was a slave to protocol and logic. She thought it best to put her at ease.

"But nothing can ever happen because we fight together, because you're afraid of being betrayed like before. But I won't. I'll never, ever betray you like that. I'm not capable of it. Vibs—"

"No! You want to know why I don't want you? Because I can't trust you. Because you *would* be Mishka all over again."

It was exactly like pain training—a punch in the stomach that ruptured the lining. Violet didn't speak.

"Nothing to say now? No sex jokes? No innuendo? Then you know how I feel. I don't want you because the one time I fucked a girl like you, it was her. Yeah, I love you back. *Almost* as much as I loved her. Her strength, her wit, the way she held me, exactly like you're holding me now. But I loved her like I'll never love you because I wasn't afraid back then, and I paid for it. Got that? I will never, ever love you the way I loved her."

Violet was shaking and not because of the cold.

"Stop."

"You never stop. You flirt and fidget every goddamn second, and you've done it for a year now, and I put up with it. I'm not going to anymore. Whatever you think can happen between us wouldn't be what you want. I'm damaged goods. I'll never trust anyone enough to love them. I'd be faking it with you."

Vibeke stewed. Violet wouldn't care if it were fake. She was too thick, too single-minded. And Vibeke was too tired to fight her anymore. She gave up.

"You want something to happen between us? Fine. Plow away. Spit out the blood and fuck me right here in this fucking corpse. If that's what you want, take it. Just don't expect me to like it because you can tongue and finger any spot you like, and I'll be thinking about killing Mishka. If that gets you off, go for it."

Violet didn't move a centimeter, or say a word. She was horrified. Vibeke was suddenly far too human to objectify easily. She wished desperately that Vibeke had told her long ago how Mishka had truly hurt her. She was furious at her for not telling. And deeper down was an animal inside her that didn't care. Vibeke said it in anger, but she said it. Fuck me. That overrode any sympathy Violet might have felt. If Vibeke told her before, if she hadn't told her in spite, she might not have done a thing. But Vibeke was fighting her. Tempting her. Part of Violet wanted to stay noble and be a friend for Vibs after her admission. But a bigger part wanted to grab her tit.

Violet reached over Vibeke's side and pressed her hand down. Vibeke didn't move. Didn't object. Didn't say a thing. Violet held on more firmly, squeezing harder and harder. Still Vibeke didn't move, wouldn't even give her the satisfaction of objecting. That's how it was to be. Not a word. Violet grabbed harder. And harder. Nothing. She grabbed as tight as she could, angry and taken aback that Vibs would rather go into full pain training mode than let out a gasp or tell her to stop. Violet had never felt so worthless or ashamed. She let go and sniffled.

"Fuck you, Vibs. Just fuck you."

Vibeke ignored her and tried to sleep. Violet never learned she had in fact been groping the guardthing's kidney.

IN THE morning they shook the innards from their suits and walked on. They encountered no more guardthings, but robots became a problem. The Yakuza had several monitoring the landscape and reporting back. The landscape offered little cover so they kept Tikaris at high altitude, as high as they could fly in the thin air, to watch for the robots.

Violet and Vibeke said nothing to each other. And nothing felt different. For all that had transpired in the night, neither wanted to admit any of it happened. So they walked on side by side, both burning too deep inside to let a thing show. As they plodded through the monotonous landscape, the buried anger and lust absorbed into their aching legs and didn't register at all.

They had to constantly adjust their course to stay out of the treaded wanderers' field of vision. Vibeke estimated it added another half day to the journey. They looked into Nelson's feed. The Yaks had built up something around the Ares tanks, along with a network of building pods and modules. They were serious about taking the Ares, unlike the Wolves.

The security perimeter wasn't too bad. More robots but not enough to form a complete line. Eight more guardthings, but only the three they'd killed would be on their path inward. Dozens of Yakuza. Vibs counted forty-three unique outdoors, likely seventy-five or more total present. They walked closer.

Finally they came to the plateau overlooking the Ares zone. The Yaks were building a rocket right around the tanks. It was short, only tall enough to encase them. It had small fuel tanks, enough to lift off but nowhere near enough to get to Earth.

"We're going to head for the conveyor and get ourselves home before these eggs die off," said Weasel.

Veikko nodded. Neither the PRA nor Valkyries were prone to long good-byes, so after Varg snogged Spit for a solid five minutes, the rebels left for home, leaving V team alone on the plateau. Nelson returned to Violet shortly after they left. She felt whole again with her Tikari back in her chest after so long. Nelson recharged greedily.

They elected to wait for nightfall to make their incursion into the Yak base. They were close enough to venture a hack into the Yakuza network, so each went for a different Yak. The first few Violet found were hack armored and would need bores to read, but one technician was wide open. His mind gave some idea as to why the rocket was so simple. The team shared their findings at dusk.

Violet spoke first. "They've carved out Enyo, a tiny natural satellite. This rocket will only take the tanks up into orbit where they'll put them inside. Enyo has been fitted with the thrusters necessary to take it into Earth orbit. I'm sure they have something ready to take them over there."

Vibeke had hacked a communications officer. "There's concern about that. The Unspeakable Darkness are attacking Yak interests on Earth. They expect they're going to attempt to steal the Arcs when it comes into orbit. Both are UNEGA, but the political situation down there must be going berserk. If we set off the nuke, there's almost no question there would be an intra-UNEGA war."

"Also it would vaporize us," added Varg.

"The sabotage option seems our best approach," said Vibeke. "We keep them from taking off. No nukes, no risk."

"Agreed," added Varg, "but I caught something else from my hack into one of the security team. The UD isn't just attacking on Earth. They think they have a platoon on Mars."

"The Darkness on Mars?"

"They may try to take the rocket here and bring it back themselves with Yak equipment."

"That would certainly complicate matters."

"Yes, it would. But it can work to our advantage. When the UD come, we'll have a chance to destroy the thrusters, security will be occupied, and it'll be the perfect distraction for the rest. All we have to do is survive the attack."

"I'm still not convinced," said Veikko. "No battle will end this. Even breaking open the tanks wouldn't stop it. They'd just ship the mud back to Earth. The Ares water seems determined to stay existent. All we can do is delay, and with the UD coming, there'll be two major forces trying to bring it home. We'd have to stay here indefinitely to keep each new threat from securing the water. I say we get on the conveyer and nuke the thing from Barsoom. It's the only way to be sure."

"It's not an option anymore," said Varg. "The Geki would kill us all."

The four considered it; it seemed likely. They'd have to find a way to permanently sabotage the Yakuza efforts.

Mishka's eye left their conversation and returned to her in the abandoned Wolf stronghold.

Chapter VI: Vastitas Borealis

V TEAM prepared a simple Mug-For-Disguise incursion. They'd knock out a couple periphery guard teams of two and, once in their uniforms, start by checking out whether the nuke was still intact.

On one hand there was no reason it shouldn't be. The organic warhead would simply appear to be part of the Ares tanks to anyone who didn't know what the tanks were designed to look like. On the other hand, a simple alpha scan would reveal there was an atomic bomb strapped to the things. There was far too much built up around the tanks to see from a distance and too many people working there to send a Tikari, so Yak suits were the order of the day.

The four descended from the plateau and lurked just outside of the guard perimeter. The first couplet of guards was rotating in to place. They matched Varg and Violet in stature so they headed out first.

Vibeke and Veikko monitored with microwaves ready in case their teammates' stuns were ineffective and the guards had to be killed. Vibeke moved in closer for a better shot and hid behind a large rock. There she saw two corpses.

Violet and Varg moved closer, microwaves at the ready, sticking to the blind spots afforded by the guards' breathing apparatuses.

Vibeke examined the bodies. Both had Yakuza tattoos. Both had public link labels as guards 37 and 38. Vibeke looked at the guards Violet and Varg were about to stun. Publicly labeled as guards 37 and 38. She linked immediately to her team.

"Those aren't guards, someone beat us to it!"

The message hit Violet the same instant she fired a stunning beam at the first. It had no effect. The guard's replacement turned around, and Violet saw its face. It looked like four black hands opening up to reveal a single bloodshot eye. Violet stumbled back. She set her microwave to kill and fired again. It burned off the front of the suit's chest, but the creature was undisturbed. From the hole came two tentacles with spiked suckers, reaching for her face.

Varg's sword chopped them off. The thing let loose a howl that sent a shiver through Violet's chest.

The Unspeakable Darkness. Bodies modified to the point of inhumanity and beyond.

Varg swung again to behead the monster but only shattered its helmet. The second guard impostor broke out of its suit and grabbed him with the taloned claw it had in place of a head. Its true face became visible as its suit tore off, four eyes in its chest with a gruesome toothed set of three flaps for a mouth. Two legs unfolded from each leg of its suit, two arms from each arm. The thing had made a spider of itself.

Varg ran it through with no effect. There was no telling where an Unspeakable kept its vital organs. It pushed him off, throwing him past Violet. She fired again at the center of the thing that threw Varg. Her beam hit its "face," and she could see its eyes burn. She was certain she'd blinded it. She turned to the other Unspeakable. It had torn out of its suit to reveal that it was two bodies, one on top with the bloodshot eye and one below with no eyes, just a mass of limbs. A question shot through her head of what kind of human beings would modify themselves into such abominations. She fired again at the top Unspeakable at full strength.

Vibeke's microwave hit it too, and then Veikko's. The crossed beams resulted in a protonic reversal, and the Unspeakable exploded. They realized what happened and fired again at the lower beast, vaporizing most of its torso.

The spidery creature grabbed Violet with the claw it had in place of a head. She ejected her Tikari and sliced at its "neck." The segments were armored, and she couldn't get her knife between them.

Veikko and Vibeke fired again at its back. Its skin boiled and puckered, but it remained. Varg's sword emerged from the face on its chest, run through again but to no avail. It began squeezing Violet's head. The crushing force was immense, seconds from knocking her out or crushing her skull completely.

Veikko ejected his Tikari and rammed it down the creature's throat, then let go. He set it to berserker mode and let it wreak havoc inside the thing. Slowly it let go of Violet and collapsed to the ground. Veikko recalled his Tikari and wiped it off on the guard suit's sleeve.

A massive blast hit one of the Yakuza barracks. The shockwave knocked V team off their feet. Violet looked up for the source of the blast. She saw a contrail leading to the destroyed building. It came from a flying bundle of worms.

The UD ship was massive and grotesque. At first glance it looked like worms tied together with more worms, but from within the mass came spines like an urchin's. It had a shield, a shell of some sort on its front, rendering it completely unaerodynamic and asymmetrical. It was slick black but painfully visible in the Yakuza's bright work lamps. Violet almost wished it weren't. Something about its appearance got under her skin the same way as the Unspeakables themselves. Their ship hurt to look at, to think about. It fired again.

One of the spines bloated and disgorged a missile that armed and flew for another structure, demolishing it in a colossal red blast.

All hell broke loose as the Yakuza shuttles unleashed projectile fire at the Unspeakable ship. The construction site was now an inferno, burning dim in the oxygen-poor air. Only the rocket under construction seemed untouched. Both sides were avoiding harming their prize.

"Mission's still on. Confirm the nuke. Sabotage the rocket," Veikko shouted. And they ran.

Violet found herself dodging shrapnel and corpses alike. Running as fast as she could for the rocket, her suit's breathing apparatus spraying mist up toward her eyes. Another blast from the UD knocked them all back, but they scrambled to their feet and kept running.

Yaks stampeded around them, running from the Unspeakable ship, for cover, in any direction they thought would save them. Except for one guard. Violet knew from its stance it was another Unspeakable in disguise. She drew her microwave again and fired. The others took her cue and fired, disintegrating its suit. That left a horrible sight, a burning monster, this one with an elongated double-lobed head that split in the front to reveal long, spiny teeth.

The Unspeakable figures were like a symphony of horror, every limb tweaked to make skin crawl. The burning monster's arms looked broken, jointed in the wrong places, and pierced with gold rings. Violet fired again with no effect.

Varg ran straight for it and cut it in half with his sword, but not before it had launched a dozen spines into the side of his face. He didn't stop running as he yanked them out, ignoring the barbs and letting them tear his skin.

He ran to the left of the team as they headed for the rocket, and he got detoured on a ramp. Violet stopped under the end of the incline and linked to Varg that they were right beneath him. He jumped off the incline onto a soft canopy, then adeptly let himself fall onto a soft mound of packaging, and then, less gracefully, facedown into a hard pile of nails.

He didn't even bother to remove the ones that stuck. He and Violet just started running, and they fell out one by one. Closer to the rocket, Yaks were standing their ground against UD troops, some even charging against them with drawn swords. A fierce battle raged around them as they ran. Flaming Unspeakables unperturbed by microwaves, mutilated Yakuza fighting to the last breath. Total mayhem.

They arrived at the rocket, surrounded by Yakuza. The Yaks ignored Valknut completely. Violet jumped up onto the rocket's superstructure, a square around the tanks with thrusters at each corner. She made her way inward toward the tanks and caught the first glimpse of the nuclear warhead. It looked simple and downright pretty compared to the monsters that were attacking, something like a cephalopod disguised as a structure across the top of the tanks. It opened its eye as Varg approached, recognizing its trigger.

Violet linked out for anyone who didn't see it that the nuke was intact. Half the mission complete. Now it was time to sabotage the rocket.

Vibeke was already looking over the thrusters and comparing their designs to records in her partitioned memory. Trying to find a weakness. She was interrupted when a shake rattled the superstructure.

At first they all thought it had been hit by a UD missile, but when they looked for the flames, they found them directly below. And sustained. Coming from the thrusters. They hadn't been hit—the Yakuza were launching prematurely with a half-finished ship to get the tanks away from the attack. The rocket began to lift.

"Stay or go?" asked Violet.

"We get off and nuke it as soon as it's in space!" shouted Veikko.

"The Geki would kill us all," replied Varg.

"We stay and sabotage, crash it before it breaks gravity. Let 'em clean up a kilometer of mud to get the Ares," voted Vibeke. "Might make it financially unfeasible, and they'll give up."

"I'm with Vibs," called Violet.

"Same," called Varg.

Veikko cursed and grabbed a pipe leading to the thrusters. "Then we take it down slow, disable one thruster at a time."

Vibeke called back, "Thick red pipe on each is O_2. They're far enough not to ignite if we cut 'em."

Varg immediately took his Tikari and brought it down on the nearest pipe. It cracked and pressurized gas spat into the air. The thruster seemed to be working fine, though. He swung again, and the pipe was severed completely. The thruster began to fizzle.

They were already thirty meters up and still rising. The thing seemed fine on three thrusters. They began scaling the remaining scaffold to reach the next. With two down, it would have no way to remain stable. It would crash slowly. They'd just need to jump when it drew low to the surface. Inertial negation fields and low Martian gravity would keep them safe.

Violet reached a catwalk that, though rumbling violently, provided a path to the next thruster. Gravity was increasing with acceleration, and atmosphere was almost gone. Mars was falling away fast beneath them.

Vibeke and the others made it to the catwalk after her. Violet looked back after them. As soon as Vibs was atop the metal grate, she drew her Tikari. Violet didn't understand until she turned around.

Mishka crouched on the catwalk, microwave in hand.

Mishka drew and shot Violet with a killing beam. It hit her in the center of her chest armor, which absorbed most of it. The remaining sparks burned horribly, as if she'd swallowed acid. She fell to the inner scaffold and clutched her chest, then struggled to pull an internal coolant from her Thaco pocket. She barely caught sight of a melted coolant pack in her hand before her vision began to fade.

Valhalla was half an astronomical unit away. They were in space already, and even if they could get back to Mars, she was doomed without a coolant pack. As her vision flickered, Varg arrived with his own and forced it into the Tikari slot on her chest. Nelson ducked out of its way, butting into her xiphoid process. The coolant field activated, and the relief was phenomenal. A soothing feeling like nothing she'd felt before. Varg hit her with an adrenaline syrette, and her vision returned.

"Stay down, you can't move yet," he said. She could hear Vibeke and Mishka fighting on the catwalk. She tried to prop herself up to see but couldn't move without pain ripping through her chest. She was forced to lie down as Vibeke fought her nemesis to the death.

Vibeke drew her microwave and fired a wide beam at Mishka. She countered with her own. They knew it was a stalemate and ran for each other, beams conflicting and sparking.

Vibeke kicked Mishka's microwave from her hand, off the rocket and into the Martian sky, then readied her microwave to fire the final beam. Mishka grabbed her leg and threw her off the catwalk. Her microwave fell from the rocket alongside her. Veikko tractored her back in place before she fell away, then switched back to kill, ready to take any shot at Mishka that came clear.

Vibeke and Mishka fought in a barrage of slugs and kicks that betrayed their precarious, shaking spot. Gravity was growing less and less now, acceleration altering to freefall. Vibs got a kick in that nearly sent Mishka into the void, but she caught a pipe and scaled back down.

A fistfight was hopeless in zero-g. Both would be thrown into space. Mishka clawed her way to the other side of the rocket and locked herself to the scaffolding with a diamond filament tether. She checked her oxygen, 90 percent. She had almost two days left. If they docked with a larger craft, she'd be fine. If they headed for Earth, she'd scale the rocket and drag Vibeke into the void with her.

V team regrouped. Vibeke was on top of her rage and didn't waste a second finding Mishka. The thrusters were off. Gravity was over, she and Violet tied into the catwalk, Veikko and Varg to the scaffolding. They all checked their O_2 constructors and vacuum shielding. All working at maximum capacity. They could last almost a month at regular metabolism. Over a year if they took internal cryo-tabs.

But the mission had failed. They were on their way to Earth with the Ares water.

Veikko linked, "Don't worry, I won't nuke us in space."

"As if I'd let you." Varg tightened the trigger around his neck.

"What are we gonna do?"

"We can't risk sabotage between planets. If the Ares falls into the sun, it ends the solar system. We need to get off when we get to Earth and nuke it there."

"That *will* cause a war, without question."

"We cannot allow the Ares to exist on Earth. It's not an option."

"I disagree."

"Well, we have a month in space to argue about it, Varg."

Enyo appeared overhead, first as a bright dot, then as an asteroid, technically Mars's smallest moon. They could tell on approach it was only a bit larger than the rocket. It had a hatch carved into its side.

The docking procedure was simple and smooth, and the five apparent corpses latched to the rocket were ignored. As the rocket docked, they got a better look at Enyo. It was fitted with one massive thruster on one side and a tiny cockpit on the other. A cheap interplanetary craft, but it would do the job.

As the rocket passed through into the hollow rock, Mishka detached and pushed out against the rocket, hurtling into space.

She had only one chance to survive, and she took it, aiming for the cockpit. Her jump was spot on. She was obscured by the door to V team and went unseen. The cockpit slowly loomed closer and closer to her until she approached the ties holding it down and caught in their web. She held on to the thickest line of the bunch and pulled her way toward the cockpit. All over its side were handholds leading to the airlock.

She felt around for active links inside and found two. She broadcast.

"Sanchita Patel, Havildar CMP for Bharatiya Sthalsena, on your hull."

A Yak ran to the cockpit side window and looked out. Mishka smiled and waved with her free hand.

As soon as the massive door closed, V team began scouring the rocket for Mishka. First in the darkness, looking for light, then in the dim light of their Tikaris, then in the bright light of their uniforms. After seven hours of searching, they determined she wasn't there.

She could have fallen, but somehow they all knew she'd made it to the cockpit. She didn't have Valhalla's armor anymore, only Bharatiya Sthalsena space capables. She couldn't live in deep space for months. She had to stay indoors.

And V team had to stay inside of Enyo. The door was closed, and no exit presented itself. A stalemate. The Valkyries tied themselves to the innermost scaffolding in the rocket. They took a month's worth of their cryo-tabs and their metabolisms slowed for the ride back to Earth.

VIOLET COULD feel the cold, inside her and out. Her suit was sealed for prolonged space travel. It didn't grow fur or cycle heating elements. It was designed to be used in conjunction with cryo-tabs, to let her freeze. The cryo-tab included analgesics, so it didn't hurt, but it still felt cold. An overwhelming cold, a deep cold unlike anything else. It also carried with it a strange sense of calm. Coupled with the vacuum silence and darkness of the Enyo interior, it felt far more deathly than any time she'd died.

Their links still functioned in low power mode. They could still talk and still see time pass one distorted second at a time. Mercifully with their bodies working at 1/30 of their usual speed, time felt fast. Hours felt like minutes, minutes like seconds. The trip would feel like a day.

All four went into deep immersion. There things seemed almost normal, though the net was far away, and all they had was each other. In their lucid dream, they plotted ways to kill Mishka, ways to destroy the Ares, all the relevant mission issues they could think up. But there was little resolution beyond their admission they'd have to ask Valhalla to advise once they got in range.

Before long Varg receded into his porn partition and Veikko started playing solitaire, leaving Vibeke and Violet just as they were on the trip to Mars and inside the guardthing. Alone together.

In her few waking moments outside the link, Violet was completely aware of her proximity to Vibeke. Though there was no light and no air to convey warmth, she could feel Vibeke centimeters away from her, floating before her. Through the cold vacuum, Violet swore she could feel heat radiating off of Vibeke's back, an impossible feeling yet more real and urgent than anything else in the ship, more intimidating than the mission ahead and more intense than the shaking thruster behind them, rushing to Earth on a constant burn. They were willing to melt the thruster to get there fast.

She let her suit illuminate a sliver of light and stared at the back centerline of Vibeke's armor. Run a finger down the seam to unzip the back, peel off the front to expose the chest, pull that down, the metal all falls off, and the rest just slips away. Vibeke did that every day they were home, she thought, every time she jumped into the showers, every time she undressed to wander the ravine in a thin shirt and shorts (And how cold she looked in that shirt). Mishka undid Vibeke's armor once too, on some hot day in a distant jungle. And they did more. All the things Violet would never do. She should have tried on that night in the monster. Gross, covered in gore, the least romantic setting imaginable would have been better than the nothing she'd have now. She couldn't open Vibeke's armor now without killing her.

So she just crouched there behind her, doing nothing. Thinking everything. Indulging memories of brief glimpses of a bare breast or a towel that shifted to reveal another stretch of skin. Imagining sex with Vibs in comically exaggerated fantasy.

"It doesn't feel like space without the stars," linked Vibeke.

"I wasn't thinking about stars," Violet replied.

"What were you thinking about?"

She was thinking about bending Vibeke over the scaffold and fisting her up to the elbow.

"Potatoes," she replied. "I haven't had potatoes since before I came to the ravine."

"You had chips just before we left."

"Chips are potatoes?"

"Yeah, crisps too."

"Wow, you learn something new every day," she chirped. A few seconds passed, nearly an hour in reality.

"What are you really thinking about?"

"Zero-g sex."

"No wonder you can't read. Your brain only has one compartment."

"I should have fucked you in that guardthing."

"You would."

"I almost did."

"Thanks for restraining yourself. You're a real mensch."

"So you can never love me. I'm fine with that"—she wasn't—"so we have nothing to lose. Why not just feel good together? Friends with benefits."

"Because we are friends. Maybe you don't value that, but I still do. But keep it up, that might change."

"And then you'll have sex with me?"

"How do you even remember to breathe?"

"Around you, sometimes I forget."

"How sweet."

"Yeah, Vibs, it is sweet. And it's not just sex. Maybe you think you're incapable of love, but where do you get off denying mine? If I just wanted to fuck you, I would have the second you said it. I didn't because I'm not after your body. I mean, I am but not only your body. I want the girl that disemboweled Veikko on her first sparring match. The one who killed her father and survived prison for it. The Valkyrie who fought by my side, the woman who stood angry next to me in Cato's office. The smart one who actually gets that Cloutier shit. Cuz I sure as hell don't. It's fucking gibberish half the time, but I packed a series of it because I feel closer to you when I load it. That's not sex. It's love. And it's not my fault they come packaged together."

Days passed. Vibeke's mind cycled through an impossible loop of love, and even lust, for the woman behind her. And hate for the way she could act.

"Isn't there anything that could make you give up this stilted bullshit and just... give in?"

Vibeke gave it genuine thought. "Only if we could go back in time and make Mishka never happen. Or if you were no more than an AI, programmed never to betray me. If you were subhuman, if you belonged to me."

"I'm willing to belong to you."

"You're a Valkyrie. Not a slave. I'd rather have you as a warrior friend than a love slave."

"I'd trade."

"I know."

"I'd leave the team for you."

"I know."

"I'd give up Wulfgar. The thrill of any mission. There's nothing on either planet I wouldn't do for you."

"Except shut the fuck up."

Violet stopped talking. She'd happily prove that one. She wouldn't talk the entire way home. If that's all it took, it would be the easiest day of her life. But that's not what it would take, was it? Vibeke was only kidding. The best she'd ever get was a grope or maybe on some lucky day another kiss on the cheek. Vibeke was a waste. She'd be better off tying Gabrielle to a bed. At least that was a person she could stand to hurt. Or worse.

She had to push Vibeke out of her mind, somehow. To give up. Move on. She'd done it before, for a while. Pushed Vibeke out of that part of her mind. It worked for months. With practice she could do it for good. Violet had no experience with any other addiction, but the sort of mind that can stay calm through murder, through torture, through the worst the world had to offer wasn't completely helpless against a schoolgirl crush. She knew what she had to do. Abrupt withdrawal. Immediate cessation of all action, all thought, all talk. Vibeke told her to shut up, and that she would do. She'd do it better than Vibs ever imagined. She'd never speak of it, nor feel it again. It was over.

Or not.

"How about online? We could just have sex online, you know."

"Shut up, Violet."

CAPTAIN PRESTON got his dream job. Delivery: 1 crate. 88kg. From Sidi Bouzid Spaceport to UNEGA 07. Payment: 1,375,000 euros. It would keep him alive for years, a massive paycheck just to stay on retainer for a few days in August. He hired on Burke and Samno for the trip. He didn't need them, but he owed them, and it was the best way to pay them.

He kept thinking it would fall through. It was too good to really happen. But it was happening. Launch date approached, and just as they said they would, Underwood/Dawson LLC delivered the crate. It looked like any other crate, hardly worth what they were paying. But he didn't question a thing. They paid him what they paid him because word got around—he didn't question. He didn't care what he was delivering so long as it paid enough. And 1,375,000 euros was more than enough. For that kind of cash, he'd deliver the crate if it were screaming that it were only a child.

He fired up the main engine on the Lampyrid and took off with the crate in the high security hold. From there the computer took over. It sorted out his place in traffic, it secured the right orbit, it adjusted toward UNEGA 07, and the rest was a matter of what to eat on the way.

He ate some extra spicy chili garlic jerky.

UNEGA 07 came in to view. Preston told his men to get to the cargo bay. He stayed for a moment in the cockpit to see the station. It was a beauty. Forty years in the making for a slick silver crystal in space. Not a ring or a clump of modules but a genuine Gehry VI design. Ruined, of course, by the dozens of shuttles and ships stuck to its exterior but an astounding sight nonetheless. He turned over his controls to UNEGA 07 to dock him where they pleased.

The dock was his smoothest ever. Not like UNEGA 04, which crumpled his aft docking brace. It was like a gentle caress guiding him in, like the airlock was kissing his side.

The hatches opened, and a friendly voice welcomed him. It was so real, he expected to see a woman there to greet him, but that was just 07's computer. Truly it was a masterpiece station. He floated out into the main hall, and the cargo floated behind him. The trio guided it gently down the hall toward bay 16. He opened the locker with the code they'd given him and pushed the crate inside. Job done.

He patted the crate with a laugh and joked, "Enjoy your stay!"

"Thanks," said the crate.

Preston wasn't surprised. He didn't feel betrayed or the least bit alarmed. After all, people didn't pay him 1,375,000 euros to ship carrots.

THE CRYO-tabs began to thaw as they approached Earth. Alopex knocked at their heads as soon as her signal was strong enough to be secure. They let her in, eager for news from home. Violet didn't know what she expected. Whatever was happening couldn't have been good. Alf spoke.

"Your mission rated a 96 percent efficiency in design but a 7 percent in practice. Better than E team's 0 percent effective. They were caught by the Yakuza and took two weeks to escape. With Mishka and without E team, you simply had no chance. It looks like our best course of action would have been to detonate the nuclear weapon on Mars."

Veikko tried hard not to look smug. He was 0 percent effective at it.

"The effects couldn't have been much worse than what's already happening. Zaibatsu has split in half. UNEGA is nearing a state of civil war. GAUNE is considering hostile takeovers of up to 80 percent of their assets in the crisis. UNEGA has accused GAUNE of readying illegal wave bombs for deployment. Paranoia abounds."

"What's our best course of action now?"

"Alopex suggests it's to steal the Ares and keep it unassembled in Valhalla. Too close for comfort, but at least we'd control it. This would also guarantee an assault on our base by Pelamus. We may be in for a long night under the rampart."

Veikko spoke. "If we're going to keep it at Valhalla and defend it there, we might as well give it to Pelamus. We'll be defending the critical half anyway."

"There may be means to render it impossible to use that we can discover while it's in our possession. H team suggests we rush research into chemically destroying the Ares. Balder suggests we hide it. C team suggests we dissolve it in the ocean. That would in fact flood the Earth, but without the YGDR S/L kick, it would take millennia. Valfar suggests we all buy boats. As you're the only team onboard, you have a say in the matter, V. What say you?"

"We nuke it as soon as we can get out of the way," said Veikko.

"A nuclear blast on Earth on UNEGA soil, Veikko? You would all but guarantee a nuclear war."

"All but."

"Veikko, I realize you can set off the warhead. I realize you want to despite the risks. I won't pretend I can stop you. But don't forget the Geki, the treaty."

"Right, we all know what the Geki will do. But if we nuke it, what will *you* do?"

Alf was silent for a moment. "I'll rejoice that the Ares dilemma is over, Veikko."

Veikko pursed his lips.

"And then I'll sweep up your ashes and polish the floor. Any other ideas, Valknut?"

Violet thought of any scrap of a plan to propose. She might have felt worse, but even Vibeke had nothing to offer either.

"Very well, the Ares is coming home. Your mission is now to capture the Ares water by any means necessary and bring it here. If you lose the Ares…. You make the call. We read you at twenty minutes to orbit. Our intel suggests they plan to dock at UNEGA 07 and transfer the Ares to a cargo shuttle currently docked there.

"UNEGA 07 will be over Prešov when you arrive, and there's an alarming buildup of Yakuza and UD shuttles in that area. It's clear the Unspeakables intend to steal the Ares on its way down."

"Any sign of the Wolves?" asked Violet.

"None. We're inclined to concur with your analysis that it was a feint to distract the Yakuza. Yak assets have fallen apart in the last month. We can't even tell who seized what yet. Regardless, when this is all over, we'll head to Hashima and slay the Wolf. And Varg?"

He was almost startled. "Yes?"

"Our teams online keep getting requests to buy the Skunkworks Blackwing, so we can assume the entire net knows we have it. Would you happen to know anything about that?"

"I might have confirmed something to that effect, yes."

"If you survive, your next mission will be to rectify the situation."

"Will do."

"Stay frosty, kids, or rather thaw out and get ready to fight. We have four teams en route to Prešov right now, but there's nothing to suggest the Yaks or Unspeakables intend to keep it in the region. Orbit's a long way up. You're the only team we know will be there wherever they go. Capture the Ares and get it back to Valhalla. That's your mission. Don't Fuck Shit Up."

Alopex sent them link dumps of all the relevant information. There was little time once they were thawed. UNEGA 07 was only forty minutes away.

GRISTLE CHECKED his scope and waited for the hall to empty. When it was, he got out of his crate and entered the locker code. He floated out into UNEGA 07's main storage hall and took a deep breath. It was finally time.

His entire life had lead up to this moment. Seventeen years prior, he was born in Qabis to a pathetic family of farmers. He was the first in his line with any ambition to do more. To that end he got a job in town. It annoyed his parents at first, but in time they agreed to let him follow his own path. They were even proud when that path led him to Ez-Zitouna University. He took his tests and made his way in as an adult at sixteen.

There, majoring in medical ethics, he met Gloom. Gloom was a transhumanist. He didn't look human. He was tall, sleek, glowing white with big, deep green eyes. He was beautiful. And he taught Gristle, named Moncef at the time, that he too could be something more. But Moncef became greedy. The mods he wanted weren't, well, they weren't legal. He confessed it to Gloom and expected to be let down, but he was not.

Gloom knew some people who would do those mods. They were in fact his "other" employers. They called themselves Underwood/Dawson LLC or "UD" for short, but they had another name for those among them who leaned toward darker, less legal modifications. Thus Moncef left college early to join the Unspeakable Darkness.

He traded his arms for tentacles. He got new eyes like Gloom's. He had his body lengthened and twisted, and he got those illegal suckers he wanted, the kind with spines. He got the illegal legs he wanted, not armed but copyrighted and not affordable by anyone but the richest CEOs. But most importantly, he took the traditional jet black skin. The glossy, slick black of the Unspeakable Darkness. He took it after an oath of loyalty and after learning its symbolism and severity.

He survived the initiation in which the black was injected into his every pore over the course of five days, the Dark Trial all Unspeakables withstood. And he was reborn as Gristle of the Unspeakable Darkness. His parents were informed of his death, as Moncef was indeed dead. The obsolete larval stage of a new man.

His first mission was a high honor. And an easy task to perform. All he had to do was get in a crate and withstand a bit of zero-g. He was there on UNEGA 07 before he knew it, flown by a particularly polite pilot.

His mission came with some degree of freedom. So long as he finished by 1500 hours, he was free to wander the station. Heaven. He was free to wander heaven. He floated about, guided by his phenomenal legs, which had pressure ports for swimming or null gravity. He looked out the windows and saw Earth far below, far behind him. He felt only vaguely sad he would never return.

And then he saw a woman. A woman in uniform. She was beautiful, floating in her blue jumpsuit, arms covered in patches, hair short but free floating. She would be his last sight. She screamed of course. Humans weren't used to the UD. It was sad she had to die scared, a bittersweet end. But no problem for Gristle. He had been spotted, and it was time to perform his mission before someone might prevent him.

He detonated his marrow bombs and ceased to exist.

UNEGA 07 took longer to fall apart. There were fires and shrapnel, the ugly demise of a beautiful place. Most of it fell back to Earth, burning up over the Caspian Sea or splashing down in voluminous sprays of water.

All crew were lost, the worst disaster in the history of space exploration. But all to a purpose. Somewhere out there was a ship that was to dock there. It wouldn't anymore. It would go down in the atmosphere, all except for one part that the Unspeakable Darkness could now steal and sell at an extraordinary record profit.

Worth every life.

ALOPEX REPORTED the destruction to V team. With nowhere to dock, Enyo could enter orbit and be swarmed by the UD, or it could fall to Earth. The UD would have a plan to harvest it in the sky, the Yakuza might not.

Alopex reported that the buildup of UD and Yakuza fleet over the High Tatras was monumental, a massive battle had already begun. She confirmed the UD had one vessel of massive cargo capabilities. None of the Yakuza vessels seemed to. As soon as news of the station's destruction had reached Valhalla, T team departed in the P0S to grab the Valkyries in space if necessary. But the space flight was almost over. Alopex confirmed Enyo didn't have enough fuel to adjust its course, and without the station's tractoring system to slow it down, it would enter the atmosphere and crash in the High Tatras.

V team began cutting their way out. The rock was thick, and the microwaves were small, but their best hope was to jump in space and hope the P0S caught them. The microwaves quickly proved incapable of penetrating the rock.

Alopex linked that the cockpit had left Enyo and was coming in for a soft landing over the mountains. Mishka was safe on Earth. Vibeke hoped that, if nothing else, Enyo would hit her when it fell.

Suddenly a blast cracked the small moon in half. The sides fell away in seconds, leaving the spent rocket falling through the atmosphere. The wind was too great and the rotation of the rocket too unpredictable to risk unhooking themselves. Violet called out to T team.

"ETA three minutes," they replied.

Vibeke shouted and linked at the same time, "We impact in one!"

The mountains hurtled toward them, jagged and gray. As they grew closer, they could see the UD cargo vessel. It was massive and under attack. Closer, they saw dozens of pogos, UD wyrms, unidentifiable vehicles in the insane furball of combat.

Suddenly, the rocket jolted. They knew instantly that it was a tractoring beam because it flexed their suits. It hit again, and again, until it caught the rocket and began slowing its descent.

The massive magnetic force also began deforming their Thaco armor. They hit the emergency bolts and broke off their armor seconds before it twisted into shapes that would have killed them inside. That also broke their connection to the rocket.

Very suddenly they were falling free over the mountains in only the internal, soft portions of their suits. No more Thaco armor, no more inertial negators, no more emergency parachutes, or anything that could halt their fall.

Chapter VII: Prešov

THE ENYO cockpit set down in a small clearing. Mishka linked to her tank. It was only minutes away.

"There are two Yami fleets, one to the east and one to the south," said Supika.

Sonohoka reviewed the Yakuza datastream. "We have seven carriers, fourteen destroyers, nineteen battle pogos. All fire is focused on the Yami cargo vessel."

"Where are the stowaways?"

"Not detected. They don't appear to be on the Ares rocket."

"Find them, now."

"Yes, Havildar Patel, but the Ares—"

"The Ares is a secondary concern compared to the stowaways. I need their location now!"

"Yes, Havildar! Scanning!"

Mishka's tank was under a kilometer away. She stepped outside. The thick air was like pudding in her lungs, the smell of rock overpowering compared to the synthetic air she'd breathed for the last two months. She crouched down and gathered some dirt in her hand. It was mostly pebbles, gray and chipped. She heard the tank and stood.

It limped quickly up to her position and stopped, its underside steaming. Mishka linked it to open its cargo hold. Inside were her two cutter rifles. She took both and strapped them in an X on her back. She stormed into the cockpit hatch.

"Have you found them?"

"I believe so, Havildar. They've fallen from the rocket, nearing terminal velocity. They'll die upon impact in one minute and forty—"

"They won't die," she said. "They never do."

She looked at their position on the map and left the cockpit. She opened the top of her tank and hopped in, leaving it open to keep the rifles on her person. She linked the map into her tank and told it to run at top speed. If they splattered on the rocks, she'd be there to vaporize the remains.

V TEAM drifted farther apart as the wind rose up from beneath them. The crags seemed to fly toward them. The wind ripped the trigger from around Varg's neck, and it fell toward the cliffs.

The P0S hurtled toward them, pointing straight down and matching their speed, it swept forward to engulf Violet in its open cargo hold, then Veikko and Vibeke. It pulled up as it captured Varg and closed the hold only seconds before it started scratching the mountains. It was still planing upward when it hit the mountainside full force, tearing off the bottom of the fuselage and shaking V and T teams to their bones. The smart foam inside the shuttle expanded and cushioned them, nearly suffocating them.

The P0S shattered through more rock and slowed, breaking its nose cone beyond repair and tearing off the left wing. It came to a screeching stop at the bottom of a rugged valley, steaming and shattered. Violet stumbled out of the cracked hold, Varg behind her. They looked back to see Veikko and Vibs climb out uninjured.

T team was close behind, pouring out of the cockpit. Immediately they came under fire. Projectile shots from a Yakuza force rattled across the spent hull. V team was painfully aware of the loss of their armor, which generated projectile shields and defended against microwaves. They were essentially naked to every weapon. T team provided cover. They all ran toward the rocks.

"Well, no more P0S, thank God. We'll have to use the Burp," coughed Toshiro.

Tahir linked back to Alopex, "Tell H team the die is cast. We have crashed the Rubicon."

"Thanks for the... for the uh... the saving and shit," Veikko called out.

"No problem, it was worth it to wreck that thing," said Trygve.

They looked around the sharp rocks and tried to get their bearings. The landmarks weren't pleasing.

To the north was an air battle, dozens of Yakuza shuttles and pogos firing on one massive ugly UD cargo ship. The battle was gradually spilling south toward them. To the east was a land battle where a legion of Yaks fired at rolling masses of deformed Unspeakable. To the south, as best as they could estimate, the trigger had fallen, and in the distant west, Violet saw for the shortest instant a three legged tank.

"We head south. We need to find the trigger," said Veikko.

"We can't detonate it on Earth, Veikko, the Geki—"

"Fuck the Geki!" he shouted. "Fuck the Geki. It's on Earth, Vibs. The Ares is here, on the planet. There's no way to capture the Darkness ship that's tractoring it. The UD has the Ares. They will escape, and they will sell it, and the world will flood."

"The nuke will—"

"You know I'm right, Vibs! You know it. Look!"

She looked toward the aerial fight. The UD ship had the rocket tractored in midair. It was extending a sharp fueling pipe. It was going to siphon the Ares into its own tanks.

"If you have a better idea, Vibs...."

A series of blasts hit the nearby rocks, shattering their scant cover. Violet looked over to see Yaks with Gat-Zooks on a nearby plateau, loading another ribbon of rockets into the massive machine.

Before anyone in V or T could run, they fired again, but this time hitting well over the teams' heads. Violet looked up. Deformed black body parts were raining down on them. There were Unspeakables up the hill, the Yak's true targets. They had little time before the Yaks eradicated them and turned back to the Valkyries.

V and T began running south. All seven with flying Tikaris ejected them and sent them to scour the landscape for the trigger. None could activate it, and none could lift the heavy organic, but left to their own AI search patterns, they'd be perfect for finding it. Violet was very aware that without her microwave or Tikari, she was now completely unarmed.

They heard a scream, a guttural deranged scream coming from overhead. A Darkness shuttle was broken and trying to land. Its organic engines belched out a bloodcurdling howl. Its flight path was erratic, and there was no telling where it would touch down. V kept running south until they had reason to expect it would hit them.

It rammed into a rock face and fell down to their southeast. Unspeakables poured out. They looked at first like a stream of black guts. It was impossible to differentiate between them. But soon the distinct beasts became clear, and they were headed for the teams. Veikko linked to Alopex and asked when the next teams would arrive. Nearest ETA twenty-eight minutes. Useless.

Mishka saw the two teams form a wedge against the oncoming Darkness. She sent her eye closer to get a good look. T team was in full armor with microwaves drawn at the front. V team was armorless and weaponless. All too easy.

She drew her left rifle and fired at V team. Plasma ripped through the air and cut off a chunk of Vibeke's cheek, cauterizing it with tremendous heat and setting fire to her hair. She ducked and rolled back away from the beam.

Tahir saw it and looked for its source, then fired a suppressing beam. His teammates fired full force at the Unspeakables, with no effect.

"Mishka!" shouted Violet, now certain she'd seen the tank. Vibeke jumped up and recalled her Tikari to find and kill Mishka. It turned around in midair and flew back toward them.

Another beam shot past Vibs, incinerating deep into the rock beside her. Then another, but the second beam was warped, twisting off target. The Yakuza were coming over the rocks to Mishka's south, firing every microwave they had at the Unspeakables, burning half of them to dust and deforming the air like a lens to Mishka's cutter rifle.

They had only seconds before the mass Yakuza microwave barrage hit them. The teams again ran south. Mishka set her tank to watch them and pursue with a fifty-meter gap, close enough to aim, far enough to remain safe from T team's microwaves.

Tahsa's Tikari spotted the trigger worm. It was caught on a cliffside, two kilometers southeast of their position. The terrain was unforgiving, sheer rock faces and jagged ground, nearly impossible to traverse by foot but mercifully impossible to traverse by tank. Again they ran. The teams reset their Tikaris to find Mishka.

Two Yakuza pogos flew overhead, and Violet looked up. The battle was closer, the great cargo ship now busily slurping away at the Ares tanks as it flew south to avoid the numerous Yakuza vessels throwing microwaves, bombs, projectile fire, and rockets. All seemed useless against its dragon-like armor.

"If the cargo flies low enough, we could tractor on, seize the ship and fly it home!" shouted Varg.

"That's a modified fang freighter. There's no way in," replied Vibs. "They armor themselves inside, have to disassemble the whole ship to get—"

Another cutter beam flew millimeters from her throat. She cursed loudly. Two of the Tikaris spotted the beam and began calculating its point of origin.

Mishka was already tired of near misses. Time to use her rifles like they were intended. She fired upward at the mountain looming over the teams. Slowly she cut through, breaking off sixty tons of rock that began to fall onto the team.

They heard it and knew the sound. T and V ran to the other side of the valley, narrowly escaping the falling crumbling rocks. Mishka fired again, this time directly at them. The beam hit Tasha and Trygve's armor, bouncing off randomly and cutting one of the Yakuza pogos in half.

Half of it flew on and crashed into the eastern cliff. The other half fell straight down and blocked their way through a pass to the south. They'd have to climb.

A Darkness APC rolled up behind Mishka, a vehicle like a bundle of Unspeakables sewn together, now splitting up and rolling down the rocks toward the valley. She kicked her tank and sent it farther south toward the pass. One Unspeakable tried to latch on to the tank's back leg. She cut it in half without slowing down.

Vibeke's Tikari stabbed into Mishka's shoulder, just missing her heart. She shrieked in pain and anger. The Tikari pried itself out of her collarbone for another strike. The other Tiks were quickly on the way. Mishka hit the top of her tank and lowered it, leaving only a slot for one of her rifles, smaller than the Tikari could pry into.

Violet ran up the rock wall until her legs began to slip, then started taking handholds and climbing. She was directly over the crashed pogo half when Mishka fired another mountain splitting beam. The landslide knocked her down into the open pogo backside and showered her with dozens of heavy rocks that beat her down into its floor.

She couldn't see her team, but she immediately recognized motion inside the pogo. Yakuza. The man leaped at her with a microwave and fired, singeing her shoulder badly. She kicked the microwave out of his hand and caught it midair, then fried a hole through his neck. Veikko and Toshiro landed in the pogo, exchanged brief glances, and then Violet fired at a window at the bottom of the tilted pogo, warping it and knocking it out onto the ground.

"Here!" Veikko shouted, and the teams followed into the new cave.

The terrain grew only more difficult on the other side of the pass. There was nowhere to run, only spires of rock to climb around, upward to the cliff across from the fallen trigger. They wasted no time lamenting it.

THE HEAT of the microwaves wreaked havoc with the atmosphere. Aside from bending Mishka's cutter beams, they created vortices in the sky that dragged clouds down toward the battle. It rained only briefly before the tips of the clouds were tugged to the ground, throwing hailstones onto the crooked battlefield.

The rocks grew slippery, and Violet had trouble climbing, sliding down and knocking Veikko and Varg back. She had no time to apologize. A glance upward showed the Ares tanks still connected to the UD ship. There was no way to know how long it would take to siphon the entire thing. They had to get to the trigger.

Suddenly a cutter rifle fell and stuck nozzle first into the ground. It fell between Vibeke and Toshiro. Vibeke couldn't imagine how Mishka could drop one of her rifles. She looked into her Tikari. Mishka was holding it at bay with her microwave as she closed her tank's canopy. She had thrown the rifle. She realized a second after Toshiro that she'd set it to overload. She turned and ran. Toshiro did not.

The rifle was sticking up in the center of their group, in proximity to kill everyone on T team and half of V team. Toshiro thought quickly and knew he was dead no matter what; the sheer rock on either side of him meant he couldn't escape the blast. So he decided to make his death as useful as he could.

He leaped onto the rifle and held open his armor, letting it slip over the particle accelerator. The blast vaporized his chest and head and threw plasma onto the surrounding rocks, burning off one of Tahir's arms and digging into Vibeke's back, burning off chunks of her remaining suit and through her skin down to the muscle. She screamed, but her voice was nothing compared to Tahir's. Trygve froze, and Tasha fired indiscriminately into the sky, trying to hit Mishka.

Toshiro's Tikari went ronin instantly and flew to their position, permanently stuck on AI due to the fast death of its owner. It hit the ground and began digging at the spot where Toshiro died, trying to uncover him from rubble that didn't exist. Out of mercy for it, Tasha fired point-blank into its core, ending what was left of her teammate.

Mishka cursed and closed her tank before the oncoming flock of Tikaris could make its way inside. Battered by hail, they were only flying at 60 percent efficiency. They were the least of her concerns. The blast was much smaller than she anticipated: she didn't see the epicenter and couldn't fathom why. She'd wasted one of her rifles on what should have been an unquestionable victory. It hit next to Vibs. It should have annihilated them all. But she climbed out only burned. Mishka cracked her canopy a centimeter, leveled her other rifle, and fired again directly at Vibeke.

The air was still thick with microwaves between the Darkness and Yakuza. The beam missed. The Yak ground forces were flooding south toward the crashed pogo half, and the Unspeakables were coming north straight to Mishka's position. She set her tank to climb the hill behind her and reach higher ground.

Hail pummeled Violet's hands and head as she climbed toward the edge of the cliff. The Unspeakables began firing at her, assuming she was Yakuza. She dropped down and felt microwaves burn past the top of her head. She led the teams downward, west through a thicket of rock spires into an alcove.

Tasha wasted no time and started tending to Tahir and Vibeke's burns, slathering them with analgesic and stasis gel.

Trygve wept Toshiro's name. There was nothing left of him to save. He was completely, irreparably gone.

Vibeke was resolved to kill Mishka. She looked into her Tikari and caught it flying overhead, but there was no sign of her.

"The trigger is on the cliff opposite this coming incline," explained Veikko. "It's crawling with UD. There's no cover."

"T will cover. We can keep the Darkness off you while you climb," promised Tasha.

"We've got our Tiks on Mishka," said Tahir. "They should keep her from firing once she emerges. We've got your backs. Just run."

Violet took no time to question, nor did her team. They left the alcove and ran for the incline.

Mishka spotted them as soon as they did and opened fire through the slit under her canopy. The microwaves distorted the beam just enough to miss Vibeke's head and slice an Unspeakable's wings off. It was only then that Mishka noticed the squadron of flying Unspeakables.

They began diving toward V team, grabbing Varg first and ripping into his chest. His Tikari unraveled and chopped one of the monster's claws off on its own. The team kept running.

T team laid down an expansive field of heat, sending most of the groundling Darkness behind the rocks. V was almost out of the rock field and to the incline when another beam from Mishka shot over their heads. Well over their heads, cutting the mountaintop.

The rockslide that followed was incalculable. Massive chunks of the mountain hurtled down toward them, fatal crushing weight in every boulder, and hundreds of boulders. Mishka narrowed her canopy again seconds before T's Tikaris hit.

The teams ran for the opposite side of the hill, into a patch of crouching Darkness who stood, only to run with them. Suddenly Yakuza began firing from the nearby cliff, microwaves coming down from the western sky, a mountain from the right.

Most of T team was out of the rock zone and let loose firing at the Yakuza. A flying Unspeakable teamed with them for an instant to pull several Yakuza from the wall and send them plummeting between the cliffs.

Violet was closest to T team and ran quickly out of the landslide's path. But when she looked back, she saw her team wasn't close enough.

The first rock hit Varg, killing him instantly as it crushed his chest and waist. The second sharp rock cut across Veikko's gut, crushing his pelvis and eviscerating him, sending a torrent of intestines out of him like a squashed bug. The third crushed Vibeke's legs, pinning her. Her Tikari made it back into her chest a fraction of a second before the fourth hit her back, killing her.

The rocks stopped short of burying them all. Violet ran toward them but had no Valkyrie microwave to tractor them out. The flying Unspeakable had turned on T team; their microwaves were busy.

Without thinking Violet ran straight through the center of fire and from speed alone made it to her team unscathed. The last rocks fell, one landing on her right leg and fracturing it against another stone.

Veikko called out, "The trigger! Hit the trigger!"

"I have to get you three—"

"We're dead! Now! The trigger!"

It was up the incline and across a chasm. She heard a great growl from the UD carrier, now south of them and still fending off dozens of Yakuza vessels. Its thrusters were warming up. Its tractors were powering down, ready to drop the Ares tanks. There was no more question of capturing them. Violet had to destroy them. She had seconds.

"Run!" shouted Veikko. She pulled her fractured leg from the rocks and ran.

VIOLET SPRINTED uphill as fast as she could. Every muscle burned. The fracture stung. Darkness fired, burning spots across her chest, into her ribs. The Yakuza fired, a dozen blasts from their Gat-Zook rockets pounding the rocks around her and pushing her off course. She ran faster, up the hill to where she could see the chasm.

It was impossible to jump, at least seven meters. She ran faster. From behind her, a flying Unspeakable ripped into her back with its claws, following her to the edge of the cliff.

She jumped and caught the Unspeakable by the leg. It started kicking immediately. Its talons cut up her neck and back severely but didn't sever any muscles she needed. She swung from its legs and managed to grab its tail and pull to the left. That steered it, briefly toward the trigger. Close enough.

She let go and fell toward the rock; her hands hit it, grabbing for any hold. She caught one, but it only broke her fingers, dislocated her arm, and sent her on down. The worm was only a decimeter away, caught on a small jagged ledge. She tried to grab the ledge but kept falling. She tried to grab the chain-link worm, but it slipped between her broken fingers. Finally as she came to the end of the worm, she dug her fingers into the links, mangling her joints completely.

The ligaments broke and pulled from her hand, hanging on by skin alone. But she stopped falling. Hanging from the worm and her broken fingers, she pulled herself up with her dislocated arm, stretching the skin and sending pain all the way to her shoulder. But she managed to grab the worm with her other hand and pull herself up farther. And farther.

Mishka fired. Violet was barely moving. If not for the microwaves, it would have chopped off her head. Suddenly Violet felt it easier to pull herself up. She looked down for a second and saw that her legs were falling severed to the ground. She pulled herself on up. Mishka cursed and let her rifle warm up to cut down the entire cliff.

Violet glanced to her right and saw the UD ship drop the tanks. It had suctioned the entire Ares out and was ready to leave. There would only be another fraction of a second before the nuke fell out of range to vaporize it. Violet pushed down against the worm, raising her up the last few decimeters as she swung her broken hand toward the bulb. She hit it. She meant it. It detonated.

The brightest light she'd ever seen struck her and blinded her and set her on fire. On fire inside and out, worse than the microwave, worse than anything in pain training, worse than any pain she dreamed could exist.

She fell back down the burning cliffside as the shockwave hit. It threw her back to the incline and put out the flames, then sheered the top off the rocks only a meter from where she rolled.

She rolled fast into the rock that crushed Veikko's stomach and hit her head on it hard enough to fracture her skull. She was knocked out. Only Veikko was awake to see the burning dust shoot down toward them. Then the buzzing began, a feeling like burning mixed with buzzing like the taste of rotten milk, like an electric shock across his body.

He had no armor to put up radiation shields. None of their pockets held radiophonic gel, none of their medicine. They were lying bare before the mushroom cloud and its heat and gamma rays. Veikko and Violet had seconds to live.

R team arrived in seconds. The airfoil fields from their pogo flickered with red sparks, trying to keep their form in the irradiated air. They set down as Ragnar tractored the rocks off of Vibeke and Varg in one powerful discharge from the pogo's microwave. He fired the tractor again to pull them inside. Ripple and Ruger ran down to pull Veikko and Violet in, Veikko's intestines unraveling as he came up.

The last of Valknut's Tikaris flew into the pogo just before it shot up into the sky. It rocketed toward Valhalla as B team arrived to pick up the survivors of Tiwaz. Ragnar stuffed Vibeke and Varg into the rescue pogo's stasis chambers. Ripple went to work on Violet, clearing the blood from inside her skull first, then starting radiation and burn therapy. Rebecca tended to Veikko's stomach and Violet's legs, putting platelet fabric on all the open wounds. All temporary, but enough to keep them alive until they reached Valhalla.

They got to work on Varg and Vibeke in stasis. Merely crushed, burned, and dead, R splinted the bones and jumpstarted them. They'd be awake and intact to walk to med bay. Veikko protested that their triage left his guts hanging out.

As they careened northward, the measures took effect and Violet awoke. The pain was omnipresent and severe, but Violet laughed. The mission was over. She'd just saved the world.

The pogo fell down into the ravine as the nurses ran out to bring in the corpses. But when the door opened, they found V team walking out on their own feet, at least those who still had them. Varg on the right held Veikko up. Veikko held his intestines in and carried Violet on his shoulder. Vibs did the same with her shredded, broken arm on the other side. They walked in triumphant.

Until Veikko slipped on his intestines and pulled the group down onto the floor. Still they laughed.

A few minutes later, they sat in med bay with the remains of T team, free of their radioactive sizzling inner suits. They were cleansed under a powerful radiophobic field and a half dozen other medical array features. Vibeke and Varg had been aligned and sealed, their organ damage and plasma burns erased. Veikko's stomach was finally under repair by a speedy robotic arm, and Violet's new legs were growing in a tank, wire frame models projected onto her person as she sat on the side of the table.

She was euphoric, the cool air on her naked skin, the feel of a reset arm and fingers, and analgic legs. And of destroying the Ares. It was finally, truly over. Concerns about the global reaction and Geki were far from her mind. Vibeke was foremost on it.

She was standing there, naked in front of Violet, grinning with the same satisfaction. Euphoric and relieved on a level reserved for sufferers of the most intense stress humans can survive. She sauntered over to Violet and put a hand on her shoulder.

Violet felt free. Completely free, and she knew Vibeke wouldn't push her away this time. Wouldn't worry about the future or decorum or rules or laws. Wouldn't worry about the woman who'd just tried to kill her.

Violet grabbed her and pulled her close and kissed her on the lips as hard as she could. Grabbed her shoulder blades and sunk her nails into her smooth skin. She wrapped her nonexistent legs around Vibeke's sides, the wireframes tightening across her back.

Vibeke kissed back and held her tight, ran her lips over Violet's. Wet and soft, sucking on her lower lip, letting Violet nibble on hers, slipping her tongue across her tongue and playfully sucking it into her open mouth. They grabbed each other as hard as they could and mashed their faces tight, let their breasts squish against each other, and felt across each other's backs in utter ecstasy.

Slowly Violet let go of her lips and tried to breathe. Her breath was stuttered and uneven. She couldn't breathe right. She felt Vibeke's nipples withdraw from her chest and opened her eyes. They stared at each other for an instant that seemed to last hours and let their hands drop and hold each other on the table. And slowly, Vibeke backed away just a bit so they could see one another clearly.

Violet's eyes, irises vibrant and striated, her pupils contracted in the bright med bay light, showing off all the more purple. Vibeke's, so light they were almost white, like crystal, like opal. Violet could see deep into them, smell Vibeke's cool skin over the clean chemical sting of the room.

The med bay finally came back to her. The world intruded again, having granted her one flawless moment of pure pleasure. And she noticed Dr. Niide and Varg and Veikko, and the dozens of Valkyries outside the glass wall. All staring at them. Everyone staring.

Some aghast, some aroused, some happy, and some perplexed, but all staring. A wide grin slowly bloomed across Veikko's red face. His lips moved, finding the right words. The only proper thing he could say after seeing that kiss.

"May your first child be a masculine child!"

Violet and Vibeke laughed, Veikko stepped back, Dr. Niide returned to his work, and Varg quietly departed for the barracks. The occupants of the ravine slowly wandered off. V team was okay and returning to good health. Their mission was over. The world was safe from an apocalyptic flood. And already, Vibeke began to feel the sting of doing something horribly, dreadfully wrong.

THE LAST Wolf was finally back from Mars. Wulfgar personally oversaw their return. Countless men he'd risked, and every one of them was home safe. The venture was complete and soon to pay off.

As the last fat man reached Hashima, Wulfgar accompanied him to the vomitorium. There, the men performed the least enjoyable portion of their missions: coughing up all the water they drank at the strange Martian outpost. They'd all been through it before, drinking normal water on Earth and regurgitating it on Mars, then drinking the strange water on Mars and heading home for Earth. They knew they'd be smuggling, but the water was a surprise, as was the grotesquerie in how they delivered it. Most of them suspected something surgical, but apparently the simplest way was the best.

Wulfgar watched the Ares filter and drip and distill, capturing all the extra bodily fluids just in case the filter was too strong and removed some of the precious, expensive water.

After only fifty men, he was worried. They were short of calculations by almost a kilogram, unacceptable. Pelamus demanded at least 99.9995 percent of the fluid. Wulfgar consulted the doctors.

They'd hoped the special stomach bladders they'd implanted would contain every drop, but in the end, they were living tissue, and nothing living is perfect. A full .2 percent had been absorbed into the bodies of the smugglers.

Wulfgar contacted Pelamus and asked a question he hated to ask.

"Does it need to be pure, or can it have debris in it?"

Pelamus was angry. He wanted 100 percent of it pure, but there was no going back. What was done was done, and he had to make do with the situation. He consulted his scientists and understood that debris was inconsequential; it could be mixed and littered with anything and still work, but it had to be complete to affect the entire ocean. An incomplete sample even by .1 percent would only affect 30 percent of the world's water.

Wulfgar received the note and, with a heavy heart, did what had to be done. He had Blue Boots head online and purchase an industrial 300-liter blender.

Chapter VIII: Home

VIOLET HAD missed the ritual before, for two entire teams. Aside from Rasekrig, she'd seen no permanent Valkyrie deaths in her time in the ravine. She was told the last man to die permanently was Rygar in 2229, killed by a giant illegal genetically engineered snail.

She didn't know what to expect. Funerals, from what she could tell in Kyle City, were solemn sad services where people shared memories of the deceased, cried, buried them or burned them or had them dispersed at the molecular level. But there was no body to bury for Toshiro, and she didn't expect to see anyone cry.

Nearly everyone in the ravine was present, from Governor Quorthon and Snorri to the members of every team and many civilians. Sad as she was, she feared it would be a long affair and that she'd be asked to carry out some ritual function. She looked into Norse funeral customs as soon as she heard there would be one. She wondered if there would be a boat set on fire or a slave girl passed around, then slaughtered. She doubted the latter.

Once everyone was in the mess hall, Alf waved for the crowd to be silent, then spoke.

"Toshiro has died permanently, as will we all. He died in battle on his own terms. What's over is over, what's done is done. Let his name not be carved on any wall, let no goods be wasted upon his grave, let no ships be burnt. We have moved on, and we will not come back. G Team, begin the search to replace him."

He stepped down, and the room began to mill about. The funeral was over.

Violet should have expected it. She'd been as cold when her parents died, didn't bother to give them a funeral at all. And she was among kindred creatures. Here it was an institution. The sobbing and moaning she'd feared weren't to be found in the ravine.

There was only one more ritual to perform, one less formal. Kjetil opened some oak barrels while Balder and Varg passed out large hollowed-out horns. The kitchen staff poured each person on the teams a large horn of mead, and everyone drank.

Violet wandered and drank slowly, absorption implant off as seemed to be the tradition. Some drank their entire horn in one swig and took another. Others held their horns but didn't seem to drink at all. Balder and Varg were among the former. Violet was almost surprised to see Vibeke drinking liberally.

She found T team, and they pulled her into a group hug, then drank together. Tahir congratulated her on the mission with no sign of sarcasm. It was the mission Toshiro died for, and Tahir wanted her to know that his team deemed it a mission worth dying for, nothing less than the salvation of the planet. Valkyries had died for far less. Violet felt uneasy staying with T team for too long, so she went to find Vibs.

She passed Veikko, who was drinking quietly with Skadi, talking in whispers. Violet had always felt a bit uneasy seeing them together, but as she passed, she felt completely different. She was happy to see them together. Whatever sting it was in the past was gone. She knew why. She'd always been alone before. Everything was different now. She was on her way to find her own girl to squeeze. She found her on a distant bean blob.

Vibeke had the dim ghost of a smile on her lips, and her eyes were set in the distance. Violet took a chair beside her and just stared at her for a moment. She tried to guess what Vibeke was thinking. About Toshiro no doubt, a good memory judging by her expression. Vibs didn't seem to notice her, or if she did, she didn't care that she was there. Violet hoped she was simply unseen and hoped selfishly that she was thinking about that kiss, as Violet had been through the funeral.

Violet felt hot in her suit, an unnatural heat that would persist even if she were underdressed topside in the snow. She'd missed it when the two teams died, still stuck down south wrapping up her own loose ends, and flirting with Gabrielle. She pushed that disaster from her mind and considered if she should lean in and kiss her again. She didn't know if it was a free-for-all now or if she needed permission to do it again.

Vibeke startled her when she spoke. "We should inject it. It tastes awful, stings. I guess it would sting in our veins, but…. You know?"

"I like the taste, much better than beer. More warming," said Violet.

"I like the feeling at least. I can see why so many people used to get hooked on it. Did you know people drank themselves to death? They wouldn't stop, even after it made them sick."

"Why?" asked Violet.

"Stops the pain."

"It does at that."

They sat for a moment as people milled around them. They caught the name Toshiro a few times.

"I'm glad we only do it on days like this," said Vibeke.

Violet said nothing.

Vibs continued. "Funerals, I mean, not victory. Hey, you remember that time we saved the world? You know, yesterday?"

Violet laughed but didn't say anything. She leaned back in the chair.

"What were you thinking about during the funeral?" asked Vibs.

Violet answered before thinking. "Kissing you."

Vibeke didn't change her expression, or react at all.

Violet pressed, "That's all I've been thinking about since I did it."

Vibeke kept staring into space. It made Violet angry.

"I think we should do it more."

Still nothing. The warm fuzzy feeling turned into a sharp icicle.

"We should probably start fucking too."

Clearly she wasn't even listening.

"Right here on this table."

It was almost fun.

"I'll invite Umberto for a gangbang."

"Did you know," Vibeke reminisced, "Toshiro wrote a kids book before he joined up? He let me read it. It wasn't long. But it had drawings, the main character with his horn, copper dragons, a seed fairy. It was really cute."

Vibs snorted. Violet stewed. She was tempted to keep going and see how raunchy she could get before Vibeke noticed, but it seemed too frivolous for the night. She scooched her chair closer and put her hand on Vibeke's. She didn't notice or didn't say anything if she did. Violet let the anger fade and the pleasant buzzing return, let her mind wander.

She took another sip, and another. She thought drinking sounded like a great way to die.

ATARGATIS HATED her job. She worked online, and she felt her body pay for it. She was growing limp and atrophied. Every day she spent two hours working out. She ate only health cubes. All to no avail, eight hours a day of lying inert still took their toll. She decided it was time to quit.

Unfortunately B&L decided she would stay. Her contract was for another twenty years and she was doing a fine job, so they told her she could stick with the job or go to prison. That was that.

Or at least it would have been for anyone but Atargatis. She logged right into her department head's office and demanded they renegotiate her contract. They wouldn't, of course. And after that the job got worse and worse. The pay went down, despite a contract clause stating it wouldn't. They didn't honor their own word. Atargatis sued, also to no avail given the company's lawyer system. Then her hours got cut. Then she got reassigned to synapse debugging, which she simply couldn't do. They were torturing her.

At the end of her rope, Atargatis picked up her bow for the first time in years. She hadn't had time for archery in so long, but well, they cut her hours so she had to do something. Once again she enjoyed the sweet thokk of an arrow flying and penetrating the soft target.

She did some digging and found the names and exact locations of her chain of command, all the way up to Will Fredard, its CEO, and she began shooting them. First came Cecelia Wongraven. She woke her from her dreamscape and put an arrow into her brain, penetrating just past her link. Cecelia's boss Alexei Bodom suffered the same fate, one arrow, halfway into the brain. His regional manager, Johnathan Mäenpää, was found alive but pierced the next day. She had shot her way up the corporate ladder all the way to Vice President of Acquisitions Martha Amon by the time police caught her.

The doctors noted that none of the victims were dead, or really in any danger of it. Every arrow had penetrated just far enough to sever the wetware matrix. None of the victims would ever work online again. In their careers, that was an ending blow. They were all back to square one, jobless and without the ability to do the only things they were good for.

The courts didn't care about poetic justice. Sentenced to life in prison without the possibility of parole, Atargatis considered jumping from her high ring of the George C. Fisher High Security Panopticon, a prison infamously nicknamed the Gallery of Suicide. But she wasn't the suicidal type. Nor was she the type to live in a panopticon for the rest of her life. She vowed to escape or die trying.

Her first attempt was sloppy and brief. She attempted to wrestle the microwave from a guard and got her arm burned off.

Her second attempt was more subtle and clever but roughly as successful. She snuck from the floor detail to an out of-prison work detail and managed to run four kilometers down the road before she was caught and sizzled by four broad beams.

The one armed, heavily tanned inmate made one last attempt to escape, and it was quite ambitious. She began by dunking and nearly drowning Frosty Haraldstadt, the kitchen supervisor, in a giant pot of chicken soup. Taking a knife, she stabbed one guard in the back and the other in the belly and took possession of one of their microwaves. She barbecued five more guards on her way to the gate. But despite her hostage, Tomas Tveitan, they refused to open the gate.

Atargatis did something nobody expected. She gave up the hostage and microwave and lay down to be taken. The prison didn't really care, nor did they care that all her attacks were skillfully nonfatal, nor did they care about her clever reasoning in giving up—the gate was her only way out. Once it was clear it wouldn't open based on a hostage situation, she knew the game was over and laid down her king. The prison guards were far more vicious to her ever after, and her sentence grew by centuries. Nobody at the prison was grateful for her restraint in the least, and certainly nobody there was a fan of her remarkable fighting skill.

G team, however, was very impressed.

MISHKA KEPT the radiophobic beam on her tank for half an hour longer than was necessary. She'd piloted an irradiated pogo on a mission for Valhalla, and her butt itched for weeks.

She wiped the gel off her eye and put it back in. She ran through the recording. There was no doubt it would be enough for the client. Vibeke was clearly visible and clearly crushed. She sent the video in to Red Boots. Almost immediately he linked back.

"Decent work, if a bit late. But Mars is Mars. The second half of the funds will be transferred tonight at midnight, minus the interrogation bonus. Little Boots is also willing to grant you right of first refusal for other assassinations. We need a good woman outside of the gang."

"Thanks, I'll keep it in mind."

"First refusal runs out in thirty minutes after each offer if we don't hear back from you. Out."

R team had arrived far too early for comfort. She wouldn't be surprised if all of V team survived. She cursed Toshiro, at least she thought it was Toshiro. What kind of damn Valkyrie sacrifices himself? Vibeke was centimeters from the blast. Centimeters.

Mishka revved up the tank and trotted out of the cleanup system. She checked her Hashima nodes. No Valkyries had flown to Hashima, but with the Mars mission blindingly, spectacularly over, they'd be sending in a team to research it if not destroy it. Mishka had two distinct interests when they did: First, she had to be certain they didn't send V team. If Vibeke had lived, and she knew deep down that she had, Mishka couldn't have her showing up at the Wolf Gang's door. And less importantly, they were a paying client, and she didn't want Valhalla to erase them from the planet as they tended to do.

She set the tank to head to Nakanoshima, where she could monitor Hashima closely, and immersed herself online.

The news planetoids were going wild over the nuclear blast. It was the first in the lifetimes of anyone on Earth. UNEGA was publicly blaming GAUNE and throwing accusations like mad. GAUNE had more nuclear weapons than UNEGA. GAUNE wanted to destabilize the (mostly empty of any financial interest) region during their sensitive time of intracompany dispute.

But the company actions betrayed the truth. UNEGA truly believed it to be an act of either the Yakuza or the Unspeakable Darkness in their own fight. Prešov marked the start of a full-scale earthbound civil war between Zaibatsu's subsidiaries. UNEGA was putting the utmost pressure on Zaibatsu to take care of the problem peacefully, but the YUP was disassembled, and there was no legally usable peacekeeping force powerful enough to suppress either subsidiary.

GAUNE denied any involvement, honestly, but there was no chance whatsoever they wouldn't try to take advantage of the situation. The nuclear blast was not an act of war, but it would be a perfect excuse for one to UNEGA, and GAUNE would want to take over as many assets as possible before they had the chance. With UNEGA in shambles, nobody on Earth expected GAUNE to sit back and let things resolve themselves.

Peacekeepers were at a loss to control the situation. Most of them had plans to drop a squid on it in one way or another, but the companies were closed off to their projections and pleas. Even the famous Nate Sanderson was at a loss to compel the companies to work toward a peaceful solution.

Mishka watched the situation closely. Not in the hopes of a lasting world peace, but for her next job. Assassination requests would soon be booming.

ATARGATIS, NOW named Thokk, arrived without ceremony and knew her place from the outset—replacing a long honored member. It was T team's mandate that G send them the first replacement possible. They all had the intense urge to move on, to avoid any mourning period, and to become an effective team as soon as possible. Tahir would admit the three-person team's prospect of constant walrus duty might have been a slight motivator.

Her adjustment was not without some problems. Firstly, she was upset that bows and arrows weren't used at all in the ravine. She kept one for sport, but it wasn't a Valkyrie standard. She insisted on using hers with her new arm for kill training but in time had to depend on her Tikari. She was disappointed again that Tikaris weren't flexible enough to act as bows, either. Of course nobody who gets a Tikari objects for too long, but she was never happy about her most treasured skill going to waste.

Her age saw her butting heads with a few senior team members who didn't recognize her life experience, reminding her it was all outside the ravine and therefore meant nothing. But she was a couple years older than anyone in O and P and felt they condescended a bit much.

Her biggest rivalry was with Balder. The first time they met, he was impressed by her name and suggested she simply shortened it to "Targ" to fit in with T team. She took offense to the name, explaining it was the name of a type of horned furry pig. Balder didn't grasp her reference, and things were awkward for them ever since.

She didn't take well to his dislike of religion and challenged him on it frequently, even going so far as to write an article in *Håvamål*, on her first day, which Alf enjoyed but Balder found to be a personal attack. But still he set out to teach her and teach her well.

She got along with Tasha and Trygve far better. Fitting their psychological profiles as G predicted, the team grew tight within a day. Tahir and Thokk grew more than tight within a day, and it pissed Violet off in the extreme. The notion of an in-team romance starting instantly filled her with envy and regret. Thokk never understood why Violet was so cold to her, but Tahir explained it was her own problem and nothing that reflected on Thokk.

It might have been the loss of his closest friend, it might have been Thokk's thrill at escaping her miserable previous life, but the two bonded fast. As if they were caught in a whirlwind, desperate for each other. Tahir didn't hide it well. He was like a schoolboy with a crush at first, oblivious to how hot she found his timid act. She kissed him first, and after that first kiss, when he felt her finger on the back of his suit, he grabbed her as tight as he could and pounced on her.

She missed training with Balder that morning, an extreme rarity among new recruits. Balder was quite disappointed.

DR. NIIDE looked over Violet and the other six for any signs of residual problems from their repair a few days prior. He began to mutter his usual subvocalizations of "severe" and "permanent," but the teams' faces forbid his usual remarks, and he left, almost apologetic.

Nurse Taake explained, "He's sad you couldn't bring Toshiro back."

"Poor him," muttered Tasha.

"It's not sympathy. He wants to try out some new mods, wanted to build someone from scratch."

"I'm sorry our partner's death didn't suit him."

"We stay detached," the nurse defended. "What we lack in bedside manner, we make up for in efficiency. You're all clear."

They hopped off the medical tables and headed for the tailor.

Eric was solemn but still congratulated them on destroying the Ares in the nick of time. He had their new suits ready. They were completely identical to the originals and even felt broken in. Valknut kept trying to find any fault so they wouldn't have to head to their next meeting. Though the mission was a success, the matter of the nuclear bomb was sure to be a topic of discussion in the meeting with Alf and Balder. There would be no avoiding it, and they couldn't have anything nice to say about it. As the team entered the library, Alf handed a small black book to his Tikari and sent it to deposit the book on a high shelf.

"Twenty-nine years of nuclear arms intelligence I've logged in that book. I never expected to write in it that one had gone off."

Violet swallowed.

"Don't tell Balder I said this"—Balder stood right next to him and pursed his lips—"but I'm glad I lived to see it. A mushroom cloud, hot and bright in our day and age."

Violet remembered the bright heat, the fire that burned through her inside and out. She was certain Alf was happy enough to have seen it only through their visual memory.

"I must have watched every old clip of the testing, seen every film-caught photograph of every cloud, and I never thought I'd see a new one. The Ares vaporizing within it was a mere bonus by comparison to see the fireball rise, sucking the dust up with it. Mmm. But we are to deal with another matter first. Varg."

Varg stood at attention, an odd habit of his, considering he'd never been in any military.

"We need to convince the world that the Blackwing has been destroyed. H suggests that simply using its main thruster will provide a large enough explosion to catch everyone's attention and that a specialized fluff bomb will convince them of its demise."

"Easy day, I'll get right on it."

"The day may be easy, but the months to follow will be a longer affair. You are to fly the Blackwing to Mars and leave it in the care of our Phobosian friends. You will not be able to use the thermobaric thruster again despite the speed with which you would reach Mars, as it would betray the illusion of its death. So you'll need to fly there on ramjet momentum and Hall thrusters, and fly home on mass transit."

Veikko spoke up. "You're taking one member of our team for two months?"

"Yes, we are. We have work for the rest of you as well while you're a three-person team."

"Oh God," said Veikko, "not walrus duty…."

"Not walrus duty, though I don't think you'll be happy with what we need you to do. First however, Vibeke and Violet."

Violet was suddenly afraid he'd be lecturing them about their kiss.

"Hashima," announced Alf.

Violet's chest swelled with relief.

"We intend," he continued, "to eradicate Wulfgar and whatever gang he's built. The first step to that end is a surveillance mission. Though Balder suggested a team of four would be best suited, a team of two has its advantages in such missions, and I thought you would appreciate this one and that perhaps you deserved it in light of that spectacular worm striking business in Prešov. I trust you don't object?"

Violet and Vibeke both shook their heads emphatically. Alf saw Violet's actions as impressive, or so it seemed.

"Then lastly, Veikko."

"Glad you didn't forget me."

"You won't be shortly. The Geki visited us last night."

Veikko gulped.

"The Geki hold Violet responsible for the nuclear explosion on UNEGA soil."

Violet gulped.

"But primarily, they put the blame on you," said Alf.

"They 'blame' me for saving the planet from flooding over. I'll accept that blame."

"They would like to speak with you."

"I'd… like to avoid that."

"You won't be able to. Balder and I have defended you vigorously to them and justified your actions 100 percent. In the end, the explosion has not done significant harm beyond what Zaibatsu is doing to itself, and it has destroyed a global threat. That is why you aren't burnt to a crisp already. But they're monitoring the effects for more fallouts than nuclear. Essentially, you'll be held responsible if the situation deteriorates as a direct result of the bomb but ignored if they're negligible."

"That's fair."

"I thought so."

"And I don't," said Balder. "Veikko, I'd like to speak with you in private. Shall we head to the gym?"

Veikko nodded with a clear lump in his throat. He stood up and left the library with Balder. Alf addressed the rest of the team.

"Varg, we'll need you to head out as soon as possible."

"I can head out right now."

"Very well, be sure to say farewell to Veikko as you run."

Varg nodded, then turned to Vibeke and Violet. He couldn't think of anything to say, so he nodded again, smiled, and ran out of the room.

"As for you two lovebirds...."

Violet felt the lump move to her own chest. She didn't know how he would react to their public display of affection. Part of her feared the worst, that he'd order them onto other teams or simply order them to somehow fall out of love. If Vibeke loved her back at all. She'd been so distant since they kissed, she wondered if it really was all in her mind.

"There are no rules here beyond the treaty. So follow the treaty. As long as shit stays unfucked, you aren't required to stay unfucked yourselves. But tread cautiously. This sort of thing has ended teams and ended lives. Whatever happens, you have your next mission together. Consider it a test case."

"Don't worry," Vibeke jumped in, "it was really nothing."

Violet's eyes widened. She felt like she'd just been slapped. Alf clearly picked up on her surprise.

"Ah, very well, then. I won't make much ado about it. Off to plan your scout for Hashima, then. I'll be playing the new Zelda if you need me."

Vibeke walked out of the library. Violet stormed out after her. She jogged up behind Vibs, and as gently as possible, tapped her shoulder.

"Nothing, then?"

"Violet—"

"If it were nothing, then you wouldn't mind doing it again now, would you?"

She grabbed Vibeke by the arms and moved to kiss her.

"Stop!"

"Nothing?"

"I mean we're not… together. Romantically."

"That's news to me."

"Hardly, you know what I've said about this. One kiss because we saved the planet doesn't mean—"

"A peck on the cheek doesn't mean diddly, but that was a buck-naked tonsil massage of walrusine proportions, Vibs."

"Well, it means the same thing as a peck on the cheek."

"Not to me."

"Then make it."

Vibeke turned to walk away.

"Vibs, I swear to God, you know this is a good thing, and if Alf is okay with it, you have no damn excuse."

"I don't need an excuse not to get romantically involved with anyone. It's my choice."

"It's a daft choice. I should get a cerebral bore and—"

"See? This. This is the problem. You're threatening to bore my skull to change my mind. That's the problem, it—"

"For the love of Odin, Vibs, I was kidding."

"Then it's my concern for it! You make me nervous now, Vi. I don't know what to expect from you, and everything we do is built on predicting each other. We need to end every ounce of this, right now. Nothing will happen. Agreed?"

Violet stood and stared at her, feeling a mixture of anger and lust that swarmed behind her sternum like bees. She wanted to hurt her, deeply but, at the same time, couldn't stand the thought of her hurting.

"I won't agree to anything that would hurt you," Violet assured her.

"Oh you think you know what's best for me now."

"Well, you clearly don't."

"You want to play that game? Then I won't let you make an ass of yourself anymore. I won't let you keep on in the delusion anything can ever happen. I won't let you throw away your closest friend by trying to fuck her, and I won't ever, ever kiss you again like I did in med bay."

"Yes, you will."

"What the hell makes you think that?"

"Neither of us wants it your way. We both want it mine. It's inevitable."

Vibeke couldn't think of any response.

"We're both stubborn as rocks, Vibs. But gravity's on my side. No matter how far up you push—"

"You'll still try to go down on me?"

"I was gonna say 'love you,' but I'm up for whatever."

Vibeke tried her hardest not to smile, then turned away before Violet could see her fail. She walked away so Violet wouldn't, deathly afraid and allured that Violet was absolutely right.

VEIKKO AND Balder bowed. They circled each other in the dojo, and Balder spoke.

"What would you have done if the bomb were a dud?"

"What do you mean?"

"The bomb failed, the Darkness took it, it's in the open. What would you have done?"

Balder feinted to Veikko's left with a quick punch.

"Destroy our half."

"That's what I thought." Another feint. "So we've got a problem."

"What's the problem?" Veikko launched a kick, Balder adeptly avoided it.

"You'd turn on Valhalla to get your way."

"My way? We're talking about saving the world!"

"There's always more than one solution to a problem. Alopex put our best solution at keeping the Ares here, researching a way to destroy the water component. Surely there were more."

"We can't risk them! We had to end the threat. If both parts were here, every Cetacean in the seven seas would've been beating down our door."

"Valhalla can survive such an attack indefinitely. But no, every Cetacean would not have been at our door. Most Cetaceans are peaceful people, they—"

Veikko kicked and connected with Balder's chest. They continued.

"I know them better than you ever will," said Veikko. "They're not peaceful, and they're not people."

"You're right, I've never met them. Not on one mission. Because we've never had a mission against their establishment. We've never needed to."

"Until now."

"What do you think power is for, Veikko? Valhalla has the power to rule the world. We don't. Because power isn't action, it's the potential for action. Companies rule because they have armies, not because they use them. If they used them, there would be no people left to govern."

"Irrelevant."

Balder slugged Veikko in the stomach and sent him to the ground. He quickly recovered.

"Not irrelevant, Veikko. Not irrelevant. GAUNE and UNEGA have the power to kill all the Cetaceans. Why haven't they?"

"Mystery to me, they should."

"But they don't need to. They are subjugated. Why do you think the Fish wanted the Ares?"

"To kill us all! To flood the world!"

"No. Mutually assured destruction. It's ugly, Veikko, damn ugly, but it saved the planet before. Pelamus Pluturus has no reason to flood the globe."

"Of course he does; he's a Fish!"

"He's not you, Veikko. No Cetacean has ever shown a hint of genocidal behavior, not even Pluturus."

"But he tried to capture the damn Ares!"

"You don't understand. You just don't understand that a weapon can be for the threat of fatal self-defense."

"You don't understand how Fish think. I grew up with them. I know them better than anyone else in this ravine. Pelamus would have killed us all. He'd have activated the Ares the second he took our ravine, and he would never stop until he took it. Don't forget that—we were sitting on half his prize. Even if he'd let the world be, he'd have killed *us*."

"But you too would've destroyed Valhalla to destroy the Ares."

"Yes."

"You risked war to destroy the Ares."

"Damn right." He launched a series of hooks. "The world might be better crispy. We're the masters of warfare, the experts. If the world's at war, we're the most at home, the most free."

"Your essay in *Håvamål*."

Balder ducked the last throw and fought back with a sweep. Veikko dodged.

"Tell me I'm wrong." Veikko aimed for Balder's arm and connected. Balder seemed unaffected.

"You're not wrong. You're a cruel bastard, but you're not wrong. About that."

"Then what am I wrong about, exactly?"

"You would tempt the Geki."

"I did, and it worked!"

"You may not think that when they come to visit. You know if they ask, I'll turn you over to them."

"You won't have to turn me over. I'll go."

"You would go with them willingly? To die? Or worse?"

"Everyone has to face their fears."

"They go beyond fear. There's a reason they enforce that treaty."

"Right, you know what they are and why they do what they do."

"I have my theories. And some proof. I'd have told you if you ever asked."

"Tell me."

"One is owned by UNEGA, the other by GAUNE, they—"

"Wait, they're owned?"

"Do you think their technology comes free? They're the most advanced warriors on Earth. Of course they're company-funded."

Veikko unleashed a barrage of punches in pure anger, none of them connected.

"Who watches the watchmen, Veikko?"

"We do!"

"And who watches us? We operate above the world, over it, beyond it. We're the force behind it that keeps it alive. Don't you think the world should have oversight of us?"

"No!"

"Then we would be monsters!"

"We are monsters!"

"Don't Fuck Shit Up! Don't you get it? The Geki are the ultimate check and balance, the final safeguards, the people's will over the secret kings."

"How can you let Valhalla be controlled by company men?"

"We have no choice. The Geki are a superior force."

"What are they? Robots? Ghosts?"

"They're human, what else would they be?"

"They're mortal."

"Humans are."

"We could kill them."

Balder suddenly snapped into a series of hits that knocked Veikko down and pinned him in a stance so powerful Veikko couldn't even begin to fight it. Balder had been playing along the whole time. He could have beaten Veikko at any moment. That restraint had ended.

"You could try. And they could kill us all in a heartbeat. Let me make this clear to you: write all the angry letters in *Håvamål* you want, but if you threaten this ravine, if you threaten Valhalla, if you threaten *me,* I will erase you. Is that understood?"

Veikko choked to speak. "Yes."

Balder stood and returned to a neutral pose. Veikko struggled to stand up.

"Then we have an understanding. Good job saving the planet. We meet the Geki tomorrow. Alf's Library at 0900." He bowed. "Have a nice day."

Veikko failed to bow. He was still coughing. He sat on the dojo floor and tried to breathe. He stirred, angry, furious. At the fish, at

Balder, at himself. But above all at the Geki. They were owned men. They were no different from any other group Valhalla could trump, just a bit heavier in the purse and advanced in their weaponry. And whatever Balder said, they were human. They were mortal. They could be killed, and then Valhalla would truly rule the world.

REID AND Haglaz arrived at the ice hangar. Ragnar aimed the pogo's microwaves and melted it. Varg gave Rebecca a kiss and seated himself in the Blackwing, then closed the canopy overhead.

R team headed immediately south to set off the fluff bomb. Varg sent two radio transmissions, first to Mars on conventional encryption reading "Taking Spit up on her offer," her offer on Mars having been some innuendo about occupying her secluded hangar. Then he sent a simple note to Valhalla reading only, "En Route." He sent a thoughtwave up into the system, and the BIRP took off with a thunderous rumble.

R team prepared. Ruger looked over the sky for any sign of the thermobaric thruster.

"Is that it?" he asked, pointing to a conventional contrail.

"No," explained Ripple, "I think we'll know it when we see it."

Varg flew on ramjets up to 5,000 meters and prepared to activate the thruster.

"How about that one?" Ruger asked of a slightly larger contrail.

"Trust me, you won't need to ask."

Varg activated the thruster.

An explosion of incomparable size obscured half of the daytime sky from view. Ruger didn't ask if that was it. The explosion raced south at incredible speed, propelling the small craft at its forefront faster than any other object had traveled in Earth's atmosphere before. It reached R team in only seconds after their flight of an hour.

R team launched their fluff bomb at the exact proper time and hit the Blackwing, setting off a charge that made a tiny explosion of deep red that Skunkworks would recognize as the craft's demise. Simultaneously, Varg cut off the thruster and fell into the ocean. The illusion was complete, and within minutes the news logs were streaming with reports of the long lost BIRP's destruction at the hands of incompetent thieves.

Varg propelled the Blackwing slowly south out of the zone in which searchers might look, then launched unseen that night from the ocean.

He rose to the edge of the atmosphere on ramjets, then set the BIRP to head to Mars under conventional Hall thrust. The thermobaric thruster could have maintained a localized atmosphere in space and sent him there in a matter of hours, but it would tip their hand. It would take a month at regular speed, so Varg took his cryo-tab and went to sleep. The orgy he dreamed up was phenomenal.

THE NEXT morning Veikko walked to the edge of Kvitøya and ejected his Tikari.

"Hey, Sal."

Sal fluttered its wings and stared at him, on full AI.

"We've got some rough times ahead, little guy. I'm gonna need you to do me a big favor."

An hour later, Balder and the remains of V team met in his office. Balder looked oddly disheveled. He saw that they picked up on it, and he explained.

"My dream software is acting up, happens when I try to do too much in my sleep. Nightmares creep in."

"Are you okay?" asked Vibeke.

"Yeah, just a malfunction. We have things to deal with. Varg is going to be two months out, to and from Mars. He has to travel slow and silent. Project Daunting is over, but we have to see to its repercussions, the Geki."

Violet took a deep breath. She wasn't looking forward to seeing them again.

"We're summoning the Geki at 0900. Any questions before we begin?"

Violet was unnerved by the word "summoning" and wondered what dark ritual would call the black-cloaked enforcers. She wanted someone to ask a question to delay the inevitable but couldn't think of any herself. She just wanted it to be over. 0900 came slowly.

"Very well, then, take your last calm breath."

The team did so, and then Balder enacted the complex and mysterious ritual that called the Geki to his presence.

"Geki!"

They appeared. Fear hit Violet and the others like ice-cold water in the Tikari port. She stumbled back a step away from them, the anxiety thick in her chest. She looked to Veikko, who was clearly even more affected by it than her. Vibeke was frightened but on top of it, standing tall. Three kilometers over Balder's office, Sal noted a minuscule air distortion moving at a slight curvature.

"Who is the third?"

"Vibeke," said Balder. "She stands with her team."

"Leave."

Any other time Vibeke would have stayed, stoic, but the Geki's voice commanded her to her deepest neuron. She couldn't disobey, so she left without a word.

Outside her distress turned to empathy. She was free, but Violet and Veikko were not. Her thoughts went to Violet most powerfully. She was heartbroken that she should suffer another second of it. Her pity grew harsher and more raw as she waited. Seconds passed, feeling longer. She wondered how long Violet could take it, if she should return and rescue her. But she couldn't. The Geki's suggestion was still active in her mind. She was helpless.

"You are responsible."

It wasn't a question. The Geki's accusation was an order, a demand for acceptance of their crime, motivated by its voice as if they'd been holding back a confession for years.

"Yes," Violet admitted quickly to stave off the pressure.

Veikko seemed frozen again. Violet feared he was stuck in a miserable loop the way he'd been the first time they met the Geki. But he was lucid and able to speak. And somehow, Violet couldn't imagine, he had the strength of will to disobey the Geki's order and say something other than yes.

"I'm responsible. Violet acted on my orders."

"Your kind do not give or follow orders."

Again, Veikko disagreed and somehow had the strength to tell a half-truth to the inhuman gaze. "I did because the world was at stake. I am responsible. Violet just pushed a button."

"Did you?"

The question was directed completely at Violet. She could feel it focused on her, restrained to her and more intense than the other words. She wanted to do as Veikko did and oppose the force, but she couldn't. She answered.

"Kind of?"

Her answer surprised her. She knew she was incapable of lying, but she thought she'd take responsibility for the mushroom cloud. It was as if the Geki's will filtered into her, and it didn't want her to say no. As if the Geki were, somehow, for one fleeting moment, protecting her.

"Then leave."

It was an order. Violet walked out and fell to her knees outside the library. Vibeke ran to her side and hugged her. Violet had no energy to hug back, let alone flirt. For one brief moment, they were friends again and nothing more, nothing tainted or complex. United in their concern for Veikko, who remained.

"You take full responsibility for the detonation of the nuclear bomb?"

"Yes!" Veikko shouted, the question rooting the word out of him.

"You will choose. You may die now, or you may come with us until Valhalla undoes the damage you've done to UNEGA."

The option of death stuck out at him like a release, as if he were forced toward it. The option to stay with the Geki was a promise of living hell. The Geki's words were swaying him, pushing him toward death. He pushed back.

"I'll go with you."

"Balder. We will keep Veikko until the civil war declines commensurate with the damage of the nuclear incident. Your senior teams will undo that damage now. If they fail, we will keep him forever. Act quickly, we are watching you."

The Geki disappeared, and Veikko disappeared with them. His microwave fell to the rocky ground. Balder was suddenly alone in the room. His breath returned to him. Veikko was gone. He'd made his choice. There was nothing Balder could have done to protect him. He left the room.

Three kilometers up, Sal detected an air distortion moving on the exact opposite direction of the previous one, along the same curvature. The Tikari did a quick calculation and pinpointed the distortion's point of origin and return—13,000 kilometers away. Two days with available power. Sal activated his rocket and flew southwest.

"Where's Veikko?" asked Violet.

"They took him," said Balder, as grim as if they'd killed him on the spot.

"Took him where?" demanded Vibs.

"I don't know. I don't know where they go when they disappear. They gave us an ultimatum: our senior teams fix any escalation the bomb caused and they let him go."

"We'll cancel Hashima, we can—" said Violet.

"No," Balder interrupted. "They made a mandate. They said senior teams. We do what they said, exactly as they said it. You know we can't refuse or beg them to change."

The three stood silent. Balder looked sick.

"Are you okay?" asked Vibeke.

"Okay, but afraid," said Balder.

"It stuck with you? Or you're afraid we'll fail?"

"No. Afraid of what Veikko will do."

Violet didn't understand. "What can he do?"

"He can get us all killed," Balder sat down against the library wall. He looked broken, far from his constant powerful aura. "My dreams have been so bad these days. So very bad. They won't be any better tonight."

He waved for Violet and Vibeke to leave. They did so quietly. They tried to think of what Veikko could do, of what he would do. They weren't as concerned as Balder because they trusted him fully. But their minds dwelled on the worst possibilities. Of the Geki coming to destroy Valhalla. The deaths of project Rasekrig compounded tenfold. Or, with the Geki involved, of something even worse.

THEY HAD called it project Rasekrig because it was intended to end a race war. Vibs had to explain it to Violet. It was literally a fight over skin tones. They had been more common in the past, but they weren't completely dead in some regions.

"The stupid zone, apparently," Violet remarked.

"Just don't say that when you work with them."

"Why should we work with them? If they want to fight about who's blonder, let them kill each other."

"It's the innocents in the region we're concerned with," Vibs went on. "We can't stand by while people who don't want to fight are kicked out of their homes or killed."

Violet had to agree with that much.

There were four belligerents. There was Kigali, a city company that wanted to drive the light-skinned people out of the region. There was Swastikult, the obnoxiously vocal and occasionally violent minority. There was Bruise, Swastikult's online presence, and there was Kigali En Ligne, their opponents. The online halves had long since fought a different war from their real world counterparts, a war of hacks and takedowns rather than the machete-based fight in the real world. *Shameful*, thought Violet. Every briefing she heard of it. But Alf called it a good simple start for political missions, a perfect introduction to the field for junior teams.

V team was assigned to Swastikult; W team to Kigali; X team to Bruise; and Y team to KEL. Each team was to pose as new recruits and convince their respective target to go pacifist or assassinate whoever wouldn't until the leaders were more amicable. They knew it would be a bloody, nasty project, and some had doubts about sending the most junior teams in, but the youngest of them were merely online, so it wasn't too big a risk.

V team ended up with the easiest job. Swastikult proved happy to go peaceful. They were just waiting for a ceasefire. That left V team with very little to do beyond protecting their target until the others stopped fighting.

That's where Violet met Gabrielle. Gabrielle looked nearly identical to Vibeke. Pale with white hair, the same hair Vibs would have had if she hadn't dyed it. Same round face, same shape of body, slightly larger breasts, slightly broader hips. Violet had long since given up on Vibeke romantically, or so she thought, but her near-doppelgänger wasn't off-limits and well, Valknut had little else to do.

Violet wasn't quiet about her conquest, so Balder ventured to give her a warning.

"These racial types are very backwards, you know."

"About race, certainly," Violet admitted.

"About more than race. Swastikult is from a long line of conservatives. They can be very closed-minded, even religious."

"I'm sure Gabrielle is above it," explained Violet. "She's very smart and not at all about the war. Moving her into a more powerful position was on our list from the start."

"Just be careful, Vi. Make sure she doesn't... take anything the wrong way. Conservative types can object to some things that the civilized world, that *you* might take for granted."

Violet wasn't certain what he meant but agreed anyway. And got to know Gabrielle better. And better. She wasn't as smart as Vibeke, but Violet wasn't looking for her teammate over again. The looks were just coincidental. She wanted a fling like one of Varg's, and Gabrielle seemed chipper around Violet more than anyone else in her gang.

Then X team was dead. And Y right after. V team got the signal an hour after it happened. There was nothing to do. KEL and Bruise were fighting each other on the Black Crag, hemorrhoid of the net. X and Y fought there too. And they got hacked, hacked into living spyware.

C team recognized it fast and put them down like rabid dogs. It was the blackest day in the history of the ravine. Two junior teams killed because they stepped onto the wrong website.

V and W took over the online aspects, which died down after the same mass hacking killed off 90 percent of Bruise and 99 percent of KEL. There was just some simple cleanup work to do, but the easy work was made next to impossible by the loss.

Gabrielle hugged Violet as soon as she got offline the first time. Violet hugged back harder. It was the strangest feeling. She was angry and sad and hurt, but completely transformed by that embrace. If she didn't have a crush on Gabrielle before, she was head over heels after that.

The rest of the mission wound down, and Valhalla broke its last ties with Swastikult. Its last battle ties at least. Violet stayed behind a night for personal reasons, and Gabrielle was happy to welcome her. There were two bunks in her room, one recently vacated by one of the deaths online. It was morbid but not so perverse Violet turned it down.

She and Gabrielle sat on her bunk that night and talked, mourned the dead but held hope for the future. The war was over. V team had ended it. Gabrielle was impressed.

Violet stroked Gabrielle's hair gently and leaned closer. If her eyes were open, she'd have seen Gabrielle was getting weirded out. She kissed her on the lips, a gentle kiss like she'd dreamed of with—well, it didn't matter who she dreamed of before. She was kissing real lips, and she was ready to do a whole lot more.

Gabrielle jumped back.

"What the hell are you doing?"

Violet was startled. "Kissing you?"

"Whoa, we…. What are you doing?"

"Kissing you, you know, lips and things? What's wrong?"

"You're a girl!"

"No shite, what's going on?"

"You're a… lesbian."

She'd heard the word before. It was an antiquated word like Tory or Whig. She assumed it was a political party or nationality. "No, I'm Scottish. What the bloody hell is a lesbian?"

But Gabrielle seemed panicked. Violet couldn't fathom why or what she'd just been called. Had Gabrielle thought she was male or something?

"Why don't you…? Just wait here. Just wait here for me. Then I'll come back, and we can…. Okay?"

"Okay," Violet said, still at a loss for what was going on. Gabrielle left, but she'd said she'd return, and she seemed suddenly amicable. Violet lay back on the bed and waited. And waited. She figured she'd give Gabrielle a pleasant surprise when she returned and took off her suit, then crammed it behind the bed. The door clicked as soon as she was undressed.

Two large bald men walked in. Violet pulled the blanket around herself. "Who are you?"

"We're with Gabrielle," one of them laughed.

"Yeah, she sent us to uh... set you 'straight,'" said the other. They seemed terribly amused about themselves. Violet didn't understand. She sat upright in bed, and the two men moved toward her.

A moment later, the door burst off its hinges. Violet emerged covered in the men's blood and looked around the hall. She was sickened enough by what the men intended to do, but she was more than anything pissed the hell off at Gabrielle. Luckily, she spotted her in the hall and could have a discussion with her.

Violet shouted, "Oi!"

Gabrielle ran as soon as she saw Violet but didn't stand a chance. Violet caught up with her in seconds and grabbed her by the hair and pulled. Gabrielle's feet fell out from under her, and Violet tugged her hair again, making her head hit the floor hard.

"What the fuck was that?" Violet demanded.

"You're a freak!"

"*I'm* a freak? Do you know what those men wanted to do?"

"They wanted to give you what you deserve. You unnatural.... You're not fucking natural!"

"What the hell do you think is wrong with me?"

"You like girls!"

"Duh! But what's wrong with me?"

They had reached an impasse of understanding. Violet gradually figured out what the problem was at least but couldn't fathom how Gabrielle could see it as a problem. It made her all the angrier. She heard footsteps coming down the hall and looked back to see a dozen Swastikult men looking at them: Violet naked and covered in blood, holding her suit in one hand and Gabrielle's hair in the other. She stood and pinned Gabrielle against the wall as the men came closer.

She was angry but growing somewhat amused at how awful it was. Jilted but she had the instincts to transmute it into skill and focus. She thought quickly of a proper fate for Gabrielle.

She kissed her on the lips, even more passionately than she wanted to in bed. She slobbered on her, rubbed her face on her, and bit her lip. Then she spoke loud enough for her conservative pals to hear.

"Thank you so much for showing me how hot it could be with a girl. I'd never have tried being a librarian if not for you."

She kissed her again and walked away. The men didn't chase her, but they seemed quite angry at Gabrielle. Violet left surprisingly happy for such a nasty turn of events and headed back north to where people had fucking brains.

"It's 'lesbian,'" explained Vibs. "Librarians deal with books."

"Whatever, it worked. They probably raped the bitch to death."

"Violet!"

"What?"

"We... we don't do that to people!"

"Well yeah, we don't. But they do."

"Violet, you can't set someone up for... for that."

"Why not? And why don't we rape people exactly? We torture them to death. Why can't we top 'em off with our—"

"I can't believe you! It's sick, it's wrong, nobody should ever face that. Not even the worst."

"Oh, so you don't want Mishka to get raped? Were it possible, I mean."

"No!"

Violet considered it.

"Well, you're a kinder woman than I."

"Violet, we kill rapists. We kill anyone who turns an assault sexual. It's the worst thing people can do to each other."

Vibeke seemed genuinely disgusted. Violet knew she had to relent.

"Well, I'm sure Gabrielle explained her way out. She'll be fine. Better than she deserves."

"Violet, we need to talk about this."

"No, we don't. I get it, it's wrong. I'd never actually do anything. It's just... philosophical."

Vibeke brooded on it. She acted for the next week like she had more to say but never got to it.

In time things went back to normal, or so Violet thought.

Vibeke actually never thought of her quite the same way after that brief but profound disagreement. She knew Violet wouldn't have understood why if it came up again. Vibeke wouldn't tell anyone else about it. There was no reason to deflate their opinion of Violet. And Violet surely knew better than to say or think the way she had again. Vibeke alone would bear the burden of knowing what she knew. That Violet, in one serious way, had been completely backward.

But then, who in the ravine wasn't in some way? In the end Vibeke decided not to judge. She'd corrected the problem and checked in on Gabrielle, who had indeed explained the situation to Swastikult. All was well on that front. X and Y were the pressing matters of the month. Worse things had just happened.

Chapter IX: Hashima

VIOLET WALKED the branches with Vibeke and Alf. They asked once more to participate in the Zaibatsu cleanup, but Alf declined.

"Even if it were not a Geki request, political matters this fragile are always handled by our most senior teams. Junior teams are great for sneaking in and blowing up, assassinating warmongers, but the experience necessary to forge treaties takes decades to learn, let alone master. Zaibatsu is more complex than Swastikult. Infinitely more complex. I'll be overseeing it personally. Don't worry, we'll have Veikko back."

Violet wondered what would be left of him if the Geki subjected him to their fear all the time he was with them. She pushed it from her mind. It was too horrible to consider. She could only be thankful, infinitely thankful he'd saved her from it.

"I've reviewed your link dumps about Hashima," Alf went on, "I approve them fully. You'll depart tomorrow to implement them."

The three stepped off the branch by the barracks and defuzzed their feet. Vibeke nodded to Alf and headed for V team's room. Violet stayed for a moment.

"Alf, a question."

"Go on."

"Veikko told me last night that the Geki were simply men working for UNEGA and GAUNE. Is that true?"

"We suspect it. Balder is certain of it. I have doubts and suspicions myself, but Veikko wasn't lying."

"Then why don't we kill them? Why do we let them have power over us?"

"It's uncertain we have a choice. If their abilities are all just tricks or if they truly could annihilate the ravine in an instant. But our teams have seen their fire, the Geki in action. All who have believe they constitute a superior force to all Valhalla can muster. But more importantly, they have always acted righteously. If they are the arm of the world governments, I don't mind submitting to them. I consider it reasonable and just."

"I did until they took Veikko."

"And I question it too. But I remain inactive against them. Fear is a powerful weapon. It takes the Geki to instill fear in Valkyries, but we're certainly guilty of the same."

"What? We don't use fear as a weapon."

"Of course we do! We are feared, even more than the Unspeakable Darkness. And we use that fear to get our way. The Hall of the Slain has a dreaded reputation for a reason. We earned it, and we keep it alive."

"We act fairly, though, don't we? Aside from a few indiscretions...."

"Those indiscretions are the meat of who we are. We do act cruelly. What seems normal to you after two years in the ravine was once enough to kick you out of Achnacarry. You have no monopoly here when it comes to childhood cruelty. We aren't the noble poet warriors of old."

"Snorri said you were a poet warrior before you came here."

"Snorri calls me such as a joke. Nobody called me a poet warrior. They called me a serial killer. I snapped easily and blew up big when I did, and not metaphorically. When the police harassed my parents I blew up their headquarters. When my parents saw the carnage and called me a monster, I killed my parents. Your Lilliputian eccentricities are nothing compared to my youthful lows. I was a monster, and I haven't changed all that much."

"But you did change when you came here?"

"When I came here, here was a pack of savage Wolves. Clear walls to mock the injured, sharp rocks to cut those who fell out of line. They hazed the new flesh in ways to make Achnacarry look like preschool. When I came here, the last boy in a four-man runeless team—it was all men back then—they beat me my first night for not using the right towel. They beat me all night and beat me more in the morning. The next night I killed them all in their sleep. In all the time you've been here, you never wondered where my team was? They're buried under the library. Every foundation in this ravine is built on buried men. Valhalla is not a place for good men and women. It's a place for you and me."

"Still, we save the planet. We don't torture anyone to death unless they really deserve it."

He almost laughed.

"Yes, we have saved the Earth forty-three, sorry, forty-four times. But it is not our responsibility. It's what we do when we're bored. We're killers and crackpots, and we fight those who would end the world only because they taunted us as children. You think Veikko wants to stop Pelamus to save humanity? He wants to stop him because he hates his relatives. He hates Fish and won't see the world taken over by them. Why, Violet, did you save the world from deluge? For the good of the weaklings who made your childhood so dismal or for your own sense of reward?"

"But someone has to defend the weak and—"

"No, nobody has to. If it can't protect itself, it deserves to drown, let it die off. If someone wants to champion the human cause, so be it. If you want to then feel free, use our microwaves, but it's not our responsibility. Our only responsibility is to ourselves."

She didn't know if he was playing devil's advocate or trying reverse psychology, all to teach her why it really was a cause worth fighting for. She could have asked, but she was afraid. She knew deep down that he would tell her it was the truth. That he believed it. By implication she knew she might have agreed with every word of it. She could call herself a bad girl in taunt, but there were some things too dark to admit of herself. Alf broke the uncomfortable silence.

"You should read *Håvamål* sometime. It deals with all these trifles."

She was about to say she couldn't when he dropped the pretense that he wasn't disappointed. "And you really should learn to read paper text. You're the last girl here who can't."

He walked away. That hurt. It was the first time the inability ever felt like an inability. It was the first time Alf had ever said anything that really distressed her. It was the first time she ever saw Alf as a flawed man and not the fearless leader of the pit. It was also the last time she would ever see him.

VEIKKO FELT nothing. No fear, no pain. It occurred to him suddenly that the Geki had killed him anyway. There was only darkness. But there was a feeling, something there in the space with him. He realized quickly that it was fear. He was afraid, only so afraid that it didn't register like the usual Geki fear.

Like the dead nerve endings of a terrible trauma, the fear had knocked out part of his brain, overloaded it, numbed it. But it was coming back. And it was bad. It was worse than ever before. He was swimming in fear, drowning in it. A vortex of fear. As if the Geki's voice was omnipresent and incarnate, flowing around him. Like he was melting away into the whirlpool.

He tried to scream, but the fear stifled him. He couldn't move his arms or legs. He couldn't even be certain he still had them. He tried to think, but it was hopeless. Soon he was overcome by fear completely. His mind focused in on it like the worst imaginable pain. He was unable to avoid it. He searched for something, anything to focus on instead, but nothing else existed. Until a dim light appeared.

A dim light moving closer. Becoming clearer in the darkness. He could make out the texture, the color before long. Then the ears. He knew what it was, but he couldn't understand why in the depths of hell he was seeing a walrus in a pair of pink bunny slippers.

VIOLET WAS angry. Angry at Alf, angry at herself. She stormed out to Special Arsenal 2 to pick up a razor-chain whip and practice against some meaty but nonsentient grown targets on the range. Shredding something that could bleed always made her feel better.

She reached SA2's door and kicked it open to reveal Tahir and Thokk having sex on a crate of field knuckles. They were shocked to see her and quickly covered themselves with their discarded armor. They separated, stood up, and quickly became annoyed at Violet's lack of flight.

Violet couldn't move. She was transfixed by the sight of them naked together, violently thrusting and bouncing. She felt an instant envy like nothing she'd felt before. It was animalistic, beyond that it was an all pervading stink as if the Geki of Envy had burst into the air before her. The image tore through her rational brain, the part that might have told her to get lost.

She stared at Thokk, thinking of her pale, spread thighs from a moment before. Her moans, the way she grabbed Tahir's back and pulled it in toward her again and again before they jumped up at the sight of her. She saw their faces, angry at her and shouting for her to get out. It all skipped over her head. She could only see their faces in ecstasy a moment before.

They were on the same team. It was possible, not only possible, but it had happened after only days. She was furious. It should have been her and Vibeke. Without question she should have been fucking Vibeke on that damn crate for the last two years.

"For the love of shit, Vi, get out!"

She had no intention of leaving just then. She walked straight in, grabbed a chain-whip, and made sure to stop by the door and thoroughly sign it out. She pressed the fingerprint button and spoke properly. "Violet from Valknut team checking out chain-whip zero one from special arsenal two, on October seventh in the two thousand, two hundred and thirty-second year of the common era at fifteen thirty-two hours and seventeen seconds."

The two just watched her, Tahir going flaccid and Thokk staring daggers at Violet for it. Violet linked the light off and slammed the door on them, then marched to the meat range.

She ordered out a standard target and went to town, slashing meat off its sides, splattering blood on the walls and floor. She gave up on skill within seconds and went for power. She cut the target in half, then cut it from its hanger. She kept whipping, with all the anger she could muster, and that was a lot. She shredded the target until she was cutting into the floor without any semblance of form or aim, finally throwing the whip down at the target and walking away, cursing under her breath.

She shoved her way past an onlooking citizen and headed for the barracks. She threw the door open and walked in. Vibs turned to her, her face pale in the room's light, her roots glowing under the black, her mouth slightly open, surprised.

"Tell me I'm not a useless bloody idiot."

"You're not! What happened, Vi?"

"Nothing." She sat on her bunk, right next to where Vibs was standing. She was eye level with Vibeke's breasts, centimeters away. The image of Thokk's chest bouncing with every thrust flickered through her mind. Vibs didn't step back.

"What's wrong?"

"Things… things just aren't…." She exhaled. She couldn't even put it into words.

Vibeke looked her over, genuinely concerned. She saw blood spatter.

"Is that from the range?"

"Yeah, the range." The useless range. There was too much anger, too much regret to whip out of a simple target. Because it wasn't anger and regret. It was lust. The image of them pounding away had Violet furiously aroused. She was sick of talk and dispute. Sick of Vibeke's insolence. Sick of restraint.

"Take off your suit."

Vibeke feigned shock. She practically expected it of Violet at that point. What she didn't expect was the strike of heat she felt herself at being ordered to undress. Despite all the calm logic filling her head, the thought of doing as ordered occurred to her and held a sharp appeal.

"What?" Vibs took a breath and turned away. If Violet stopped, she'd be okay. It would go away.

Violet didn't stop. "I said take off your goddamn suit."

Vibeke turned to face her. "For the hundredth time, that's not something we can do."

Violet saw through her. "You want it too, damn it."

Vibeke looked down. She couldn't look Violet in the eye just then. She spoke to the floor. "It doesn't matter what I want. I chose to be a Valkyrie, I chose this life for myself."

Myself. Violet's anger boiled up again. She didn't even think to tell her that it was working for Thokk. Vibeke had said she chose it for herself. For *herself.*

"Then how about me, you selfish bitch? You can beat yourself up all you want, but you have no right to take it away from me."

"I don't fucking belong to you! I don't *owe* you!" Vibs snapped back. Talk about selfish.

"Yes, you fucking owe me! I just saved the bloody fucking world. The least you could do is eat me out or something!"

"You're out of your mind. Just think about what you're—"

"I've thought about it for two years, Vibeke! I've thought about you and craved you. I've wanted you naked in my arms since I met you, and I'll go insane if I have to wait another second."

"You are going insane, look at yourself. Look at yourself, Violet. A team can't work like this."

"I don't give a shit! I just want you. Now. Just get in bed and—"

"Violet! Stop! It's not gonna happen."

"I love you, Vibeke."

"I don't love you, Violet."

It wasn't true. Even then, Vibeke felt a force behind her chest telling her to give in. She could throw it all to the wind and give in. She could be in bed with her in seconds if she just gave in. It might be better for the team if she gave in. She wouldn't let herself think it. She had to get out of there.

Violet stared. She wanted to speak but had nothing to say, no words came. There were no words strong enough. She wanted to command Vibeke, to order her to act like she knew she should and walk straight back to her and kiss her and fuck her.

But she couldn't. Vibeke turned to leave. She was simply walking out. Walking away. Like a Valkyrie would ever walk away from a fight. Violet was beyond furious, beyond rage.

She grabbed Vibeke by the shoulder and spun her around and slugged her as hard as she could.

Vibeke was spun around and thrown across the room, completely unprepared for it.

Good, thought Violet. *She's halfway to her bed.*

Violet ran her finger down the back of her own suit, undoing it and letting it slip off. No thought crossed her mind. She just pushed Vibeke the rest of the way onto the bed and climbed in after her. Vibeke squirmed, lying on her front. She was pushing to get back up. Violet grabbed her by the hair and held her facedown on the mattress, then ran her finger down the back of Vibeke's suit. It pulled open across her back.

Violet took a deep breath and kissed her skin, and it was like an explosion of warmth across her lips. For years she'd dreamed about kissing that skin, and it was beyond her fantasies. Her mouth open, she dragged her lips across her back, kissing her more, harder and harder.

"You're worse than Mishka," said Vibeke coldly.

It pinched her ego, but Violet didn't care. She was too happy just then, too turned on to consider it fully. She was being bad again; she knew that much but couldn't possibly bring herself to care.

"Yeah, I am," she replied. Let Vibs deal with that. She pulled Vibeke's suit farther down around her ribs and touched them with her free hand, moving closer to her bare breast, dying to feel it. To squeeze it as hard as she could. To hear Vibs whimper and moan and give in and ride her face until—

"You're worse than my dad."

Violet froze. She was, wasn't she? Her dad never molested her, never raped her. Violet realized it was going to be rape. What was she thinking? She pulled away from Vibs like she'd been stung. She took a deep breath and tried to bring herself back to the real world. Had she even just done what she thought she'd done?

Vibeke propped herself up on her elbows, then sat on the bedside. Violet couldn't look at her. She'd gone too far. Much too far, incalculably too far. And she'd lost whatever scrap of Vibeke's heart she ever had. She was worse than her dad. Violet shuddered.

Vibeke stood up and walked toward the door, pulling up her suit. God, she'd started undressing her, kissing her. Violet felt sick. Vibeke turned around and faced Violet. Violet couldn't look up.

"You—you can't do this, Vi," Vibeke said in a broken voice.

Violet had to look. She had to look her in the eye and say something. She looked up and saw Vibeke staring at her with a crushed cheek. She'd broken it, snapped her skull inward. It was black already and starting to swell. Violet gasped. She'd done that. How was she even capable of it? She tried to apologize, but nothing came out. Nothing was good enough, strong enough.

"I'm—"

"Nothing will ever happen between us, Violet. Nothing. Not ever."

It hurt more than her knuckles, which she realized were also broken. She couldn't breathe right, something was grabbing her lungs.

"Vibeke, I didn't—"

"Shut up. Just shut up and get it through your thick fucking skull. We're never gonna kiss, we're never gonna fuck, and…," she lied, "I'm never gonna love you."

She walked out the door toward med bay. Another sob hit Violet in the chest. Tears started to cut their way out of her eyes. She was crying, for the first time she could remember. She was ashamed, of the tears and of all she'd done. She felt such shame that it choked her, that it took control of her breath and her face and contorted her into a sobbing weakling. She'd felt nuclear fire, and it was nothing compared to this. She screamed at the top of her lungs.

WULFGAR WATCHED as they threw the last man into the blender. He'd lost too many men bringing the Ares back, but it had to be done. Unfiltered, the Ares now took up almost eight times its original mass. Filtration experiments had failed. The water was now a part of the living tissue of the men who drank it. Without every cell they read .2 percent short. With the gore intact, the analysis read 99.999997 percent intact. Enough for Pelamus.

"But you promised more, Little Boots," said Pelamus. "I let you attempt the Yakuza contract because you said you had the other half."

"I said I know where it is, your giant glowing tree," replied Wulfgar.

"Where is it?"

"Kvitøya. I was interred there briefly in a ravine containing the device."

"Then you will seize that ravine and ready it for my arrival. Then your contract will be complete."

"There will be expenses."

"Invoice the YUP; they will be paid."

"Very good. I have to admit, Pelamus, I'd have done that part for free."

"I have to admit, I'm a socialist. When you're done, you can have the entire YUP and all our topside assets."

"Thank you, Pelamus. I do hope you won't flood the planet as soon as I do."

Pelamus signed out without replying.

Wulfgar had no desire to see the world end for the sake of his profit margins. His spies in Pelamus's sub were certain that he had no intent to activate the device. He'd not have brought the Ares back if he expected him to. So he offered a better contract than the Yakuza and proved himself by stealing the Ares before they ever approached it, and he did the deed that could end the world but did so with the utmost confidence he would be safe on the surface.

That didn't stop him from invoicing himself a ticket back to Venus just in case.

VEIKKO'S HALLUCINATIONS shifted rapidly. Random at first but succumbing to the fear. From trees and cacti to the notion he was in lung surgery, then to the visions of a flood, to Violet and Vibeke torn open and burning in radioactive flames, to Risto.

"It's called a 'Farnesene Pulse.'"

There was diseased flesh, the stink of rot, of rotting alive. Seafoam washed over him and seeped between his teeth, choking him with salt.

"You can find Farnesene in apples. Do you like apples, Veikko?"

"Yes," he gagged, the answer forced out of him. Veikko couldn't breathe regularly. Air came in minuscule bursts. It was a prison whose bars were surgically impaled through him. But he remembered the Geki. The pain hit his teeth again.

"It's a fear pheromone in some insects. RAND weaponized it for humans."

He thought he threw up but couldn't tell. He could hear, but he was blind, unable to feel with his hands. He tried to look, but all he saw was fear. It was visible. He could touch it. It stung his fingers and made him shiver uncontrollably.

"There's no defense against it. It seeps through airtight seals. It works in a vacuum. It inflicts fear with no escape. There is only one way out."

"Death!" shouted Veikko. Then he heard a bloodcurdling laugh, a deep laugh. Laughter in the Geki's voice. It cut into his brain through his temples. Like an electric shock. Suddenly he realized he was blind because his eyes were closed. He tried to open them but couldn't.

"You build up an immunity to it in time. We had to. To be Geki, we spend months inside the fear. We ingest it, we become it. We become toxic but immune."

Veikko opened his eyes. He shut them just as fast, leaving only the impression. The Geki stood before him. He was tied to a steep diagonal panel of some sort. But he must have been hallucinating. Behind the Geki he saw his parents, slick and gray, dolphin-skinned with giant eyes on the sides of their heads.

The fear crawled like ants up his spine. He tried to open his eyes again. He expected blood and fire, but he didn't fear blood and fire. He opened his eyes, and he saw water pouring in. He breathed it into his lungs and vomited into the water around him, then inhaled his own vomit. He was drowning.

"The first day is the worst. After your first year of it, you'll hardly notice it anymore."

SALVAGE. THE word kept going through Violet's mind. She would salvage what she could. In time she might be able to speak casually to Vibeke. She might be allowed to stay in the ravine. Or they might not even allow her that, she thought, and another sob hit her from inside.

Her eyes stung, either from the lack of sleep or the tears, or both. She wanted to know where Vibeke spent the night. It seemed important to know.

She hated herself for wondering. All the reasons for self-hatred came pouring out of the back of her mind. Not just for the horrible climax but for all she'd done before. The jokes, the constant pressure, begging. What the hell had she meant to do? To wear Vibs down? To erode her until she did what, fucked her out of pity? She couldn't believe herself. She couldn't reconcile her own name with the pointless mistreatment of a friend, Vibeke of all people. What seemed so important to her felt like nothing compared to what she'd risked with every stolen touch. Like she'd traded her closest friend, so much more than a friend, for a second's indulgence of petty lust. The clarity of it all was so sharp it was a cutting edge, a slice into her skin. She felt tears and snot covering her face.

There was a knock on the door. Violet was suddenly afraid of who it might be. Balder to tell her she was kicked out. Alf to tell her something even worse. "We kill rapists," Vibeke had once said. Violet was very aware the knock on the door could have been her executioner. She sprang upward and sat up in Vibeke's bed. She quickly skipped over to her own and wiped off her face. At that point she was ambivalent toward death. If that's what was coming for her, she'd let it.

"Come in!" she called.

The door opened, and Vibeke appeared. Her cheek was healed, but her eyes looked like Violet's felt.

"You don't need to knock on your own door, Vibs."

"It seemed right."

Nothing was right. Violet averted her eyes and looked at the floor. At the tiny blue and black pattern in the carpet.

"I told Dr. Niide it was a sparring injury."

Violet knew it was a statement for convenience, not shame or any attempt to protect her. "Did he believe you?"

"I don't think so. I'm not a good liar when I'm not on duty. He probably peeked at the memory."

Vibeke sat on her bed and felt it with her hand. It was still warm. She knew Violet had slept there.

"I'm sorry, Vibeke."

"I know."

No sense of forgiveness presented itself to Vibeke. Violet was unforgivable. If she begged for it, she vowed to slap her. If she even said she was sorry again, she would kick her damn face in.

"This doesn't have to be the end of... everything," whispered Violet. "We can salvage it. Maybe we can even stay on the same team. If we just need some time apart, then—"

"I don't want to lose my friend and my team on the same night, Vi. Not over this," she said despite herself. She sounded too lenient.

"I'm so, so sorry."

"Stop."

"I'm just—"

"I swear to fucking God if you say 'sorry' again, I'll bash your goddamn fucking teeth in."

Vibs was certain that was less lenient. Violet felt relieved at the threat, like Vibeke was still herself. Violet's face must have betrayed a trace of relief because Vibeke made sure to erase it.

"You retarded fucking cunt," she muttered. Even that wasn't enough. "You ruined *everything*."

Vibs almost felt guilty for it, kicking her while she was down. Almost. She shook her head. She felt angry at Violet for just taking it, for looking down at the floor like a guilty dog. She wanted a fight. She wanted to drag Violet to the mat and pound her into putty. To break her arm if she tried to punch back. Or hang her up on the range and whip her. She erased the latter thought from her mind because it inspired something else that she absolutely couldn't be thinking.

Violet felt on the verge of tears again. She had said "salvage." The only word that was running through her mind. She had nothing else to offer. It all tumbled in her head. They sat in silence for too long.

Vibeke wanted to sweep it all under the mat. She'd called her names and said her threats, and it did nothing to make her feel the least bit better. She had to move on.

"We have a mission. Alf said it would be a test of us together. I think we should stick to it. See what we really can salvage."

"I agree." Violet snapped it up. God did she agree.

Vibeke was disgusted by her supplication. She still wanted Violet to fight back. To fight back so she could hurt her more. Grab her breast and wrench it as hard as she could and see how she felt assaulted. She quickly pushed the thought away, proud she'd never do such a thing, even to her, even then. And pushed it away fast because, of all possible things, she didn't want to think about her hand on Violet's chest. Nothing sexual could ever happen between them now. Not even a wink.

"It has to be on my terms. We work together. Nothing more."

"No, no, nothing," she agreed, and suddenly hated herself for her groveling candor. She hated groveling, apologizing. She hated herself for wanting to so badly. Though she hated herself for other things much more.

They sat across from each other on their beds for several minutes, soaked in hate and regret, tired with it. More tears escaped Violet's eyes, and Vibeke saw them shimmer. And she felt for a second like hugging Violet tight and stroking her hair. Beyond all the hatred she could muster, she loved Violet more than anyone else alive and couldn't stand to see her so hurt. The conflict was unbearable. She had to get out of there, to kill someone. To hunt again. She needed a mission.

"Wipe off your eyes," said Vibs. "Let's go kill Wulfgar."

"WHAT ARE your names?" Veikko asked. There was no response. Veikko wanted to talk. Anything to distract from the fear, from the nausea and pressure in his head. And in his heart, he feared he'd have a heart attack. It had beat so hard for so long. How long had he been there? It felt like decades. He suspected it was a day.

"Do you even have names?"

"Yes."

Veikko tried to open his eyes again. He could make out a red carpet. Black walls.

"There you go. Get some conversation started. How's your mother?"

No reply.

"You're bullies, you know. Overgrown bullies."

"Valhalla is an overgrown bully. We are the schoolmasters."

"That's great, Professor Geki. That's really great. Why don't you teach me a few things?"

Silence.

"How do you do that disappearing trick?"

Silence, a wave of fear.

"Or your cloaks, what's up with that? It's *so* 1600s."

Nothing.

"Okay, how about why you didn't care… that a doomsday device made it to Earth? You care about one nuke, but you let the Ares come back to Earth, an indestructible doomsday machine."

"A hundred doomsday machines exist on Earth, ten thousand nuclear warheads. We only care that they are not used, as you used one."

"You don't care about shit," Veikko managed to laugh. He tried opening his eyes all the way. He saw the room and the two Geki inside it. He tried to remember why he was there.

"Balder said… you used fire?"

Silence. Fear.

"So what is it, some kind of plasma lattice? Ionization fields? Do you call it down from a satellite, or is it under your cloaks?"

"Implants."

"God! You're so fucking forthcoming, I love it!" Veikko laughed. He wondered if he was going insane. The fear stabbed him for laughing, and he wept.

"Are you male? Female? Anything?"

Silence.

"Cuz you know, I'm free later if you're not doing anything. Thought we could hang out, maybe get some dinner. I could tell jokes, you could send the waiters into agony and terror, make a night of it, you know?"

He opened his eyes again. The black room. No Geki.

"It's fucking rude! To leave when someone's fucking talking! God, you're so fucking rude!" He laughed again and no longer questioned that he was going insane. "Does that fear crap wear off on people? Cuz if I scare everyone when I get outta here, I'm gonna be pissed."

THE POGO crossed Mishka's net. She was alerted instantly, awakened by the system through her link.

The pogo was black. It looked like a common driver's vehicle. Fake tags, fake licenses, only Mishka knew they were Valhalla's. She knew she should have killed them there and then, but the alert showed only two people. Likely a passive observation mission. If she waited and followed them, she could get superior intel on her employer's lair. Vibeke could grant her one last advantage before her death. She ejected her eye and sent it flying toward the pogo.

It arrived as the pogo landed in the ruins, unchallenged. Wulfgar's fortress was nothing but decayed and collapsed buildings on the surface, any weapons would have given it away as something more. Surely the surface was monitored, but that was of no concern to the Valkyries. They were content to walk straight to the front door.

But there was no front door. They sent their Tikaris to scour the small island for any sign of an entrance, but for forty minutes they found none. Nothing came to oppose them. If the surface was monitored, nobody cared. They began to think they might get a free element of surprise. Violet cracked her repaired knuckles and tried not to think of the way Niide had stared at her as he fixed them.

The Tikaris found their way over the crumbling concrete and finally came to an eroded maw in the rock under one of the abandoned concrete towers. The Tikaris sensed warm air coming from the mineshaft, moist and laden with human breath. There were men inside but not near the entry. They set their suits for dull illumination and headed inside.

They were both completely at ease. On familiar ground, the ground of a mission. The night before didn't exist. They felt nothing for or against each other, only complete focus. So complete Violet couldn't even feel the relief it gave her, the absolute calm as she monitored the surroundings for threats.

At first there was nothing but rock, jagged teeth of coal around the sides of the tunnel. Graffiti marred the walls, somewhere between obscene and grotesque, all abstract and sloppy yet somehow deeply offensive to the eye and the mind.

They came to a sharp drop-off, an ancient vertical esophageal passage with a brand new plastic spiral staircase. The Tikaris scanned for traps as they headed downward. Several small rooms branched off, and within them the Tiks could see men, all men at work. As light from the doors took over, they dimmed their suits and went into full quiet mode, passing unseen by the chambers of what appeared to be file clerks and hackers in their offices. Deeper down were chambers containing apparent collections of meat and hair, doors emblazoned with human teeth, and a dim hallway full of what appeared to be men savagely gangbanging a stuffed giraffe.

They reached the bottom of the staircase and found a constricting aperture on the coal ground. It exuded the stink of a crowd on the other side. Luckily a quick look around the edges of the aperture revealed the start of an open-air duct system. They crawled inside behind their Tikaris and looked down through the grates into the massive room below.

It was a bulbous space with a wet floor and raw coal walls, wrinkled from mining and filled with tables and men, all eating. The cafeteria. The stink of the men mixed with the urungus odor of bad cooking. The humidity of the room was overwhelming even from above. The men below bickered and spit as Violet and Vibeke slowly crawled above them toward the opposite end of the room. There the air shaft went straight down. They slid through it.

They could see into side rooms to the main hallway, which curved around and downward. One cavernous room was painted bright green and appeared to be a research lab of some sort, with a large phallic drill at its center. A vicious looking drill with wires and hoses attached, presumably for coal mining but possibly for something else. Whatever it was for, it was still in use.

Farther down the hall was a room that smelled strongly of blood, or at least of iron. But somehow they knew it would be the former. They tried to look into the room, but the ducts didn't favor them, and the hall was too crowded to breach. They continued downward.

The halls became a total labyrinth, and the air ducts even more so. Zones of dampness became more and more frequent. Clumps of mushrooms had begun to grow in the corners and junctions of the maze. But they could see from vent to vent that the manner of personnel was changing. The brutes from the upper regions were growing more and more sparse, and men in black rubber business suits became more frequent. Locks on the doors between segments of the tract all faced back upward. They seemed to be moving in the right direction.

Then the air ducts stopped. There was a door visible in the hall beyond the final grate, and they'd seen no people for several minutes. They left the ducts and stepped into the cave.

The cave was still cramped but felt like an open field compared to the ducts. They were covered in soot and matched the coal walls even without their suit camo. The Tikaris perched on their shoulders and waited for instructions.

The door was another constricting aperture, but it had no visible controls. Violet reached out with her link but found no operating system. Touching the curious gate suggested it wouldn't open by force.

Vibeke whispered, "Open Sesame?" and they heard a low beep. The door didn't open, but they now knew it was voice activated.

"What would his password be?"

"Hrothgar," beep.

"Hrothgar Kray," beep.

"Orange Gang," beep.

"Fenrisulfr," beep.

"Violet MacRae," ding. The aperture opened.

"You should be flattered," whispered Vibeke.

"You can't see me blushing under the soot."

The Tikaris took off and stuck to the ceiling, monitoring ahead. There were no people for at least several meters. The hall offered a slow curve, and it turned back upward. As they walked through the strangely round, lobed corridor they saw one brief hallway leading down, but it came to a short end and appeared utterly useless. Up was the only way to go.

The round walls were covered in wallpaper, far nicer than the cave they'd been in. And they noticed a red carpet floor, which they almost felt bad about dirtying. But there were plenty of footprints on it already. They were giving away no tactical advantage. The area resembled a nice hotel, even if it was clearly still in a mineshaft, and the open rooms branching off suggested the same. There was a pool in one, empty. One appeared to be a kitchen, cooking up far more aromatic food than that of the cafeteria.

As the hall leveled out, it was downright opulent. Sconces decorated the walls, and the floor was finally clean. The doors were made of rich wood and had gold knobs. They had entered Wulfgar's mansion. As the hall turned downward again it became almost garish. Wood paneling, gilded chandeliers. They felt terribly underdressed. Their Tikaris kept pace, warning them of detector systems and alarms, but there were fewer and fewer. They'd clearly entered the inner sanctum where security ended.

Their Tikaris found a meeting room with a closed door, betrayed by their superior hearing. Nelson flattened himself on the outside of the door, and Violet listened through his tympanum.

"I think what's important is that Wulfgar not feel we're keeping a secret from him."

"Agreed, if he finds out, our plans will be ruined."

"The risk is incomparable. I can't stress this enough."

"Steel Toes has us covered, I assure you. Little Boots won't find out until it happens."

"Then it's settled. Tomorrow morning as soon as he leaves his room."

"We'll be waiting outside his door."

"I'll have the cake."

"I have the streamers and confetti planted in the ceiling and on remote."

"I think he'll really enjoy this. He'll never expect it."

"He doesn't even think we know his birthday. It'll be a real treat."

"What did you get him?"

"*Mass in G* by Goggly Gogol."

"Oh he'll love that!"

Violet withdrew her Tikari and cringed at Vibeke. They proceeded on down the hall, and after a sigmoid twist in the corridor, they came to a central hub with a beautifully engraved door.

At no time in all their caution did they notice the tiny black sphere rolling behind them all the way from the surface. Mishka saw everything they did from her perch on the surface. She was losing link resolution so deep in the tunnels, but she could recognize an emperor's door when she saw one.

Violet and Vibeke recalled their Tikaris and approached the door. They drew their microwaves and set their Tiks to kill anyone with a giant metal jaw. Violet scanned for traps and found none. She took a deep breath and opened the door.

She saw Wulfgar seated in a leather chair behind a luxurious desk. He looked up as the door opened. His expression flickered from surprised to angry at being disturbed. He hadn't yet recognized them. She was struck again by his eyes, the animal eyes that stared at her, the demented piercing eyes that stood out in Aga's mind. And the jaw, silver and exaggerated, filled with sparkling teeth that shifted loosely along their track as he moved. And he was bigger than she remembered, enlarged in surgery and now terribly intimidating, though not disproportional. He looked simply strong, powerful. Above all dangerous.

But terrible as he was, Mishka, Violet, and Vibeke were far more alarmed at what was behind him: Violet's corpse.

RISTO WAS born in 2207, six years before Loki. He learned fast and started speaking very young. He learned to swim young as well, and his parents were thrilled. It was as if he were born with an awareness of his great future underwater, as if he were eager to get moving, to get sinking.

He never cried, never spoke disrespectfully or stepped out of line. He questioned everything, of course. He was no robot, but when his parents explained the rules, he saw the value in them and followed them without further discussion. He avoided trouble when he saw it until he could avoid it no longer, that is to say, until Loki was born.

Risto was six when the little monster barged into the family. Loki cried constantly. When he learned to speak, he shouted and acted out. He wouldn't follow any rules, wouldn't hear the explanations or even listen when they spoke at all. And he never did learn to swim. He screamed the first time they took him to the pool. As soon as his feet touched water, it was like he'd been dipped in acid. The kid just couldn't stand it.

Had Loki's parents been sterner, things might have been different. But they didn't believe in striking the child. Such things were better left to history books. They loved him and cared for him with the utmost compassion, but that did nothing to quell his violent outbursts. Before long he had harmed another student in school and was removed.

"Take him topside," they said. "Let him learn online."

So Loki became the first in the family ever to get a link. Linked in, he saw the human world. So different from the Cetacean. Everything was bright and loud, everything was easy and painless, and everyone loved a good fight. There were fighting games, news of fighting in the streets, classes on how to fight better, and more.

By the age of seven, Loki couldn't understand why Risto was so happy down undersea. Everything was hard work. Everything was quiet and stagnant. The colors were brown and gray. Fighting was unheard of, except when it was Loki who started it. Loki certainly couldn't understand when Risto got his gill. The operation was long and bloody, and Risto was clearly in pain. The coming of age ritual was a gruesome affair, yet his parents stood proud, proud like they'd never be of Loki.

Loki resolved never to become a full Cetacean. No gills, no fins, no set of big silver eyes. He'd move topside as soon as he could.

Before long, Risto turned eighteen and finished his surgeries. He was the very model of a perfect Cetacean. Tall and slick, gray with the huge eyes and translucent skin. *Gross as hell*, thought Loki. Risto was no fan of Loki either. In the last few years, he'd been kicked out of online education, and that's no easy task. He'd been in brigs twice at the age of twelve, once for breaking a stanchion in a restaurant and once for attacking Risto with a knife. Risto pitied him. Something was clearly wrong with his brain. They could fix such things topside. Perhaps someday Loki would be fixed, but not on their euro. They had no money. Money was for land folk. Risto had everything he'd ever need. Why would he need a medium of exchange to get more?

He joined the Valkohai. The strongest sea force on the planet. And the most secret. He kept it a secret from Loki, of course. If Loki thought there were a navy, he'd join to "kick ass" and other such primitive things. That could not be allowed. The Valkohai were strictly a defense force. They'd never been deployed. Only in the event of a major attack from the humans would they ever unleash their terrible power. And humans had calmed down since the olden days.

Except for Loki. He didn't see Risto after he left for who knows where. He thought his parents knew but wouldn't tell him, which infuriated him to no end. He was an angry teenager. He landed in brigs twice more for violent acts, and his next would kick him out of the colony for good. A day he longed for. The only thing keeping him from exile was his father. His mother had practically disowned him. She cooked for him and cleaned his dry, land-made clothing but only out of care for her husband, who still held hope his son was something more than a total disaster.

When he turned sixteen, they argued. He felt it was time to leave. His mother felt it was time to leave. His father wouldn't let him. He would fix the boy first, make him acceptable before unleashing him on the world. It was his duty, he said, to see that Loki could do no harm. Loki of course wanted to leave, and the old man was in his way.

Cetaceans are somewhat fragile out of water. They have floppy feet, and their underwater eyes don't work, just their atrophied air eyes. And they have long necks. Loki seized his father's and squeezed. His mother shot him through the chest with a harpoon gun.

He knew he had only seconds to live. He used them to pull his mother onto the barbed spike that stuck out from his chest. The barb caught in her and pulled out of him as she fell back dead. By then his father was too, choked quickly—a disadvantage of having only one lung. Cetaceans were weak, thought Loki. And they were dead.

He was still alive. The harpoon had missed his vital organs, though there was a hole in him, and the hole was losing blood. He was turning pale.

Leaving his parents bodies behind, he took the boat and headed topside. It took thirty minutes to get to the beach, and by then he was unconscious. Almost dead. But crashed on the shore, his boat was seen by hundreds and poked and prodded by those curious about the first Cetacean vehicle they'd ever seen. They found him and took him to a hospital.

Loki healed quickly and found himself alone on Earth. He had never been so happy. No police from below came topside to hunt him, or if they did, they never came close enough for him to see them. He enjoyed the hospitality of those he ran into, curious to hear tales of the great below. Before long he was set up doing odd jobs for an acquaintance of one of the nurses that saved him.

Odd jobs such as beating up debtors, catching traitors to the organization. He was never invited to join the gang completely. Hrothgar didn't trust anyone from the sea, but Loki made do and made cash and settled into a decent thug's life.

But he craved more. More violence, more impact. He sought out the Unspeakable Darkness. They were all as modified as Cetaceans, not for Loki. He sought out the Yakuza, but they didn't trust a sea-born either. He looked into the myths, the fairy tales of darker organizations. He heard of the Hall of the Slain.

The stories were few and unreliable, but they grew clearer as Loki asked around, finding people nearer and nearer to the incidents that inspired the rumors. The Hall had not in fact killed five hundred men from Gang Green. It never had so many men. But a team of four, with

Sowilo runes on their belts, had killed twelve of them when they were plotting a bombing. And they had left survivors.

Loki spoke to them and heard the account. It was mostly just the same thing he heard before, told with more clarity. But the new information was the location of the fight. 2722 Ankkurikatu, a warehouse on street level. He found the place and broke in.

It was a dark, dank place. An empty one. There were microwave scars on the walls, chunks broken out of the concrete from years prior. He hunted for any clue and, in his thorough search, found something far better than a clue. A tiny gold pebble stuck to a ceiling corner. They had left a monitoring device.

Loki chipped it down from the ceiling and looked into its lens.

"My name is Loki," he said. "I am a skilled warrior, a hunter of men, a born fighter. There's no band of soldiers on land or sea good enough to deserve me, except perhaps you. If you hear this, watch me and see what I can do, then come get me."

The observation pip informed S team of new material, and they watched it, amused. They turned it over to G team who watched it and gave him a shot.

He was impressive. He was working for gangs and taking up mercenary work where he could find it. He had only street skills and little more, but how he used what he had was impressive. He was clever, clever in the extreme. He had instincts, the kind one can't learn. The kind G team looked for. In the end, they decided to bring him in.

They arrived to fake his death. He recognized the trick and spoke plainly.

"You don't need to fake it. Nobody cares if I die."

He walked into their pogo and headed for the North.

The Hall of the Slain—they called it Valhalla—was all he hoped for and more. A land full of strange weapons, extraordinary armor, and the prospect for spectacular training and spectacular missions to use it for. It was heaven to Loki, especially because he also got to choose his new name and shuffle off his Cetacean-given moniker.

It had to start with a specific letter, so he looked through the history pages and after a couple days of consideration, selected Veikko, after Veikko Korpiklaani, president and CEO of Suomi from 2150 to

2156, who slaughtered the first Cetacean divisionists and set the seas back many years.

THE INITIAL shock of seeing herself dead gave way almost instantly in Violet's mind to the rationale of how he had come by it. Valhalla-grown to replace her and presumed disposed of, Wulfgar had repaired her false body and preserved it. But that wasn't enough for him. As soon as she saw her corpse move, Violet realized he had granted the body a simple AI, some artificial brains. He had it programmed only to react to torture and scream in fear at the sight of him. Violet could have been offended or disgusted or felt terribly violated, but she never did waste time on such things. She quickly broadcast a hacking signal, broke into its brains, and told it to strangle its owner.

The corpse leaped down onto Wulfgar and reached its arms around his neck. It wasn't strong, and he threw it off in seconds, but it was enough time for Vibeke to send her Tikari straight into his chest. Violet sent hers into his head. Both bounced off, he'd been implanted with heavy armor. He ran.

Violet and Vibeke gave chase, the eyeball right behind them. They spotted raw coal walls and didn't risk firing their microwaves. Wulfgar ran down a short corridor and through another aperture in the rough wall. It closed tightly behind him. Violet reached it first only to get thrown back by a shockwave as the aperture burst open and outward. Her suit reacted automatically to protect her from the concussion, and she was merely thrown into the opposite wall. She dropped down from it and ran back toward the door.

It had been a pneumatic escape valve. She looked up in time to see daylight appear from the top of the long shaft as the capsule left with her nemesis. She cursed loudly.

"This is why we have four goddamn people on a team!"

Vibeke caught her breath. She checked the shaft for any way to tractor outward only to see it begin to collapse. A one-time-use escape route. There was nothing left to do but get out and report back to Valhalla. But Wulfgar knew they'd be coming for him. He wouldn't return to this base. They'd lost him.

Unless there were clues. As men who heard the bang flooded in from outside the office, Vibeke severed the first three heads and affixed a bore to one of them. Violet turned to guard the door, and Vibs monitored until it had a complete relevant memory load, then stowed it on her arm clingers.

"We head out, hunt for any clues on the way," said Violet.

"What about your body?"

"What?"

"The other body?"

"What do we need it for, the carpool lane? Leave it!"

Vibeke smirked for a fleeting second. Violet caught her and suddenly felt better than she had in days, despite the loss of her enemy only seconds prior.

Leaving the office and Violet's corpse behind, they navigated the lowest levels adeptly and returned to the conventional hallway of the mine. They wasted no time with the air ducts. They ran through the humid, winding passage at top speed, striking ahead with their Tikaris at anyone who emerged around any bend.

Soon they came near to the top of the passage and smelled blood. Not any they'd spilled, the smell was overwhelming. The strange room they'd passed before.

Violet was curious about the stench. For some reason it stuck out to her. She let her Tikari take a long last glance.

The room was a giant ventricle of the mineshaft. There was ancient equipment for moving coal scattered about. But there were also three giant tanks of blood. And guts. She recoiled at the thought. Then she saw the blender. Wulfgar had blended and tanked what must have been a great number of men.

And in a pile of clothing by the blender was a pair of yellow boots. Something snapped together like two puzzle pieces in her brain. They were the bulbous Wolf men from Mars.

"Vibs, wait."

"What?"

"This room, come back."

Vibeke scurried back through the shaft, and the two jumped down into the ventricle. Vibeke looked around as Violet spoke.

"He's blended God knows how many men, and he's keeping them in water tanks. One was Yellow Boots."

"The men from Mars," said Vibeke. She had it too. But Vibs went further. "They smuggled it back inside of his gang. They got to it before the Yaks."

Violet realized what she meant. "The Ares is here on Earth, intact."

Violet sent a brain-to-brain link to Veikko. It couldn't be encrypted, but it would hit him wherever on Earth he was. "Ares safe on Earth."

Vibeke sent the same message to Valhalla through Vladivostok's Alopex connection. They looked at each other. There was nothing they could do on their own. They didn't dare sabotage the tanks on an island where it could seep into the ocean. They leaped for the vent and started outward again. The great cafeteria chamber was ahead, so they took to the vent shafts.

Violet's mind was racing. They had failed. Nothing was saved. Worse than that, Wulfgar of all people had the thing to sell to Pelamus. There was no question he would, and he would gain exceptional power in doing so. If Pelamus was behind the YUP's disintegration, Wulfgar would stand to gain a significant chunk of UNEGA.

And the way he did it, to sacrifice his own men to bring it home. And that she failed to see it on Mars. So did Vibeke, of course, so she didn't feel that bad about it, but still the notion was sickening on every level. They traversed the ceiling duct over the cafeteria.

Until it broke. A section gave way, wrenching downward and dumping Vibeke onto a table. Violet moved to look down in.

Vibeke was surrounded by a hundred men in the place's main mess hall. She already had her Tikari in hand. Violet had high ground, but it was too high for a wide microwave to do more than make the men itch. It had to be far more personal than that.

Violet jumped down and stood beside Vibeke. She caught her Tikari. Dozens of men moved slowly toward them.

AT TIMES, Veikko felt like the fear was waning, softening. But these times seemed like a cruel joke as the sensation rocketed up again from his stomach to throttle his brain, as if the fear knew he was growing slowly immune to it, so it fluctuated to trick him into letting down his guard.

The hallucinations were growing stronger. He was certain that Violet had actually sent him a link that the Ares was safe on Earth.

But then, he'd also been reliving his childhood. Undersea—the most fearsome place. Not for the giant squid or the threat of drowning but for seeing them again, the last people who could control him. Anger surged up and fear, briefly, ceased to press in on his temples.

He thought of the Geki, and anger rose up again. It couldn't replace the fear, but it seemed to dampen it, to make it almost manageable. He focused on the anger and hatred of the Geki, the common-owned bastards in the black cloaks. And fear was only his state, not his master. As soon as he found that foothold, he devoted every free scrap of himself to anger. He lingered in its different chambers, repulsion, disgust, annoyance, exasperation, but it was raw fury that proved most effective of them. In fury he was able to think again.

The Ares was safe on Earth. He was certain he heard it, standing out above the synthetic delusions. He checked his link records. It was like crawling out of a pit under fire, trying to navigate his partitioned memory. The fear was still on his heels. Every time he opened a partition on his way to the link records, there was another blast of it. A cold feeling in his chest, or the shameful jolt of being startled anew. He turned it into rage. Every prick in the soles of his feet was a reason to run faster. Soon he was running at full speed toward the link.

The Ares was safe on Earth. It was there, clear as crystal. Not an illusion. He tried to absorb it. He couldn't fathom how. The nuclear blast had surrounded the Unspeakable carrier. There was no way it could have survived.

But Violet was going to Hashima. Wulfgar's lair. She was going to check on the Wolf Gang. Who had lingered on Mars without doing a thing. They must have done something, something that got it home and into their control. It had to be true.

He had to destroy it. He had to get out of there. He had to get what he came for.

For the first time, he made himself aware of his actual surroundings. He was trapped by strands of black fabric, like the Geki cloaks, like a blackened burnt spider web. He struggled to no avail.

A kilometer away, Sal reached the zone where he calculated the air distortion originated. It was easy to pinpoint once he saw the citadel. There was nothing else for kilometers. Sal landed by a river and used the water flow for a quick, slight recharge. Just enough to find Veikko.

The citadel had defenses. It was covered by a black canopy, threadbare with thick ropes. Not ropes on a closer scan, metallic tendrils covered in imaging arrays at their junctions. Sal plotted out the coverage zones, then deployed his sniffers. The long delicate antennae reached out of his head and electrified. Particulate matter from the air covered them. They withdrew.

Analysis showed Veikko's skin cells in the air, originating from a hole in the ground near the periphery of the canopy. Sal projected a possible route through the air and on the ground that would avoid all the detectors. It would be thick enough for Veikko to escape through as well. It prepared the information to download into his mind once docked.

The Tikari took flight and adeptly navigated the gaps in coverage. When he swooped low, however, a puff of dust was kicked up by his wings. Sal froze. Monitored. No reaction. The imaging arrays weren't motion detectors. Sal moved more freely.

He entered the hole and found a room filled with more black tangles. He avoided them and quickly found Veikko tied up in their masses. He jumped straight into Veikko's chest and recharged properly, simultaneously loading the information into Veikko's head.

Veikko immediately told Sal to jump back out and start cutting him free. Sal wouldn't leave his chest. He was afraid.

No, he thought, *a Tikari can't be afraid. It's me. It's only me.* Veikko brought himself to hate the fabric, hate its tangled look, hate the way it pressed on his skin, hate the very idea of the Geki trapping their quarry in those brambly wires. His Tikari emerged and began to cut into them.

Seconds later he hit the floor. He'd fallen only a meter, but the pain was crippling. No, not pain, just more fear. The fear of pain.

Worse even in common life than the pain itself. He stood up and grasped Sal, forming a blade in his hand.

The room was drenched in black and grotesquely surreal. Like the inside of an old cathedral dipped in tar. A palace patterned on frightful aesthetics. Anger. He hated the place, and it let him walk through it. The Geki surely never found this shortcut themselves. If they could function so calmly in their work, they must have truly become so immune to the fear they produced that they didn't need constant anger to navigate their own shrouds. Veikko's heart ran too fast. His teeth gritted themselves near to the point of shattering in his mouth. No, he had found a way through that they didn't suspect. They'd never see him coming.

The air was thin. High altitude, or elevation perhaps? The air was 2,500 meters thin. He was 2,500 meters up, more or less. The air was cold. But rich in its scents, pine and grass. He was on a mountain.

There was no door. Only an endless wall of gothic decoration and black gossamer.

He felt his way along the tangle, looking for any exit. Fear kept kicking him in the stomach. Insisting on itself. He wondered how much hatred was left in his system. It was tiring to be so angry. But anger has a way of snowballing, increasing itself. He fell to the floor and beat it with his fists, clawed at it with his nails. Red carpet. The decadence, he screamed with rage.

And looked up. At the base of the wall was a gap. An open gap into a cold blue light. He began to crawl.

Veikko found himself outdoors under the night sky. There was a canopy, though, more black webbing overhead like a threadbare tent. But the ground was rocky nature. Clumps of weeds and dirt. Ugly ground. He began to walk, looking back at his cage. It was a hole in the ground, in a hill. Like the entrance to an old mine. The discordant world played into his anger. All the better.

He crossed a road, an ancient paved road, cracked around its sides. He scanned the horizon. He could see dim mountains and hear a creek. And he could see red. Red lights, like a boat far away. He climbed over a fence at the roadside, black wire with barbs. They dug into his skin, and it felt sublime, pure sharp pain to piss him off. It granted him a moment of perfect clarity.

In that moment he saw the unquestionable core of the Geki's home. Draped in their signature coarse black cloak was their fortress, an unholy mixture of Egyptian temple and mutant porcupine, sticking out of a squat mountain. Veikko stepped toward it slowly and noticed the bizarre fortifications and fences, all at strange angles, all twisted and warped from any notion of linear architecture. Dim red lights spilled from what might have been windows under the cloak. Red lights also lit the moat surrounding it, making it glow like lava. Veikko walked toward the heart of fear.

He crossed a curvy bridge across the moat and came to a massive door in the building. Another strike of fear pierced his chest and told him not to open it. That whatever was inside was too vile to imagine. It sent him to his knees, demanded he turn back. Veikko hated demands. He rose up and burst through the door.

"'Land of Song!' said the warrior bard, though all the world betrays thee."

It was music.

"One sword, at least, thy rights shall guard, one faithful harp shall praise thee!"

It was Irish music. Veikko was caught by surprise and barely registered the rich, Victorian hall he stood in. He stood on a red carpet in a wood-paneled hall. He thought suddenly of *Alice in Wonderland*.

"The Minstrel fell! But the foeman's chain could not bring his proud soul under."

Panic crawled over him and urged him on, Tikari at the ready, looking frantically around him. All the doors in the hall were closed except for one, from which a golden light shone.

He approached it. Fear of the unknown replaced panic, and it wasn't so bad. Veikko still boiled with rage, and the unknown held little sway over him. He felt proud. He was surviving. He was functioning. He came to the door.

Inside was a massive library. Thousands upon thousands of books covered the walls, putting Alf's collection to shame. In the center of the room was a chair sitting next to an antique record player.

"The harp he loved ne'er spoke again for he tore its chords asunder."

And in the chair was a Geki.

Fear cut through him again like a kick in the face. Veikko cried out despite himself, robbed of breath before the black cloak. But the cloak didn't stir.

The Geki didn't move.

Veikko forced himself to walk forward, to lurch step-by-step with his blade drawn until it pierced the cloak. Just the cloak. His blade went through it into the chair. He realized it was hanging on the chair. He'd been looking at the chair's backside.

"*And said 'No chains shall sully thee, thou soul of love and bravery!'*"

He stumbled back and fell on the floor, fear of his mistake gaining a foothold into his mind and attacking again. No rage came to him. Nothing he could use. He was trapped within fear again, so close to its source and so helpless he froze.

The chair began to turn, slowly. Creaking as it swiveled to reveal the true face of the uncloaked Geki sitting before him. Pale, eyes sunken, creased, and elderly. Setting down her book with a wrinkled hand and wincing at the sight of him, her cheeks peeling back to reveal her teeth.

"You came into my house."

Veikko recoiled at her voice, his anger shattered, his mind raped again. The woman stood.

"You damn Valkyries, you never do as you're told."

Her voice grabbed his heart with an icy hand. He pulled in his arms and legs, shriveled up like a dead bug. The Geki raised her hand.

"You will burn, now."

And suddenly fear was his ally. His fear of death, his fear of pain, they rose up in him and took him over. A spark began to form in her palm. Veikko felt his arm flex. The spark became a flame. His arm began to swing. The flame became a fire. He swung his Tikari blade.

It severed her arm and sent it flying to the ground, where it set the carpet on fire. The old woman began to raise her other hand, but Veikko acted from pure instinct, from pure fear. He leaped up and stabbed her in the chest.

"Aaauugghhhh!"

Her sickening death cry burst his lungs, stabbed needles into his stomach, shattered his brain. Veikko felt his sanity torn in half. Felt himself snap from the fear, from the horrifying sound, from his own empowering rage, from all the monstrous terror held in the reservoir he'd just cut open.

And then suddenly, he felt nothing.

"Thy songs were made for the pure and free, they shall never sound in slavery!"

The record cut off. The room went silent. Veikko had been held in rapturous fear so long, he wasn't certain what was left when it ended. He was in a library. An old woman was dead in front of him, impaled on his Tikari. Her arm lay by her side. It was on fire. She was a Geki. That's what this Geki was. A grotesque old witch casting a spell. And she was dead.

Veikko spent a moment on the floor catching his breath, trying to reset his internal workings. He felt as if he should be gathering his guts and stuffing them back in, but there was nothing to gather. He was fine. It had all been nothing more than fear. He tried to wrap his brain around it but couldn't.

He remembered the implant. He looked to her arm. Burning in the center of its own fire. And the fire was spreading.

Veikko reached into it, catching fire himself. He examined it for a moment before the burning pain finally struck him. He started a vacuum field from his suit and the fire on him went out. The rest he left to burn. He examined the arm, burned and ancient, its skin sloughing off like paper.

He cut open the palm and found a metal prong inside. He grasped it and pulled. The implant slid out from between her radius and ulna. He saw where it replaced some of her wrist bones, where it held its power source and emitter. He wiped it off on the Geki's chair where her body had fallen back.

And the rage returned to him. After that brief numb moment, it wasn't the fear that returned but his anger, the rage he'd developed to combat it. That rage wasn't gone. It was all the more pure and intense.

He grabbed and swung his Tikari and beheaded the old woman, letting her head drop off the back of the chair. He attached her implant to the clingers on his arm and headed for the door. He snapped into Valkyrie mode again, very aware that there had been two Geki and that one would be hunting him very soon, if not already.

He made his way to the door where the cold mountain air caressed him. It was pure air, air so clean he'd never felt anything like it in his lungs, not the refined air of interior Mars nor the ocean air of his former home, not even the comfortable familiar air of Valhalla. Slowly it was tainted by smoke.

He walked out into the beautiful night landscape and out from under the Geki web into the vast mountain range. The Geki web caught fire behind him as he walked away. His geolocator slowly came back on and told him he was in America with a village eighteen kilometers along that black paved road. He set out toward the village.

As he walked, Veikko set his Tikari to the sky to watch for any sign of air distortion. It might give him a fraction of a second's chance against it if the other Geki came. He set his link to half immersion. He didn't tap into Alopex, the anger stuck to him, and he didn't trust his old friends just yet. He wanted to see Valhalla through his own eyes, to check on it on his own terms.

When he'd first arrived in the ravine and learned his first spy tactics, he'd set a few bugs around the place, bugs he never got around to using. Furious and betrayed to the Geki by his home, he logged into the spyware and took a look around, viewing the ravine for the first time as an outsider.

"DO YOU have any idea who we are or what we're going to do to you?" Vibeke asked. The men seemed unperturbed. They bared their teeth and moved in closer. They all attacked at once.

Violet and Vibeke both set their Tiks to berserker mode and let them orbit. They ran quickly away from each other so as not to harm the other, cutting into the crowd and sending body parts flying.

Violet ran for the exit to the room, to make her way up topside through all the Wolves who crossed her path. But the field of men was incredibly dense. Her Tikari couldn't cut through them all. She had to recall it for a boost from its thruster again and again to stab and slice at those immediately in front of her. She glanced to Vibeke and saw she was making the same slow progress.

There was no way around it. They fought their way out, killing swaths of men, drenching the floor in a decimeter of blood and taking no shortage of blows and microwave bolts themselves. Violet was tired after only a few meters of the mass, and the room was twenty meters across.

She made her way to the wall to take some of the pressure off, but that was hardly a break. The energy was sapped from her by her suit to maintain the antimicrowave field. Bullets hit from time to time, and they took even more. She felt cold, freezing cold before long.

By the time she made it to the wall, she was getting alerts. Frostbite would set in within seconds. Her Tikari would need to recharge soon. She was two meters from the exit. Vibeke was running out before her.

For the briefest moment, she was angered at the sight. Vibs was leaving without her. And why shouldn't she abandon her? After what she'd done, she deserved it. But she wiped the line of thought from her mind. Vibs was running because she knew Violet was right behind her, that she could take it and live just fine. She didn't want to disappoint her.

Violet cut through the last men and turned off her fields just in time to prevent internal freeze damage. Her Tikari rushed back into her chest to avoid getting left behind. She caught up with Vibeke, and the two continued to run through the hall.

Before long they came to the aperture and spiral staircase. Vibeke closed the aperture behind them and welded it shut with her microwave.

"That was a hell of a room," linked Vibs.

"I got forty-eight."

"Thirty-seven, guess I got the shallow end."

Violet laughed silently. She was sitting at the base of the stairs behind Vibeke, nose right by her boot. She knew she was looking at her foot enamored again. Of all the times—she got two seconds of rest after thinking Vibs abandoned her, and already she was thinking about rubbing her feet.

I'm insane, she thought. *Vibeke was completely right, and I've been too crazy to see it.* In that moment she thought she could push her love for Vibeke away and focus only on teamwork. It would be hard, but she'd done harder things. If she could cut through forty-eight men, she could beat down her libido. And that's all it was, she told herself. It wasn't love. It was sex. And she'd just proven that in spades.

Vibeke stood and began to climb the stairs. Violet followed and succeeded in not staring at her butt. They passed the side rooms with caution and stepped into the shaft leading out.

Mishka sat in an abandoned ruin over the entrance with her cutter rifle ready. This time she wasn't going to bring a building down on them or stop at anything short of two severed brain stems. She prayed, the best way to focus she knew. *Deliver to me my enemies, O Lord.*

Vibeke walked toward the entrance. She saw a black dot fly out through it. She recognized it instantly and fell back.

"Mishka!" she shouted, then ran back.

She bumped into Violet, pushing her back down the shaft. A cutter beam sliced through the air, burning deep into the coal as they fell down the first spiral of stairs. A fire suppressor hit the flames with a vacuum field before the entire mine went up. Violet briefly thanked Wulfgar for following proper safety procedures in setting up his tunnels of horror.

Mishka cursed. She should have risked hitting the eye to kill her. Now she was underground hunting for another exit. She had another chance, though. She didn't know where they'd come out, but she knew where they'd go—she had seen the pogo land. She ran for it.

Violet and Vibeke ran for the first rooms branching off from the stairs. There had to be another way out. Violet ran first and microwaved two Wolves who came across their path. After a couple minutes, they realized there was no other entrance. Impossible, there were too many people there to use a single portal. The new Ares tanks—the drill, far too large for their entry route. There had to be another way.

"Side," said Vibeke. Violet ran for the steps down to the welded aperture. There had to be a dock of some sort on the side of the island, which was built up on its edges like a battleship. They came to the aperture, and Vibeke drew her microwave just in time to see it burst open from the other side. She switched from cutting beams to killing beams and fired into the pit. But no fire came back.

They cautiously stepped down into the cafeteria hall, and then into the cafeteria ready for another slaughter. The few remaining men who saw them, though, ran for dear life, leaving them standing in an empty room, shin deep in blood and body parts.

"That must have sucked for them. I mean it was their lunch break, wasn't it?"

"Yeah we're… we're not friendly people."

Mishka came to the pogo and hacked its lock. Not one of Valhalla's standard pogos, it was easily opened. Mishka crawled inside the back. She pulled a Carlin Knife from her ankle band and cut her way through the backseat into the trunk. There she lay in wait, linked into her rifle's scope, keeping it aimed at the driver headrest with only a fraction of a centimeter sticking out of the seat. She had them.

Violet and Vibeke walked calmly through the room and into the next hall, where they found the Ares room and the obscured but large door through which it could exit. They looked and linked around for a door opener, and Vibeke found an open protocol. She linked it open, and it began to rise. She let it open just enough to slip through and rolled out with Violet.

Violet burst into sunlight at the side of the island. There, a platform jutted out of its side to hold several black pogos. She felt the subtle sizzle of the thermoptic field that had hidden the platform from their Tikaris. She recognized one pogo as the vessel that rescued Wulfgar from the island, that flew off into the aurora. She ran for it, and Vibeke followed.

"Oi! You ain't registered on tha—girls?"

Vibeke elbowed the guard Wolf into unconsciousness and took his key box. They leaped into the pogo. Vibeke found the proper key, and Violet started the pogo, then lifted off at top speed.

Out of the windshield, through her scope, Mishka saw the pogo take flight. She knew instantly who it was. She cut her way back out of the seat and threw her rifle aside. She hacked the pogo to start and lifted off.

They were both in conventional pogos. Mishka knew how to catch up. She overrode the safety features on the engine and gunned it almost to the point of failure. She sped toward Violet and Vibs at nearly the speed of sound.

Vibeke saw the pogo chasing them and warned Violet. Violet overcranked the engine and steered out over the sea. But the other pogo was gaining on them. Vibeke crawled into the back and shot out the window with her microwave. The air suddenly left the pogo leaving a near vacuum. Vibs shot out the windshield past Violet, who knew to put up an inertia field to calm the air. They could breathe again.

Vibeke began firing at the pogo behind them, which continued to gain. Then suddenly, a cutter beam appeared, firing past them. Violet began evasive maneuvers, flying wildly from side to side. But Vibeke knew who it was.

"Slow a tenth!"

She wanted her to catch up. To kill her.

Violet should have gone on. But she felt a pang of guilt. She owed Vibeke everything after what had happened. She knew as she thought it that she was wrong to consider it, that it was a mistake caused by romantic thoughts on the teams, exactly as Vibs said. But she did it anyway.

The pogo slowed, and Mishka's sped up to them, almost passing. As it reached them, microwave fire and cutter beams burned the air between them, but with the evasive driving of both, nothing connected.

"Toshiro!" called Violet.

It took only an instant to click. Poetic justice. Vibeke set her microwave to overload and waited. It approached critical. More cutter beams sliced through the air, one cut off the rear bumper. The microwave was ready. Vibeke threw it.

The explosion went off right on Mishka's windshield, blasting it out of its grooves and into her face, splattering plasma through holes onto her arm and stomach. Her pogo shot down toward the water. Mishka tried to eject, but the windshield blocked her seat. She was trapped. The pogo hit the water at hundreds of kilometers per hour. The water spray was colossal.

Vibeke shouted at the top of her lungs, "Chug brine, you fucking cunt!" then fell back into the pogo's seat. She caught her breath. Then came the realization that she hadn't just shot Mishka down and delayed her. The crash would be fatal, and Mishka didn't have Valhalla to take care of her anymore. If she died, she died permanently.

Vibeke realized it might suddenly be over. She ran through the odds in her mind. It was certain. Mishka was dead, there was no way she could survive that crash. Vibeke smiled more broadly than she ever had before. She had to control her breath to keep breathing. She shifted her way into the passenger seat. Violet looked at her and laughed.

"'Chug brine'? What the fuck, Vibs?"

Vibeke laughed out loud, then froze to let the idea sink in. As wind struck her face, she thought about the years of hatred, a hatred so intense it blinded her to everything else. She felt it even then, victory did nothing to rid her of it. She was angrier than ever, the adrenaline surging behind it. If anything it had spilled out, where Mishka gave anger a place, that place was now gone and rage permeated every other thought.

More than anything else in that moment, she hated Violet. She had thought once that if Mishka were gone, she could finally accept her similar gaze, her strength, the things she loved that she could never love again. Instead she felt only fury that Violet had ruined it. She tried to calm her mind, thinking it was a mere momentary derangement. But as Violet kept staring at her with a coy grin, Vibeke was absolutely overcome by hate for her, and she finally realized why.

She was angry at Violet for losing control, for the last year of flirting and looking and begging, for her backward notion of consent, for attacking her the night before, but none of that rage held a candle to the fury she felt when Violet held her down to the bed. Because in every fantasy Vibeke had ever had, she was the one holding Violet down by the hair. The idea struck her like no revelation before it. She turned back to Violet and looked her in the eyes for only a second before she slugged her as hard as she could in the face.

Violet was too surprised to block. She had no idea what was going on. She barely took a breath before Vibeke slugged her again, spinning her head to face away from her. She felt Vibs steal the weld clip from her hair, and before the wind could take it, Vibeke grabbed the loose strands, tearing half of them out. She grasped her hair tight and forced her face into the seat of the pogo so fast it spun her body around.

Vibs wasted no time in clawing down the back of Violet's armor, peeling it off and reaching inside and around and down, making Violet squeak. Vibs wanted to hear her squeak again. She pulled her hair to the side and jumped closer to kiss her, her mouth open as if to suck Violet's tongue out by the root. She grabbed her breast with her other hand and rubbed it with vicious force as Violet struggled out of instinct, still completely unaware what was going on.

Vibeke kissed her neck and her back, then withdrew her hands and shoved Violet into the backseat, slamming her head into the center armrest. With Vibeke's hands off her for an instant, Violet turned around to see her peeling off her own armor. Somewhere around this time, Violet finally figured out what was happening. Her promise to herself in the caves vaporized. Her regrets and shame failed to disappear and only confused her further. She forgot the mission, the wind in her face. She forgot how to speak and fell powerless under Vibeke as she climbed back on top of her and grabbed, groped, and rubbed herself against her with every second of lust that had built up over years past.

The pogo slowed to its regular top speed as its passengers ravaged each other in the back, and flew aimlessly over the Korean Peninsula, another car in a traffic of millions.

The younger Geki recoiled its sensors and stopped watching, giving them privacy. It was content that Violet was safe. It descended into the mineshaft unseen and found Violet's extra corpse. With its flame, it incinerated the double, then damped out the flames that took to the coal. It was time to return to the citadel. It jumped home.

ALF AND Balder walked together around the perimeter of his library.

"A Geki came to me as I slept, a single Geki," said Alf.

"I've never heard of such a thing."

"Veikko has killed the other."

Balder said nothing.

"The Geki demanded we kill him," said Alf. "I suspect even a single Geki could do so easily, but it wants us to. A show of loyalty perhaps."

"I'll do it as soon as he returns."

They walked on in silence for a moment.

"What do we do with V team?" asked Balder. "Split it up?"

"To say the least."

"Vibeke should stay in the ravine. As a consultant or on a new team." Alf nodded.

Balder went on. "I can take Varg into B team. He belongs there anyway."

"Did you read Dr. Niide's briefing on Violet? On her and Vibeke?"

"Yes. What do we do with Violet?"

"This ravine has never suffered a sexual predator in any way, shape, or form."

"No, it hasn't."

Alf scratched his cheek. "Kill her the instant she arrives."

Veikko logged out from his library bugs and took a deep breath.

Chapter X: Ragnarök

VIOLET SLOWLY woke. She felt wind on her shoulders, cold and bare. But also hot on one side. And soft.

She'd been dreaming offline, of such wonderful things. She'd never had so good a dream in her life, nor one that felt so real. She had to go back a day to think just where the dream began. Assaulting Vibeke, that was real, as was the torturous regret. Seeing Wulfgar again, the pain told her that was real. Mishka dying in a great ocean spray seemed less likely, too good to be true. And what happened next was completely impossible....

Vibeke gently ran her fingers through Violet's hair. Violet shifted, inhaled with a choppy breath, and realized it happened. The hot skin on her arm and chest were unquestionable. She was genuinely pressed up naked against Vibeke. She opened her eyes and adjusted to the bare sun and dark blue sky. To the cold, angry wind.

She kissed the stretch of Vibeke's side that appeared right before her face, then the side of her breast and her collarbone. Vibeke pulled her closer and kissed her on the lips.

Violet tried to think and wake up, but it was like the dream kept its claws in her, the sharp heated pinpricks of memory that spoke to an entire day of squeezing each other close against the cold, highlighted with several hours of sex in every form they could think up. There was no question it was the best day, dusk, night, and dawn of her life—despite the starving feeling, despite the pain of microwave burns and what was likely a fractured arm. Vibeke was hers for that day, hers in a way nothing could take back from her. *Or*, she thought, *the other way around.* No mission, no revelation, no hour online with the Patumias pleasure spool could compare to it. She thought if she only had another day to live, she'd die happier than she'd ever been. And that no day to come, no matter how good, could possibly top the recent past.

That is to say the sex was *really* good, and plentiful. Violet took stock of the morning after. They were in a pogo high above...

somewhere. An incursion into the Wolf stronghold had met with mixed results. Wulfgar escaped, and the Ares was on Earth, but then again, Mishka was dead, and Violet and Vibs had a whole lot of sex. Alopex would rank the mission at 100 if she knew Violet's priorities. She stared up into Vibeke's eyes. She tried to think of anything to say and felt compelled to say at least one thing.

"I'm sorry for breaking your cheek and trying to rape you."

Vibeke grunted. She still felt no sense of forgiveness. She simply wasn't the type to forgive. It wasn't in her range of emotion. She'd hold it against Violet until the day she died, but like every other feeling, she could ignore it utterly. Push it down so far it couldn't matter. She was angrier than ever at Violet for souring the love they could have had. It would never be pure now. But then, what in her life ever was?

"You want me to say I'm sorry for waiting so long?" she asked.

Violet didn't care. It seemed like the least important thing in the world.

"I'm not sorry for anything," said Vibeke.

They stared at each other, felt each other's skin.

"I'm gonna make you pay for every glance you stole in the shower. For every joke you made, every time you brushed your arm against mine."

Violet didn't know what to make of it. Vibeke hunched down and grabbed her hair again.

"And you're gonna pay for what you did in the barracks every damn night of your life."

She grabbed her hair harder and pulled her up to kiss her.

"Okay," said Violet, "but if this hair thing is what you mean, I'm gonna go bald."

"Shut the fuck up."

Vibeke kissed her with tooth-shattering force. Violet rubbed against her naked body again, hips against hips, breasts against breasts, lips on lips on tongues on teeth. She felt burning hot, Vibeke's skin on one side and cold wind on the other. It felt so alien to her. As if the world knew the importance of the night before and the walls of reality had broken open to the surreal state she felt. She held Vibs tight and nuzzled again behind her ear.

"Violet, no Alopex," said Veikko.

"What?" Violet asked, bolting upright.

"What?" asked Vibeke.

"Veikko," she replied. Then she realized it was a link.

"Violet, don't sign into Alopex. They'll kill you. Tell Vibs I killed a Geki and said 'Hi.'"

"What about Veikko?" asked Vibs.

"He says 'Hi.' And he killed a Geki."

Vibeke sat up. "Okay...."

"He just linked to me from... from over Newfoundland. He said if I signed into Alopex, someone would kill me."

"What the actual fuck?"

"I don't know."

"He killed a—how? Are they after us too?"

Violet didn't have any answers. She instinctively pulled on her suit, a foot of which had never left her in the previous day's commotion. Vibeke began to dress as well.

"Where are we?"

Violet checked the geolocator. "Holding pattern over Neo Seoul. I'm setting it for Valhalla. It'll be a day in this thing."

"Are you sure we should go back? If Alopex is gonna kill you?"

"I don't know. I don't know what's happening."

"We have to meet Veikko. He must know."

"I'll set course for Vadsø. We can risk an open communiqué to him, right?"

"He did for us."

Violet sent a link to him across the open net. "Lost Collar."

Vibeke knew immediately. They'd meet at the restaurant where they took her for training, where she'd forgotten her collar and Veikko and Vibeke brought it back to her. *Clever*, Vibs thought.

"What now?"

"Well, we can't sign in," said Vibeke.

"It'll be a day before we meet him."

"Well, what can we do all day?" Vibeke smiled broadly.

Violet pulled her suit back off, and they lay down in the back of the pogo. She began to kiss Vibeke again but stopped, awash in shame for that night in the barracks. Vibs seemed to pick up on it.

"How...?" Violet whispered.

"How do we do this after what happened?"

Violet looked into her eyes. Vibeke looked somber, concerned.

"You fucked up, and I'm not the forgiving type, I'm not gonna lie, but...."

"But?"

"Maybe if we fuck hard enough nonstop until we die, we can keep our minds off it."

Violet exhaled and nodded, and then started kissing her chest and stomach and on further down.

WULFGAR LANDED at the Nagasaki office. The pod ride was miserable. It wasn't made to be comfortable, of course, but given the likelihood he would need to make an escape, he made a note to make the next escape pod more spacious, perhaps with a minibar and unquestionably with a bathroom. The high gravity of the rocket out of his chamber was killer on the bowels.

Steel-Toed Boots greeted Wulfgar and offered him vodka, which he happily accepted. The medical team immediately flocked around him to tend to his superficial wounds. As they worked, Wulfgar got right down to business.

"How great a delay will that break-in cause?"

"No delay to the invasion, sir."

"None at all?"

"No, sir. They did no damage to the Ares or the drill. They stole one conventional pogo but not one from the fleet."

"Excellent. Then we head north tonight and arrive in the morning."

"Yes, sir."

"And our man in the North?"

"Ready, sir."

"Excellent.... Toes?

"Yes, sir?"

"Did they happen to find... in my office...."

"The duplicate Violet was destroyed, sir, burnt to a cinder."

"Ah. Well. We'll have to take the real one, won't we?"

Preparation had lasted months, and there was little else to do. Valhalla would be coming, and they'd be sending a massive destructive force for Hashima as soon as possible. All the better reason to head north with the fleet. And hopefully the girls would be there too.

Violet MacRae, in person. He questioned whether he should have stayed to bite her head off then and there. But no, she had the advantage. Two of them with blades, one of him with a Thunder 5. One had penetrated one of their necks before but not the suit. He'd have had to aim for the heads. And he wanted Violet's head intact. He had plans for that head.

Not to mention the knives in his chest and face. Violet's friends had made her into a killing machine. Quite unlike his own machine Violet. A shame, a true shame they destroyed it. But surely the real girl would head back home, right where he was going. And he knew she would accept his challenge. She'd do it to save her base. To save her friends. It was the perfect design.

A fleet of sixteen armed pogos, four battle pogos, and two cargopogos departed Hashima. Wulfgar stood in one cargopogo and examined the drill. A mining drill he'd purchased from Zolfo while awake on Venus, rebuilt to the specifications of his contact within Valhalla, able to penetrate their rampart.

It was small, only two meters in diameter and four meters long, but it would prove sufficient for its purpose. He linked to Steel Toed Boots.

"Take command, I'm getting in."

"Roger H. Wilco."

Wulfgar climbed into the drill's capsule and closed the trap door, sealing it shut. He wanted some time to think.

He wanted to kill Violet. Badly. And he was heading toward her home. But not for her, for business. She would be icing on the cake, nothing more. Though Wulfgar's favorite part of the cake was always the icing.

THE DAY he chose his name, Veikko promised himself he'd never be called Loki again. He was not Loki. He was a new man, born fully grown and native to Valhalla. Eric had granted him new skin. Niide gave him a new body, or a new body part at least. And Balder had given him new purpose. Not the ideal purpose, though. Balder was adamant that Cetaceans were harmless critters to be left alone. Veikko, of course, knew better.

But such things were quickly forgotten. Training had begun. Veikko learned a hundred ways to kill. Then a hundred more, and after that another hundred with the promise of hundreds more to come. That he learned to fight was no surprise. What surprised him was that he quickly learned to laugh. He had been a somber, angry child. But in the paradise of the ravine, he quickly manifested a humorous streak. Timid at first, in his first month, he grew rapidly outlandish, especially where Skadi was concerned.

She was stunning. Tall but far from gawky. Buff but not visibly in her armor. Veikko loved that armor, not just on himself. It was as if the front carriage showcased her small, firm breasts. He was shocked one morning to see her showering off outside of the gym, naked in front of him without a second thought. It was clear, though, she saw him, that nudity was nothing to her. The opposite of Cetacean thought, in which any dweller topside would be expected to wear an armor suit over their air suit over their wetsuit over their underwear over their skin suit over their lipid layer. So the sight meant everything to Veikko. It was by far the best memory he kept in his head, and indeed he made sure to back it up in several cloud partitions.

But Skadi didn't laugh. At anything. Everyone in the ravine enjoyed his jokes, his practical jokes, his general demeanor. Skadi was as cold as cold got, and in winter on Kvitøya that was saying a lot. So he tried constantly to no avail. The hopeless quest fell back to second place after his training, which, to his delight, literally included "kill training." He had to kill someone. *With pleasure*, he thought as they revealed his target. A Cetacean pirate. A nasty one who had tortured families topside. Veikko didn't want to show off his delight. Years of Cetacean social mores told him not to be proud of killing, so he did it painlessly and regretted that ever since.

Then he was given a daughter. He knew he'd be getting a team as time went on, but he was surprised when R team dropped a beaten, wrecked girl in his lap. They fixed her up, of course, but she was clearly a victim of an incredibly hard life. Yet she was not a victim at all. She was angry, feisty. She was furious they'd hacked her brain to determine her bedding preferences, though, in fact, they'd merely done their research. She told him she'd been in prison, in a riot. He told her that in her new prison, he was the riot. He proved it by making the girl laugh and felt a pride he'd never felt before. He felt as close as he'd ever feel to a parent, and it suited him well.

Until he taught her to spar. She didn't like his sparring music. She disemboweled him for it. As Dr. Niide stuffed his guts back in, Veikko lost the fatherly vibe. He had no choice but to see Vibeke as anything but an equal. A rarity for a girl, given the Cetacean sexual dimorphism he'd been raised with. He'd never imagined a girl could be as vicious as he'd always felt. And so unapologetically so. He was amazed by landloper girls and tingly all over to imagine Skadi was such a warrior at heart.

Not too long after his disemboweling, he and Vibeke monitored a Scottish girl for their team. She caught G team's eye by killing the men who killed her family. She seemed like their type of girl, so they kept her on the list of potentials as G team continued the hunt. Then Violet beat the living shit out of her entire barracks rather than be hazed. Veikko and Vibeke agreed she was their next team member. The three watched a Deutsch boy for the last, and the team was complete.

They grew together through the trial of Udachnaya, through the takedowns of the Orange Gang and Sasha Suvorov. And all the while, Veikko felt just a millimeter held back. It was Alf mostly, an older man who reminded him a little too much of his father. He was restrained. Reserved and smart, to be sure, all the positives of age, but he was also afraid. Alf was afraid of the Geki. And that fear, even though he'd experienced the fear they caused firsthand, was a shame to let linger the way he did. He felt Valhalla was wrong to remain subservient to anyone or anything. But it was of little concern. He was on Earth, he was killing for a living, and he was still in a place infinitely better than under the sea.

That outlook changed quickly when he heard of the Ares. The power to deliver the world to his nemesis. And the elders wouldn't let him nuke the damn thing. He snapped then and there on their first order to use restraint on the nuclear option. The Geki had to go. Veikko would happily die fighting them, but he couldn't resist fighting them any longer. He vowed to use the nuke if only to summon the things and deliver them into his hand. Then he would take their fire weaponry and be a god among gods.

He realized as he plotted out the Geki demise that their fire was what he was really after. Not merely their deaths, but their ability to induce fear—not by the Farnesene Pulse but by their ability to destroy Valhalla. That was what Alf truly feared. The solution was unavoidable. He had to kill the Geki and take their flames. Then Alf would fear *him*.

Violet heroically nuked the shit out of the offending device. And for their accomplishment, they were punished exactly as Veikko had hoped. The Geki would come for them. Not only that, but the Geki were, in Balder's estimation, no more than common human beings with advanced weaponry. The kind he killed for breakfast. Finally, it was time for the Geki to die.

He planned it out. He set Sal to find him when they took him. It was a huge risk. He had no guarantee their transportation tricks would leave any trace. But Sal found it, the brilliant bumbling bug, and Veikko accomplished his ultimate goal. Or half of it. Upon escape from the realm of fear, he gained a new concern to keep him afraid—there was still another Geki out there. He didn't know why it wasn't there to begin with or why it didn't come back to kill him when its partner died. But his hacks into Valhalla solved that. The Geki wanted them to kill him. Easy day—if he could kill the Geki, he could handle his old pals.

He was to meet Violet and Vibeke in an old grill they'd once visited. On the slow GET there, he formulated his plans to handle the ravine. It was a difficult task, in fact, the hardest puzzle he'd ever solved. But solve it he did, and by the time he arrived in Vadsø, he knew each step of the plan.

He knew how to deal with Alf and Balder, and Cato too just for fun. He knew how to deal with the Ares, now that it was known to have survived. And he knew how to deal with the restraint he'd been given over the last year. His plan solved more problems than it needed to. He only needed to stay alive. But now he was going to reign in a world of fire. With only a few sacrifices.

Violet and Vibeke landed in the parking lot and stepped out.

"We don't tell him anything about us, right?" asked Violet.

"Right, absolutely, he can't know. Nobody can, not yet."

Veikko turned the corner and saw them. The trio walked in together and took a seat in a booth.

"So, you two have very clearly had sex."

Violet looked away, Vibeke face-palmed.

"Oh wow," said Veikko. "I was kidding. Did you seriously?"

"Why is Alopex gonna kill me?" asked Violet.

"The elders are under the impression you're a sexual predator."

"Shit."

Veikko tried briefly to be polite and not ask but failed. "Are you?"

Violet simply didn't know. She could hardly deny it after what she'd done, but their lovers' quarrels weren't any of the elders' business. Or was what she'd done so severe that it was? Did she deserve to die for it? In her lowest moments since, she'd have said yes. But with Vibeke, together, the thought was doubly sickening—Vibeke didn't deserve to lose her, not now.

"Okeydokeythen," said Veikko.

"I can log in," said Vibeke. "Explain it to them. They wouldn't do it if they knew we'd… reconciled."

"You might be surprised. They sounded pretty resolute. But if you do log in, can you tell them not to kill me too?"

"The Geki?"

"Yeah… I sort of kind of killed one of them. The good news is I stole her fire implant. But there are more pressing issues. There's no question, the Wolf Gang is going to invade Valhalla. I'm sure we can repel them, but we need a backup plan in case he takes the ravine, assembles the Ares."

"Actually I consider that second priority, after you know, making sure Valhalla doesn't kill us."

Vadsø was just close enough to log into Alopex. Vibeke did so. Alf and Balder were above contact, but V team had a message: Come home immediately.

"They want us in person."

"Then you'll have to go. Violet and I will find a safe house that Valhalla doesn't know about."

"The Frasers," said Violet. "They're against protocol, from my old life. They'd never expect us to go to them."

"Excellent," said Veikko. "Vibs, you take the Wolf pogo. We'll wait here. And can you do me another favor while you're there?"

"What do you need?"

"A little black book...."

MISHKA WAS very upset. She'd failed to kill Vibeke for what seemed like the hundredth time, and she'd nearly died herself. First the overloading microwave, the plasma burns, then the windshield stopping her ejection, then the impact with the water—that had to be her favorite part, barely turning on her inertia field before hitting the sea, getting the windshield blasted into her face again, almost drowning. The entire day was just a total write-off.

She had to swim for hours before she came to Hirado Island, and by the time she arrived, her body was so spent she collapsed on a small stretch of beach. She called her tank and went to sleep on the sand.

She woke hours later in the darkness with her tank gently prodding her with its hind foot, digging the other two into the sand to stay upright. She stood and stretched and looked at herself. She was a giant walking bruise, swollen all over and mostly black and blue. She didn't bother with an analgia field. She was too pissed off. The streak of near misses had to end.

She linked to the tank and told it to carry her to Valhalla at top speed. It would take only a day and a half. But she had to end it. To kill Vibeke or be killed herself. If she had to take on the whole ravine, so be it. She could visit her old stomping grounds, kill all her old friends. It would be a jolly good time.

The tank raced into the water and propelled itself toward the Korean Peninsula. Whatever happened when she arrived in the North, in one day Valhalla wouldn't be hunting her ever again.

An urgent message loaded in the back of her head. Red Boots wanted his money back.

VIBEKE STORMED off the pogo pad. She found Balder and Alf in his library and headed straight there. She burst in and interrupted.

"Did you get my link? The Ares is intact and in possession of the Wolf Gang."

Alf and Balder stared at her. Balder spoke as Alf walked out.

"Yep, that explains why Vladivostok just detected them incoming."

Vibeke was dismayed by their seeming lack of concern. "Veikko has killed a Geki."

"And he'll die for it," claimed Balder.

Vibeke was disgusted. "Grow some damn balls! He killed one, why don't we kill the other?"

As he turned, Vibeke ejected her Tikari and sent it to the top of the library.

"I won't discuss this with you."

"Then how about this, is it true you want to kill Violet too?" asked Vibs.

"Yes," stated Balder, emotionlessly. The Tikari scanned volume after volume.

"Don't."

"From the report it seemed you'd be the first to agree that Violet is dangerous."

"We've reconciled."

The Tikari found its target, a small black book. It pried it out from between the others and waited.

"She assaulted you. We do not allow such people here. We kill them."

"Then cut her from the teams, but do *not* kill her. I love her."

"If this situation arose under my predecessors, the solution would be very simple. You would have to kill her to stay alive yourself."

"You're not your predecessors."

"I wonder sometimes if I should be." He headed for the door. As soon as he turned, the Tikari flew to Vibs and deposited the book in her hand.

"You won't," she said. "Let her go. She can leave the ravine if she has to, but I won't let you kill her."

Balder turned back and spoke brusquely. "Then let me offer another deal, one more to the point. Veikko must die. The Geki have— *has* demanded it. There is no question nor debate. Kill him or convince him to return and be executed, and Violet may leave the ravine quietly."

"And if I want to leave with her?"

"After this grotesque emotional display, we won't miss you."

Vibeke didn't feel the least bit hurt. She linked out on high encryption to Veikko.

"Have book. They demand I kill you or you return to face execution. We can't count on Niide to make a fake, but we can fake your death at my hands easily enough."

"Negative, I've anticipated this. Tell Balder I'll return to Valhalla."

"Veikko, I'm not asking you to sacrifice yourself."

"There's no sacrifice, Vibs. I have no intention of dying. Tell him I'll be there in two hours."

Veikko logged out of the communication. Vibeke didn't know what he had planned, but she had to take the chance. Veikko could take care of himself. And soon, she and Violet would be free agents, together out of the ravine. She'd miss it, she thought, but this was the only way.

Alopex spoke. "Wolf Gang approaching Kvitøya, ETA 170 minutes."

Balder linked in and spoke over the system to the entire ravine.

"Middle teams to defensive positions. Nonessential civilians and junior teams to depart the region, rampart to close in thirty seconds."

Vibeke was confused at his orders. "Since when has Valhalla evacuated because of a threat?"

"Never. Civilians evacuate. Valkyries fight. Half of us are going topside to deal with the assault. Half of us will destroy Wulfgar's base while Alf kills him."

Balder walked away, and the earth shook. A deafening grinding noise began to sound. The rampart was moving into position. Vibeke ran for the pogo pad and climbed in, then flew straight out as the rampart closed.

"THAT SETTLES it, then," said Veikko. "I'll take the north road, and you'll take the south road, and you'll get to Scotland before me."

"What are you going to do?"

"Stay alive. Destroy the Ares. Maybe get some Thai food."

"But how?"

"At a Thai restaurant, Vibs, do I have to explain everything?"

"Veikko, what—"

"Don't worry. I'll be fine. Just get to the safe house, and I'll resolve the situation. Situations. Take the Wolf pogo. I'll steal something nice for myself."

"Veikko, you need to tell us what you're planning."

"Maybe a Hyundai if I can find one."

"Vei—"

"Shhh. Trust me, there's a method to my madness. Wait for me with the Frasers."

"What about this book? Why do we need Alf's old intel?"

"Did you look through it?"

"Briefly, his handwriting's not the best."

"Just hold on to it for now. I'll let you know if we need it."

"Veikko, you've never in two years not informed us of every detail of an operation."

"I didn't tell you about my hangnail on project Thanatos."

"Veikko, what's going on?"

"I'm solving the problem, Vibs. Trust me. There's a reason for everything."

Veikko stood and bowed, then jogged out of the restaurant. Violet and Vibeke looked to each other. They didn't bother to link. They were both thinking the same thing. Veikko seemed to know what he was doing, but it was completely unlike him, unlike any Valkyrie to leave his teammates out of the loop. He was planning something unusual, irrational.

They had to trust him. That's all there was to it. They stood and headed for the Wolf pogo, still silent. Vibeke started it up and set it for Arcolochalsh. Violet felt nothing at the thought. It was a tactical decision devoid of sentimentality. It had to be done.

Because they were going to kill her if she returned. Everything had changed in an instant. She had lost the ravine by punching Vibeke and gained Vibeke by—something she didn't fully understand. Mishka was dead, but Violet couldn't comprehend how that changed matters, or even if it was what did. She grew concerned that Vibeke's love for her might be as impermanent as the prior rejection of it. They boarded the pogo and set course.

She tried to tell herself it was different now, that it had changed forever. She had an instinct to enjoy it while she still could.

"Wanna make out?"

"I'm worried about Veikko."

"Me too. Wanna make out?"

"Not right now, Vi."

"'K, how about now?"

"You have fewer settings than Wulfgar's copy of you."

"It's a long trip, Vibs."

"It's a long life, Violet. We have plenty of time."

"Yes, and we should spend it kissing."

"We'll have to make a living."

"We should apply as orbitliner attendants. Spend the rest of our lives alone in zero-g."

"I was thinking assassins."

"We did just kill the competition."

Vibeke sighed in relief. Mishka was gone. Probably. Vibs had tried not to let herself gauge the actual odds again. Part of her said Mishka was unquestionably still alive. If you don't see a Valkyrie's liquified brain, they're still alive. But Mishka wasn't a Valkyrie anymore. No more Dr. Niide. No more friends to save her. She had to have died.

Violet looked over Vibeke. For the first time she was thinking of Mishka and smiling. She shifted around to behind Vibeke's seat and put her arms around her, hanging them in front of her chest.

"I've wanted you so long I don't know what to do now that I've got you."

"I don't know what couples do either. I think we're supposed to, like, have dinner together and talk about... stuff."

"Well, we've done that for two years."

Vibeke took one of Violet's hands and kissed the back of it. She didn't put it down, but kissed it again and held it on her lips.

"Two more hours to Kyle," said Violet.

"Talk to me. Tell me everything," Vibeke replied.

"About what?"

"Everything," she said.

VEIKKO USED an emergency link carrier to call the police. They arrived within minutes. Two officers, one pogo. They found Veikko lying on the cold ground.

"Sir, are you awake?" asked the first officer.

The second approached him and prodded his body. He didn't move. One readied his scanner to take a pulse. Veikko sprang into action and attacked both simultaneously. He knocked both out within the first second of his attack, then continued to break both their necks. He piled them into the back of their pogo, alive but paralyzed. Just in case he needed them.

He flew north and examined the police sensor array. It wasn't too shabby, standard collision avoidance and terrain survey equipment, but also a long-range com landscape tool and high-end defensive arrays. He set the longest scope to observe the ravine.

CATO WAS busily hacking the GAUNE meteorological database. If the weather was going to be bad in Maynila, GAUNE's conglomerate, Graco would delay their attempt to take over UNEGA's conglomerate, SM Prime Holdings. Then Cassandra would have time to hack in and crash their stock, making GAUNE give up its Maynila operations altogether, operations they'd never have started if the UNEGA monitor junction in Poprad hadn't been evacuated due to a nuclear event.

"Veikko," he muttered under his breath. All of Valknut. The upstart team had been a nuisance since Udachnaya and this, this was the last straw. If the Geki didn't kill Veikko, Cato would. If Violet returned, he'd be first in line to end her, for ever touching her teammate. With some luck Vibeke would turn civilian, and Varg would stick with the PRA. There was some dim hope of ending the accursed team forever.

With all that was about to happen, V team had to detonate the first nuclear blast to grace the globe in 200 years. How did the damn Geki not kill them all in that instant? As far as Cato was concerned, they deserved what they got at Veikko's hand. They'd gone soft. Everyone was going soft. Everyone but Cato.

Cato was about to do for the ravine what Balder never could, what Alf never would. He logged out of GAUNE but didn't return to Alopex. He stayed offline. That would be critical.

Cato crossed his arms and leaned against the rock wall. Truly he was above and beyond any other Valkyrie. He had more guts, more vision. Or so he thought. That's why he never saw Veikko coming.

THE FRASERS door was lit. They were home. Violet knocked.

Mrs. Fraser fainted as soon as she looked. Mr. Fraser stared at the video-door for a full five seconds before he understood why. He opened the door and let the undead in. He didn't even ask her companion to explain. He tended to his wife first. As she came to, the duo explained a standard Valhalla contingency tale to spin when encountering someone known previously.

"They had to make the Wolf—the Orange Gang think I was dead, or they'd have pursued me till I was. They gave me some work with—"

"No need to explain, lassie. I'm so happy to see yeh, yeh could tell me you were brought back t' earth by the devil himself, and you'd be welcome in these walls, and I migh' buy the old man a drink for havin' brought yeh."

"Another friend may be joining us soon," said Violet, suddenly worried he might not.

Vibeke picked up on it too, "may be." There was every reason to think he'd lied, that he intended to die to get them free and clear of the ravine. And every reason to think he did have a plan, something brilliant. Or at least audacious.

They observed the niceties and then retired to a guest bedroom.

"What do you think he's going to do?" asked Violet.

Vibeke only cringed.

THE WOLVES appeared on the HMDLR's outer field. A large pack of them, bearing fangs. Alf linked the external defenses to activate. The array outside the rampart erupted from the ground, shaking the earth beneath Balder and his team. The Bs rode individual roving guns. Balder stuck to his old Ice-CAV, a giant horseshoe crab of an armored tank. Perth team took his right flank, Wunjo team his left, both teams in APCs. Alf's tank made the surface on HeR Mode to lend its arms and legs.

Othala and Sowilo manned the small battle pogos, two per vehicle. Everyone else was on the way to Hashima or busy trying to ease the tensions of a postnuclear cold war.

Alf monitored the incoming fleet. All glossy black, classy pogos. One of them a Rolls-Royce. Wulfgar hadn't lost his sense of business style. It would be business for him. Wulfgar was not a master of warfare. He'd not start shooting, and indeed his fleet circled the ravine without firing a shot. He was there to do business. He would begin with an offer. There were two cargopogos. One surely contained the Ares. But the other… Wulfgar had something planned.

VEIKKO ARRIVED two kilometers south of Kvitøya. It was no longer a ravine, but a dome. The rampart was closed. And under siege, pogos circling. *A hopeless endeavor*, he thought, but it afforded the opportunity he needed. As he flew closer he saw Balder's Ice-CAV on the surface. Balder was the only man that ever drove it. The enemy acted strangely. They weren't making any kind of assault. Their patterns were merely defensive, protecting the cargopogos.

Veikko logged into the police pogo's mainframe and dug his way into the personnel files for William Testling of Sydney, Australia. UNEGA police records appeared. Testling had died in action in 2212. Veikko knew, of course, that he had not. He'd hacked Cato's files the first time they had a run-in with the old bastard. He'd gone no further. There was little to learn and no point in learning it, but now he had a cause and a necessary effect. He looked through the records. He found Will Testling's link frequency and carrier ID. Something that wouldn't change, even when he entered Valhalla. And with that information, Veikko could forge his messages.

Cato would be among the teams calming tensions between UNEGA and GAUNE. The likelihood he'd be signed into Alopex was almost nil. Veikko had to risk it. No plan comes without risk. He signed in, and no alarms tripped. He was the only Cato online within the system. Internal voices were hard to mimic but not as hard as real ones. He didn't have to mimic Cato's voice, only his cadence, his mannerisms. Easy job, being a total dick. He'd test it on the one girl certain to forgive him if it didn't work.

"Alright listen up, Skadi," he said, imagining an Australian accent, "need you to veer away and check out the blip to the south, looks like a police pogo."

"Cato? I thought you were—"

"Don't pay ya to think, sheila. Get on it."

On his sensors he could see Skadi turn toward him, away from the action. It worked. He linked into W.

WULFGAR'S CARGOPOGO lowered the drill. Alf armed the defense array but didn't fire. The drill was small. It wouldn't afford entry to any pogo. He remained calm and linked out through Alopex.

"Do not fire on the drill. We could use another drawbridge anyway. I've anticipated this. If Wulfgar wants to speak to me, let him come."

The teams stayed ready to fire.

The drill fell from the cargopogo and rocketed toward the side of the rampart, bit spinning at terrible speed.

WEATHER HEARD Cato over the link.

"Weather, emergency incoming! Fire on 66-86! Wire-guided!"

"Negative, Alf has ordered us not to strike," she replied.

"Pig's arse, fire now!"

"Negative, Cato. I'm not even detecting the drill at 6—"

"That's because you're blind, doll. Weather. Trust me. Fire at 66-86!"

"Cato, I need to—"

"No time! Fire!"

It was on W's project Harbinger that Weather last directly disobeyed Cato. She paid for it. He had told her to detonate the charges exactly one hour early. Out of contact from her team, she couldn't risk them still being in the blast zone. The charges remained still. An hour later Weather finally heard from her team. They had been out of contact at the critical moment but got a message to Cato through his Tikari, which had been monitoring them for purposes of his own.

Cato informed her of the new time, the new brief moment in which they could have destroyed the bridge. But she didn't. She didn't trust her elder blindly, and for it, Harbinger was a waste of two months of planning. The arms made it through on time, and a tribe was slaughtered. She ran to Veikko and told him everything. He remembered.

"Weather. Fire."

Weather fired a wire-guided missile at the coordinates, trusting Cato blindly.

It hit Balder's Ice-CAV exactly on the side. Molten copper shot through its armor and into the cockpit, with white fire behind it. Balder was engulfed in the blast, killing him instantly and burning his body to a cinder. Veikko's plan was going perfectly.

VARG WOKE from a digital orgy as soon as Balder's link went dead. It snapped him out of his cryostasis and left him freezing in the Blackwing cockpit. He turned the vessel around and hit the thermobaric thruster. It deployed and ignited a field of gas behind it, creating a light brighter to Earth than any star but the sun. The entire planet would see the Blackwing, know that it survived. But he'd be home in hours, for whatever he'd find.

THE FORCE of the drill's thruster chipped the first half meter in and gave its bit a chance to grab. The rock began to shatter around it and the drill burrowed in.

The drill entered the rampart practically unnoticed. Balder was off link. For the first time, Balder had died. A death nobody knew if he could survive. Skadi turned her pogo around and darted for the rest of S team, which had been engulfed in the blast and crashed.

Alf too ignored the drill, in shock at W's missile. He said nothing. Nothing needed to be said. Weather knew what she'd done the instant it happened. Her Tikari saw it from atop the APC. She lamented her choice to see through it. To trust Cato. She vowed she would kill him the instant the Wolf crisis ended. But before she could resolve, she got a link.

"Weather," said Veikko, "I need you and Wunjo to listen to me very carefully."

He had killed one Geki. He had the fire implant. He had killed Balder, and sadly a few more. Sigvald and Snot's pogo was in the blast. Good thing he'd directed Skadi and Svetlana away. He didn't want to kill any more Valkyries than absolutely necessary. But they were necessary, there was no question of that.

The framing of Cato had succeeded absolutely. Veikko didn't know it, but he guessed correctly that Alf marched straight for C team's office. With some luck he'd kill him on the spot. With equal luck Cato would kill him. Alf would need to die too; there was no question. But he could live to see Veikko's plan unfold just a bit further. He linked to Skadi and gave her the same link dump he gave W. Every step, every point, every reason he had. He knew she'd understand.

Then Veikko saw B team amid the rubble. He watched in horror as they lifted Balder's remains from the wreck. His head and one shoulder were intact. His brain was unharmed. He'd be back. And then Veikko would be doomed.

ALF KICKED C team's door open.

Churro began, "We're looking into—"

Alf shot Churro with a confined beam, cutting him in half through the heart. He swung the beam through Claire and Cassandra, killing all three. Then he leveled the microwave on Cato.

"You may take them to med bay once you've answered to my satisfaction. You lose a part for every dodge. Now. What have you done?" he demanded.

"Alf... that wasn't me... I—"

Alf shot him, cutting off his left ear.

"Damn it, Alf, why would I—"

His right.

"It wasn't me! For the love of God, Alf, let me explain!"

"Explain." He kept the microwave on Cato's head and walked up to him, holding the weapon to his temple, ready to blind him.

"That wasn't my link, I wasn't in Alopex, check the log signature!"

"I will as soon as we're not being drilled. Take your team to Niide. When this is over, the log will determine your fate. I'll investigate if you've told me the truth. If you've not, you will live forever in pain to regret what you've done."

Alf walked out and climbed the power plant branches toward the drill site.

MISHKA'S TANK emerged from the water. She saw the CAV get hit. Balder's Ice-CAV. Impossible, a shot from their own APC hit Balder. An unthinkable accident. An unthinkable opportunity. She rode up onto the land and set her tank to run at top speed for the wreckage.

The tank limped wildly toward the destroyed CAV. Everyone on the field saw it. The Valkyries recognized it. Everyone knew without question that Mishka was to blame, except those few who Veikko had told the truth. Those were the only Valkyries not firing at the tank. Everyone else let loose.

The tank outran all they threw at it and skidded down into the crater surrounding Balder. She fired at B team, killing Bathory and Borknagar. Brock made it to his gun and fired at the tank to no avail. She ran him down, impaling him on the tank's right leg. That put her right over Balder's remains.

She opened the escape hatch under her tank and grabbed his remains, then set the tank to head for the water.

The fire ceased. Valkyries knew what she had taken. None of them even gave chase. None of them would be fast enough.

Except for one tank. Alf's. Eight legs, the fastest tank of its kind. The smartest too, on HeR mode. He sent it for her. She couldn't outrun it, but she had to talk to them anyway. She stopped her tank just short of the water.

"Mishka?" asked the tank in Alf's voice. He was immersed in it atop the YGDR S/L.

"I want Balder to live. As much as you do. But I want to live too."

"Say it, Mishka."

"I want everyone in the ravine to stop hunting me. Every Valkyrie."

"Done."

"Link them! I want to hear every voice say it!"

Mishka knew that they would have to keep their word. She had offered a fair trade. If they kept their promise, Mishka would be free and have no reason to pester the ravine again. If they broke it, they'd have a new active enemy with near omniscient intel.

Alf immediately sent the question out to every Valkyrie. Affirmatives flooded in from across the globe, everyone was willing to promise for Balder's sake.

Alopex sorted the requests and located each Valkyrie across the globe and beyond, then contacted them in whatever way would reach. When the link hit Violet outside of Alopex, it was uncoded. And it hit Vibeke.

Violet looked to her. Vibeke had only hours earlier watched Mishka die. She was so happy at the prospect that she lost all control, and for that brief time, she was a completely different person. Free, happy, and in love. Now Mishka was alive, and she had to promise not to hunt her. She had to, there was no choice.

She had seen Mishka die, so she thought, and somehow she could tell herself that was enough. She had the catharsis she wanted. And she had Violet. Everything would be better, she just had to let go of the past.

"Yes," she said. Violet too.

The link finally hit Varg in space. He replied yes instantly.

Veikko signed out of Cato's link and sent his own into Alopex without signing in again. He said, "Yes," then thought fast. He couldn't allow Balder to live. This was his only chance to end the man. He hacked into Thokk's new link. She didn't stand a chance. She knew nothing of link warfare yet and didn't even know that her affirmative reply wasn't heard, or that the "no" that flashed involuntarily through her head for an instant was sent by Veikko in its place. To Mishka and everyone else listening, Thokk said no.

A hundred voices linked her name in anger and exasperation. They knew her disputes with the man but never imagined anything so cruel of her. G had made a mistake. They had brought in something terrible.

Mishka cursed and fired a microwave beam directly into Balder's brain, destroying him.

Tahir in extreme shock, betrayal, and rage pulled his microwave and shot Thokk through the head.

Mishka headed into the water. They'd never stop hunting her now.

WULFGAR'S HUD told him the bit door was free. He stopped the drill, leaving its back end like a plug to the hole. Nothing would get in or out. He opened the door.

It swung down with him latched to it, landing him right on his feet. He walked over the bare rock.

He kept away from the edge of the ravine. Surely he'd be shot instantly by their security systems. He looked instead for a slick incline, a drop into the rock. A walrus trap.

He'd been dead the last time he passed through it, but the place still felt oddly familiar. He found the trap in only seconds, marked as promised by his spy. He walked down inside. His implanted sensors betrayed a dozen traps around the inner lining to the room below, but all were turned off. Again the spy came through.

He stepped onto the rafters, and they pivoted down, allowing him into the room of his death. They hadn't cleaned up the scars from his men's microwaves, nor the stain of his blood on the floor where he had been crushed. *Filthy*, he thought. *Unsanitary*.

The storage room door opened, and the golden ravine burst into his eyes. It was beautiful, the rock lit in vibrant gold, the hundreds of towers built into stalagmites, into stalactites hanging from the outcroppings overhead, and in the center a glowing tree with hundreds of branches. And on its highest branch stood a man with a spear.

"Wulfgar," said Alf.

"You have me at a disadvantage."

"In more ways than you think."

"You lead this ravine?"

"You could say that."

"Then I have an offer for you. I assume that, as any good leader would, you have no wish for bloodshed?"

"You assume wrong."

"So an offer to avoid a battle would mean nothing to you?"

"It would mean little. We can annihilate your fleet."

"But surely some of you would die."

"What's your offer, Wulfgar?"

"Champion warfare."

"Intriguing."

"I hoped you might think so."

"The terms?"

"If my champion wins, you turn over control of the ravine to me. If yours wins, my fleet departs."

"And how do we know you'll comply?"

"Because I represent myself, and the match is to the death. If I am dead, the fleet will dissolve."

"I accept."

"Then I want to fight Violet MacRae."

"Violet MacRae?"

"Blonde girl? About yay high, wears purple? Kinda cute?"

"Violet has been expelled from the ravine. If she returns, she'll be killed. And you don't get to choose your opponent's champion, Wulfgar. You'll be fighting me."

Wulfgar was damn angry. No Violet. And a very different opponent. He grumbled at himself, how stupid to have expected such fortune.

"Too great a letdown. To be honest, I'd prefer to go back to the battle."

"Too late, too late. You'll honor your agreement. Stab me in the back now, and I'll do the same, literally as you turn."

Business, he reminded himself. He'd made a deal, and he had a job to do. And if he failed, he wouldn't be alive to regret it. Wulfgar stepped onto the power system and kicked off his little boots. His feet had a good grip on the warm branch. His compound mechanical jaw was ready to tear the man to shreds.

"Very well. But I still don't know your name."

"Alföðr."

"Your real name."

"It's long and Tibetan, and it would be a waste of time to recite to a man about to die."

Alf's Tikari lengthened, a formidable spear. He held it high and waited for Wulfgar to come. Wulfgar walked toward him. All the man had was a spear. Wulfgar had the finest fighting body money could buy. Even impaled on a spear, he was confident he could—suddenly he was impaled on a spear. He quickly realized it wasn't just a spear. Its legs began to writhe inside his wound. The Tikari sprang inside him and stabbed in eight directions.

It pulled itself out of him and formed a tarantula. The tarantula attacked, viciously. Alf was quick behind it. He delivered a punch with an unnatural arm that knocked Wulfgar off the branch and down to a branch below. He landed with a painful thud that seemed to squeeze blood from his wound.

Alf didn't stop attacking. He jumped down and landed on Wulfgar's stomach. The spear leaped into his hand, and he stabbed Wulfgar again, only his rib breaking protected him from death. Alf kicked him, his leg splitting into two spines as it connected, piercing Wulfgar's side and sending him down to the next branch. He bounced off it and fell down to another, almost five meters below.

Wulfgar was scared shitless. He had at least expected to throw a punch, but he never even—his line of thought ceased as the spear launched itself, rocket ended, into his right arm, nearly severing it. Wulfgar now intended to run, but he couldn't. Alf was on top of him with a double kick, breaking his hip. Suddenly Alf pulled back his thumb like the fore-end of a shotgun and fired. Wulfgar barely moved his head in time to keep it from getting blown off, still the ricocheting pellets bounced back at him from the branch and embedded in the back of his head.

Alf wasted no time. He kicked Wulfgar again, sending him down to the next branch. Wulfgar managed to pull himself up just enough to fall down to another branch, then another. He had enough time from the falls to catch his breath, and then the tarantula landed in front of him and knocked it back out of him. He fell again, hitting a branch with his face, then falling to another below it. Nothing was under him except the rocky ground now. He jumped down the last four meters and broke his shin on the stone.

Alf landed on his feet next to him and kicked, spinning Wulfgar around on his spine. And again, spinning him the other way. The tarantula landed and formed a spear. Alf raised it high into the air and aimed for the center of Wulfgar's skull.

Cato fired his microwave into Alf's back, paralyzing him. He fell to the rock. Cato stowed his microwave and offered Wulfgar a hand, pulling his massive, heavy body up to stand.

"I'd say that's for my team, mate," he said to Alf, "but I'm content to let them die. Truth is, I planned to sacrifice them to bring back the Ares if Wulfgar here hadn't done it himself. My contract with him required that much. Killing you wasn't part of our deal. You weren't even a subsection. Or how did you phrase it when you took me in?"

Alf didn't try to speak.

"A side letter to Cassandra's induction? You thought I was a by-product? This by-product's your death, mate. This by-product ended you."

He patted Wulfgar on the back.

"Took you long enough," muttered Wulfgar.

"Patience is the greatest of all virtues."

"I never liked Shakespeare."

"Not Shakespeare, mate. Do it."

Wulfgar pulled Alf up from the rock and extended his jaw to its maximum length. He activated the teeth, which cycled like a chainsaw. He bit down on Alf's head, destroying his brain in a wide splatter, leaving only his lower jaw. He let the corpse fall back to the rock.

"Now, Cato," he said, blood spilling down from his mouth, "lower this rampart. And more urgently... get me to a—"

Wulfgar passed out on the rock, beaten and broken from the fight. Cato slowly dragged him to Dr. Niide.

Chapter XI: Arcolochalsh

BATTLE POGOS appeared on the horizon of Hashima.

They flew over the island and let loose every conventional bomb they had. Buildings were blown off their crumbling foundations. The blasts flooded the air, splitting off the surface of the island and leaving barren waste across it.

Then the Valkyries landed, nine of them with Tikaris orbiting, plunging down into the holes left by the surface assault. They cut the remaining Wolves to shreds. Blood poured down through the tunnels. So much blood issued that the Wolves on the lowest floors drowned before the Valkyries could slaughter them. Each Valkyrie fired twenty scanner bullets.

The scanners imaged the lair and mapped out its tunnels thoroughly. They sent the telemetry to H team's pogo, the pogo with the Gerðr System. The system took in all the data and prepared a cutting field around the tunnels. The Valkyries inside made their escape and tractored onto the passing battle pogos on their next pass. Once safe, H team activated the system.

The field cut into the rock and held the tunnels in place. Then the field rose up above the ground bringing the internal structure of the mines up onto the surface. The field turned off and the structure began to fall apart. But as soon as the Valkyries were inside, the battle pogos turned around for their final pass. Their guns began to fire. Every projectile they had shattered the tunnels, disgorging the blood and meat within them, breaking Wulfgar's lair into nothingness, leaving Hashima utterly annihilated topside and below, ruined, a bloody stretch of crushed land in the middle of the sea.

DR. NIIDE sat back and lamented his oath, the mind-locking oath that forced him not to break it.

After a short time in the medical center, Cato led Wulfgar toward the com tower.

"Alf always suspected, since you were a prisoner," said Cato, "soon as I kept 'em from tinkering with your Gulliver."

"Assuming you mean you kept them from reprogramming me to be a tofu merchant, I'm endlessly grateful."

"As you should be, mate."

"I believe you had one final duty to me before I make you my general."

"Ah yes, about that...."

"You wouldn't be trying to avoid your duties, would you, Cato?"

"No, not at all. Just... I never got Valknut's pip frequency. He's harder to find than expected."

"You will find him, Cato. I have plans for him."

"If I may ask what plans, perhaps I—"

Wulfgar turned to him and stopped on the walkway.

"You said, Cato, that I died in that box because a walrus crushed me, yes?"

"Yes, Wulfgar."

"Then my order stands. You'll be my general as soon as you bring me that walrus."

"Yes, Wulfgar."

He turned and continued up the walkway, with a hand on Cato's chest to tell him not to follow. In the com tower, he sat down on the bench in the middle and linked into the clean line. He didn't dare link into Alopex. They would have to dismantle the Valhalla broadbrain and restore it to the Ares control system.

From the clean line, he loaded the contact protocol from a partition the Cetaceans had assembled in his mind when he took the contract.

"Valhalla seized, Ares ready to assemble."

"Good, good!" replied Pelamus. "I'll be there within the hour. I'll transfer ownership of the YUP to you in its entirety, along with the other assets we spoke of. You have done well, Wulfgar, and secured peace for your kind."

"For my kind?" he asked.

"Of course. If we didn't have the Ares to kill you all, we'd have killed you all one by one. For *our* safety."

Wulfgar snorted.

VEIKKO'S PLAN was back on track. It was time to deal with the Ares. Ideally, Violet and Vibeke would be willing to hijack a fission warhead and send it straight to Valhalla. Veikko knew from the start that it was unlikely they could successfully break into a nuclear silo and complete the task, and even less likely they'd be willing. He could handle the willing part, but he simply couldn't bank on them succeeding.

As a backup plan, he hacked into UNEGA's security mainframe and piggybacked from there into the DHS. He went straight for the slush pile to deposit his intel. He'd masterfully crafted it in a partition as he flew to Vadsø: proof that the Prešov nuclear blast originated from a GAUNE base on UNEGA's own soil, an island called Kvitøya. On this island, GAUNE was constructing a Cobalt Thorium G device. Conventional and fusion attacks would activate the Cobalt and poison half of UNEGA. But a pure fission vaporization warhead would annihilate it. UNEGA would have only one choice—to nuke Valhalla and destroy the Ares. Naturally this intel would be ignored by the bureaucrats.

Until its prophecy came true: that GAUNE intended to break into UNEGA's nuclear base at Dimmuborgir shortly and launch a missile as a black flag operation. Then the ravine would be annihilated at the atomic level. And GAUNE and UNEGA would be in a de facto state of nuclear war. Then at last the world would be warm and on fire. The evacuated Valkyries, as the ultimate force would reign supreme, with Veikko at their helm. He'd need only deal with the final Geki, and with all Valhalla behind him and with the Geki's own weapon, there was no way he could lose. He only had to learn how to use it.

He flew south to Arcolochalsh. Skadi and W team had the plan. They'd both be heading to Arcolochalsh to rendezvous with him and begin the next phase. Start the war. Evacuate Eric and Niide. Take the weapons. Find a new home.

The only real variables were Violet and Vibeke. He simply couldn't be sure, no matter how well he knew them, what their reaction would be. He wasn't even certain how much they knew. He'd have to approach it all in the most discreet, subtle way possible.

"I killed Balder and framed Cato who killed Alf. I don't suppose you two would be up to hijacking a nuclear bomb to destroy the ravine?"

"What?"

"No!"

"That's what I thought. Give me one thing, though, that's all I ask—just think about it and sleep on it. And in the morning, if you don't want to do it, that's that."

Vibeke and Violet slept in the Fraser's guest room. Violet fell asleep with Vibeke's breath on her cheek, warm and sweet. Her hand stayed on Vibeke's side, where it dipped down under the covers before her hip. Violet's fingers soaked in the heat of her skin and felt merged with it, stuck to it, and part of it.

Veikko used every tactic of silence to open their door and walk in without waking them. He slowly crept up to the sleeping couple and pulled down the sheets with Valkyrie subtlety, not waking them as he exposed their backs. The top of their spines, where they'd never look for marks. There he put the cerebral bores and began the hack.

As the bore mapped their brains, Veikko ejected Sal.

"You up for another, little guy?" he linked.

Sal nodded.

"Your aunts are gonna need help. Okay?"

In the morning, Violet and Vibeke consulted Alf's black book. Violet couldn't even make out the handwriting to have her link read it for her, but Vibeke found the key intel. The nearest active nuclear missile silo. They headed for the GET station on the roof and hacked two tickets to Iceland, reserving a berth for the trip.

Veikko headed for the seventy-sixth floor atrium, which was always empty according to the Frasers. He found it devoid of residents.

He sat down and took the Geki implant from his arm. It looked simple enough. Connections for nerves along what was clearly a power source, body-kinetic like their suits from the looks of it. He produced a bore from one of his armor pockets and removed the shell. He connected each nerve node to one of the bore's intakes and linked in through it.

The instant the implant activated, the other Geki appeared. Veikko had only a fraction of a second to feel like the biggest idiot in the universe for not expecting the device to call it like a dog whistle before the fear hit him and tore into him with a vengeance. He could find no rage. It had been scared out of him. He screamed.

Flames erupted from under its cloak, burning the area around Veikko and supercharging his suit field with its heat. It held against the flames, but the air inside still grew impossibly hot. He ran. Trees burst into flames behind him, rocks cracked from the heat. The fire burned so intense it finally ignited the air inside Veikko's field, and he still caught aflame.

Using a succession of breath stealing vacuum fields to extinguish the flames, Veikko made it to the atrium lagoon and jumped under the water. Hallucinations returned to him, deep in the midst of the oppressive fear. He could barely tell he was in real water at all.

Then the water was gone, boiled in a flash. He kept running. He tried to link into the Geki implant to no avail. Something inside it wouldn't recognize him despite every hack in his partition. Then he saw it—part of the old Geki's ulna. The implant was like a Tikari, embedded with bone from its owner so it couldn't be tricked. He dropped the implant and ducked behind a concrete beach shower.

Flames surrounded the shower and hit Veikko from both sides, burning him badly. His protective field was stronger than ever, using the energy from the flames to stay at maximum strength, but the Geki fire continued to ignite the air within and every vacuum he created weakened him drastically.

For a moment, the fire stopped. Veikko knew it was a trap. The fear told him to run. The instant he moved, the Geki would burn him front on and kill him. But he had no choice. Suddenly the Geki was above him, throwing fire straight down. He was burned again, half his hair singed off, his skin blackened. He ran.

The flames followed him, and fear permeated him. Terror and flame and no escape.

VARG TURNED off the thermobaric thruster as he neared land. He searched for Alopex, but there was no Alopex to link into. He searched for Balder, but he wasn't online. He searched for his team. He found Violet and Vibeke over the ocean, and Veikko in Kyle City. He was closest to Kyle so he used the last of his transorbital momentum to reach the place. He had many questions to ask.

As he approached Veikko's location, he found it on fire. Veikko was somewhere on the 76th floor, the source of the flames. Varg flew the Blackwing straight through the wall into the building's atrium. He saw a black cloak hurtling fire. The word Geki flashed through his mind, and he thought he saw Veikko in the flames. He aimed his razor sharp wing at the Geki and flew straight through it, cleaving it in half. Both halves warped away. It happened so fast the fear never even struck him.

He landed as close to Veikko as he could, hovering down into the burning plants. He opened the canopy and jumped out, then ran for Veikko. He pulled the burn packs from his chest pockets and approached his charred comrade.

"Veikko!" he called.

Veikko forced his burnt eyelids open and saw Varg. Varg was back on Earth. All he'd planned was based on Varg being halfway to Mars. He was Balder's man through and through, and if he was back, it was surely for revenge, there could be no other explanation. He tried to stand.

"Veikko!" Varg called again.

He breathed in, his lungs burned. If Varg didn't understand, he would figure it out within seconds. The fires crackled around him. The fear clung to him. He ran. He had to run. He ran into the pond.

Varg saw him run, and instantly, he became a hostile. Varg had to know why. Balder was dead, and Veikko was running. The Geki, one Geki—he thought they came in pairs—was trying to burn him to death. Veikko had done something terribly wrong.

Varg ran back to the BIRP and opened its hold. He took out the emergency skiff and hopped on, then darted for Veikko in the pond. Veikko had made it nearly all the way across. Flames erupted around Varg as he skated across the water, boiling it and billowing with steam. Varg's field barely kept him alive, the steam penetrated it and burned his skin. He didn't stop.

As Veikko approached the opposite side, Varg tilted his skiff and gave it a full burst, rocketing him into Veikko and knocking him onto the landscaped rocks. He stood, and Veikko rose to his knees in front of him.

"Dude, what the fuck?"

"Balder would have killed me, and Violet! I had to."

Varg figured it all out. His mind burned in anger hotter than the fire behind him but still he spoke rationally.

"No, Veikko. You can't have done what I think you've done."

"Balder wanted us dead! The Geki took me. I killed one of them. The Ares! It survived, Varg! It's in the ravine, right now!"

Varg absorbed it. "But Veikko, Balder was clear, we—"

"Fuck Balder, Varg! Balder was wrong! He'd have let the Fish take over and—"

"Didn't it occur to you he knew what he was doing? That he—"

"No! I came ashore to find the infamous, the dreaded Hall of the Slain. I dug through rumor and lies and the scum of the earth to find a hint, a clue of how to get in and when they took me, I found old men and little girls, Varg, pathetic weak fools! More of the same that calls itself the elite of the underground. It's bullshit, Varg, and you know it. Weakness! They'd let the world drown. I did what had to be done."

"Damn it, Veikko, this isn't *Håvamål*! This isn't a place for philosophical arguments. This is the real world! We're not just kids running around Vadsø anymore!"

"You're damn right we're not! We cannot restrain ourselves! We cannot be weak now when the tide's at our door! We have to fight! Fight like men! Not like the bitches we tried to humor but like men! And men don't hide and seek, men kill! Fucking hell, Varg, you're the best man I know, you have to understand!"

"I understand, Veikko. What we do has consequences on an extraordinary scale, that's why the Geki—"

"That's why I killed the damn Geki! I'm ending the consequences! I'm ending the peace! We can rule this world in a war. You have to understand. You have to join me! Put *Håvamål* behind you and join me now."

Veikko pulled his microwave and pointed it at Varg.

"Now do you want to die, or do you want to join me and Fuck Shit Up?"

Varg caught his breath. He was now in a terribly complex situation for a man to deal with. The villain before him had saved his life countless times, had brought him out of the depths of loneliness and uselessness and into heaven itself. He had also betrayed heaven and home, and himself, in the worst way Varg could imagine, and that, above all, corrupted all the good Veikko had done, made the highlights of his life into falsehood. And so what Veikko expected to be a long time of deep consideration lasted less than a second. Varg took his Tikari and stabbed the traitor through the heart before Veikko even saw him move. Veikko died with a grin still stuck on his face, a revolting grin that angered Varg as though Veikko, even in death, mocked him for his choice. Varg cut off his face in a single swing and left his corpse to burn.

The arcology was collapsing. Varg could hear the fire pogos swarming in, but he knew it was too late. The entire place was burning down in Geki flames hot enough to melt the supports.

He got into the Blackwing and took it to hover outside the arcology walls. Hundreds of residents fled to their porches and waved for him to help them. Varg moved the Blackwing to within centimeters of the walls and let them climb aboard, as many as he could fit on the wings. Then slowly he lowered the Blackwing to the ground a safe distance from the arcology. They leaped off the low, sleek wings, and Varg looked back to rescue more. But the fire pogos were swarming the building. He could only get in the way.

Then a microwave hit him in the back. It burned his skin through his armor, but it had been from a distance, he'd live. He turned fast and drew his own microwave to see Wart fire again. He dodged the beam and fired back.

W team had done a lot of soul-searching, and all four found that they had no souls to hinder their changing allegiance. Veikko brought them into Valhalla, taught them all they knew, and what he showed them in his memory package taught them the rest. The team understood.

The Wunjos detected Veikko's dying link as soon as they stepped off the APC. The great fire consuming the arcology they were to find him in explained it. Varg flying out of the flames explained the rest. W team would not let their leader's death go unavenged. Varg had to die. He didn't see them at first. They readied their microwaves and Tikaris and took positions on the street. Varg came between the four of them. Wart fired first.

Varg's suit absorbed most of it. Wart fired again. Varg ran, evading. The next instant he spotted Weather's Tikari. Knowing she was blind without it, he kicked it into a wall. It was damaged but still moving. As more microwaves tore through the sky, Varg danced his way from their aim and traced the fire to the other shooters. He sent his Tikari on foot toward Weather's and leveled his microwave at Wart. He fired at the same time as Wart, and the beams bounced off each other into the alley walls.

Weather's Tikari didn't stand a chance against Varg's giant centipede. The heavier bug finished hers and left her blind. Having completed its orders, the AI kicked in, and the Tikari decided to attack the next most likely target, Widget. She was trying to take slow perfect aim at Varg, who had rushed Wart and engaged him in a fistfight. The Tikari climbed Widget's leg and formed a sword through her heart, then head. Widget's Tikari fell from the sky. Walter saw her killed and, in a rage, ran at Varg. Wart and Walter could have killed any normal man in hand-to-hand combat, and any twenty men together. But Varg bested them both in seconds by sheer strength and speed. He knocked them cold and took back his own Tikari from Widget's corpse.

Three of the team were down and one was blind. Their Tikaris were dead or twitching from the abrupt loss of their owners. He knew they still posed the greater threat so one by one he crushed the insects under his boot. Weather, though blind, was the next greatest threat. He showed as much mercy as Veikko had taught them. He cut off her head and microwaved her brain. Then he zapped the minds of her team. He surveyed for other Valkyries, linked and scanned the area for anyone who might be loyal to Veikko.

He saw another gold pogo landing. From it walked Skadi, Veikko's girlfriend. Closest to him of everyone in the ravine. But he could see on her face that she wasn't there to fight, not for revenge nor anything else. She was the most betrayed. She was crying.

Varg watched her take a last look at the carnage of W team and set her eyes on the burning arcology. She walked straight for it, into Veikko's funeral pyre. She didn't look back.

Varg boarded the Blackwing and headed for Valhalla. Veikko's last words had made matters very black and white. He was one man, but that made him a one-man army, and if he was to die with the rest of his kind, he would die trying to take back the ravine from whatever legacy Veikko intended to leave it. The Blackwing flew north at top speed, breaking the sky in half and setting fire to old wooden churches in the mountains of Norge as it passed, deafening sheep with sonic booms and delivering Varg to his destiny in only minutes.

VIOLET AND Vibeke reclined side by side on the GET observation deck's floor window, watching the Atlantic pass quickly below them. Other people surrounded them, most fiddling with their links trying to find a signal. Despite the crowd's oblivious nature, they managed to keep their hands off each other.

"It seems like everything is ending," said Violet, "the ravine, everyone we knew."

"And we're just getting started."

"Rocky start." She could still feel the echo of Vibeke's fist on the skin of her cheek.

"That's not exactly surprising, is it?"

"Was to me. I always thought it would be perfect if we got together. All sex and laughter. Sure as hell didn't think I'd be the one to wreck it. I can't even—I don't know. But my fantasies definitely didn't have Alf and Balder putting me on the kill list."

"Yeah, you never mastered the whole rejection thing." Vibeke's frustration showed through. "See, for future reference, when a girl says 'No, I'm not gonna fuck you,' you're supposed to leave her alone, not break her face and rip her suit off."

"Yeah, I think I learned that in school at some point. Right before reading text."

She lowered her head so her forehead touched the floor window. She felt its slight vibration through her skull.

"If I hadn't done it, would we have…?"

Vibeke didn't want to admit that Violet's horrendous behavior might have actually kick-started her own action.

"Yes. And it would've been a whole lot closer to your fantasy."

Violet saw through it. "You wouldn't have pounced on me, would you? We'd still be in a stalemate."

"If that were true, it would probably make this the unhealthiest relationship in the history of the ravine."

"This *is* the unhealthiest relationship in the history of the ravine," she admitted.

"I knew we never should have started. I was right from the start. You and I aren't capable of having a courteous affair."

But Vibeke wanted it. Once Pandora's box opened, she wanted the monster it set free. Sex with Violet was a highlight of her life. Knowing Violet loved her, knowing she'd be wrecked if anything happened to her, the perversity of the bond was alluring, exciting. She just wished to high hell it had been born peacefully. She wondered if that were even possible.

"Just an intense one," she added.

Violet mulled it over. Vibeke was right. It wasn't just a rough start. It began with abuse because Violet didn't know any other way of expressing affection. It devolved into worse abuse because she got frustrated, and it only turned mutual when Vibeke realized she wanted to abuse Violet back. *We shouldn't be together*, she thought. *I should have been executed, and Vibeke should have moved on.*

"Well, at least we get intense," said Violet. "Maybe someday we'll get more."

"More what? You really think this is ever gonna be a happy hunky-dory thing? Hi, honey, I'm home and two and a half kids? No. We're gonna fuck until we hate each other, then throw each other away. I give us a couple months."

"No, this is more than that, it—"

"I could have been your friend forever. I love you like fire in a frozen hell, but fire burns out. A couple months. A year if we can play nice. But neither of us wants to play nice, do we?"

Violet was hurt by her outlook. The idea of it not being permanent had never even occurred to her. She was taken aback at the thought it could be a fling and nothing more. After all they'd been through, all they'd done, what was the point if it wasn't forever? Then she remembered. It had never been about her one true love. It was something simpler that brought her to do her worst.

"No, we don't," Violet answered. "That's fine, I don't need a wife. I need to fuck you. Desperately."

"I didn't want to waste you on that."

"Please waste me. I want to be wasted. I'd rather be wasted than—what else? What else was I ever good for?"

A hundred answers hit Vibeke's mind, but it hurt too much to think of them all, all lost. She would never confide in Violet again. She would never trust her, never fight by her side the way they used to. All that was in the past, she thought, the beautiful chrysalis for the ugly moth they had now. Most moths don't even have mouths. They don't eat. They live on what they ingested as larvae and die quickly, their only purpose being to mate. Vibeke found the metaphor all too accurate.

A ship shot in and out of view from the GET window. Vibeke felt a sour taste that Violet would say such a thing. That she thought so little of herself. And that she'd forced it. Vibeke suddenly understood Violet more than she ever wanted to. Violet was capable of what she'd done not because she was a hormone-driven animal, but because after all they'd done together, all they'd accomplished, Violet still thought she was a bad girl, one to be used and thrown away. Only someone who thought so little of herself would be capable of what Violet had done to her. She felt such empathy for Violet then that she could have taken it all back, hugged her tight, and said forever. She wanted to tell Violet she was worth everything to her. But she said nothing and didn't know why. She shivered. Violet spoke.

"That's what I thought."

Vibeke had to set her straight but couldn't speak. She felt herself blush.

Violet knew she had admitted too much, shown her weakness. The last thing a Valkyrie would do. But then, she wasn't a Valkyrie anymore. She bit down hard on her teeth. She had to move on.

"I wanted you since before I met you, you know. I wanted a girl like you, exactly like you in every way. I hunted for her online and wished I'd run into her on the streets. But I knew deep down she didn't exist. Nobody so perfect could. And when I met you... it...." Violet tried to breathe straight. "I'm sorry I wasted you too. You deserve so much better than I ever knew how to give. But maybe, just maybe after this mission, we can put all the pain and all the broken stuff, all the… just everything behind us. Can't we just…?"

"Start over?"

Vibeke wanted to so badly, but she knew the score. Valkyries don't forgive.

"Maybe in another life," she answered.

And that was her revenge. For all Violet had done, Vibeke had her revenge, and finally they could move on. With that stab Vibeke knew there was a chance they could last forever, a chance they could grow past their mutual harm and be truly happy. She'd never tell Violet. She'd insist until they were in their hundreds it had to be a cheap fling and nothing more.

Violet was stabbed through the chest. After days of self-loathing, the real depth of what she'd done hit her full force. Not any worse than what she'd already felt, but coldly, logically clear. She finally understood how much she'd given up, how wrong she'd been. In that second she grew up, finally, and knew what a responsibility love was.

And Vibeke knew that if she ever lost Violet now, she would lose her own soul.

VARG FOUND Valhalla's airspace devoid of any invading force. There was one submarine in the water but scans showed nobody aboard. He hovered the Blackwing over the water and opened the canopy. With one last bolt, he signaled it to close up and sink, with sensors to rise and open again only on Valkyrie contact. It sank. He jumped. Varg walked to the drawbridge and set his suit to match the photonics. He immersed himself in the rock and stepped through, then entered the golden hall, now lit in red by a gore-enveloped power system. The Ares had survived like Veikko had said, writhing and sinewy from the remains of Wulfgar's men. Shining deep red where it once shone gold.

He thought he'd seen the Ares nuked. But there was no question that was it, on Earth and intact. He thought back to Mars, to the mystery of the inactive Wolves and knew they must have done something, found some way of smuggling it back under their noses.

Varg drew his microwave in one hand, Tikari sword in the other, prepared for a fight. He tried to link into Alopex to no avail. The computer was set 100 percent on the Ares. The AI was nowhere to be found. Varg implemented the critical protocols to shut down the drawbridge in case of Alopex deactivation. The system was back to Leo, the simple Ares AI.

There was nobody to fight. No Cetaceans, no Wolves, no teams or Valhalla civilians. But the architecture wasn't in shambles; the hall was fine. The Ares undulated and throbbed overhead, horribly grotesque, mixed in with the innards of the Martian tourists. And thankfully without any water to infect. With the rampart up, the world was safe. But the rampart was up so someone must be inside. He looked around at the top of his guard.

The only motion he could detect was a walrus pod trapped along the edge of the ravine. He walked up the spiral walkway and observed the area. Motion nearby, and not from Umberto. There was someone in the communications tower. Hanging like a stalactite from the ravine's top, it was the highest structure in Valhalla. It was covered in antennae and protected by a heavy magnetic shield to clarify any signals. And there was something yellow inside it.

Varg approached with great stealth, and as he entered, he caught Pelamus off guard. But he did not attack. Pelamus had armor that could defy any sword and any microwave beam. It also made him nearly deaf. Varg planned as he stepped silently into the room. He wanted to take Pelamus without a fight, without ever letting the Fish know he was there. The idiot was alone. Varg didn't care why he was alone, and he didn't care why he hadn't set off the Ares yet. None of it would matter if he could just kill Pluturus where he stood. He needed a weapon that could get through that armor. What did the com tower offer? The place had no tactical benefits except that mag shield.

Varg had a stroke of true genius when he thought of that shield. In that instant he thought back to Balder, who had hidden the Mjölnir somewhere in Valhalla, somewhere so well hidden that nobody could find its magnetic signature. An obvious magnetic signature that only a huge magnetic shield could hide. It was in that com tower, it had to be. Somewhere in that very room was a generator designed to crush anything in metal armor, armor like Pelamus's. The cannons wouldn't be there, but his Tikari could channel a charge if he could just find and power the generator. And then he found it. How had he never noticed in a hundred times in that room that the bench in the middle was shaped like a horseshoe? The thing wasn't even disguised, merely painted. And Pelamus was reclining on it.

The only question was if the thing would still work. The com tower field wasn't only strong enough to hide a magnetic signature. It was enough to render most magnets useless. He calculated quickly. Checked his partitions for field strength and frequency of both the tower and the Mjölnir. Every calculation came out at 50 percent likelihood of functionality. It would happen or not. He'd deal with not if it happened.

Varg became the essence of stealth. He approached with no sound, barely a displacement of air that could have given him away. He saw every reflective surface and denied Pelamus sight of his reflection. He made it to the generator and with ease hooked his Tikari into its negative port. His suit could channel the positive without harm to himself. He was ready. He only had to charge the generator, which would make sound but perhaps he could distract the fish, who would have no clue why the bench was making noise. He only needed a few seconds.

"Hey, Fish, where's the school?"

Pelamus turned around, and bless the idiot, he gave a monologue.

"Fish, you call me! Cetaceans are not fish any more than you are an insect. We are men, young human, men. And we will have the same rights as men, the right to live. And to that end, I, Pelamus Pluturus, have taken this ravine and its intended experiment! Now, we have the power to end your civilization, as for a century you have threatened—"

Crunch. Varg's suit froze in place with the magnetic field. When he could move again, the armored suit before him was utterly collapsed in on itself. So passed Pelamus Pluturus, who stood seconds from conquering the globe but died because he couldn't shut up and kill the man before him. Or could he—Varg felt something in his shoulder. Then he felt the room shudder. There was a dart in his shoulder. The Mjölnir had shaken the com tower from its metal fittings. Pelamus had shot him with a tiny dart as he was talking—damn it, he wasn't talking to boast; he was distracting Varg from his own attack. The com tower was shaking. It was going to collapse.

With Pelamus crushed to the size of a pebble and the room breaking up around him, Varg knew to get to the catwalk. Within three steps, he knew that the dart must have been poisoned. In three steps more, he felt it overtaking him. The nearest med kit was one junction away. If he could only make it there, he could at least delay the effects before losing consciousness. But in another three steps, he fell to the floor, paralyzed.

Soon after he felt the tower supports give way. The room was falling from Valhalla's overhangs. Varg's nervous system was failing. He would be dead before he hit the ground.

In his last lucid instant, he felt something he had never felt before, a feeling that might have been death itself and might have been something else. He had never known fear in his life. But now he was afraid, filled with trepidation, the sense of something approaching, something dangerous and final. Varg passed out, terrified, fear upon fear like he'd never imagined could exist. The room fell to the jagged floor of the pit and was crushed with its contents into unsalvageable ruin.

Chapter XII: Dimmuborgir

THE MONITORING guild authorized the escalation to "red." The world was at the brink of war. Much of it had already fallen over that edge. Zaibatsu was no more. The Yakuza and Unspeakable Darkness had reduced it to such rubble that UNEGA dissolved the company. What was left of it didn't want to be dissolved and threatened to march on the offices that destroyed it. The greedy vultures that coveted its assets had already fired on the rallies or seized assets prematurely by force. UNEGA tried to legislate what would go where, but by the time the bureaucracy got around to locating it, it had already been stolen.

Blame went in every possible direction. Amorphis accused OMC of hijacking the entire Zaibatsu Pacific shipping fleet. OMC insisted it was taken by the TOT. TOT didn't even exist anymore, having been entirely absorbed by Fyntr Oil in the confusion. Silentium, meanwhile, launched a hostile takeover of Asda subsidiary, ND, which kicked 7,000 Asda supervisors out of the job. They immediately flooded UNEGA's relocation sector and plugged the cash flow to the Jourgensen Ministry, which seized the loose Nigerian assets of Zaibatsu to keep its payroll running in an attack for which they hired the Whiplash Militia, leaving DHG undefended. DHG was devoured by Nork, which stood by for its Nigerian offices to be overrun when the Militia returned.

GAUNE meanwhile pushed the limits of legality and decency by appropriating Ireland and Kalaallit Nunaat, and to the latter act Danmark couldn't respond to as it was busy preventing the secession of the more lucrative Faroe Companies. UNEGA vowed retaliation, which, of course, it couldn't do in the least. Unless, said GAUNE, they intended to use illegal force like that nuke they showed off in Prešov only days before.

D team had their hands full at first, and overflowing before long. Dani attended to COF's merger and prevented it from turning violent by convincing the Bydo Empire not to illegally seize and liquidate the numerous type R funds it had its eyes on. Death came swiftly to EnsiFerum and freed their kidnapped CEO, thus keeping Ensign and

Ferum on track to absorb Green Carnation Pogo Emporium's contract with Sam I-L. Deva and DeMurtas traveled eastward to prevent Xerox from stabbing westward into Shaw's snowy territory.

E team, by contrast, abandoned the business world for assassinations, killing any GAUNE CEOs bent on using conglomerate armies to delve into Zaibatsu's remains with illegal weaponry that would see UNEGA declaring war within the hour. J and L teams found themselves on Luna, trying to convince Tycho Under not to use the confusion to secede from UNEGA. Mars was a complete write-off, having been under direct Zaibatsu control. The PRA rejoiced, now the only ruling body on Mars Ninna considered her nuke well spent.

But no team was present to prevent the sale of Verizon to Uniquity XL. It wasn't even on Valhalla's radar. It would have been had Alf lived to monitor it, but alas, with his death the company fell, and liquidation of its assets began immediately. That meant the link went down in much of northern Europe for almost seventeen seconds.

The results were catastrophic. Euronext went offline for the first time in seventy-nine years. That alone would have been enough to cause mass panic and financial ruin, but when Euronext went down, MATIF and the ÜberBörse went wild trying to take over the sum total of Euronext company traffic, including Uniquity XL, which as a result, shut down its net link later that day, including the recent acquisitions. All of Europe went offline. Most of Africa and Asia, including UNEGA's Headquarters in Tokyo, 404'd, and GAUNE took notice.

Canada was now poised to take over the entire net and charge UNEGA to use it. New York was placed on alert. NASDAQ and NYSE militaries were put on call for the first time in history to shuttle over to the former Verizon territories and bring them online under GAUNE aegis.

All in all, UNEGA was in shambles, and GAUNE was prepared to take over 60 percent of it with military force. Despite the net outages, UNEGA was very aware of this and began massing its own troops for war.

The only saving grace to the degeneration was that neither side appeared to want to go nuclear. There was no benefit in it, no reason to do it. And despite what GAUNE perceived as a show of nuclear force, they armed no ICBMs, scrambled no bombers, activated no satellites, and this conspicuous absence of escalation was intentionally reciprocated by UNEGA. Nobody wanted a nuclear war. Except, of course, for Veikko, who in death had no means to recall his sisters, who he'd consigned to oblivion along with the rest of the globe.

THE GET slowed down and pulled alongside the Husavik station. Vibeke watched the landscape grind to a standstill out the berth window and nudged Violet.

"We're here."

Violet didn't move. Vibeke shoved her.

"Get up, time to nuke our home for the last two years."

"I'll nuke it later," said Violet as she hugged her pillow.

In time Violet arose, and they pulled on their suits to face the mission. An odd mission to Violet, but she couldn't quite place why it seemed odd. Neither could Vibeke. But Violet felt unnaturally certain they were doing the right thing. She couldn't fathom how she was so opposed to it when Veikko first asked. At the same time, she couldn't think through the logic of it. She was certain but unsure why she was certain.

Valhalla taught all its recruits to recognize a bore inception. Veikko deleted that training when he was in, knowing from his own training where to find it in the human brain. His hack, if such things were studied, would have gone down in history as one of the most subtle and flawless direct-brain codings of all time. A computer hack is simple and straightforward, a 1 or a 0—it's either done or it's not. Brain recoding is more an art than a craft, and Veikko was a grand master of the art. Violet kept her mind on the job and ignored the odd jingles and tweets of cognitive dissonance, just as Veikko programmed her to.

They departed the train and took a lift down to the station's pogo park, which was thankfully almost empty of people. Violet spotted a speedy if antiquated Suzuki Ninori and hacked its lock and starter. They headed south.

Vibeke clung tightly to her back as they flew. She tried to contact Veikko, but his link was off the map. The map was off the net. The net was flickering between GAUNE ads and UNEGA ads. Alopex couldn't be called up. Her address was simply listed as "Leo, pending." With Alf and Balder's deaths, the ravine seemed to have ceased to be. It was a lifetime away.

As they flew, Vibeke's arms tight around Violet's waist, the only concern she felt was the deathly prospect of losing her. Not from betrayal or anything related to the rules of the old ravine, but on the mission to come. Violet was right; they should consider a life in transorbital transportation. Vibeke resolved on that short flight to tell her they could last. They could retire together and hack themselves a nice salary and position with whatever company ended up owning the orbitliners.

Violet thought about retirement as well. She was almost twenty and getting old. She'd had a good run as a spy. She needed only to accomplish this one last task. She couldn't quite place why she couldn't abandon it as well. But the thought was somehow unthinkable. Not unpalatable or wicked, but simply unthinkable. They had to destroy the Ares. Then there would be absolute freedom.

They set down north of Dimmuborgir in the civilian zone. Oblivious tourists looked over the strange rocks, positioning their heads to record memory files, bobbing around chatting with their families. It was as alien a lifestyle to Violet as those of the people on Mars. It was the life she suddenly coveted.

"Doesn't look like a missile silo," she linked.

Vibeke checked the black book.

"Alf's old intel suggests it's under the civilian park. The launch tubes are concealed in the rock, but there should be a long tunnel to its conventional access half a kilometer north of here."

They headed toward the location. Sinister volcanic rocks jutted up around them, coated in tourists. The two approached a rock whose picture was included in the intel. The tunnel would be hidden in plain sight, completely unmarked and designed to fit in with the surrounding features. Violet spotted it first, only given away by the most subtle difference of black shades. The two climbed up the rock unseen and dropped down into a long, black tunnel.

Microwaves drawn, the two walked through the darkness, eyes straining even with their tapeta lucida on full. The tunnel was nearly a kilometer long, angling 150 meters down into the stale smelling pumice rock.

They walked quietly, expecting guards. As they turned a gentle corner to the left, they found light. Violet sent her Tikari to the ceiling to observe. There were two men, armed to the teeth, standing guard. Armored as well, common microwave beams would do nothing, stunning beams even less. They'd have to get under their helmets to stun them.

Vibeke improvised. She clingered her microwave and started talking loudly with an American accent.

"Becky, I don't think we're supposed to be in here!"

Violet played along. "Shut up, Carla! There's a light ahead. If we weren't supposed to be here, there wouldn't be lights!"

"Oh my God, Becky, you're gonna get us stuck or in trouble or somethin'!"

They walked straight up to the men, who stood still by the door. One was about to speak and held up his hand.

"Excuse me!" shouted Violet. "Excuse me, but can you tell my sister that—"

They sprang, each taking the soldier on their side of the tunnel, cramming their microwaves fast into the gap between their helmets and collars and firing stunning beams directly into their heads. Both fell to the ground. Vibeke began to undress one for a disguise, but Violet stopped her.

"They're in UNEGA aus-guard uniforms. If they saw them inside, they'd know they were stolen."

They were better off staying agile in nothing but their own armor. Vibeke began to hack into the door.

It was incredibly complex, the most secure door Vibeke had ever seen in her days with Valhalla. Alarms inside security walls inside hack armor inside undirectoried systems inside of a heavily guarded locking mechanism.

Suddenly, it opened by itself.

Vibeke and Violet both knew it meant a trap. They leaped back and kept their microwaves on the door. They waited. Nothing came. Violet sent Nelson to push open the door, keeping her microwave on the space. It opened to reveal nothing but the pink light of motion detectors in the hallway within.

Cautiously they headed toward the door. Nelson leaped to the ceiling and began scanning for the frequency of the detectors he'd need to jam. He found them offline.

"Something's drastically wrong here."

"Agreed, what do we do?"

"The mission as planned."

They entered, microwaves at the ready. They found only round halls, every surface covered in a network of red pipes. The halls were filled with hairpin turns, winding up and down and around themselves as if wadded up from a larger complex.

The Tikaris scanned ahead in every direction but found the halls empty. They continued down the wrinkled path until they came to a junction. A cortex node protruded from the ceiling. They didn't dare hack into it, but its ganglion would lead to the control center. They followed it through more wrinkles and came to the control center hatch. It was hanging open, and slumped limply over its sill was a corpse.

"What the hell is going on here?"

"I killed him," said Veikko. "I killed them all."

Violet and Vibeke looked around in a hurry.

"Veikko?" It hit Violet like a splash of cold water, a chill as if he'd appeared right behind her.

His voice came from the speaker system. "Sal actually. Pleased to speak to you finally."

"Sal?"

"Sal, as in Veikko's Tikari. Praying mantis looking fellow? The one that was splashing around in the tomato soup on your birthday. He sent me along to help you. Sorry about the soup by the way."

It was impossible. Tikaris couldn't speak. It had to be one of Veikko's jokes. But he wouldn't, not on this mission. It became all the more unnerving.

"How are you talking?"

"Well, it's a funny thing. He sent me into the mainframe with a couple simple directions. But when I took over their base broadbrain, I could incorporate its speech functions, internal systems, I even learned a new game program. Have either of you heard of 'Chess'?"

"This dead body—"

"Oh, I activated the vacuum fire system and locked the hatches. Reopened this one just for you. It killed everyone inside. I thought it would help. I also deactivated the security systems, did everything but launch the missiles. They're on an unlinked system. How about a nice game of chess?"

"Negative, Sal," said Vibeke. She looked to Violet, still in disbelief. The voice was like Veikko's but hollow, fallen deep into the uncanny valley. She had to consciously treat it like an AI, or the perversity of speaking to it would continue to grate on her.

"Highlight the missile targeting panel in the control room."

"I can highlight it, but you won't be able to use it. It only powers up with direct orders from UNEGA high command."

"We'll have to program and launch the missiles directly," said Vibeke. "Sal, highlight a path to the launch bay."

"Compliance."

A route lit up along the floor. They followed it through the crumpled curves of the compact base. Violet could sense an overwhelming curiosity coming from her own Tikari—the proper unformed instinct that filtered in from it that she'd gotten used to over the years.

There was something perverse about a part of Veikko speaking to them without his direct control. As if his hand had left his body and pointed the way for the mission he'd designed. Violet felt oddly supervised, like Veikko didn't trust them to accomplish the mission on their own. Resentment flickered dimly in her mind. But more than that, surprise at the Tikari's efficacy. It had already done the hardest part of the mission, killing off the crew when she'd planned to stun her way through the corridors. As they approached the massive bay door, it swung open itself, two meters of metal thrown aside by the small Tikari.

"How did you manage all this?"

"It was surprisingly easy," it said lifelessly. "Veikko sent me the night before you took off. A little sneaking, a dash of hacking, and a side order of mass extermination later, here we are."

They entered a massive open space, an indoor tarmac filled with storage crates and vehicles. It was almost completely dark except for a dim spot of light in the distance. The light reflected off the red piping along the distant ceiling, which they could faintly see had the wrinkles of other corridors all around it.

"But why did he send you before us? What did he send you to do?"

"To ensure the mission succeeded."

"More specifically?"

"First I was to lift off at a velocity of 7.2 kph within the Fraser's kitchen. Then at an angle of exactly 67 degrees, I—"

"Okay, okay. Never mind," said Vibeke. She was clearly weirded out by the Tikari as well.

They continued into the chamber. Violet's Tikari reported launch tubes to their east in the light. Cautiously they traversed behind the storage crates toward the launch area. Behind the crates they saw a line of SSS Robots.

Violet had taken a course on them at Achnacarry. Each was a dual gun system designed to work in tandem with its line. Each held 80,000 expandable rounds, 0.5mm in storage but 15mm once fired. They could each hurl 250 in a second. And this line held at least fifty robots. An enormous security system, beyond deadly.

"Don't worry, they're all inactive," added Sal.

How could he tell they were looking at them? He must have been watching them through the internal security cameras. The Tikari had become the AI of the entire complex.

"What could activate them?"

"I could if you'd like. I don't recommend it as you'd die horribly."

"Thanks, Sal."

They approached the tubes and found seven. Each one was massive, thicker than expected.

"I don't suppose you've spoken to Veikko lately?" asked his own voice.

"Aren't you in contact with him?"

"No, I've been running on full AI since I left. His link is off the map. Though this may be due to the fluctuations in link service. Low power, immediate area link communications are unaffected, but I believe the global link system is severely deranged. No communications, everyone is on their own."

"Seems like it...."

"You can't imagine how lonely we are when we're not in your chests. We miss you terribly."

Talking to the Tikari grew curiouser and curiouser. It seemed far more intelligent on its own than Violet would have expected. She quelled the thought of her own Tikari speaking to her with her own voice. Nelson was on the ceiling of the silo, a vast dome. She sensed him on AI scouting the area but not thinking, not the way Sal seemed to be. Even online, the Tiks remained silent. Sal had clearly hacked into something above and beyond the common broadbrain. She wondered what else about him might have changed.

"Sal, what kind of system was the broadbrain?"

"A bit flirty at first, but once you get to know her, she's very reserved."

"What kind of electronic system?"

"Neural selective."

That answered it. Sal's AI was now integrated with nerve tissue. It could think for itself. That posed the question, though, was it still Veikko's Tikari? It was a new mind, a fusion, a different AI. In a way it wasn't Sal at all.

But why had UNEGA used such a mutable system for something so important as a nuclear missile silo? The only weapons that required a neural network to program were—

"Here I become suddenly useless. The missile launch systems are not connected to the main base system, and the local controls are unpowered. Their only link is a lead locked hardline to UNEGA headquarters."

Vibeke moved to examine the tubes, checking them against the intel in Alf's book. Violet went through her partitions on silo mechanics and compared them to what she saw.

"Each tube has an Ehren Plate," said Violet. Emergency taps to shut down the devices in case of an accidental launch code. "They're old designs. They can be jury-rigged to launch the missiles if we can hardwire in. We just need to be sure the warheads are able to arm. Sal, the diagnostics should be part of the local system, can you detect them?"

"Affirmative. All diagnostics are part of the base's system."

"Run the nuclear armament diagnostics."

"Negative. There are no nuclear armament diagnostics in this system."

"List all nuclear diagnostics."

"No diagnostics pertain to nuclear systems."

"Impossible. How can there be a nuclear missile silo with no nuclear diagnostics?"

"Well, let me just diagnose the cause of that by running the nuclear diagnostics. Oh, wait...."

VALHALLA WAS a dead zone. The remains of T team arrived first, having merely traveled to Tromsø to feed Thokk's body into the power grid. They found the photonically selective gateway offline. The drill hole plugged by the drill. Valhalla was sealed shut.

Alopex was offline, replaced by an inactive system called "Leo." T had no way of learning that there was nothing alive in the ravine save for the walrus pod.

As K team returned in their battle pogos, H, N, and M in regulars from Hashima, the Valkyries put together as best they could what had happened. They knew from the broad link that Mishka had killed Balder, thanks to Thokk. Wulfgar was to attack, and the drill hole suggested he got at least one person in. Alf wasn't responding and never would have sealed the drawbridge to them. They saw Pelamus's sub, too small for an invading force. There was no question: Valhalla was taken. But nothing was happening as a result.

The link was erratic, and all the teams across the globe were out of contact. The net was silent, utterly silent. Even attempts to find ads from down south proved ineffective. It seemed very much as if the globe had been shut down or gone insane. In contrast to the conglomerate mayhem on the mainland, Kvitøya was a peaceful ruin.

The remaining Valkyries headed south to join the Keres on Karpathos, or the Zhnyetse in Vladivostok. The events that had taken place were uncertain. Plans were unclear.

SAL REMAINED silent as Vibeke opened the seal to the first Ehren plate and hardwired in. She scoured the system for its own diagnostics.

She found the old glitch that could be tricked into launching. She found the targeting override systems, everything she needed to launch except for the protocols to arm the nuclear warheads. Not only were the diagnostics and protocols missing, but all references to nuclear technology.

"Something's wrong," linked Vibeke.

"Don't say that when you're working on nuclear missiles," whispered Violet.

"They're not nuclear missiles."

Violet looked at her.

"Beg your pardon?" said Sal.

"The controls are all wrong," she explained. "These have no airburst measures. Whatever they are, they go off on the ground. And there's no yield control, only range and intensity, and 'temper.'"

"Temper?"

"Temper, settings A and C."

"What the hell are these?" asked Violet.

Vibeke checked over her partitions. Valhalla didn't have anything in its arsenal for which one would set A or C "tempers." And there was only one weapon Valhalla would never use. Only one weapon that would have an organic neural programming system to program the projective RNA sequences.

"These are wave bombs," said Vibeke.

"What?"

"This is an illegal wave bomb silo."

"Oh snap," said Sal.

Violet thought only briefly. "We'll report them to the courts later. We need to find fission warheads, or at least fusion warheads we can drain."

"Alf's map only shows one launch door, this is it. We need to deactivate these and get out."

"Forget deactivating them. It's not our business, and we have bigger concerns. Let's go."

"Valhalla never leaves wave bombs intact."

"We're not in Valhalla anymore. Let's get out of here!"

"We have to boil the warheads. These seven tubes are a hundred times more sadistic than the Ares."

"If I may?" interrupted Sal.

"What is it?"

"Veikko planned for this contingency. Launching the wave bombs will still result in the destruction of the Ares."

"Sal, you can't be serious."

"I am one of Veikko's body parts. Serious isn't in my repertoire. But we can complete the mission."

"We're not launching wave bombs, Sal!"

"That is exactly what you must do, Vibeke."

"It's not an argument, Sal. Close down the base. We're deactivating these and finding another."

"Negative. Time is a factor. Proceed to launch."

"Not a chance, Sal. Our mission is in another silo."

The Ehren Plates would still have a fail-safe, a way to deactivate them completely. She looked deeper into the systems. Specific shaped fields. Genetic targeting. Wave dissipation patterning. Fail-safes.

"Stop, Vibeke," sounded Veikko's voice.

She opened the fail-safes and found a subroutine labeled complete dismantle. That had to be the boiling protocol. But it was inaccessible. It was made only to go into effect if the missiles were about to launch.

"Vibeke, I wouldn't do that if I were you...."

She input a null firing solution into the first Ehren Plate, and only the plate so there was no chance of launch. She activated the solution and began the destruction protocol for the first missile.

"Firing Solution Detected" read the link label.

"Peterson, we have another false on the UNEGA labels."

For the tenth time that month, the system was reading a launch solution in Dimmuborgir. Since the day GAUNE realized they had a wave bomb installation, Peterson had sat at his post monitoring it for firing solutions on their tubes.

The spybots had been introduced two years prior by an agent disguised as one of their maintenance crew, an agent it took three years to deposit. He'd adeptly placed a remote tap under each Ehren Plate, designed not only to detect a solution but to activate the plate and destroy the missile's capability.

But the bots were susceptible to radio waves. Whenever an UNEGA soldier made an off-link call in the room, Peterson got a false firing solution.

Singh checked it out. It was a simple matter to shunt the bot's power to its radio shielding, and then the signal would go away. He sent a link to the bots to do so. But the detection persisted.

"Still on," said Peterson.

"I did the thing, did you refresh?"

"Yeah, it's still there."

"Well, what else could it be?"

"They could be launching wave bombs."

Singh and Peterson looked at each other. It dawned on them slowly that the system could actually be working. The horror pulled their cheeks downward.

"Get on the damn red link! Now!"

The link flashed in General Glover's office. He accessed it.

"Situation?"

"We have a firing solution detected at Dimmuborgir!"

"I thought we solved that."

"Rechecked it, sir. This appears legitimate."

"Are you certain?"

"Yes, sir, we have a solution detected on two missiles." Peterson checked the label. "Three now, sir."

The general dimmed the link and hit the emergency line to the CEOs. He sent a link dump of the entire situation on priority into their heads. He could sense the panic that must have reigned in their link silence. Six CEOs of various genders arguing in their boardroom. The link came back.

"Burn Dimmuborgir, now!"

The General had his order. He linked to the satellite command for Iceland and gave the order. The satellite warmed up for a 150,000 Kelvin cutter beam to annihilate the area.

UNEGA wasn't so slow and bureaucratic. The instant the GAUNE satellite warmed up, an automated ground laser system shot it out of the sky. GAUNE recognized the laser signature and fired on its source with a suborbital rail projectile. UNEGA launched a fusion interceptor and vaporized the projectile. GAUNE saw the nuclear explosion and retaliated in kind. It only got worse from there.

Chapter XIII: Oblivion

HØTHERUS HAD previously considered many of his works to be his magnum opus at the time of their creation. When he was only nineteen, he thought he'd never top the complete sequencing (from scratch) of the phospholipid polarity drive. Far superior to neural net computing, it wasn't prone to changing thought patterns or forgetfulness. At the atomic level, it was unlikely any computer would ever top it for memory efficiency, and indeed by the end of his life, nothing had.

At twenty-two he invented the advanced growth field. All that cloning of body parts that took up age progression silos for the last hundred years was finally obsolete. A body part could be grown on demand, from a cell to a limb in hours, not years. He was praised by the medical establishment, lauded as the most important doctor since... ever. And he was young! He had so much more to contribute. He improved net-link wetware by leaps and bounds. He invented a better analgia field. He invented organic living tools that could revolutionize Martian colonization. He created... a few things people didn't talk about.

The medical community was dismayed by his first weapons systems. The living nuclear trigger. The prototype for a guardthing. And his next work to trump his previous works—the rapid mutagenic beam. On a wide focus, it could reduce an enemy army to a mindless mass of agony. Høtherus considered it the ultimate weapon, a deterrent to end all wars. How little he knew of what he'd do next! But the beam was quite enough to get most of his prior research banned. UNEGA and GAUNE both signed the accord stating they'd never develop or use any mutagenic weaponry. They "confiscated" the triggers and beam cannons and forty-seven other patents, those they could freely develop and copy in secret without paying a cent to the man who spent his short life creating them.

That was only a part of his disillusionment with humanity. The real tragedy of the species he discovered in his research. He had dug deeper into the human genome than anyone before him. He saw things that the pure scientists missed. The meaning behind the base pairs, the poetry of them. And he saw how feeble nature had made life—all life on Earth. Høtherus could do better. So he did.

Long deprived of love for his revolting appearance, he first created a bride. She would be the perfect woman, in his opinion: no brain, no eyes, no teeth. Only raw sexual instinct and lust for him. He programmed the most voluptuous figure he could imagine, and whatever his faults, nobody ever claimed Høtherus didn't have an imagination, especially when it came to his fetishes. She resembled something from Hans Bellmer's nightmares, something too obscene to be explained beyond its orifices and protrusions.

His wife was poorly received by the public. She was deeply offensive to the minds of every gender. Words like "abomination" and "thing that should not be" were thrown around. In an illegal seizure, blind to the philosophical dilemma of what could have constituted the first artificially engineered human being, the bride of Høtherus was confiscated and cremated. He was finally banned from all future genetic research and confined to his modest house in Iceland.

He'd have been confined elsewhere if they knew the kind of lab he kept in its subbasement.

The world heard nothing from the imprisoned madman for three years. The world thought it was safe. Laws upon laws were written and signed to prevent anything remotely like the horrors he'd wrought. It seemed the world was free of him and free to use the works of his golden years. The simple organics, the straightforward computer systems. The good things.

Few noticed the people that went missing. None cared about the departure of his supporter, Haring Koeller, from his tenure at the University of Reyjkjavik. He wasn't missed. Not a soul could imagine what they were doing together until the first monster appeared.

It was born Tom Wis. It had a troubled childhood and an aimless adulthood. It went missing in 2202. It reappeared in 2205 as the penultimate masterpiece of Høtherus and Koeller. A beast, put simply, Tom Wis was the most profane abomination imaginable. A human turned into something like its creator's first wife (he and Koeller had a harem of them now) but geared toward inflicting terror upon the population that had ostracized its maker. And it was only the first of many.

By the end of 2205, no less than seventy monsters wandered Iceland, causing nightmares and insanity in those lucky enough to survive their coming. Those less fortunate they digested alive, their internal mechanisms designed to keep victims alive and awake as they melted into proteins and prions. The armies were called in. The creatures, called "The Agony" on official reports, were all destroyed. Høtherus's labs were incinerated, but the news logs reported he was never found, nor was his comrade Koeller. As the last of the Agony were erased and various lesser monsters rounded up for study, UNEGA admitted publicly that their creator was lost and at large.

He was, of course, not. UNEGA had found and imprisoned him and forced him to work. They weren't about to let the fiasco rob their weapons divisions of his genius.

Koeller went missing too but not before leaving his final legacy: Koeller's Gravy. A fluid composed of RNA coding chambricles, controlled by a liquid neural network, that could be transmitted broadly by use of a superintense omega wave.

Under the most absolute secrecy possible (meaning GAUNE got a spy in on the first day) Høtherus continued his research by designing his final masterpiece: the Wave Bomb.

Targeted mutagenic warfare on a scale that put his original beam to shame. With its radius determined only by the strength of the omega wave, one bomb could be set to mutate a single room or the entire planet. Of course, nobody would ever set it to planetary scale. No less than eighty-six bombs were manufactured by UNEGA to target smaller regions in GAUNE. GAUNE manufactured sixty-eight of the devices, with one notable difference.

GAUNE's bombs were made from their own Koeller's Gravy, not the original substance. That was both a blessing and a curse. GAUNE wave bombs were predictable. They could turn an entire city into quivering sticky masses of pain, but they did nothing else.

An UNEGA bomb, however, was unpredictable. It could reduce a population to slime, or far worse—it could reduce them halfway to slime, leaving just enough of them to perceive their state. Tests on Deimos found they could turn people into what could only be described as zombies. Though alive, the victims were capable only of feeling pain and hate, and tore each other apart, devouring each other's flesh. In some tests they caused nothing but massive suppurating tumors on all they affected. In others it would mutate them into a variety of Høtherian monstrosities. The UNEGA bombs could even fuse individuals into vast conglomerations of flesh or produce new bacteria that caused unspeakable disease. The only thing they never did was nothing at all. They always, always resulted in pain and horror.

Høtherus never explained that the original Koeller's gravy was in fact made with Haring Koeller's brain. He had used nervous technology to liquify the man's cerebrum and grow within it a network of sadistic intent. UNEGA wave bombs were living, thinking organisms. Able to alter their composition, thinking constantly of new horrors to inflict. That was the grand master work of the evil genius—a weapon of mass affliction that even those who commissioned it found too appalling to ever use.

Høtherus was finally quietly executed in the UNEGA High Command's basement. But his benefaction lived on in GAUNE and UNEGA hands. The most hateful weapon ever devised, literally, for it could feel hate, misanthropy, a greed for fulfilling its purpose to cause unthinkable suffering on an unthinkable scale. A weapon mind with which Veikko's Tikari was now fused.

FIVE MISSILES down, two left. Vibeke jumped down from the plate and began to climb the next tube. Violet watched. She trusted Vibeke with complex hacks more than herself.

"You must not disable the missiles, Vibeke. You must launch them. Veikko has planted intel that will result in the destruction of the Ares in the event of an armed launch from this silo."

"If there's a wave war, then what's the point?"

"That is a rhetorical question."

"Yes, it is. Shut down and head back to Veikko, Sal."

"Negative. My duty is to ensure the mission is successful."

"Sal, the plan is to nuke Valhalla. These aren't nukes. We can still accomplish the original plan. We just need to deactivate these first."

"The probability of success decreases substantially if we diverge from Veikko's intent. This mission cannot fail, Vibeke. The planet is at stake."

"You're ticking me off, Sal. Shut down, or I'll shut you down."

Vibeke began broadcasting a jamming signal, as powerful as she could manage.

"No, no, don't do it!" called Veikko's voice. "Please, stop!"

"Shut down and return to Veikko!"

"My mind is going, I can feel it." His voice grew distorted, slower and deeper. "I can feel it... Daisy, Daisy, give me your answer do.... No, but seriously, I'm hardwired in, so you can't do squat."

Vibeke worked faster. She opened the sixth seal and began to activate the fail-safe. A sound echoed from across the chamber. Violet recognized it.

"He's arming the SSS robots!"

"Yes, I am. Launch the remaining missiles now, or I will kill you."

"Kill us, and the mission fails," said Vibeke.

"I was talking to Violet."

Vibeke looked to her. The loud screech of the SSS tracks shattered the air. Violet took a breath.

"Don't launch 'em. I'll run. They're on tracks, I just need to get to the—"

Hundreds of rounds began to strike Violet's projectile field. She felt the cold instantly. The energy sucked out of her to keep the field active against the incoming fire. But this was unlike any fire she'd taken before. The sheer number of rounds hitting her was enough to freeze her to death within seconds. She ran.

"Goddamn you, Veikko!" Vibs shouted.

"Sal. Launch the missiles now, or she will die."

"Are you insane?"

"I am an AI. I am not capable of insanity. Insanity is a human malfunction. You have only seconds."

"Goddamn it! You can't believe Veikko would want Violet dead!"

"You can't believe it's worth losing your girlfriend to stop some kid in Timbuktu from growing a third arm."

"Turn off the robots, and we'll talk!"

"We are talking. I estimate Violet has forty-seven seconds before her projectile field sucks the last joule out of her and she hits absolute zero. Launch the missiles."

"She'll outrun you. This mission will only succeed if you stop this now."

"She will not outrun the robots. She is already pinned down."

"You're a liar."

"Tikaris can't lie."

"Yes, you can!"

"I know, I was lying. Vibeke, you're wasting her life for nothing. Launch the missiles."

Vibeke hit the charge and boiled the fluids. There was only one bomb left. She hopped to the next tube and opened the seventh seal.

"Do not boil the warhead. Leave it intact, and I'll stop the robots. We can talk."

"Talk is over."

She wired into the plate and found the boiling fail-safe. Right next to the launching glitch.

"You're killing her, Vibeke. She's running out of time."

"Violet will live."

"If you launch, yes. Destroy the warhead, and I assure you, you destroy her with it."

Vibeke knew Sal was right. She chose instantly. She chose wrong.

THE ROBOTS in line kept firing, their arms shaking forward and backward from the recoil, making each whole robot vibrate drastically as the rounds seared the air toward Violet.

Every round connected with her projectile field; every round was deflected. But every round cost three megajoules from her body to deflect. At 250 every second from each robot, she had gone cold in an instant.

She ran for the crates and climbed on top. The fire ceased as the robots stacked themselves to get to her height. Fire began again. The cold surrounded Violet and made it hard to breathe, but she kept running. From feel alone she had a chance of making it outside. The air within her field was already cold enough to desiccate, and her skin was going numb. Rounds flooded into her as the robot line gave chase. In a few seconds, her shield would run out of heat to suck out of her, and she'd hit absolute zero, inside and out. When the shield failed under their weapons, she would be frozen solid when the rounds hit. She would shatter, and there would be nothing left of her to recover. Not that Valhalla was there to recover her.

She ran as fast as she could, over the tarmac and toward the vents. The fire was relentless, the cold piercing. She ran faster than she ever had before, her muscles breaking inside her, brittle and stressed. The pain grew and grew as she passed over some sort of crane boundary, marked by text but nothing else.

And then she froze. Not her temperature but her motion. She couldn't move. Her suit was rigid. The robots moved closer, all fifty of them firing a barrage into her field.

She knew then what the text must have said. Magnetic Crane System. She'd run into a heavy magnetic field, and her armor was frozen in place, impossible to move. The robots kept firing. Thousands of rounds sucking the energy out of her.

Alf was clearly right about learning to read. But he only merited a fraction of a second in her mind. Vibeke took the rest. A hope that Vibs would launch the missiles and save her, somehow. But she knew there was no chance, no way. She had no choice but to save the world, the entire world over one bad girl.

Her mind grew calm as the water within her neurons turned to ice. Supercooled into a sublime state of perfect clarity.

In those last seconds, fear abandoned her. Sadness crept in, telling her Vibs would be wrecked without her. She forced the thought away. She felt Vibeke by her side, lying on the window of the GET to Iceland, her voice emotionless and her expression cold. But Violet didn't feel cold. Not at all. She remembered what Vibeke told her. It hurt at the time, but now her words resounded with hope. About to die, those words were a promise. A warm thought in her frozen brain. "Maybe in another life," Vibeke had said.

Maybe in another life.

 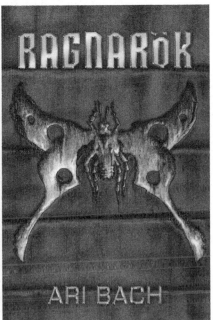

Check out the Valhalla series official blog at
http://the-walrus-squad.tumblr.com.

ARI BACH'S artwork can be found online at http://aribach.deviantart.com/.

Ari also runs a webcomic at http://www.twistedjenius.com/Snail-Factory/ and has a Tarot deck at http://surrealist.tarotsmith.net/.

But Ari is probably best known for the humor blog "Facts-I-Just-Made-Up" at http://facts-i-just-made-up.tumblr.com/.

All the Devils Here

By Astor Penn

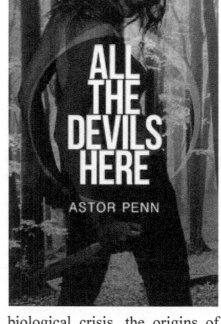

Brie Hall, a sheltered and privileged teenager, is in her final year of boarding school in New York City when disaster strikes. A worldwide biological crisis, the origins of which are unknown, quickly decimates a large portion of the population, and there is no known cure. The threat of contamination is always present, and she cannot trust anyone she sees on the road, and as time goes on, she sees fewer travelers.

While journeying to find her family, Brie meets another wanderer, a girl with a past she can't or won't divulge. Circumstances force them together to escape notice of government-issued hazmat vehicles sent to deliver them to unknown conditions. With no hope of a cure, they do only what they can to survive and remain free, picking up new skills and hardening into people they never meant to become. While struggling to answer the question of how to survive a plague, they must also ask how they can survive the version of themselves they've become.

http://www.harmonyinkpress.com

The Little Black Dress

By Linda Palund

Carmen is the most beautiful and desirable girl Lucy has ever known, and when Carmen is savagely murdered, Lucy's teenage life crumbles. She is devastated by the loss of her first love, and when it appears the killers might never be found, she vows to solve the murder herself.

Together with her best friend Seth, who is not only a master computer hacker but also the son of LA's new Chief of Homicide, they gain access to the gruesome autopsy reports. They learn the true extent of the horror inflicted on Carmen, and Lucy gets closer to understanding the secret behind Carmen's little black dress.

After another beautiful girl is murdered, they uncover the brutality lurking within the corridors of their privileged Los Angeles high school. They put their lives on the line to come face-to-face with the murderer himself.

http://www.harmonyinkpress.com

Noble Falling

By Sara Gaines

Duchess Aleana Melora of Eniva, future queen of Halvaria, is resigned to the gilded cage of her life, facing a loveless marriage to Tallak, the prospective king, and struggling under the pressure to carry on the family name despite her wish to find a woman to love.

When her convoy is attacked on the journey to Tallak's palace, Aleana is saved by her guard, Ori, only to discover her people have turned against her and joined forces with the kingdom of Dakmor, Halvaria's greatest enemy. Her only hope is to reach Tallak, but she and Ori don't make it far before another attack and an unlikely rescue by Kahira, a Dakmoran woman banished from her kingdom for reasons she is hesitant to share.

Though Kahira is marked as a criminal, Aleana's heart makes itself known. Aleana is facing danger and betrayal at every turn, and she fears giving in to her desires will mean she will enter her marriage knowing exactly the kind of passion she will never have as the Halvarian Queen—if she survives long enough to be crowned.

http://www.harmonyinkpress.com

Geoff Laughton

Under the *Stars*

http://www.harmonyinkpress.com

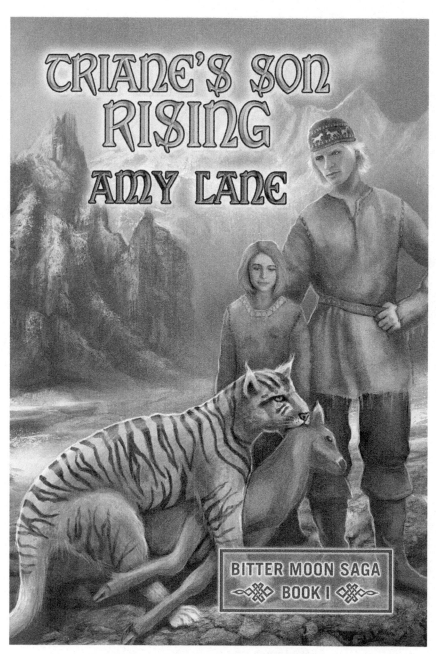

TRIANE'S SON RISING

AMY LANE

BITTER MOON SAGA
BOOK I

http://www.harmonyinkpress.com

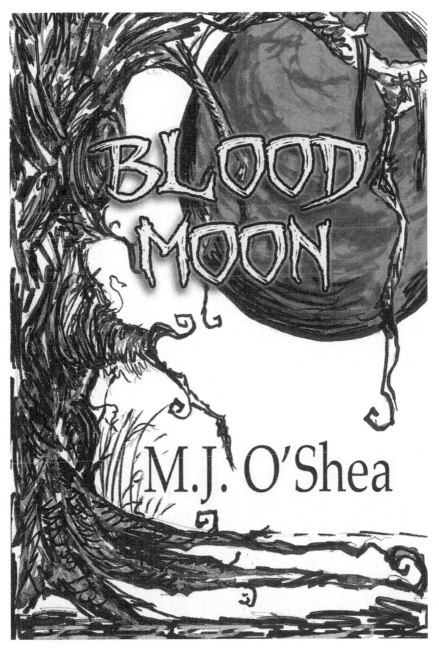

http://www.harmonyinkpress.com

JOHN GOODE

Straight GAY Straight STRAIGHT

Tales from
FOSTER
HIGH

http://www.harmonyinkpress.com

Nail Polish
and *Feathers*

Jo Ramsey

http://www.harmonyinkpress.com

BINARY BOY

RJ Astruc

http://www.harmonyinkpress.com

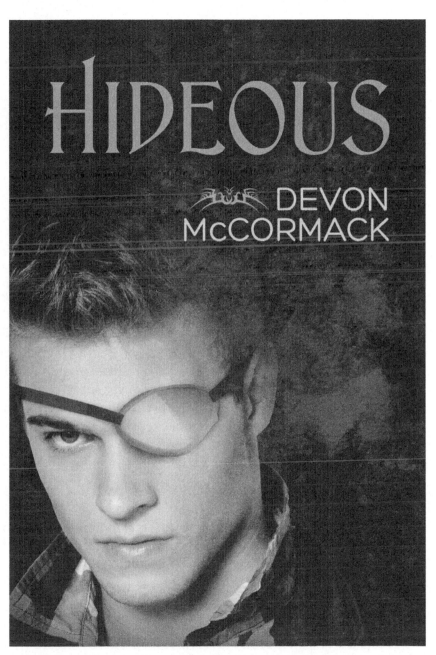

http://www.harmonyinkpress.com

Pukawiss the Outcast

By Jay Jordan Hawke

When family complications take Joshua away from his fundamentalist Christian mother and leave him with his grandfather, he finds himself immersed in a mysterious and magical world. Joshua's grandfather is a Wisconsin Ojibwe Indian who, along with an array of quirky characters, runs a recreated sixteenth-century village for the tourists who visit the reservation. Joshua's mother kept him from his Ojibwe heritage, so living on the reservation is liberating for him. The more he learns about Ojibwe traditions, the more he feels at home.

One Ojibwe legend in particular captivates him. Pukawiss was a powerful manitou known for introducing dance to his people, and his nontraditional lifestyle inspires Joshua to embrace both his burgeoning sexuality and his status as an outcast. Ultimately, Joshua summons the courage necessary to reject his strict upbringing and to accept the mysterious path set before him.

http://www.harmonyinkpress.com

Ben Raphael's All-Star Virgins

By K.Z. Snow

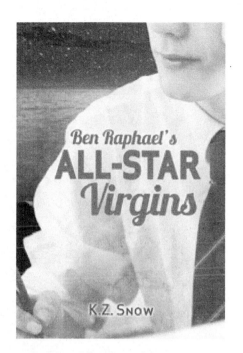

Sixteen-year-old Jake McCullough and his friends Rider, Brody, Carlton, and Tim are the invisible boys of Ben Raphael Academy, an exclusive coed prep school. Brody decides they need "mystique" to garner attention. "Nobody has more mystique than a desirable virgin," he declares. Thus is born Ben Raphael's All-Star Virgin Order or BRAVO.

The boys polish their appearances. Brody launches a subtle but canny publicity campaign. Soon, the boys are being noticed. But they're emotionally fragile. Two have succumbed to a seductive female teacher. Jake and Rider, roommates and best friends who are attracted to one another, fear the stigma of being gay.

It takes an unspeakable tragedy to make the BRAVO boys realize what's important in life, and that "virginity" has more than one meaning.

http://www.harmonyinkpress.com

CPSIA information can be obtained at www.ICGtesting.com
Printed in the USA
BVOW06s2245210116

433591BV00010B/21/P